OzHouse

They built it for children. There were certainly going to be children. There was no doubt about that. They had always planned on children. Lots of children. They were artists and writers, and their favorite books were the classics. They called it the Oz House. It was emerald green. It had turrets capped by giant Witches' hats on the east and west corners. Yellow bricks led to the separate entrances and all around the yard. And all over the lawn were statues and topiary depictions of their favorite scenes. Inside, the house was filled with books and art. And every room had a theme. It was a magical house. Everyone who saw it said so. It stood as a monument to creativity and to fantasy and imagination and friendship and family. And it was meant for children. They had always planned on children.

But life had other plans.

Years passed, and no child's footsteps ever shook the halls. And in the room for which the wardrobe was the only door dust settled and cobwebs grew.

Other books by Dennis Anfuso
The Winged Monkeys of Oz (Interset Press)
The Astonishing Tale of the Gump of Oz (Interset Press)

Other books by Alan Lindsay
Ambaguam, Beginning at the End (an eBook)
A, a novel (Red Hen Press)
Death in the Funhouse (Peter Lang)

Forthcoming by Alan Lindsay and Dennis Anfuso
Intruder in the Realm
OzHouse Revisited

Chronicled by
Alan Lindsay
& Dennis Anfuso

Chapter Heads by Dennis Anfuso

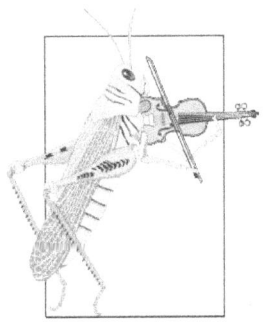

Interset Press

OzHouse by Alan Lindsay and Dennis Anfuso
Text Copyright © 2012 by Alan Lindsay and Dennis Anfuso
9 8 7 6 5 4 3 2 1 /0 1
Interset Press
35 Burns Hill Road
Wilton, New Hampshire 03086
Interset Press is a registered trademark and "Fiddler," the Interset Press colophon, is a trademark of Linda Anfuso.
Designed by Marcus Mébès and Geimle Burzeen.
Printed in the United States of America. First Interset Press edition: July 2012.
Library of Congress Cataloguing-in-Publication Data: Lindsay, Alan and Anfuso, Dennis

Oz House

Summary OzHouse finds itself threatened when foster children start to disappear—again. Years ago it was Suzy Bishop. Now it's little Buddy Samson and Jessica Holton. In the desperate search to find the children, no one could guess that Buddy is wandering the streets of Mother Goose Land, in search of his family that perished in a fire, or that Jessica, to find him, is opening dangerous doors in one magical world after another until all of fairyland is threatened, from the Forest of Grimm to the Emerald City of Oz. No one, but Charles Emerson. And he can't tell.

[1. Fantasy. 2. Suspense. 3. Oz. 4. Anfuso, Dennis. 5. Lindsay, Alan.] 1. Title [Fic.]
ISBN 978-1-57433-042-7

For Jenny, who would have been the first to find the door.

~Alan

For my big sister Arlene, who can now get a glimpse into my head as she reads this book. It may answer a lot of her questions.

~Dennis

CHAPTER 1

*"There was an old woman
Who lived in a shoe
She had so many children
She didn't know what to do
So she gave them all broth
Without any bread
And whipped them all soundly
And sent them to bed."*

"WHY DID SHE DO THAT?"

Buddy's mother closed her eyes and drooped her head as she closed the book.

"You're not spose to hit children." Buddy's whole body shook as he said it. He knew when something was right and when something was wrong. His mother never hit him—or Ellen, or Donna or Scnapsy. Sometime she hit Scnapsy, but that was only if he peed on the rug.

"She was old." His mother was tucking the blankets in tight around him. She handed him his teddy bear. "And she was poor. And all those children were just too much for her."

"But you're not spose to hit," Buddy insisted. "You wouldn't hit."

"No, you're not. And I wouldn't. But sometimes even grownups...." She kissed him on the forehead. Her breath was smoky.

"But you don't," said Buddy.

His mother turned out the light. Scnapsy jumped on the bed. He always jumped on the bed. And then his mother picked him up and carried him into the hallway and closed the door down to a crack, so just a little light came in. The light made a line across the bed, and he could just make out the stars on his blanket.

"Good night, my angel," said his mother through the door.

The smell of smoke came in the room. That happened every night. It floated all the way up the stairs and down the hall through the crack in the door. Like a ghost. Mommy was downstairs in the chair. And Scnapsy barked. And you're not spose to hit people. And he didn't like soup anyway. Bread was good. Scnapsy wasn't allowed to bark. And then it was dark and then the lights came on and got little and got big and then the wind blew loud and the oven was on and the door was open or the sun turned on and the house rose way up into the sky and then—crash. The glass broke.

The monster had him, the yellow giant. The world screamed. Everything was hot and wet. He was all sweaty. The red light swung around like a puppet's head. And the faceless yellow giant dragged him to the broken window. And he couldn't scream, he wanted to scream but he couldn't breathe. His mother's smoke was in his nose like pudding. And he fought the yellow giant but the faceless giant dragged him outdoors in the wet cold, down the cold ladder, down the steep ladder. He coughed and he wiggled until he almost fell.

"You'll be all right. Everything's all right," the yellow giant said. "You're safe." And his voice was a monster.

And they gave Buddy to a man who wrapped him in a blanket. And the fire roared like a lion and jumped at the stars. And he could feel it.

CHAPTER 2

GWEN'S JOURNAL:

Beth says there's no need to panic. I'm sure she's right. But the new boy has been missing all afternoon. "Just calm down," she said. "You're supposed to be the calm one around here." (That British accent always seems to have the right effect, doesn't it?) She told me I was no help right now, and she insisted they don't need me. He's probably just sitting in a closet somewhere.

So I'm here, calming myself down. I could walk the labyrinth, but I'm not going to. I'm just going to calm down. It's a big house, plenty of room for a child to hide. I don't know. Ever since I heard his story—lost his whole family—I've been having flashbacks to Suzy. Suzy came from such trauma and we lost her so quickly.

I wish Gary were here. But Gary's gone down to bail Charlie out of some fiasco he got involved in at RISD. All very hush hush.

We need to keep better watch on these kids! Buddy doesn't understand that he's alone now, except for us. He announced at lunch he was going away to Mother Goose Land to find his mother!

Over the years we have had so many others like him that just didn't adjust.

Doug was sure he'd find him in the Mother Goose Room at the end of his hall. But there was no sign he'd ever even gone there. That leaves only 27 rooms and who knows how many corridors and hiding places he may be in in this crazy house.

He could be anywhere. But lots of people are looking for him: Beth and Doug and a bunch of the older kids. What if he's got himself outside?

GWEN JUMPED UP. She didn't even close the book.

The house was so big, she had to think of all the ways a little boy might find his way out.

Still, it was odd to feel this sense of panic this time. Did it have something to do with Gary and Charlie? Those two home bodies; they'd hardly left the OzHouse grounds in years. And Buddy wasn't the first child to hide himself away. They were always found—all but Suzy.

Now they'd lost Charlie too—but that was expected. Charlie was at college—a few years late, but gone at last and, they thought, for good. When he departed for art school, Gwen finally managed to think of him as their most unqualified success. Ten years he'd lived among them.

He'd entered as an angry, frustrated, silent young man prone to violence and left—well—better. He certainly talked more. And he hadn't hit anyone in years.

So maybe that didn't exactly constitute an unqualified success, but it was far more than anyone had expected at the start. And now the news was that maybe he hadn't outgrown the violence after all. He'd emailed with a hint of something he'd done. Maybe it was just anger that came out, but it could have been violence. Almost certainly there had been a threat of expulsion. Security had been called in. Gary passed the note around. It made people laugh at first: "That philistine Frewer, eye-candy to that stunning nothing! Mr. toothpaste *Grumbachers!* Mr. Rainbow Paintbox splayed like a frozen fawn..." Typically impressionistic, not rich on detail. Gary suspected he'd written the note in fury and sent it by accident. It was impossible to figure out exactly what was going on. No one at the school would tell him. So his foster dad ran down to RISD to get to the bottom of things.

Gwen pulled on the front doors. They were firmly locked.

The truth was, if anyone needed Gwen's mental energy right now it was probably Charlie. Buddy would be okay. Or maybe Gary. Gwen was always amazed to find how much she relied on him. Not very enlightened, she knew. More breathing, then! More yoga! More counting her steps in the labyrinth!

"No luck yet," Doug reported. He'd met her at the back door that led down past the wall and out to the woods. "I've already checked all the doors. There's no way he could've gotten out."

"That's what we said about Suzy."

Doug laughed. "That was a long time ago."

"It was ten years ago," she reminded him. "A quiet little girl comes to the house, she sulks around the house for two days. No one can get to her. And then just like that, she's gone."

Just then two little girls, Brittney and Samantha, best buddies, came up to the pair of grownups to report in, "We looked in the Mother Goose Room and Wonderland and the Library of Alexandria."

"Good, good, nice job Brittney, Samantha. Just keep looking."

"Where?" asked Samantha.

"Anywhere at all." And off they trudged.

"I think we should look in the TV room," said Brittney as they walked away. "Maybe Sponge Bob is on."

"Sponge Bob is always on."

"See, no one's worried," said Doug.

"And I'm supposed to take my cue from a six-year old?"

"Maybe you need to talk to Beth," said Doug:

"Maybe I need to look for Buddy."

CHAPTER 3

You do your best to help someone, sometimes it just makes things worse. I just trucked myself all the way down to RISD, and all I did was piss Charlie off. Some people just don't want help.

I asked him if he was coming back with me. I wanted him to say no. I wanted him to say he was going to stick it out. Well, he did say no. But not because he was eager to stay at art school. No, it was because he was afraid to come home. What the hell was he afraid of?

Maybe he was just mad. What he said was "Sometimes when you go back, everything's just the same as it was and sometimes everything's changed."

One step at a time. Here's how it went: I asked him what happened; why was he in trouble again half way through his first semester away? That was his whole reply. He seemed to think it was relevant. I never got the story out of him. And since I'm not his legal parent, I didn't get the story out of anyone. At least not all of it. Paying the bills affords you no rights of any kind in this country.

As close as I can discover, he did something in class which someone interpreted as threatening. I don't imagine he actually attacked anyone. He hasn't been like that in years. And I can't imagine he would run around the room like a bull in a china shop. (Although I suppose he'd like to do that now and again—but then again, who wouldn't? If a teacher for whom Charlie—rightly or wrongly—had little respect praised some sophomoric effort by another student and overlooked Charlie's own heartfelt and painstakingly rendered work, I can picture Charlie imagining himself doing the Christ among the moneychangers routine. But I can't picture him actually DOING it. We got him past all that. I'm sure of it.)

From what I can tell, it seems he had a problem with a particular student over a painting, I believe it was one that Charlie was working on—probably one of his fantasy pieces. What happened then? Well I think some pretentious classmate looked over from the still life or figure that they were supposed to be painting and said something to the effect: Fantasy is not ART.

Did Charlie raise his hand as though to swing at him? Did he kick his easel over? Did he scatter his art supplies around the room? The "father" in me wishes he was there to splay the philistine's hackwork over his head. After all we've done for that poor child, to have people discouraging him in the one environment where he feels he's somebody.

I know, I know. Splaying wet canvasses over fool's heads solves nothing. I'm sure I wouldn't and he didn't. What he did I don't know: pushed him, yelled at him, kicked over the bowl of fruit. Something.

Whatever the event, the student files a complaint and Charlie is summoned to the dean.

Charlie wouldn't tell me. Nor would the dean, nor the instructor. I couldn't get the name of the student. I guess it doesn't matter. I got the impression there was a girl in it somewhere.

He's still so full of anger. He knows exactly how things are and how they should be, he gets so frustrated when no one else sees what to him is so plain. Sometimes I think he's recovered. More often I think, like with alcoholics, it's a matter of endless recovering for Charlie. Maybe for all of us. But that anger, it hides away for months at a time; but it's never further beneath the surface than the depth of a fingernail. He was warned. He wasn't expelled. And he decided not to leave.

What did Charlie tell me—before I got him so angry? He said he thinks school is stifling his real talent—making him learn all sorts of irrelevant things about dead painters, stuff like that. The sort of thing a young guy says when he's full of spleen and doesn't have the experience to know better.

I said "if you don't want my help and you're not gonna fix whatever the problem was yourself, then just give up. Come home." I was hoping he'd feel challenged to stay. But that was it: he was afraid of coming back to OzHouse—funny isn't it when for all those years he wouldn't leave? "It won't be the same now," he said. "When you go back, after you've been away, sometimes it's the same—as though time hasn't passed at all; but usually it's different." Like he'd come back this time, and it wouldn't be home any more.

Come to think of it, that was an odd thing to say, coming from a guy who's never gone back to anyplace he ever left in his life. But he's read all the books—all the books in the house I think. I told him I thought he was afraid he wouldn't ever leave again if he returned before he was through with his degree. Hit a nerve with that one. He said, "Wake up, Gary. That's not a place people get to stay, is it?" And then he added before I could respond, "You and your brother, and Gwen and Beth— you're the only ones that shelter yourselves away in that pretty mansion."

Of course I denied it. But I could just tell he wanted to fight. He was just looking for something to attack.

I told him what I always tell him: Be patient, your world's gonna be big. Someone's gonna see what you can do. Someone here, at RISD, who has connections to that world. OzHouse is nothing, it's tiny compared to what's out there for it.

"There are whole worlds in OzHouse," he said.

Sometimes I don't think he and I are having the same conversation. "But that's just an illusion of architecture," I told him. He knows how art works. And for people like him the illusion may be a danger. We were never meant to be a monastery.

I thought I had him calmed down, but then there was this: Charlie said he had something to tell me. It was about the girl who ran away years ago. He mentioned her several times. But in the end, he didn't say whatever it was. At least I don't think he did. He said something, but it was pretty trivial, funny even. Maybe it was me. I didn't exactly hurry him to the point when he first mentioned her name.

"I been thinking about, you know, that girl that disappeared," he said.

"Suzy?" I said. "It was a long time ago." I didn't want to go over that again.

"I know but..." then he paused.

"We can't live that way," I said. "Some things are just out of our hands." Suddenly I felt the whole weight of the trauma that led us to convert our private Oz house into this OzHouse to help kids—the hardest

years of our lives, any of us—and how once we got over the pain of not having children of our own, there was quite nearly the pain of losing OzHouse when we lost Suzy. Charlie knew what I was feeling. I didn't want him to say anything about Suzy or those days. Maybe he thought I was wondering about his part in it. I wasn't.

"That's not it," he said when I asked him if he knew something we didn't. But then he went on, tentatively, "not that I don't." But then he paused, "I can't really say." For a second I was afraid. Funny. It was the way he said it. He didn't kill her, the way the police thought. But the thing we never got to the bottom of was the thought that he drove her away. (I think Beth has always blamed him.) Then he went into the funny thing; it was about the Narnia room. I knew he'd been there; he'd signed the guest book years ago. "It says in the book you're not supposed to mention the room to anyone whose name isn't in the book," he said. "Well, I overheard Suzy mention it to one of the other kids. I forget which one. I never got very close to them. She wasn't supposed to. His name wasn't in the book. That's why I was yelling at her."

So it came down to that. He'd never mentioned to anyone what he really knew about Suzy because of a silly rule he'd found in a book that was part of a children's game. We knew about Suzy, too, of course. At the time theirs were probably the only names in the book. She wanted to talk about it, but like all the kids she was afraid of Charlie.

Still, I should have been astonished that a room—that even THAT room—could be so important to Charlie. But I know what he means. How many hours have I spent reading in the reclining throne in the Persian room? The flying carpet, the magic lamp, the complete set of Burton, the minarets and djinn I painted all over the walls. Yes, there's something about that leather chair in that mahogany room—that ambiance, it's as close to magic as anything in this world can be: the right cup of coffee in the proper mug on the proper table by the proper chair under the perfect lamp.

At first I almost laughed. All these years, I knew the explanation he refused to make at the time would be that simple. But I didn't have any idea why he'd let himself get into all that trouble rather than confess something so trivial. I thought it was exceptionally foolish of him and I told him so.

And then I thought of something else. "Suzy never spoke to anyone," I said.

"Maybe not when you were around."

"You mean to tell me, she started talking and you yelled at her for it? Who gives a damn what she said. Do you realize you might have driven

18

her over the edge just when she was coming back? Do you realize...
Suddenly I was blaming him—the only one who never had. He yelled at
me then.

"That room was very important to me. I spent days and days
there. I wasn't going to have her destroy..."

"But why didn't you tell me?"

"Your name's not in the book," he almost screamed it. "You
never signed it."

Oh my God. Who would have thought he'd take our scribbled
instructions so seriously? "Why are you telling me now?" I asked.

"I guess it doesn't matter now. It doesn't work anymore anyway.
Not for me."

I didn't bother to ask him to explain that one. It seemed like a ploy
to avoid the issue.

He finally said, "How was I supposed to know she wouldn't come
back?"

Has he carried that guilt all these years—and did I just make it
worse? He yelled again and then we both went silent. I could tell I wasn't
doing any good. I wished him well—and I left.

Anyway, I'm back and he isn't. Nothing has changed of course.
Gwen when I got home acted as usual, as though she hadn't noticed I'd
been gone. "Oh, you're back," she said. And she kissed me and set back
to work helping Doug make supper. "Buddy's gone and hidden himself
away, but we've got to eat. I'm hoping the smell will draw him out of
hiding."

It's amazing to see someone as truly self-possessed as she is. All
the Buddhist meditation. You wonder why she even tolerates the rest of us.

GARY PUT DOWN his pen. He was remembering things about Charlie—the
times he'd disappear for days. It was after they stopped worrying about
him so much. You never really knew how long he was out of sight; it was
easy to think the others were connecting with him. There was school of
course. But a lot of the schooling was self-directed, especially with
Charlie. And an artistic sensibility like his needs room to develop. He
would always lose himself in his art—never more than in those days after
Suzy left. There was a time, during Pollack-therapy (Gwen's invention),
when he would spend days on end hurling paint at canvases—hurling cans
of the deep red rage of his beaten self at the white canvas, flicking streaks
of black, blue, and purple with brushes on top. You had to let him do it.
Sometimes you need to stop rage; sometimes you need to let it play itself
out. When the boy would tolerate it, Gary hurled paint right along with

him, though Gary had very little rage to defuse. He just thought throwing handfuls of paint at walls was fun. And he liked to keep Charlie company, and now and then he got him to laugh. He even thought it helped Charlie to see someone else hurling paint. It got the rage out more quickly. Sometimes they'd fill balloons with paint and chuck them and watch them splat like giant asterisks. This was Gary's addition to Gwen's prescription. These were the sessions that most often ended in laughter. Gary avoided red, tending more toward the chartreuse and aquamarine. Now it turns out some of those times when Gary left him alone, Charlie wasn't in the studio at all, but in the Narnia room. Reading, no doubt. Or just being in the one room in the house where you were least likely to be found. The only access to the room was through the back of a wardrobe they'd purchased in England. It looked just like the one Pauline Baynes had drawn for C.S. Lewis. Some fan of the books must have made it. They'd found it in England, ten miles from the nearest railway station, and Gary had modified the back into a door. They filled it with fur coats and just let kids find it. Behind the door was an extraordinary library and playroom the four of them had designed: a great stuffed lion was there, and a smaller one with a red ribbon, and a white rabbit with a pocket watch, and a man of tin and another of clockwork, and dwarfs and dragons, and a patchwork girl and a leprechaun with an expression on his face half a frown and half a smirk, and faeries of all sizes. And there was exactly one genie. A dwarf danced in glee by a fire, and a stuffed goose sat in a corner; it was large enough to sit on and wore a bonnet and a friendly smile. And a caterpillar sat on a mushroom. There was a nightingale on the shoulder of a Chinese emperor in splendid robes. There was a gingerbread dollhouse with candy decorations and a witch inside. Two couches were tied together in the center of the room, and on the wall was the head of a gump that would welcome you, if his batteries were charged, when you entered the room. Hanging from the ceiling over the couches was a pair of great big monkeys with wings. Books lined the walls. A very small Humpty Dumpty sat on the shelf between Mother Goose and Lewis Carroll. And just to the left of the door, visible when you first enter the room was the fancy guest book with a note and a gold fountain pen.

Gary's cell phone rang. It was Doug. He told him about Buddy and Gwen. "We're still looking for him," he said. "Beth thinks we should call the police."

"Okay, okay," said Gary. "Just hang on. I'll be there soon as I can." And once more he was off to the rescue.

THE FOUR OF THEM GATHERED in Buddy's room.

"Let's just be clear headed about this," said Gary.

"Clear headed nothing," said Beth. "The boy is not in the house."

"You remember what happened with Suzy," said Gary. "The publicity. The things the papers said, the..."

"You can't compare the two," said Gwen. "Charlie's a..."

"Charlie didn't have anything to do with it. The papers don't need... I mean, weren't you as surprised as I was that they lit on Charlie based on no evidence at all?"

Doug chuckled. He didn't think it was so unreasonable for them to latch onto Charlie. But what he said was, "Even if that's so, there's no one here they could..."

"You never know what they'll dig up," said Gary.

"Let them dig," said Beth. "We could have a dozen bona fide murderers in the cellar. It doesn't matter. The little boy is missing. I'm calling the police."

"He *can't* have gotten out of the house," said Gary.

"It's always possible..." Doug began.

"And it doesn't bloody matter anyway, does it? You worry about publicity. Imagine the publicity if we *don't* find him."

"He's perfectly safe wherever he is," Gary insisted.

"You got a house here full of guns and swords and what else, and a little boy loose, and you say he can't hurt himself?"

"A., the guns are antiques. They don't work. And B., the swords are clamped to the walls with..."

"Then think about that if you're worried about the press," Beth cut him off. "We wait and we still don't find him, and then we call the police and the press comes into the house and takes pictures of the swords?"

"I think everyone's getting a little out of hand here," Gwen interrupted.

"Damn right, I'm getting out of hand. We've waited too bloody long already..."

"Gwen?" said Doug, seeking her opinion.

"She's right of course," said Gwen. "We have to." That was all Beth needed; she went to the door.

"I'm going to call," she said.

"Doug?" said Gary.

Beth was going to make the call no matter what. But she stood there for a moment, waiting to hear the answer.

"We don't know he didn't find a way outside," said Doug.

"We checked outside," said Gary. But Beth was already gone.

21

"Meanwhile we can go back out and keep looking," said Doug to Gary. "We might still find him in time."

And then Gary had a thought: "Has anyone looked in the Narnia room?"

"How would he get in the Narnia room?" asked Doug. "He can hardly reach a towel rack."

But they checked. The three of them went together. The door was closed tight. But they noticed before they opened it that little fingers could certainly fit under the doors and pull them open.

"Could he be that clever?" asked Doug.

"Just go in," said Gwen.

Doug called the boy's name as soon as the door was open. They crawled in past the fur coats, pushed the back wall out on its quiet hinges. "Buddy," Doug called again.

"Well, hello there." But it was just the voice of the gump from the wall. "I see you have found the room of secrets. Come in, come in." The voice was accompanied by the chug and whir of a motor and hydraulic clicks.

Everything in the room looked the same as it always did. Green light streamed in through the stained glass Oz sign Gwen had made and Doug had installed below the eaves. Doug pulled a string and a giant yellow, sun-like orb illuminated the room and the gump talked again. The books were all neatly on the shelves. There was no sign of Buddy.

But then Gwen noticed something. "Look," she said. Inside the two couches of the gump's body lay an open book.

Doug picked it up, "Mother Goose," he said. "So he has been here."

"Not necessarily," said Gwen. But then she picked up Buddy's bear and a box of plastic army men he'd brought with him to the house.

Gary looked at the guest book.

"He couldn't very well have signed his name," said Doug.

The book was still open to the first page. After all these years. No more than a dozen children had ever found the room. Charlie's name was the first on the list. Suzy's was second. Most of the rest belonged to children that none of them could easily attach faces to anymore. The last one, a child now in the house.

"Jessica's been here," said Gary.

"She's never mentioned it," said Gwen.

"None of them ever mention it," said Doug.

And there was something else. Over the whole bottom of the page was a scribble. Someone had taken a crayon and scribbled over everything the way little kids do when they first discover writing, formless loops.

"Buddy?" said Gwen.

"Or Charlie in his Jackson Pollock phase," said Gary. Doug pointed out that if he wasn't in the room now, it didn't really matter that he had been there at some point.

"Unless that tells us he is still in the house," said Gary.

Gwen left the room to resume the search.

"You know why they never mention it?" said Gary to Doug as they crossed back through the wardrobe. "I realized this when I was talking to Charlie this weekend: the four of us have never signed this book."

BUDDY'S LITTLE FEET in worn red sneakers hardly made a sound as he walked along the rough street. He kept looking around to see if he could find anything that looked like things in the picture in the book, but all he could see was grass, trees, and this long rocky street.

It was a warm, sleepy kind of day. The trees in front of OzHouse were all bare and it was always cold outside. But the trees on the road Buddy was walking along were still green, and flowers were growing in thick clusters among the tall grasses.

Buddy put his hands in his pockets. He liked the way it felt when he was scrunched up tight against himself. His fingers played with a plastic army man he had in his right pocket, while his left pocket had nothing but a small hole in it.

"Gotta find that shoe," he thought to himself as he scuffled along. Twice he stopped and turned around. It had been a long walk for one so young and the road seemed to go off into the distance forever. Maybe he should go back. But he might be almost there, and he had to know if it was her and if she would take him back and they would go to Disney World like she promised. Then things could start to be like they used to be, before the fire.

He saw someone coming toward him. He was pushing something in front of him. Buddy had been warned about talking to strangers, especially men, but there was nowhere to hide, and whoever it was might have already seen him.

It was a man, and he was close enough that Buddy could see his face. He was smiling. His mouth was wide and toothy, and he had a big handlebar mustache unlike anything the boy had ever seen, not at all like

Gary's. The man was pushing a small cart, and he was wearing all white clothes with a small white cap on his head.

Buddy imagined he was an ice cream seller like the Good Humor Man who used to drive up his block when he lived in Manchester. Buddy began looking through his pockets for money, but he only had the one green plastic army man. His tummy rumbled at the thought of ice cream. He had left his lunch uneaten on the table after Jessica told him to be quiet.

Maybe there was a way to get ice cream without money.

"Hello, little fella," the old man wheezed as they reached each other.

Buddy didn't say anything.

"You on your way into town? You're kinda late for the fair. Ended yesterday. I was a vender at the fair." He waited for Buddy to speak. But the boy just looked at him, so he continued all the same, "Not a bad event though, shame you missed it. We had rides and games and all sorts of goodies."

At the word "goodies," Buddy started to speak. He really was hungry.

"I completely sold out hours before the end of the fair," the man continued as if Buddy was asking him more questions. "Even the venison sold. Can you believe that? Beef, sure, you expect to sell out of beef, right? But I usually take home several venison and a few chicken. But not this time, no sirree-bob. You live here?" The man laughed as though he'd made a joke.

"Do you sell ice cream?" Buddy finally asked.

"Ice cream? Never heard of that," the man sounded thoughtful. "I sell pies; can't you tell?"

"Apple pies?"

"Apple?" the man chuckled. "In a pie?"

"Blueberry?"

"Blueberry? You're a funny one. Blueberry? You mean Bilberry? I have chicken, beef, and venison. Real pies."

"Mommy never made that kind of pie," said Buddy. "Do you have some more?"

"Already told you, sold out. Maybe next year." The man looked up as though to leave when something seemed to strike him. He turned to Buddy again and asked, "Where do you live?"

"She might take me back. I'd be good. And then she's gonna take me to Disney World."

"But..." The old man scratched his head. "Strangest thing I ever saw."

"Maybe I could live here."

"You really don't come from here, do you? I'm sorry I seem so puzzled, young man. It's just that, you see, this just isn't a place outsiders get into." And then he seemed to be talking to himself, "Had some cautionary kids show up a while back. Strangest thing. Thought they were gone." And then he looked directly at Buddy again. "Are you a cautionary?"

"I don't think so." That was not a word Buddy knew, but it was clear the man did not want him to be one.

"Then how'd you get here?"

Buddy became afraid. Was this man going to take him back to OzHouse? But he still had to find his mother. "No, no, no!" he cried and ran past the man toward the village the man had just come from.

He thought the man might follow him; he ran as fast as he could on the rough cobblestones, but when he glanced back he could see the merchant had continued on his way pushing his cart.

"Good," the boy sighed. "Be careful. Don't tell nobody nothin'. That's how you get in trouble." He decided to avoid anybody he saw until he found the lady he was looking for.

A short while later, a few more people approached from the village, and Buddy wanted to run off and hide, but the trees were too thin, and there were no fences to hide behind, so once again he was forced to stay on the street. But he wouldn't say a word to these people. No matter what they said to him. His mind was made up.

He saw them from quite a ways off, and he could tell two were women and one looked like a teenager. They were wearing long skirts and kerchiefs on their heads, and Buddy thought they looked friendly. But he wasn't going to talk to them. No matter how pretty they were. No matter how much they giggled and laughed like his own sisters used to. One even had blonde hair just like his sister Ellen. He wished it was Ellen. But Ellen wasn't that old; she was only in fourth grade. He really missed her, and he missed Donna, and he really missed his mom.

But the lady he was looking for looked so much like his mom. Maybe it was his mom. Maybe she hadn't died like everyone said. Maybe she had moved to this town and was taking care of all these other children he had seen in the picture in the book. How happy she'd be when she saw him. He didn't know how he'd find her, but he knew he had to find her, and he hoped she lived up this street.

He tried not to look at the women as he passed them, but he had to take a peek. Just to be sure it wasn't Ellen.

The tall woman with the pink and white kerchief caught his eye as he glanced over.

"And what's your name?" she asked with a singsong smiley voice that forced Buddy to stop and look at her. He was smiling even before he realized he was doing it.

"I'm Buddy.'

"Buddy? That's a new one. Nice to meet you, Buddy," the woman said through a big smile.

"And I thought by now we'd met them all," said the teenager. "Hello, Buddy." And then she said to the older woman, "I wonder if he'll tell us his rhyme."

And then the woman looked in a kind of puzzled way, like the pie man, and asked, "What *is* your rhyme?"

"I... I gotta go, can't be late," Buddy said as he looked at the ground and started to rush off.

"Of course not," replied the woman. "Good for you. Never be late if you can be on time."

Buddy started to run, but then slowed down, afraid they might chase him. But no. Just like the pie man, they continued on their way, and he was all alone again.

As he reached the top of a small hill, he saw the village. It looked like the book, little houses close together with little patches of grass in between and white fences.

"I hope she's here," he said out loud as he started down the hill. "She just has to be. That picture was her, and she was smiling."

His head turned left and right as he looked at each house. They were all small, even close up; picket fences surrounded their little flower gardens, and there were no garages anywhere and no cars parked in front or on the streets, which were just wide enough for walking. Buddy liked these houses. They were brightly painted and had such pretty square yards. How he would love to live in such a house. Not that he didn't think OzHouse was fun, but his mom wasn't there, or Ellen, or Donna, or his dog Scnapsy. The lady from the state had said they were all gone, but she could be wrong. Grown-ups were wrong sometimes.

Once Scnapsy had run away and Ellen was crying and a neighbor had said he wouldn't be back, but a man in a gray coat brought him back two days later.

He began to imagine what it would be like to live in one of these houses with his mom and sisters, and he found himself crying.

"I don't care what they say," he said, "My mom is here and we are gonna be a family again. Maybe Scnapsy too." He looked in each yard and tried to look in windows if the curtains were pulled back.

He couldn't remember any of these particular houses from in the picture, but he felt sure he was not far from the spot where his mother would be. He saw some kids playing in a backyard and imagined what it would be like to be their friend, but there was no time for games. He had to find his mother first.

He turned the corner and stopped suddenly. There it was! Just like the picture. He knew it. His mom had to be inside. He was afraid to take another step. What if she wasn't inside, if it wasn't her? What if he was wrong?

No.

It was her, and he was going to run all the way to the front door. He'd knock and knock and then she'd open the door and cry out, "Buddy! How I've missed you." And she'd grab him up in her strong arms and kiss him and he'd be home, and everything would be like it used to be!

Before that picture could fade from his mind, Buddy started running. He ran through two yards to go directly there.

"Mommy! Mommy! It's me, Buddy!" he was screaming as he reached the front door. He knocked and knocked and kept calling, "Mommy, mommy!"

The door opened so quickly it frightened him. He was standing there staring up at the woman in the doorway. All around her were other children, some crying, some yelling, some laughing.

"You...you're not my Mommy. You're old," choked Buddy.

"I am many people's mommy, but not yours little boy," said the old woman.

Buddy's explosion of tears drowned out all the other sounds coming from inside. He had found the woman, but she didn't look like her picture. She tried to pick him up, but he pushed himself away from her, and backed off.

"Now what am I gonna do?" he said between tears. No one offered him an answer, so the little boy just cried as he stood in the doorway that led into the giant shoe that was the home to this old woman and her many children.

CHAPTER 4

Lebanon Gazette, Thursday November 21 A5

CORNISH—A massive search is underway in Cornish for a young boy who was reported missing from a foster care facility early last evening. Five-year old Buddy Samson had only recently arrived at the facility after losing his mother and sisters in a fire at a Manchester apartment complex on November 19.

Police searched the mostly wooded 50-acre property of OzHouse throughout the night. They were joined this morning by dozens of volunteers from the surrounding community.

There has been no sign of the young boy. Police speculate that he may have been trying to get home and may have been picked up on the road. Tragedy is not new to the boy whose father died two years ago, on Christmas.

Several years ago, a young girl was reported missing from this same facility. The case of Susan Bishop was never solved.

THIS TIME EVERYTHING was different. When Suzy was lost, everyone was hostile almost from the moment it happened—from the moment they mentioned on the news that a troubled child with a history of violence was living at the house. People came from all over both times to search the woods. But the first time, they'd come to find a body and haul someone off to jail. They'd wandered through the gardens looking for soft spots in the ground when they should have been looking for a live girl. The volunteers whispered among themselves to find out who among them were the owners, and when they found out, they didn't offer friendship or sympathy but looked away with pointed disgust or cast judgmental glances. Doug and Gwen thought this was just fine, "They were here to find Suzy, not waste time talking to us." "There's no reason why they couldn't say something *while* they were searching," Gary replied. "Isn't it hard enough we've lost a child. Do they have to treat us like we're a disease?"

That's how Gary remembered it. The news reported it, and the people believed it. They trampled the gardens and left tire tracks on the new lawn.

Not so this time. No one who came to search seemed to remember the tragedy of Suzy Bishop, even though the news mentioned it every time they reported the story. The volunteers seemed to think it wouldn't have been polite to mention the past in this difficult time. Everyone seemed to assume the sad little boy had wandered off or been picked up on the road trying to find his lost home. The best hope was that Buddy was right now at the home of some caring stranger who was trying to help him get back to Manchester.

BUDDY RAN UP AND DOWN the cobbled streets. He was glad that old woman who wasn't his mother and didn't look at all like her picture had offered him some soup, even if the soup was just warm, salty, yellow water with little bits of chicken skin in it, and he didn't get to eat very much, not enough to stop him from being hungry. Everyone was crazy in the shoe. And the old lady was picking up one baby and then another that was crying and then putting the first one down and picking up another one and putting all three of them in a playpen and then they broke out of the pen and the cat jumped up on the table and she hit it, but it didn't jump off, so she left it there. And then the soup was bubbling all over the stove and she put her apron on but didn't tie it, so it flapped. And her hair floated all over her face. And all the kids were running around, so she yelled at them, but they didn't stop. And they were spilling soup on the table and they wanted some bread to wipe it up with. But there wasn't any bread, she yelled. Then she yelled real loud and slapped them and said, "Go to bed." That was scary. That was when Buddy ran out the door. His mom never slapped him.

He didn't like the shoe house. He ran down the road but the confused old woman didn't chase him. He went to the right place, the shoe house. But his mom wasn't there anymore. He'd have to look for her someplace else. But where? There were all sorts of houses. One was a big pumpkin and the woman in it leaned out the window and looked sad. And there was a crooked house down a funny street but that didn't look like a nice place to visit. And up on a hill was a big giant castle. But that was too far away to get to. All the other houses were just normal houses. The ocean was down at the bottom of the hill.

And there was Humpty Dumpty of course. He was sitting on a wall that went around a farm or something. But he was just an egg. Buddy passed by Humpty Dumpty's long brick wall and looked at the funny, egg-shaped man. This Humpty Dumpty was much better than the Humpty Dumpty at Story Land, but that one was good too. Humpty Dumpty just sat there with his elbow on his knee and didn't move. He was staring up at the crooked house or maybe at the castle where Old King Cole was eating a blackbird pie. Buddy said, "Why are you sitting on that wall all the time?" But Humpty Dumpty still didn't move. Buddy said, "I'm trying to find my mommy. She's going to take me to Disney World." Humpty Dumpty's eyes, which were very big, rolled down from looking at the castle or the crooked house to looking right at Buddy, but nothing else moved. Buddy was starting to think he was a statue. "Are you a statue?" he said.

"Thin-king," said the statue slowly.

"I need to find my mommy," Buddy repeated. Humpty Dumpty's eyes shifted left to right and back again.

"No," he said. "There is the maiden who waits, like a fool, for Bobby Shaftoe, and there is the man who looks for a wife. And there's Margaret of course who thinks she has a chance with the dusty miller. But there are no children in search of their mothers." Then he stared straight at Buddy. "You, young man, are a stranger."

"My mom said not to talk to strangers."

"Perhaps I won't," said Humpty Dumpty, turning away. "Haven't had a stranger here since—what was her name?" he mumbled to himself.

"Why do you always sit on the wall?" asked Buddy.

Bat, bat, come under my hat
And I'll give you a slice of bacon;
And when I bake I'll give you a cake,
If I am not mistaken.

Buddy laughed. "What does that mean?"

Humpty Dumpty twisted himself as though to get more comfortable on the wall and smiled down at Buddy. The question seemed to please him.

"Anything and nothing," he said. "It used to mean something. Very likely. But that's been forgot. Now it may mean whatever we agree to make it mean. I used to think differently. But I've reformed."

"I'm not a bat," said Buddy.

"Mind you, it wasn't funny. I won't agree to its having been funny either in the content or the rendering. Hence your laughter was entirely inappropriate. Or else we're not a community."

Buddy had no idea what Humpty Dumpty had said. But the way he said it, it sounded to Buddy as though Humpty Dumpty was trying to tell him he'd done something wrong. He said, "I'm sorry."

"That's better," said Humpty Dumpty. "Because I find this world incomprehensible."

"In what?" asked Buddy.

"Incomprehensible. Don't you? In answer to your question, I sit on this wall all day and all night and never move because I find this world incomprehensible—likewise inscrutable."

"I read it in a book, and came through the closet," said Buddy.

"Yes, indeed. Inscrutable," said Humpty Dumpty. "I've read absolutely all the books. In most of them the world makes perfect sense, which is how I know that *this* world and your being in this world where no one comes who isn't already here to be utterly incomprehensible, *in*scrutable. And also redundant."

Again, Buddy had no idea what Humpty Dumpty was saying. "How come Old King Cole's horses and his men couldn't put you together again?"

"That's just what I mean, isn't it? Have you ever known a horse to assemble anything? And as for bureaucrats and soldiers, they couldn't fix a foot race with a yard stick."

"Can you help me find my mother?"

"No," said Humpty Dumpty without pause and as though he were getting weary of the conversation. He put his leg back up on the wall and his elbow on his knee.

Buddy yelled out, "Be careful you'll fall."

Said the preacher to King.
And for these words the man was raised.
And never said another thing.

Humpty Dumpty smiled at his own rhyme. And then he frowned. "Where is that goose when you need her?" And then he stared down again at Buddy, "Do you have a pen?"

"I'm hungry," said Buddy, his hand on his stomach.

"Then sing," said Humpty Dumpty, yawning. "I'm hungry," Buddy repeated. "I want something to eat. I didn't hardly get anything to eat at the shoe."

Little Tom Tucker sings for his supper.
What shall he eat?
White bread and butter...

"He should sing at the old lady's shoe," said Buddy. "They don't have any bread."

"Don't interrupt."

"I'm sorry," said Buddy.

"Not good enough this time. Too late." Humpty Dumpty spun himself around on the wall, turning his back to Buddy.

"My mommy burned up in a fire," said Buddy.

"Ah," said Humpty Dumpty, turning his head around but keeping his legs on the other side, "then I *can* help."

"You'll help me find her?"

"I'll tell you where she isn't, and that's anywhere around here. There are no dead people here. Well hardly any. Plenty of unhappy ones, several who've wished they were dead now and again. But as for actual dead, we don't allow it, as a rule. You'll have to try—someplace else."

Buddy started to cry. "How do I find someplace else? Can somebody take me?"

"Somebody could. But that somebody would have to be me. I'm practically the only one here who's ever been to another place. And I'm not going to do it. I don't happen to be going just now. And as for ever going where dead people are—not for me thanks. I take mine black with sugar." And then he twisted his legs around to join his head on the same side of his body and looked down at Buddy. "But you *are*!" And he raised his eyebrows so they went entirely under his hat. "Closest likely place would be the Grimms' Forest." And then he looked hard at Buddy. "But you won't want to go there."

"Why?"

And then he almost yelled: "Have you ever read 'Fundevogel'? Hmm? Bird steals a baby, huntsman rescues it from a treetop, witch puts

33

on the water to boil it, step-sister hides it... Make any sense to you? Servants hunt it: 'Nothing in the woods but a rose bush?' What in the name of the Goose does that tell us? The whole woods—and there is nothing in it but a rosebush? And what happened to the poor mother? Why a bush? Why a church? Why a pond with a duck? Sanna drowned—by a duck? Is it working for you? Your yoke boiling yet, little boy?"

"Maybe we could go there," said Buddy.

"Perhaps we could climb the cow and jump the moon. Hmmm? I'd rather visit dead people."

Buddy looked down at the ground and sniffled. Just then he heard a sound. Someone—it was a boy's voice—was singing,

As I was going to sell my eggs,
I met a man with bandy legs,
Bandy legs and cahhh-rook-ed toes;
He tripped up his heels,
And he fell on his nose...

And someone else—a girl—was laughing. She sang the next part:

As I went to Bonner,
I met a pig, I met a pig, I met a pig,
As I went to Bonner
I met a pig without a wig,
Upon my word of aaaaaw-aaaaaaaaw-aaaaw-awnor.

And the boy's voice laughed. They sang the last line together. But Buddy didn't look up. All during the singing, a long shadow fell upon him, a shadow so long that it seemed to take several minutes coming; the setting sun was behind it on the horizon. Buddy could see the black line of the long shadow moving over the ground as the singing grew louder behind him. Waiting for the body the shadow was attached to was like waiting at a railroad tracks for an unbelievably long train to pass. When the body, or bodies, finally did arrive, they announced themselves with a "Whoa, there. Dumpty, what's this?"

"Speak of the devil, little Tom Tucker," said Humpty Dumpty, "and lazy Nancy Dawson. Still in the begging business, I see."

Buddy looked up. Tom Tucker tore a piece of bread from a long loaf and stuck it in his mouth. He didn't look at all little to Buddy. He was almost as big as a grownup. Nancy Dawson had her arm around him and was staring up at his face. He popped a piece of bread in her mouth too.

34

"I earned this bread fair and square," said Tom Tucker.

"Doing what?" asked Humpty Dumpty.

"Singing at the fair," said Nancy Dawson. Wisps of blonde hair fell out from her bonnet.

"Tarts for lunch and bread for desert," said Tom. Then he looked down at Buddy. "Tart always tastes better when you're hungry. Don't you agree? Some people save it for desert, which I consider a waste."

"He could use a little bread," said Humpty Dumpty nodding toward Buddy.

"What's he done to earn it?" asked Tom, clutching the loaf more closely. Nancy slapped him on the arm.

"Lost his mother," said Humpty Dumpty.

"That's not exactly *doing* something," said Tom.

"Tommy," said Nancy. Humpty Dumpty's comment made her for the first time look directly at Buddy.

"Lost both *my* parents," said Tommy. "I never got nothin' for it."

"Nothing but a hard heart," said Nancy. "Give the boy some bread."

"I will not," said Tommy.

"You will too," said Nancy. All the while, Tommy was ripping a big hunk of bread from his long loaf. "You will if you want the privilege of walking me home," Nancy cautioned.

"Careful what you say, or maybe next time there won't be anyone there to rescue you when Georgy come out."

"Maybe not all girls want to be rescued when Georgy comes out." She looked at Tommy sideways when she said this. Tommy finally got a good-sized hunk of bread torn off and held it out where Nancy could pluck it from his hand.

"That's better," she said. "He wanted to give it to you all along," she said to Buddy. And then Nancy asked Buddy his name.

Buddy's tears stopped immediately. He took the bread and smiled. "Buddy," he said as he tried to bite into the hard crust with his little teeth.

"Don't be so sure I did," said Tommy. "I still say you don't get no rewards for losing your parents."

During this whole transaction, Humpty Dumpty's head was bobbing from side to side, as though something inside was working up steam to bubble out. "That doesn't make any sense," he finally said. And he stood up on his wall for the first time and started pacing back and forth. "I've just told the boy hardly anyone ever dies here, and now you've told him you've lost *both* your parents. It's inconceivable."

"In what?" asked Tom.

35

Nancy recited:

Old Grimes is dead, that good old man
We ne'er shall see him more;
He used to wear a long brown coat
All buttoned down before.

"Get out of here, both of you. And take him with you." Humpty Dumpty was angry.

"You forgot about Old Grimes," said Tommy.

"I never forget anything," yelled the egg man.

"He's not very nice," said Buddy, chewing on the wonderful-tasting buttered bread; this bread would have tasted wonderful even if he wasn't hungry. He'd never had such soft inside or such crispy crust or so much butter in his life. And the butter was as sweet as blueberries.

"Egghead," said Nancy nodding toward the wall.

Humpty Dumpty kept pacing. "I told him, he needs to go someplace else. No mother for him in this one."

"Mother Hubbard," said Tom.

"But I want *my* mother," said Buddy.

"Get out of here, I have to think," said Humpty Dumpty still pacing.

"Come on, Buddy," said Nancy, "We'll help you look for your mother. There's lots of other someplaces, if you know where to look."

"Won't matter," yelled Humpty, as they started down the path. "He's not going to find his mother in any of them. I've been out there. You haven't. You can't find dead people. That's what *dead* means. Do you hear me?"

But they were getting farther and farther away. "Funny egg," said Tommy.

Buddy looked back. Humpty Dumpty was still yelling and still pacing the wall. "You're not going to find her," he yelled. "Mark my words. That's how it is. You're just gonna have to accept it." Humpty Dumpty stopped pacing, but kept yelling. And then he took a step backwards, and teetered. He rolled his arms in circles real fast. But it didn't help. He disappeared, still shouting, behind the wall. And then there was a loud popping sound.

Up on the hill, at King Cole's castle, an alarm sounded.

"Where are we going?" asked Buddy.

"Good question," said Nancy. She had one arm around Tommy and she held Buddy's hand. "Where do you suggest?" she asked Tommy.

36

"Grimms' Forest," said Tommy.

"Can't get there," said Nancy.

"But it's just the place for the likes of him." He looked down at Buddy, "It's where all the children without mothers end up."

"Really?" said Buddy.

"Place is crawling with 'em," said Tommy.

"But there's no way," said Nancy, and she let go Buddy's hand. "You can't get there from here. You can't get anywhere from here."

"What about Humpty Dumpty?" said Tommy. "He says he's been to a place called Wonderland lots of times. What about those *Cautionary* kids?"

"Pfffwump," said Nancy, yawning.

"Cautiony kids?" said Buddy. He'd heard of them.

"They said they came through the path under the willow," Tommy said.

Nancy rolled her eyes and exhaled, "Just a rumor."

They stopped at a little path under the drooping branches of a willow tree by the side of the road. The path was strewn with copper-colored pine needles. It hardly seemed like a path at all, more like a little river of pine needles that had petered out by the road.

"That's the way," he said.

"We can go?" asked Buddy.

"They say it'll take you to lots of places," said Tommy.

"I would avoid some places," said Nancy.

"Aren't you coming with me?" asked Buddy.

"I would," said Tommy, "but I've gotta get Nancy home. She needs her rest. Besides, there's no need to. Just follow the path. I'm sure you'll find plenty of companions."

Nancy fiddled with her hair.

"You could come with me," said Buddy.

"Oh, I don't think so," Nancy yawned. "It was very nice to meet you," she said. And she put her arm around Tommy again and waved. "Hope you find your mother."

Buddy scrunched up his face and brushed past the low leaves of the willow tree. It was growing dark. Just past the tree, over the path, Buddy came across a very old doorway without a door in it. You couldn't have seen it just walking down the street. Buddy imagined someone had put it there to throw it away. He would have thought it was funny. But he'd seen old doors and windows beside the road in Manchester for the garbage men to pick up. He went right through.

There was still enough light to see by when Buddy started down the way. But that didn't last long. Soon the path disappeared beneath his feet in the dark. There were no lights anywhere then, and the woods were thick. He didn't know how to go on or back.

Somewhere in the distance, a wolf howled. It sounded sad.

CHAPTER 5

November 22

Dear Mum:
        Remember that situation I told you about on the phone? Well it's worse by the minute. All bloody Hell is going to break loose, I know it. Oh, we've made a right pig's ear out of it, as Uncle Harry used to say. The DCYF has sent an imbecile caseworker to us—you do get a bad one now and again. He got us all so riled up, I'm afraid he's gone to file a complaint.
        And then there's the papers.
        At first we were all relieved that the articles hadn't said as much about our "failures" as they did last time— when we lost Suzy they practically wanted to see Charlie drawn and quartered without so much as a how-do-you-do. Then came today's Lebanon Gazette.

Suddenly we are the poster child for all that's wrong with the New Hampshire child-care system. First there's a letter to the editor: "What do you expect when the state entrusts its most vulnerable citizens to a pack of flower children that never grew up." Honestly! Then the semi-literate editorialist jumps on the letter like it was the only bus to the circus: "In a state that can't even find the money to give an equally adequate education to every student, it is criminal to be in a position of having to spend money looking for runaways from an inadequately funded foster care system."

What passes for English in this country!

And now, to top things off, there's poor Jessica. She cried all morning. I know she was becoming friendly with Buddy, but this is certainly a bit OTT. She couldn't even eat her breakfast and was starting to have hiccups, so Gwen told her to go to her room and relax. I brought her a cup of tea after searching the woods one more time over by the shed.

There was Jessica crying her heart out in the Little White Horse room. I stayed with her for quite some time assuring her that we'd find Buddy and that he would be fine. (Why adults do that I will never know, but at some point I became an adult—remember the time you told me Cuddles was going to live on a farm in Cornwall?—and now I too feed children rosy little fibs to calm their fears when I have no proof that everything is all right, and in fact I fear something dreadful may have happened to little Buddy.)

So I fibbed and told her to be calm and that we'd find him. And she kept crying and hiccupping and seemed to be trying to tell me she broke the rules and this was her fault.

When I asked her, "What rules?" She cried louder and said, "You know, you know. I wasn't supposed to tell him, but I did and now he's gone."

I thought she was saying she let him out the door or something, but no, she insisted she didn't do that and that she didn't see him leave, but that she just knew that he did.

Just hysteria. She's the type of girl who takes the blame for everything. That's the kind of attitude that will make her a victim all her life; it's the sort of thing foster care is not very good at fixing.

I just know that imbecile from the DCYF will try to question the children about what happened—as they did all those years ago with Charlie—and if he manages to talk to Jessica Holton, she'll bloody well take the blame for everything and then there'll be a bigger investigation. Of course they'd have to find her first. And I'm not even going to tell you about why I say that. The way this is snowballing I don't even want to think what it will be like by week's end. Unless Buddy shows up, that's all we can hope for.

All my love, Beth

THE DAY HAD BEEN far more eventful than Beth would trouble her mother with in a letter. Walking the hall after lunch, she'd heard the sound of Gwen's raised voice. That was not a tone one heard very often with Gwen. What Gary always called her Eastern calm was not easily shaken. She seemed to be arguing with someone. As Beth got closer, she saw her sister-in-law standing face to face with a man whose worn sport coat and loose tie told her he must be a social worker. Two children were huddled in a corner, Caleb and Rachel; they had just arrived that morning.

Gwen may have heard Beth approach. Her voice adopted a tone of forced calm. Her body remained rigid. This man had, apparently, been questioning, or rather, in Gwen's word, interrogating the children.

"These are *children*," Beth heard Gwen say, "troubled, young children. Do you make a practice of subjecting your charges to a good half hour of therapeutic grilling? Is this the sort of treatment they taught you in caseworker school?"

Gary entered the hall from the other side. "What's happened here?" he asked in the type of voice that was supposed to make everyone calm down.

"Mr. Robbins, I was simply asking these two children why Jessica Holton was still in her room when all the rest had come to lunch and..."

"Good homeopathy," Gwen exploded, "rip kids from their broken homes then dump a little trauma on their heads."

"Breathe, my dear," said Beth, putting her arm on Gwen's shoulder. "And you, my good fellow..." she turned to the social worker as she bent down to comfort the children.

"It's Colin Brinks," said Gary, "right?"

"Fuller-Brinks," the man corrected. "And I am their social worker," he pointed to the two children, "and it is certainly within my rights, indeed it is my duty to..."

"Mr. Brinks was implying that Jessica was feeling guilty because she was in some way responsible for Buddy's disappearance, and that upset Rachel, and she and Caleb started crying."

"I was simply asking..."

"What? Wait a minute," Gary said more loudly than he'd intended. "What does Jessica Holton have to do with any of this?"

"She doesn't have anything to do with it," Gwen insisted before the social worker could speak.

41

"She really doesn't," added Beth simply.

"Then perhaps we should all just settle down a little," Gary said.

"Thank you." Gwen plucked Rachel from Beth's arms and, leaving Colin to Gary and Beth, took her into the Little Red Riding Hood room. Her little brother Caleb followed, holding Gwen's hand and sucking his thumb.

Colin Fuller-Brinks shrugged his shoulders. "Mr. Robbins, in cases where children go missing from foster homes, it is imperative that the state...."

"I think we can let the police do their business, Mr. Brinks," said Gary.

"Fuller-Brinks," he corrected again. "I am responsible for the welfare of..."

"Those children weren't even in the house when Buddy disappeared," said Beth.

"I was trying to find Jessica Holton. And I *will* talk to her."

"Of course no one would try to keep you from any of the children you have been assigned to," said Gary. "It's just that I think Beth and Gwen were both wondering why you did not come to an adult before questioning these two little children."

"I have gotten very little cooperation from the adults of this facility." Colin was looking over his glasses and breathing hard.

"We have been a little distracted," said Beth.

"And you give every impression that you are hiding something. I get the distinct impression that you are intentionally obstructing me in my work."

"That's absurd," said Beth. She had no recollection of this man before today.

"You are keeping me from my caseload this very instant. Now I demand you take me to the corner of this Wonderland which you have assigned to Jessica Holton. Now. This instant."

"Excuse me?" said Gary.

"We certainly will not," said Beth.

"Obstruction," yelled Brinks. He was staring between Beth and Gary like a creature whose eyes could see what was to his left and right but not what was in front of him. The tendons stood out on his neck. "You have no right to keep me from the children in my care."

"In the state you are in right now, you can do nothing caring to that little girl," Beth yelled right back.

42

"I suggest you go walk the labyrinth and calm down a little," added Gary, "then you can come back, and I'm sure you'll be fit to talk to Jessica. We are not trying to keep you from her."

"Send me out to skip through your little maze while you coach the child? Hmmm? I am not part of your fantasy world, Mr. Robbins. I don't play your games. Now you will lead me to Jessica Holton, right now..."

"Or you'll do what, Mr. Brinks?"

"Fuller-Brinks." He gritted his teeth. "Now..."

Beth and Gary communicated with a look their resolve.

"I think you had better go," said Beth.

The social worker looked from one to the other. "Wonderlanders." He said the word as though it were an insult he had stored up for just such an occasion, as though it were his private curse for the whole facility. "You plunk yourselves here with your fantasies and your millions which you unleash on these poor children. Do you think with all your money that you are helping these kids? Hmmm? Oh, yes, they'll be really grounded in their little lives when they leave this place, now won't they? Kids with fast food and day labor in their futures—if they're lucky."

"These children have as much potential as..."

"Drop outs and drug abusers unless they are very very lucky. And what do you do? You show them at a young age what they can't ever hope to have so they can give up now and get it over with."

"I think we have a pretty good record with these children," said Gary. "You can look it up. Ten years...."

"Good record? One, maybe two murdered children from this house. That's a good record? Harboring and protecting a criminal. I *have* looked at your records, Mr. Robbins. All of them. All the newspapers, all the files. You supported a murderer several years ago; you have housed that murderer in the company of an extraordinary number of innocent children."

"Charlie is not a murderer." Gary tried to hold back his anger.

"You have endangered every single child who has ever come into this facility. You have obstructed justice with expensive lawyers to keep the murderer out of jail. This fantasy of yours helps no one."

"I think you should leave," said Beth quietly. "You will not be visiting any of the children in this house today."

Colin Fuller-Brinks stared back at Beth then turned and left with a huff.

"Officious little twerp," Beth said, not caring if he could hear or not.

43

"Jessica isn't involved in any of this, is she?" Gary asked his sister-in-law when he was sure the social worker was no longer in the house.

"No, of course not. But she takes responsibility for things, you know, like when Jonathan sliced his finger cutting his chicken the other day. She announced that it was her fault because she knew she had given him a dull knife because he was so young, but that she had heard people get cut with dull knives more than sharp ones."

"Maybe I should go talk to her," said Gary.

Beth wasn't so sure this was a good idea. The girl was already upset. Hell, the whole house was upset. And more talking would very likely just make things worse. But Gary insisted.

"I know, I know. Everyone's already spoken to her—I'm sure she doesn't know anything—but I want to prepare her for idiots like Brinks out there."

Gary climbed the stairs to one of everyone's favorite spaces: the Little White Horse room at the top of the East Tower, a round room just under the great big witch's hat with the long black fluttering scarf. He always thought of it as Beth's room because she had been so involved in its creation. Beth had picked out the furniture, especially the four-poster bed, had painted the walls, made the curtains and the patchwork quilt for the bed. Finding the tiny oak front door was no easy trick. Gary himself had to make the doorjamb and lintel to her specifications just to fit the small door. Beth even took a class in metal smithing just to make the latch and tiny horseshoe doorknocker using silver.

Gary flicked on the light, called Jessica's name, and looked around. The bed was meticulously made. Everything was put away, all her toys, books, clothes; her pajamas were neatly folded under the pillow. The report they'd gotten when she arrived had said she was a careless child—that the tension that led to the abuse arose from this, according to her mother. But here she seemed meticulous. The only thing out of place was a cluster of plastic toys on the floor, her "set up," little figures of kings and queens and knights along with a dragon and a castle. The sort of toys she was supposed to be too old for, they were spread out in the midst of a story, it seemed, a knight trapped behind a dragon in a cave, a princess with a lance on a horse to the rescue.

Jessica was not in the room.

Just as Gary was about to turn to leave, he glanced over at her desk. Beside a pot of pink geraniums was a piece of paper folded under a calligraphy pen: a note.

"Oh, my God," he said, looking it over.

44

He ran to the Little Red Riding Hood room where Gwen had set up a small tea party for Rachel and Caleb, who had been joined by Brittney and Samantha. Gwen had placed chocolate cupcakes and M&M's and a celery stick filled with peanut butter on each plate and was pouring the last cup of tea when Gary called her aside.

Gwen ran to the intercom; moments later Doug and Beth had been rounded up. Gary read the note; it was carefully written on fancy parchment paper.

Dear Everyone at OzHouse,

I know that no one believes me but I am responsible for Buddy going away. I think I know where he went and I hope I can get there. But I'm not sure. I know he went to look for his Mother. I don't think he can get hurt where he went but he is so little and he might get lost. I will go find him, I promise, and bring him home and then I promise never to spoil the magic or tell anyone unless, well, you know. (I can't say too much in the letter because I do not know who will read this and I don't want to break the rule again.)

If I don't get back then you can ask Rhonda or Lindy or Francine or Charlie to have a look but I promise I will find Buddy and bring him home. Mrs. Henderson my teacher always says if you make a mistake it is your responsibility to fix it so I will.

Love,

Jessica Holton

"What is this all about?" Doug blurted out.

Gary shook his head and ran his fingers through his hair.

"She's taking this much more seriously than I would have imagined," Gwen sighed. "Now we have two to look for. But at least she can't be far. Beth was talking to her not a half hour ago."

They started to break up, Gwen rushing to the Jack and the Beanstalk playroom, Gary to the Middle Earth reading room hoping to catch Jessica before she might leave the house. Beth stopped in the doorway into the great hallway and Doug ran right into her back.

"What's the problem?" he asked. "You think of something?"

"I bloody well did," she said as if to herself. "Who are Rhonda or Lindy or Francine? And she's never even met Charlie." She waved the paper about like a small flag. "There's no one here with those names."

BUDDY REALIZED HE HAD CROSSED into a new story. The trees at the edge of Mother Goose Land gave away almost immediately to a wide-open,

45

hilly meadow. And the sun had begun to rise as soon as he'd left the last tree behind, barely a moment after it had set. He'd hardly had time to feel afraid before the sky grew pink. Now everything was bright with mid-morning sunshine, and his legs were tired. He didn't know if this was the land of the Grimms' stories or some other place in between. Far in the distance was a true forest, much thicker than the clump of trees that had led him here.

He didn't recognize anything.

The walk was proving much longer than Buddy had thought it would be. The path twisted and turned and went up and down small hills, and long before he reached the first tree the boy's short legs had grown too tired to continue.

In frustration he cried out, "mommy!" hoping somehow she would hear him and come running toward him. No one came. He stamped his sneakered feet, and in anger he sat down on a stump of a tree that was right near the path, a stump that looked as though it had been a seat to many a traveler over the years. Down the hill, Buddy could see a field swaying with tall, dark, rich grass and thousands of miniature daisies sprinkled throughout struggling to reach the sun from underneath the towering stalks of grass and weeds. His mother would have stopped to make him look at it and would have asked him if he didn't think it was very pretty.

From here, he could make out the village of Mother Goose Land in the valley behind him. It was still night time there, however. The red clay roofs and thatched cottages and the white, daub and wattle buildings all looked gray in the moonlight. Where he sat, the bright sun was hot and only a few white clouds dared try to cross its path.

"Who are you?" The voice came from behind Buddy.

Buddy turned but didn't see anyone.

"You from Mother Goose Land?" asked the voice.

Buddy kept turning and looking but still couldn't see anyone.

"You going to the gate of horror?" asked the voice.

Buddy's short temper was about to boil over.

"Who's talking to me?"

Then he saw a face hiding in the tall grass behind the oak stump he was sitting on.

Then he saw another face and another. It seemed the tall grass was hiding many children. They were dirty and ragged and seemed so wild that Buddy was instantly afraid of them.

The first boy who had spoken climbed up from the grass. Buddy could see he was much older, maybe in middle school or high school.

"I'm Philip," he said as he stuck out his dirty hand to shake Buddy's.

Buddy didn't want to touch the boy, but was afraid not to shake his hand. He shook it quickly and said, "I'm Buddy."

A girl climbed up out of the tall grass. Her long dress and apron were full of burn marks and her hands seemed very dirty. She approached Buddy and Philip. "I'm called Pauline. Most of the other children are too frightened to come meet you."

Buddy couldn't imagine why they, being bigger and taller, would be afraid of him, but he was glad that they were.

Philip slid next to Buddy to sit on the stump with him, and then he got up and walked around the stump a few times as he stuck his hands in his pockets and took them out again and again.

Buddy didn't think he liked this boy Philip. He moved too much.

"So, are you from Mother Goose Land?" asked Philip again now that he had sidled next to Buddy on the stump a second time.

"I wanted to live there, but the lady in the shoe wasn't my mommy, and Dumpty Dumpty..."

Pauline cut Buddy off as he mentioned the egg. "He's a jerk. He's the one got us kicked out."

"You don't know that," Philip said as he got up and started walking around the stump again.

"Fredrick said he heard Mary and Bo-Peep discussing us days before they gave us the shaft. I think it was a vote, and we just lost. Besides, we were never really supposed to be in Mother Goose Land, we were *Cautionary Tales*, but they didn't know what else to do with us."

Buddy didn't hear the explanation. He was trying to keep his eye on Philip as he circled the stump and sat down and got up again, but he was so nervous of the boy he felt he had to watch him at all times

"It was that stupid egg," Pauline insisted. "He's so full of himself. Didn't you think he was a jerk?" she asked Buddy.

"Well, he started out all right..."

"But he was a jerk, right?" the girl insisted.

Buddy remembered how Ellen used to insist he agree with her about things.

"Where do you live now?" asked Buddy.

"Out here," said Philip as he waved about with his arms. "They can't make us live in the woods even if they won't let us live in the village anymore."

"Why can't you live in the village?" asked Buddy.

"Because of that big fat jerk!" yelled Pauline as if Buddy had contradicted her.

Her yelling scared the little boy and he started to get up to leave.

"I wouldn't go that way," Philip said as he grabbed Buddy's arm to stop him.

"Why?"

"Paul is hiding over there in that tall grass. He's basically a coward, and since you are a stranger he stayed back, but he's much bigger than you and he might decide to be cruel."

Buddy saw the dark angry eyes of a boy looking up at him from a big clump of weeds.

"We tried to live in Mother Goose Land," said Pauline as she fiddled in her apron pocket. "It didn't used to be there. Then one day we looked up, and we could see it. We wanted to live there. But Dumpty said we were not needed now. That we are too, hmmm, what did he call us?"

"Redundant," Philip said as he lost his balance and fell backwards off the stump. "Ow, hit my stupid head!"

Buddy didn't laugh; he really didn't want to be near these new kids. They seemed like the kind of kids who played in the alley behind where his mother used to work.

Forgetting how tired he was, Buddy stood up again and announced that he was leaving. He was heading into the Grimms' Forest because that's where little boys should go to look for their mommies.

"I wouldn't go there," said Philip as he rubbed his head where he had struck a small rock. "Dangerous place. Didn't the man with the pincers come from there? He cut off Johnny's thumbs."

Buddy's eyes opened wider.

"Don't listen to him," said Pauline absently as she pulled a small match box from her apron. "You can't get to the Grimms' forest from here." She opened the box and struck one of the matches on the side.

"Unless you go through the gate of horrors," said Philip.

"And no one goes there," Pauline concluded.

"But I have to go. Tommy said so."

"Tommy? Which Tom? Tucker? The Piper's Son? Little Tommy Thumb?" Pauline asked as she watched the match burn down toward her fingers.

"Tucker, I guess."

"Oh then, I would go," Pauline said staring at the flame. "He's quite responsible, and kinda cute. Ow!" she dropped the match. Then she pulled out another.

"Will Paul bother me if I go past him?" asked Buddy.

48

"Probably," Philip said as he started stomping on the burnt out match lying in the grass.

"Are you afraid of him?" Buddy asked.

"No way," said Philip.

"Everyone's afraid of Paul," said Pauline, dramatically striking another match, "even Philip."

"Look tough," said Philip, "and he might be afraid of you and let you pass. He is really a coward you know." Philip continued stomping the match.

Buddy took a step down the path. Philip jumped in front of him. Buddy tried to step around him, but whichever way he moved Philip blocked his path.

"Let me go," said Buddy.

"I think you should stay here with us," said Pauline. She turned the burning matchstick upside down and watched the fire crawl up toward her hand.

Philip stared down at Buddy, arms folded across his chest.

"You'll never get past him, Buddy. You might as well sit down."

Buddy looked around Philip and yelled, "Paul!" Philip darted past Pauline over the hill. Buddy could hear Pauline's laughter as he ran.

CHAPTER 6

I FIND THE LATEST ROUND of children missing from this facility disturbing—very, very disturbing. We must not forget that this current stretch of unexplainable goings-on comes on top of the unresolved murder of Susan Bishop years ago, for which another child at the facility was clearly responsible. And that this unconvicted hoodlum (he could not be properly tried due to insufficient evidence; no body was ever recovered) hangs around and secures protection from the facility's proprietors. That child, Charles Emerson, is known by us, by the law, and by the owners and residents of this facility, this "OzHouse," to be unstable—a threat, at times, even to himself. Several attempts were made by his caseworker following the Bishop incident to remove Emerson from the home, none, ultimately, successful. The four characters who own and operate "OzHouse" have, to a man, denied that Emerson was present at the facility at the time of Buddy Sumson's disappearance. But this has not

51

been independently confirmed. And the fact is, children like Buddy simply do not run away.

To add further suspicion to this tangle of crimes, incompetence (or worse),we have the most recent loss, that of Jessica Holton, which is clearly related to the loss of Buddy Samson and may well be related to the disappearance of Susan Bishop. The following entry was found among the girl's papers:

One of the older kids told me about this other girl that they said ran away once like Buddy did but I don't think so. I think she found it. She could be where Buddy is. I wish I never told Buddy anything.

No one here will confess to knowing what "it" is. Indeed in their obstinate refusal to consider the note relevant, they reveal contempt for my efforts to solve this case, for the agency itself, and an almost criminal disregard for the welfare of the children entrusted to their care.

This loss of Jessica Holton is not without further disturbing elements; beyond the mere fact of another apparent loss of a child from this facility, there is the fact that this one was reported in the middle of the day, on a day in which the grounds were covered with people out searching for Buddy Samson. And yet somehow this child managed to get away unseen—on her own power, it is assumed. This hardly seems credible. We cannot overlook the possibility—indeed the likelihood—that someone older and more sophisticated, undoubtedly someone with a car, perhaps Charles himself, has helped the girl "escape." Did she, like Suzy, discover an unflattering or even incriminating secret of this labyrinthine house? Did she find incriminating evidence tying Charles Emerson to the murder of Susan Bishop? Did she find evidence of the cover up of that crime?

The owners, we must realize, are not "normal" people. They can best be described as eccentrics: artists and earth-types, "hippies" perhaps, although they do not look the part. (Cleverly they hide their true sensibilities under short hair and conservative dress.) On top of what seems to have been a huge inherited wealth, they have made a fortune selling children's books. The house consists of a group of people who have never had to do real work in their lives and who have never been under any pressure to grow up. We don't really know all the things these Wonderlanders may be. It is indicative of the sorry state of affairs of our foster care system when we are compelled by circumstances to entrust our most vulnerable children to a place like this.

JESSICA THOUGHT SHE KNEW all about the wardrobe. She'd been through it several times. She sometimes wondered if she'd been through it more times than anyone else. (This house was so big, and there were so many children in it, always coming and going; it wasn't hard to sneak away from the grown-ups to have a look around.) She probably knew more about it than anyone else too. She knew, for instance, that you could control it, a little. Anyway, you could influence it. You didn't always get to where you wanted to go. And you couldn't ever be sure exactly where it would take you. In fact, you couldn't ever be sure you'd go anywhere. Lots and lots of times you'd go back through the wardrobe and end up just in the hallway again. (She hoped that didn't happen this time!) And there were, probably, places you couldn't go ever, but other people could. The time she went with Buddy, they went through the wardrobe together. She ended up some place—she hadn't spent time to look around—and Buddy'd ended up someplace else. That was scary. She went right back to OzHouse immediately. She was hoping she'd find Buddy in the hallway. But he wasn't there. He'd ended up in Mother Goose Land she later found out. (She couldn't get to Mother Goose Land herself—or anyway hadn't managed it yet—and she thought she knew why). She had no way of following Buddy that time, of course, even if she could've gotten there, because she didn't have any idea where he'd ended up. And you could get to probably hundreds of places through this door. And you couldn't explore them all looking for one little boy. It would be like trying to find a ring you lost somewhere in Asia or something. So she'd sat in that big gump thing in the Narnia room for hours, it seemed, waiting for him to come back. When he did, she'd told him never to go through the wardrobe again until he was older. And to make sure he didn't, she'd read him a book called *The Cautionary Tales.* Then she said, "See, if you're not good, you might end up in a place like this. And you wouldn't want that."

What if he was there now?

She had to hope not. He was probably back in Mother Goose Land. That was the sort of place a boy like Buddy would find. She leapt into the wardrobe, past the fur coats, and flopped into the Narnia room. It's a good thing the floor was carpeted. Immediately the gump-head on the wall started talking, welcoming her, congratulating her, directing her to the book she should sign. She'd heard everything it could say by now, and just ignored it. She found the Mother Goose book on the arm of the gump-body. And that just confirmed it. She glanced at Buddy's scribbles in the book, right below her own signature; she touched her name, thinking that might help.

The best way to try to influence the wardrobe is to think real hard for a real long time about the place you want to go to. It helps if you've just been reading the book about that world very carefully. And it helps even more if you did it just before bedtime and you dream about it. But she didn't have time for that right now. But she thought maybe if she grabbed onto the Mother Goose book and thought real hard, and recited a rhyme in her head, and shot herself through the wardrobe quickly it would take her to Mother Goose Land.

She tried it. She grabbed the book. She opened it at random, recited Little Miss Muffet, which was the first rhyme to catch her eye. And she dived through the wardrobe.

She felt the sweep of fur on her face, smelled the smell of old, varnished wood and the cool air from the other side—then she crashed in the hallway. The book spilled from her hands.

Down the hall from her bedroom, she heard voices.

What if they'd heard her?

She grabbed the book and flew back through the wardrobe. "Shhhhhhh," she said to the talking gump head on the wall. She recited the rhyme again, from memory this time and dropped the book on the gump. Closing her eyes she said, "Oh God, make it work," and she dived through the wardrobe again.

She landed in the woods, on a cold, soft bed of snow. Up ahead, through the young trees, was a lamppost. Oh, she'd been here before. This was all wrong. She jumped back through the open wardrobe.

In the room, she stopped to catch her breath. Then she heard someone in the hall—it was either Doug or Gary. "Something crashed down here," he said. "I heard it."

They'd be coming through the wardrobe, and they'd try to stop her. They'd tell her it wasn't her fault, when she knew it was. *Humpty Dumpty sat on a wall.* Wasn't she the one who'd told Buddy about the magic wardrobe when she wasn't supposed to? And hadn't she pretended he was her brother and showed him how it worked even though she knew it was wrong, just because she didn't want to be alone? *Humpty Dumpty had a great fall.*

She hurled herself through the wardrobe again.

She swept past the fur coats, felt the doors fly open in front of her. Her eyes closed, she felt a swoosh of air on her face and heard a sound like that of an animal scampering away. This wasn't the hall. Once again she'd landed in the woods. But it wasn't the place with the lamppost. There wasn't any snow. And it was warmer.

She opened her eyes to find herself among tall pine trees. This was new. That was good. She stood up quickly and panned the scene. She didn't even bother to brush the dirt from her knees. She needed a marker so she would know: a crooked house, a giant shoe. But there was no break in the forest to see through. She might be miles from anywhere.

A bird flew by. Maybe it was a blackbird. That would be promising. But trees and birds, even blackbirds, could be any world. But she would not give up on it. It was worth a try. She couldn't go back through the wardrobe anyway because Gary or Doug was probably in the room by now. She picked a direction at random and headed that way.

She told herself not to get her hopes up. She knew the chances were slim. She was, after all, pretty sure she'd been right all along about how the door worked, that someone like her couldn't get to Mother Goose Land, not directly, because she was just too old. You could only visit places you felt were part of you.

But there was still hope. What, she asked herself, what if the worlds were connected, the way they are sometimes in books, the way they sometimes write about one book in a different book, or the way they are sometimes just bound together, then maybe there would be another way, if she just got close enough. That's what she was hoping for. It was just a guess. She had no reason to think it was so. But you've got to start somewhere.

The woods were cool and they had that early morning misty smell. The day was pleasant, not too warm. Her T-shirt and jeans, they were just the right clothes. She noticed a sound. She stood and listened. Then she looked around. Still nothing to see but the clustered trees with the early sun shining through them and the pine-covered ground. The sound was like rain falling hard nearby, or like leaves rustling in a stiff breeze. But the sky was blue, what she could see of it, and the trees were still. No wind was blowing at all.

It must be the sound of a stream.

The first thing she knew would be to find a way to remember where the wardrobe was so she could get back once she found Buddy. She walked in the direction of the sound, and she broke off dead pine branches and shaped arrows out of them and pointed them in the direction she'd come from. She and her sister had learned to do this when they went to day camp that time, back when her family did things like that, before her father left.

There wouldn't be any day camp this year for anyone, not even her sister Isabelle. They'd taken Isabelle to a different house that day when the people came in the white van and her mother threw the glass of milk at the door and yelled at them.

Jessica could still hear the words, "Thieves," she yelled. "Comin' in here and stealing my children. Don't let them take you. Don't listen to them. Don't do what they say. They're trying to steal you. Wait till I get my lawyer. Bastards!" Her mother was just standing there in the kitchen with her hand on the table. Drunk, of course. Or high, like she always was now. Even before Bill showed up.

Jessica didn't believe her mother had a lawyer. But she knew why the people had come. Because at school the nurse asked her why she had the bruise on her arm, and she forgot and said Bill did it. She just was mad at him and forgot. They'd told her not to say but she forgot. She was mad at him and wanted them to take Bill away. It was supposed to be Bill. But she forgot and she told. And then she tried to take it back. But they wouldn't listen. Grownups never listen when they're supposed to, just like they didn't listen at OzHouse when she tried to tell them about Buddy. Gwen tried to listen sometimes, but Jessica didn't like Gwen. Gwen wanted to be her new mother. And she already had a mother.

A ribbon of shadow appeared ahead of her as the sound of the water grew louder. She picked up her pace until she got there.

She was right: there was a stream. Finding a stream was very good. She knew if she followed it, eventually she'd come to some place, because, as they'd said in a book she'd read, water always leads to people.

GARY HEADED OUTSIDE, Jessica's note clutched in his hand.

The fields around the house were full of people. And now there were dogs here too. They were sniffing and winding through the high grass and leading their owners into the woods, weaving, in that odd, helter-skelter way dogs do when they're looking for a scent, way beyond and way back.

The dogs and the police and the volunteers and the media—it was strange how important this search seemed to be to everyone. Certainly it was a shame that it should be strange, but it was. It would be nice to believe it was all a response to how much they cared. Surely a lot of them cared. But the truth is, kids run away from foster care all the time. They'd been lucky at OzHouse, having lost only Suzy in all these years. Others had left—or tried to leave. They all came back before anyone had time to panic, or else they were discovered with their backpacks at the door or out on the grounds. They never really got away, so you couldn't call them runaways, even if it was clear that running away was on their mind. For some reason OzHouse had had more success than it should have had for its size and the number of kids that had come through, more success in keeping kids from just taking off, even older kids. Gary would have liked to think it was how good a job they did, how much they all really cared for these kids. But that wasn't the whole story; there were a lot of well meaning, earnest, loving people out there in the usually invisible foster care world. Not all of them could always hold on to the kids. Most of the kids he'd known were just regular kids with normal kid problems. Most came for a day or two and then disappeared back into their families. But too many were not like that. These kids so often refused love, met caring with hostility or suspicion. They were angry or scared or so withdrawn that if they showed the tiniest signs of hope it was celebrated as a breakthrough. And the system so often made it so much harder than it needed to be.

Too many kids weren't really helped at all, even if they stayed for their whole childhood. The convolutions—what Gwen called the hoops—just kept them clattering forward, as though movement were an indication of progress, down a long train of houses until they were dropped out the back on their eighteenth birthday. Gary and his brother and their two wives worked hard and cared deeply. But wasn't there an element of luck in their success? Just having the Oz house itself was lucky; it was so big and so intricate, so full of wonderful and intriguing things that a great number of kids wanted to get a look at it all before they ran off. And by the time they'd seen it, they'd been there so long, they'd become used to the place and consented to stay.

But OzHouse was kind of a fantasy world in the system. It was adequately funded, for one thing. Not even jerks like Colin Fuller-Brinks—with their overlegislated rules and their infinite dotted lines—had managed to knock the wind out of OzHouse. And the rest of the world had pretty much ignored them. The kids who came to places like this were so far on the fringes of the world that they were in danger of falling off the edge—into the place where dragons are. Their lives mattered to no one but the foster care workers. To the politicians it seemed this little constituency of nonvoters was mostly a burden.

But their runaways, unlike all the other kids, had drawn people's attention. Buddy sure had, and Suzy. Buddy mattered, Gary supposed, because his story was so touching: little boy loses his family in a fire, photos of the fireman carrying him with his teddy bear down the ladder spread across all the papers. You couldn't orchestrate it better.

Jessica would be another story. Her case was more typical: a child of divorce. Abandoned by her father. Her mother takes in an abusive boyfriend and, overwhelmed, loses her two daughters to Child Protective

Services. Officially, the woman's still trying to get her life together, to win the children back. An all-too-common story. Sometimes the women do turn their lives around and win back the children; often they don't. Sometimes they make no progress at all but get their children back anyway— pure disaster, like losing a child in a jungle. In this case, Gary had little hope. DCYF had managed to find a long-term home for Jessica's sister. Jessica was still waiting to be placed.

Jessica of course blamed herself.

Gary brought Jessica's note to the leader of the canine search-and-rescue unit.

"We've got another one to look for, I'm afraid," he said.

The woman looked at him cautiously. She seemed to be trying not to appear suspicious. When she read the note, she became visibly more at ease.

"She thinks she can find Buddy," he said. "I can get you some of her clothing or something."

"It's not necessary. If there's a person out there who doesn't belong in the woods, we'll find her." And then she smiled and put a hand on Gary's arm. "I'll pass the word along. We'll find her."

"Of course we will," he replied. The woman trotted off to talk with the other handlers.

Gary looked around, tried to figure out what to do next. Jessica's mother would have to be notified—a task he did not look forward to. She wasn't the kind of woman he found it easy to sympathize with. He'd had to deal with her on the rare occasion when she called—or rather when she was called. She was full of tears, accused everyone of stealing her child, threatened lawsuits. She was always threatening lawsuits. She seemed to think of the words of the threat as a kind of magical incantation. If she just said, with mystic inflection, "I'm gonna have your head in court," you were supposed to become as compliant as a marionette. And it never seemed to matter to her that the charm never took. She wouldn't give up. She'd get angry and throw names around. Then she'd hang up without ever talking to Jessica. And she hadn't yet come to visit. Not even once. It all made her too emotional, she said, when the truth was she just couldn't be bothered. Yes, she was relieved not to have to deal with the child, and happy in her misery because she could get so much mileage out the pity it won her when she acted the role of the caring, abused mother.

Doug approached him. "Have you considered the possibility that Jessica actually might find him?"

Gary didn't hear him. "She's gonna sue us. That witch."

"Excuse me?"

58

"For real this time. If she just stays sober long enough. Why wouldn't she? Who knows how much she could get. She'll try to take it all. We put our lives and livelihoods in jeopardy to try to help some kids, and then this. I always thought, Okay we can't have children ourselves. We've got this great big house, every board of it is designed to be the perfect place to raise a child. We've got these four story turrets with witches hats on the top. We've got all these rooms themed after stories. All these secrets places for kids to explore. The whole Narnia room, for God's sake. So let's use it. Maybe we can do more good this way and still have what we wanted while we give neglected children a chance. And now we can't even have that. The whole thing's going to be taken away from us when she hears about this. She doesn't give a damn about her kid. But now her sad little girl is going to turn into a gold mine."

"First of all, my emotional brother, we're gonna find Jessica—and Buddy. How far could she get in half an hour? And besides that, hell, we've got lawyers too if it comes to that. We're not going to let anyone destroy anything. We know how it works."

"It doesn't work."

CHAPTER 7

Who wouldn't have blown up! All right, maybe I shouldn't have shown her the painting. That look on her face! Who'd think a chick that hot would be such a princess! Maybe they just shouldn't pay students to model in these classes. Maybe they should just get some ugly old ladies so we can concentrate on what we're doing instead of what we're looking at. I thought I'd flatter her by putting her in that Barbarella *scene. I'd worked out this whole thing: I'd show her the picture. And when she was speechless with amazement, I'd tell her how hot she looked and I'd suggest we go to the Bistro. One thing would lead to another...*

But that look on her face, like I'd violated her, insulted her. Like how could I have the nerve to DO THAT to HER! She's the one standing in the middle of the room stark naked for God's sake. I was flattering her. And then that stern, self-important: "Aren't you just supposed to draw what you see." OK. Not worth my time, I suppose. But to hear her flatter the rigid "likeness" of that dweebface Frewer's—like he was sketching a wax figure instead of sweet, foxy... And then to have him look over at my drawing and snicker. He's lucky I didn't do a whole lot more than lose my temper!

61

And I don't believe no one has ever called him any of those things before.

Oh, never mind!!!! Not worth my time. DAMN IT! This isn't working.

Gary still expects me to spill the beans on the room, and he made me so mad I almost did. I caught myself just in time—so maybe all those years of counseling have paid off!

I should mention that Matt Frewer and I have reached a détente, sort of. He keeps his moronic comments to himself and I ignore him like the insect he is. I didn't even mention how bogus his last painting was: a birdcage to represent being trapped, a rainbow to symbolize hope for the future. Good Lord, I was doing better stuff than that in high school. The instructor hinted that it was crap, but everyone treats Matt like he is made of glass. His total creativity seems to consist of arranging his tubes of Grumbachers one inverted from another to make them look aesthetically pleasing when he opens his paint box. But of course it is more likely that his parents are loaded, and the school doesn't want to risk losing any money they will donate.

There are the real life lessons folks! Rich people are coddled and the rest of us get dumped on!

BUDDY WAS STILL RUNNING as he passed through the first trees into the Grimms' Forest. Paul had indeed been mean to him. He'd pushed him down and even tore the collar of his shirt. Buddy didn't have much of a chance. He'd cried for help, but no one came. Well, someone heard the cries and came, but it was Fredrick. He was as mean as Paul. Buddy was really scared of these two bigger boys. He looked around for a large stick or a rock, but he couldn't find one he could grab. Paul was already pushing him backwards and laughing. Desperate, Buddy pulled the little army man from his pocket and held it up aiming the gun at the two boys. Neither had ever seen such a thing, and they stopped dead. Philip must have been right when he'd called Paul a coward, and Fredrick was one too because they huddled closer and backed away. They threatened to throw him through the gate of horrors.

"Mr. Soldier man has you in his sights, and he might just decide to shoot you both," Buddy said with clenched teeth.

"W...what is that thing?" asked Fredrick.

"Magic!" boasted Buddy. "And he can shoot if you don't leave me alone."

"Shoot *him*," Paul cried, pointing at Fredrick as he backed away further.

"No, shoot *him*," Fredrick was shaking.

"He'll shoot you both, if you don't go away," Buddy glared. Whether either of the two bullies considered risking the danger of the little army man, Buddy did not wait to find out; he made machinegun noises and jerked the little man about, and both of the bigger boys jumped back just long enough for Buddy to bolt around them. They started to chase him, but he ran very fast. At the bottom of the hill was a fence with an open gate.

"Stop," yelled Fredrick.

"Don't," yelled Paul. And their voices were getting farther away.

"That's the gate of…"

Buddy charged through the gate, thinking, "I have to get to the Grimms' Forest." The bullies did not follow him. Buddy didn't know why.

Glad as he was to get away from the bullies, if Buddy had known how dark and dangerous the Grimms' Forest was, he might not have entered it so eagerly. But the Grimms' stories were not the kind his mother usually chose to read to him. He'd heard of some of them of course. But he did not know that most of the evil stepmothers and wicked witches he knew about lived in these woods and only thought that he'd be safer here than waiting around for Paul and Fredrick to return.

Now that he was safely away from the *Cautionary Tales* he sat on the dirt and breathed hard and let himself cry for a good long time until he got all the fear and frustration out of his system.

The only emotion he was left with was anger. He was angry with the boys who were so mean to him. He was angry with Humpty Dumpty who seemed to be able to help him, but wouldn't, angry at Tom who had to be forced to share his bread, angry with Doug and Gary and Gwen and Beth, angry with Jessica for showing him this terrible place, even angry with his mother for dying and leaving him alone. Now that all the other emotions were pushed aside, all he was left with was anger. And it was growing. He stomped away like a little giant. The woods were dark among the thick trees. And that made him angry as well. And he was hungry and tired, and that too made him angry. He didn't know if there would be a town or city in Grimms' Forest, so Buddy just looked for homes he might spy between the thick black trees. As he walked, Buddy grabbed a long thin branch from a hedge and used it like a whip to strike at bushes and wildflowers he saw near the path. He kicked and whipped at anything that caught his eye, until he became tired and threw the branch into a large flowering bush.

When he got tired of stomping, he put his hands deep in his pockets and shuffled along. It was dark enough now that Buddy noticed a flickering light coming from ahead of him in the forest. It seemed that more of the woods came alive at night, and Buddy could hear animals howling and crying, crickets and other insects buzzing and whirring, and he was sure he heard branches snap.

"Hello? Who's there?" asked the boy.

He heard more branches snap and leaves rustle. But no one answered him. The little boy charged off in the direction of the flickering light. He did not know what it was, but light was better than dark. Behind him, as though something was keeping pace, came the sound of leaves crunching and something panting. Buddy barely heard it. He was still angry, and he was keeping his eyes fixed on the light ahead. The sound behind him stopped when he stopped. He laid his hands on the rough bark of a big tree and peered around it to get a better look at the fire.

It was a campfire all right. Behind it a growly looking, dwarf-like man with a long grizzly beard was mumbling to himself as he turned the brown body of a small animal around on a spit over the fire.

Buddy was still mad; he didn't want to talk to anyone. But the smell of the meat made his hungry stomach hurt. But that was just another mean stranger. And he wasn't going to talk to him.

Behind his back, the boy heard a sound like a paw of a dog scraping the dirt and a deep panting sound like a mean chuckle. He turned his head to the sound. The reflection of the fire burned in two eyelike circles that seemed to float in the air. Buddy screamed and ran toward the fire just before the wolf leapt.

"Spies!" yelled the dwarf the moment Buddy appeared in the circle of light.

Buddy just stood there, panting, his fists balled at his sides.

"You'll get nothing from me, little one," the grumpy dwarf continued. "Who sent ya? The queen? That two-headed miller's daughter? Come on, who was it? Speak up?"

"I'm mad," said Buddy.

Something almost like a smile appeared on the wrinkled face of the old dwarf. "Mad, huh? Well that makes two of us. Me and the little spy. You alone?" he added in a creaky voice.

"I'm not no spy. I'm not spyin' on nobody! I want to sit down," said Buddy, still breathing hard

"I don't want no queen's spy in my woods."

"I'm not no spy. Can I?"

"Can you what?" asked the dwarf squinting one pale blue eye.

Buddy sat down next to the dwarf with a huff and ignored the little man's question. "They told me my mommy might be here," Buddy muttered.

"Here? Who? Who told you that? Spies everywhere!" The dwarf started yelling and jumping about on his spindly legs.

If Buddy hadn't been so tired and cold and angry, he almost certainly would have run away from this crazy little man. "Stop yelling at me! I didn't do nothin' wrong!"

The little man sat down again. He straddled the log beside Buddy, put his hands on his knees, and looked him over. Several seconds passed. The dwarf rubbed his chin, and nodded his head.

"Human?" he asked.

Buddy just sat there, limp and tired. He did not seem to know he'd been asked anything.

"Parents?" asked the dwarf, "Father? Mother?"

"I'm trying to find my mommy," said Buddy.

"Yes," said the dwarf, sounding a little disappointed. "I suppose you would be." Then he swung his foot over the log and reached out to turn the meat dripping on the spit. The smell of that meat made Buddy hold his stomach and lick his lips. The warm fire crackled in an almost friendly way, and Buddy began to cheer up. He had walked too much and been too hungry, and too many people had disappointed him for him to be really happy, but with another grownup beside him and a warm fire he was starting to hope things would get better.

The dwarf let the cold youngster sit closer to him on the log.

In the darkness behind the bushes the wolf paced stealthily, his nose in the air, his eyes on the little boy and the dwarf.

CHAPTER 8

GARY WROTE:

Charlie's home! Ha ha. Heard the news about Buddy, and rushed back. And I was worried he'd given up on us. (Yes, I admit it; I was beginning to think he was never coming back.) I think back years ago: he barely cared for what happened to himself, let alone a stranger—which is all Buddy is to him—a complete stranger. If anyone can find him, Charlie can: the builders of this place don't know it as well as he does. Hell, Doug and I designed it brick by board by tree and we probably don't know it any better than he does. If there's any place to hide a little boy—or a little girl (he just learned about Jessica)—who better to search!

Gwen wrote:

Oh my God. Good idea; bad timing. Sort of typical of Charlie. Run to the rescue without thinking what that means for everyone else. First of all, if all these people can't find Buddy or Jessica, how could Charlie hope to? Oh, I imagine he really came because he thought Gary wanted him to. They've had a tough relationship: Charlie needs a father; Gary needs a son. The difference is Gary knows he needs a son. Charlie thinks he doesn't need a father. Charlie never starts with "what can I do to help," he just jumps in like a dog chasing a ball. I wish he hadn't come.

Beth wrote:
The story's spreading like those bloody Harry Potter books. Gary's Charlie sees us on TV way down in Rhode Island! Runs back to help. Comes strutting in like the Yanks during the War. "Don't worry, I'll find 'im," he says. Now we've got to worry what happens if he doesn't keep his silly gob shut—on top of everything else. All we need is him to say something—or worse yet DO something rash and it's a complete dog's dinner.

Doug wrote:
...oh yeah, and Charlie came back to help with the search. Nice gesture, I suppose. Gary seems pleased anyway.

Colin wrote:
Things are becoming clearer now. It turns out that Charles Emerson is in N.H. after all. The Wonderlanders say he just arrived. I say he was here the whole time. Must see that the police come to question him. My guess: he somehow lured Buddy Samson away. I expect Jessica Holton really did get lost in her search for Buddy. In this case Charles may still be an accessory in her disappearance. There may be little hope in finding Buddy alive. But there is some small consolation in the hope of finally solving the case of Susan Bishop.

ON THE AFTERNOON FOLLOWING HIS RETURN, Charlie was pacing the grounds. He was worked up. It wasn't Buddy or Jessica (he didn't even know them): OzHouse itself seemed to have changed. Just as he'd feared. The place had always been stable, a shelter. A place to come in from the cold. He'd returned as soon as he'd heard about Buddy; he needed to get away from that stifling school with those self-important counselors and administrators that were just trying to make sure the ledgers were full so they could justify their existence. He had nowhere else to go.

The Buddy story would cover him.

He needed to get away from his own recent troubles. Not just that flare up he'd had in the classroom, but the doubt he'd begun to feel for the first time about his own talent. They put you in with all these truly talented people—yeah, he fit in—but did he rise above them as Gary had always made him believe? For the first time in years he'd begun to wonder if he really had a future in art. No wonder he lashed out. He hadn't ever mentioned it to Gary. Gary would just puff him up: *Are you kidding*

Charlie? You got more talent than any one your age I've ever met. The way you see things...

Maybe that's all Gary had even done, just puff him up.

He was hoping in the midst of it all to come home—if this was home, if he even had a home—and breathe for a while. But the house was in such turmoil. Gary was glad to see him of course. It's not hard to make Gary happy. Just put the whole RISD thing in a drawer and everything's April again for Gary. The others didn't seem too thrilled. No hugs, no "welcome back." Just a cool "Aren't you supposed to be at school?" Perhaps they were just too busy. They didn't even seem grateful for the help. This Colin Fuller-Brinks, the social worker, had them on edge. Charlie had never met him, but he could tell from the way everyone acted, he was a definite head case, the kind of person that says he doesn't want the state's neediest children screwed up by a bunch of artists, no matter how much money they had, but who really just has some private agenda he's working out: his own psychoses probably, just like the kids he supervises, some kind of Superman complex, inventing bad guys whenever he needed them so he could drop in and save the day, and meanwhile making everyone's life as cruddy as possible. Maybe he was even the one making up stories and passing them along to the press. The situation made it hard to relax. He'd probably have to actually find those kids after all.

Charlie knew he should be in the Narnia room, trying to set his mind right for the wardrobe. It had already been a long time since he'd been easily able to use the wardrobe as a door. For several months, he hadn't managed it at all. The older he got, the harder it was. He'd tried already of course, much of the morning, but he'd made no progress, just kept coming out in the hallway. His own bad mood certainly wasn't helping

Gary's name still wasn't in the book, of course; that was the first thing he'd noticed. Jessica's was. And Buddy had left his own mark there. But since Gary's name still wasn't there, he couldn't ask Gary for help. And he was starting to wonder if Gary even knew the magic of his own wardrobe. That possibility had never occurred to him before. But if he himself as practically an adult could no longer use the wardrobe reliably, perhaps Gary and the others never had. In which case, even if he broke the rules, told Gary about it, he'd probably never be able to get him to believe it. But the real fear was that if he broke the rules it wouldn't work at all anymore—not for him anyway. Couldn't risk that. Bad enough he'd already mentioned the book to Gary.

He had to put his mind straight, bring down the level of bad karma, so he could read the books the lost kids might have read. Prepare himself. Maybe he should just meditate the way Gwen had taught him to get rid of the anger and frustration and all the negative energy (which is what Gwen called it) that made it impossible to be "mindful " Or maybe he should just do some art—his own best meditation—put himself in the world he was aiming for. But he couldn't manage it. He'd been in such a hurry to get back. And now what if he couldn't help either himself or these lost kids? He couldn't read or paint; he couldn't sit still and count his breaths. All he could do was pace the yard.

He walked along the huge retaining wall out back they called "Doug's wall" because it had been such a project to build. And he passed through the trees below the wall that led to the labyrinth—another little Zen touch Gwen had put in. If you walked it in a contemplative framè of mind, it would help you reach enlightenment. Charlie had never tried it in the daytime.

But Gwen's gardens were pleasant and easing; it was unusually warm for November. There were still a few blooms left on the chrysanthemums.

He heard a car pull in. At first he tried to ignore it. But then he wondered if it was that Fuller-Brinks guy. There were no longer so many volunteers combing the grounds. Mostly they'd given up: assumed Buddy had been kidnapped and Jessica had gone away looking for him. The car—it could be a lot of people, of course. But it was probably him.

By the time Charlie got to the driveway, the driver of the car was in the house. Charlie looked in the passenger- side window: a briefcase and a laptop computer lay on the seat. Both were monogrammed in red letters CFB.

There were a lot of people in social services, both good and bad, just like everywhere. Maybe this Colin Fuller-Brinks was a jerk. But was he a threat to the place, really? Gary thought so. But could you trust Gary's judgment in such a case He wasn't exactly known for calm reflection—spiritual or logical. And he invested himself too deeply in a limited number of things. Charlie had felt it himself more than once growing up—like the time Gwen arranged a show for him in Boston and announced it as a Christmas present, a present as much for Gary as for him, he realized. But Gary went white when she announced it; he tried not to show how nervous it made him, but he couldn't manage it: *what if he's poorly received? What if some hard-nosed critic doesn't take to what he's doing? He's not exactly mainstream you know. A lot of people reject this sort of thing out of hand. Do you think he can take that?* That's what

Charlie imagined Gary said to Gwen when they were alone. The show went on. But how Gary hovered over him the whole time: afraid he'd get too much attention or too little. And even after it went off okay, Gary was only more relieved than happy.

Gary never understood: there's lots of different kinds of rejection, and it always matters who's doing it and why and when. And someone like Charlie is hardened to most of it. Hardened to most kinds of acceptance too. It's the same mechanism. Gary was a great guy and Charlie loved him. But there were rooms in Charlie's soul no one was allowed to enter, doors Charlie didn't unlock for anyone. Whenever Gary or anyone tries to force their way, it goes worse for them. Charlie considered himself one of those things Gary was overly invested in. OzHouse was another. So maybe Colin Fuller-Brinks was a threat, and maybe he wasn't. It was time to find out.

Charlie reached in the car and pulled out the briefcase and the laptop.

THE STREAM FLOWED through a great forest. Jessica walked and walked. She knew that if she kept to the stream, she would not lose the location of the wardrobe. But brambles grew up and the little trees on the bank grew so thick she had to wander away from the water in order to continue on. She was careful always to keep the stream in sight and to return to the bank at every chance. But the time came when the thick forest forced her so far from the stream that she lost sight of it. And when she tried to find it again, she could not. (It wasn't a big stream to begin with, and it had been getting narrower and narrower.) She thought perhaps at this point she should go back, retrace her steps, and find the stream where she had last seen it. She thought she still could. But then she thought if she did that, there would be no continuing forward again; she would certainly lose the stream once again as soon as she tried.

So she kept on, marking her way as carefully as she could, not at all sure she'd be able to find her marks again if much time passed. But if she was ever going to find Buddy, she had to keep going. And it was up to *her* to find him. It was her responsibility. She was the reason he was missing.

She stood for a moment and looked behind her, trying to take a picture in her head of these exact trees, this rock, these hills, just in case. But she knew it was hopeless. The woods looked so much the same everywhere she turned. Would she ever make it back to OzHouse, to her own world?

Well if not, that was probably just what she deserved for letting Buddy get lost in the first place.

But she had to get back somehow; she had to help her mom and Isabelle. She had to protect them from Bill. And she had to make them happy. And they had to forgive her for telling.

The woods through which she traveled were just wild enough for the wardrobe to choose them (if that's what the wardrobe did, as Jessica supposed): it always let you out in some out-of-the-way part of whatever world it brought you to. Always outdoors; never in a house, as it did in our world. That's why she believed our world was different. It wasn't as though there were all these wardrobes in all these places that led into each other. It wasn't like that at all. Our world was like the center of a wheel. It was strictly the front-door world. Yes, the front door was in our world and the back door was in all the other possible worlds. Sometimes in the new world the whole wardrobe appeared, and you got back home by going through it backwards; at other times, only a doorway appeared, or maybe just a frame or some other kind of door altogether.

Before she arrived at the edge of the woods, where the light from the open space flooded the trees, a bird somewhere in the branches over her head started to sing. It was the first bird she'd heard since she'd passed into these woods, and she stopped to listen. She thought perhaps she should not stop, but the sound was so beautiful it almost *made* her stop. She was very quiet, so as not to disturb the bird. She had never heard such a sound. It was not just a little chirp, but a real song, a tune so clear it was almost as though it had words, like a music box, but brighter. While the bird was singing she felt, without quite noticing the fact, less worried. All of a sudden she wished everyone would just take care of their own problems and let her sit under the tree and listen to the bird. And the thought didn't make her panic the way that kind of thought usually did. In fact she did sit down, very slowly, very quietly. She had to find Buddy, but a minute or two more couldn't possibly make any difference in the end. She held her breath to listen.

The little gray singer—it was a nightingale—was so impressed by the little girl's attitude that it glided down to the branch nearest her, singing all the while. And when it was done its song, it seemed to bow its head a little.

Jessica let out her breath. She was afraid to clap; she didn't want to frighten it away.

"Wonderful," she whispered.

"Thank you very much," said the bird. "I don't think I've ever met your kind before," the bird went on, and it almost sang the words.

Jessica's eyes grew faster than the Grinch's heart.

"You talked," she said.

"As did you," said the bird.

Jessica smiled and almost laughed as she tried to think of what stories she'd read in which birds talked. She knew that the wardrobe could only take you to places you'd actually read about. So you always eventually figured out where you were—even though the places were always different from the way you'd imagined them from the books. But places always are like that, even in our world, when you read about them or see them on TV before you go there. There were places she could think of where birds could talk, but none that seemed anything like this.

"Excuse me, little bird, could you tell me what world I'm in?"

The bird flew off the branch and around the tree. It lighted on a branch a little higher up. "What world?" it asked. "*The* world, of course. Is there any other?"

"Oh, yes, lots and lots of them."

"I wouldn't know. But I'm very glad you liked my song." It's possible she'd never read about this bird at all. That was the other thing about the wardrobe: sometimes it took you back into the story, not just the world of the story, as though the same story you already read was still happening. But then sometimes you just went to the world of the story, sometimes even to the parts of the story you'd never read. And sometimes the story hadn't even happened yet, or had happened a long time ago and no one there could remember it very well. You could never tell.

"Well can you tell me which way to where people are?" Now that the bird was no longer singing, she wanted to get on with her search.

"I'm ever so glad you enjoyed my song," said the bird. "Shall I sing it again?"

"Maybe later," she said. "I really need to find the people."

"I'm ever so glad you loved my song," this time the bird sang the words, and very beautifully.

"Shall I sing it again?"

"Am I heading in the right direction?"

The bird kept singing, "I am a bird with a beautiful song; I'd love to sing it again and again. I am a bird with a beautiful song, I'd love to sing…"

"Stupid bird," Jessica mouthed to herself. She put her head down and started walking. Not all talking birds would be clever.

The song stopped abruptly. "Don't go that way," called the nightingale. "That's where the emperor lives."

Well that rang a bell. "Emperor?" asked Jess. "Is he, what's the word, is he vain?"

"Awfully fond of his plumage," said the bird.

"As much as you love your voice?" asked the girl, trying to make a point without seeming impolite.

"You see he has no voice," sang the bird.

If this was the emperor she thought it was, perhaps it was best to trust the bird. "Well then what way should I go?" she called to the floating bird.

"The other way, of course," said the nightingale as it song faded in the distance.

"Which *other* way?" she yelled after.

But the nightingale was gone. "Stupid bird!" she muttered again.

Now she was sorry she'd wasted time. How was it she hadn't learned not to waste time? How many times had Bill and her mother told her she was lazy? On that very night he hurt her the last time, that's what he said. She was just listening to music, sitting on the floor of her room with her headphones on. She was supposed to be taking care of the dishes, she knew. But when Bill came in after supper was over, which meant he was drunk and he was going to have a fight with her mother, she didn't want to hear them. So she went quietly to her room and put the music on. She was going to finish the dishes later.

She didn't know what happened then, because the music was pretty loud in her head, just that Bill tore the door open and called her a lazy good for nothing and slammed down his fist on her CD player and broke the cover. "Now get out and finish those dishes." But she cried instead; she crumbled over her CD player. So he picked her up by the arms and he threw her, like a toy. Maybe he meant for her to land on the bed. But she didn't. Her ribs slammed into the side of the bed and it hurt. And he swore at her and told her to get off the floor and finish the dishes.

That's when Isabelle came in and started yelling at him and slapping at him, and he turned on her. And Jess tried to get up then, but she couldn't; she couldn't help Izzy because her side hurt.

Afterwards Izzy told her that mom was yelling at her to finish the dishes, but she couldn't hear because she had the headphones on. And Bill yelled at mom because he was trying to watch TV, and mom yelled back. That's what led to Bill coming after her and breaking her CD player, and that's what led to her telling on Bill, and that's what led to everything else: OzHouse, and Buddy running away. So it was all her fault. And then when she should have been looking for Buddy, she was listening to a stupid little bird sing about itself. She'd better stop being so lazy, she thought, or she'd never be able to fix everything.

She came to the place where the trees ended.

Before her stretched a garden: a huge, flourishing garden. It was like Dorothy coming out of the woods on the poppy field: the flowers just went on and on. She couldn't see the emperor's palace; it must be too far away. But there was a path that led by a pond, and the pond was full of ducks. A mother duck and her family paddled conspicuously near the shore, and a couple old swans hissed back and forth on the bank. The garden was even more beautiful than the gardens at OzHouse, a thousand different plants and all in bloom. But she would not let the garden distract her as the nightingale had. Somewhere over the hill ahead of her was certainly the palace of the emperor. (Did these huge gardens go all the way to the palace?) But she decided to avoid the path that led there. She took the bird's advice and walked along the edge of the garden. She came to a wall; at one spot it was old and crumbled, easy to climb over. On the other side was a path leading away.

Before long she was on the streets of a town where there seemed to be a parade going on. She told herself she mustn't let herself be distracted by a parade. But she couldn't manage to squeeze through the crowd either. It was all she could do to push past the old women in their baggy skirts to just see what they were looking at.

"Yes, fine," said a woman on the street.

"Never saw anything like it," said another.

"Wonderful, wonderful," said a third. The workmanship is extraordinary."

Jessica managed by then to push aside the last skirt and, down on her knees, get a peek at the part of the parade just then passing by.

"He's naked," she yelled. And then she covered her mouth, and then she covered her eyes too. A big fat man was walking down the street right in front of her with a high hat and no clothes at all.

All of a sudden the people all around her started saying, "he *is* naked." And, "look the emperor's naked," and things like that. And a little boy nearby said, "I thought so. I was gonna say."

In a moment you couldn't hear anything else for all the commotion. The emperor's men lined the street to protect him, or maybe just to cover him up. Someone threw the old man a dirty sheet from a window. But he didn't take it. He knocked one of his men off his horse and jumped on it himself and rode away through the town like a fat, bald Lady Godiva. And a lot of people were laughing but others were angry at the ones that were laughing. Jessica was getting pushed around

75

everywhere and yelled at and stepped on and told to get home. She pushed herself into a doorway to try to keep safe.

CHAPTER 9

(TRANSCRIPT OF PHONE CALL FOR LEGAL PURPOSES ONLY.)

Hello? Is this Mrs. Holton? This is Gary Robbins from OzHouse. I must begin by telling you I am taping this call so a clear and honest record will be kept of everything we say. Is that all right with you?

You stole my children; I suppose you can bug my phone as well.

Is that a yes, I may tape this call?

Do what you damn well please.

Right. Well, Mrs. Holton I am calling because of a situation we have here.

Yeah, what the hell does that have to do with me?

You may have heard that a small boy, a…a confused little boy has…how should I say this…has gone missing from the premises.

I don't know anything about it.

It's been all over the news.

Yeah, and? What are you... What have you done to Jessica?

Well that's the trouble, Mrs. Holton.

What have you done to my daughter, you freaks?

Your daughter decided to take it upon herself to find this little boy. His name is Buddy.

What the hell do I care what his name is. I hope they all run away from that hellhole you got. Bastards stole my kids.

Jessica feels responsible. She's a very good girl... In trying to help us find him, she wandered off.

What, what, well, serves you right doesn't.... What did you say? You...

I'm afraid your daughter is missing I, well, I just thought you should know...

Know what? What are you saying? Is my kid there or not? I want to speak with her. You can't keep her from me you know!

You can visit her any weekend you wish. But just now we are searching the grounds for the two children.

Two children? You only got my one daughter. Little Jessica, my baby. What have you done with her? You let her get lost up in that God-forsaken woods? I am gonna call my lawyer. You morons don't know what you are doing! Let me talk to Jessica.

That's the point Mrs. Holton. That is why I called. You can't speak to her just now, not till we find her. I'm sure she is fine. No reason to be concerned.

Concerned about what? Where is Jessica? Why can't I talk to her? Why are you trying to torture me?

Mrs. Holton have you been drinking? You don't seem to be following what I'm telling you.

Who the hell cares if I drink now! You'd drink too if some bastards stole your babies! What business is it of yours what I do?

Mrs. Holton I am only calling to explain what has happened. You may come up here and help us search, or I can call you back when we find her.

Find who? Who is this? Why are you bothering me? Go to hell, Bill!

My name is Gary Robbins. I'm calling from OzHouse about your daughter Jessica.

Jessica's not here. She died two months ago. Leave me alone! (click)

Hello? Hello? She's hung up. Well that went as well as could be expected I guess.

(End of transcription)

"EXCUSE ME, YOUNG MAN," Colin called to Charlie as he approached the lanky artist.

"What?" Charlie was having some difficulty trying not to sound annoyed.

Colin slowed his pace. Charlie turned his head just far enough to catch sight of the social worker out of the corner of his eye. This gesture from the child with the history of violence must have unsettled Colin. He cleared his throat, slowed his pace even further, and began rubbing his thumbs nervously over his fingers as though he were attempting to remove dried glue from the tips. Charlie knew what the social worker was going to say; he began preparing his replies.

"You are Mr. Charles Emerson, aren't you? I thought you were away at school." Colin tried to sound simply curious.

79

Charlie gave him his green-eyed stare, as Beth used to call it. He opened his large green eyes and stared right through the social worker as if he had not spoken to him or acknowledged his presence at all. The look unnerved most people, and it especially unnerved Colin Fuller- Brinks.

"I... I was wondering if you had noticed anyone near my car," the man fumbled.

"Yeah," replied Charlie after a long silence. "Lots of people. Everyone who's out looking for those two kids. Or didn't you know that?"

Colin shifted his eyes around the yard as though to emphasize that there was no one else within sight. "Yes, yes, I know that, but my car. You see I left my laptop and briefcase on the front seat and..."

"They've been stolen." Charlie finished the sentence.

"Well, I wouldn't want to accuse anyone. I just meant I left them there and now..."

Charlie cut him off again. "If you thought I took them, you wouldn't hesitate to accuse me, would you?"

"*Did* you take them?" the nervous man blurted out.

"See. You don't pull any punches when it comes to accusing people. But on paper you'd be ever so PC about it."

"You didn't answer my question," Colin cleared his throat.

"Nope, guess I didn't."

Charlie walked away with the kind of saunter that might have come from an old Clint Eastwood movie. He slid his hands into his tight jeans pockets and shuffled his feet over the few dead leaves crossing his path. He happened to look up as he neared the house. On the widow's walk stood Beth, looking, it seemed, in his direction, although with the sun behind her, it was hard to tell. He hurried inside.

"He did it," muttered Colin under his breath. He was a bad apple, that one. He had some serious digging to do, but first had to find his laptop.

BUDDY SAT ON A ROUGH PINE LOG holding his knees close to his chest and stared into the fire. The air was growing colder, and the heat from the blaze felt good. Sometimes the breeze would blow the smoke toward the boy, but before he could get up to move, the wind would shift and the smoke would go another way.

He wished the strange little man were friendlier or that he might not yell and hop about so much.

"Rabbit's almost done," muttered the dwarf.

Buddy looked from the fire at the grizzly little man: his eyes jumped suspiciously from the spitted rabbit to the little boy.

"Suppose you expect me to offer you some," his wiry whiskers flickered when he spoke. "Well I ain't. I caught this rabbit on my own. I cleaned it, and I cooked it. So why should I share it with you? You're a complete stranger to me. I don't know you."

"I never tasted rabbit before. I probly won't like it," said Buddy.

"Oh, I can hear Sarah rattling on," Rumpelstiltskin continued as though he hadn't heard Buddy at all. *"He's just a kid. What harm could a kid do ya?* Don't you think kids do their share of dumping witches in ovens, grabbing dwarfs by their toes and shaking the gold out of 'em. Isn't it just likin' kids too much got us in this mess?"

"I don't like new food," said Buddy. "Mommy makes me taste it, but I don't."

"That's my wife," said the little man. "Sarahstiltskin, case you were gonna ask. At least she was my wife. I don't know what she's gonna do when she finds out I lost that baby when it was good as mine. A little jumping, dancing, celebrating, singing—you can never know who's listening to you. You get to the deepest, darkest, remotest part of the woods and you whisper something to yourself, and the next day the whole world knows all about it. Now I gotta explain it to Sarah. And she would want me to feed you. I know it. But I'm hungry and I'm tired and it's the scrawniest little rabbit ever hopped. And I'm not gonna do it."

"So don't," pouted Buddy although he was very hungry, and despite what he'd said about not liking new foods. The smell of the cooked meat made his stomach hurt.

"I won't. I won't do it. I'm hungry. I don't want to. And I got a rule. I don't do nuthin' unless I get something in return. That's my way. That's my rule!"

"Looks burned anyway," said Buddy as he rubbed his nose with the back of his hand.

"'Tisn't burnt. Cooked to a turn," the dwarf let go of the spit and pointed at the meat.

"It is too burned. Look, it's all black on that side. Probly taste really bad like dirt or something."

"Fine rabbit, I say. Finest rabbit you ever tasted," said the little man as he tore a small piece from the flesh and stuck it in his mouth. As he chewed, he opened his mouth wide and puffed to cool the meat, and he continued to talk, which was something Buddy had never seen an adult do before. "Perfect. Juicy and hot, just the way I like it. "

"If you like it all burned," said the boy as he pointed again to the blackened parts.

"Here," shouted the man. "Taste that and tell me if it tastes burnt or not! And no lyin'!"

Buddy took a piece.

"Wave it around a bit so it don't burn your mouth," muttered the little man.

Buddy did as instructed then stuck it in his mouth. It was still very hot but also running with juice. Tough to chew, a little bit like a rubber band, he thought, and not quite like any meat he'd ever tried before. On a good day at home, he would have had trouble getting it down. But at the moment the hungry child thought it tasted wonderful. "That piece was okay, but you didn't take it from the burned spot. Over there on that side, yeah, right there."

The dwarf tore another piece from his dinner and handed it to Buddy.

"I'll bet you think this little hunk is burnt too. Look, see it's *supposed* to be black on the outside. This is what it's supposed to taste like." And he handed the piece to Buddy. "And then this piece here…"

Behind the leafy bushes, the wolf sat salivating. He paced quietly at the edge of the ring of firelight.

"So, you say you are looking for your mother," the little man said as bits of greasy rabbit meat fell from his thick lips. "You're sure you got one? Lots of kids around here don't."

Buddy nodded as he swallowed his mouthful.

"What makes you think she's here? Not many humans here. No one in my part of the forest but me and Sarah," he wiped his bushy moustache on his sleeve. "Except maybe a poacher or two. Your momma isn't a poacher is she?"

Buddy looked hard at the little man, "Don't know what's a poster is."

"No matter, I was making a little joke. Not worth the effort I suppose with a young one like yourself."

"What's your name?" asked Buddy.

"Rump… ahhh!" the man jumped up and began waving his spindly arms about. You *are* a spy. The two-timing miller's daughter sent you to spy on me, didn't she? Admit it. Admit it!"

Buddy backed away. All his fears of strangers flooded back instantly as the dwarf ranted and raved and swung his arms and legs about.

The wolf tensed up his muscles. Perhaps the boy was going to run away alone into the woods. He drooled with anticipation.

"Please stop yelling at me," cried Buddy. And then he did actually start to cry as his anger and fear and weariness took hold of him.

"Oh stop your blubbering," said the dwarf as he sat down and removed a long clay pipe from his vest pocket. "I have a soft spot for blubbering," he continued as he began filling the pipe with tobacco from a small leather pouch that hung from his belt.

"Smoking is bad for you," said Buddy as he wiped his tears with his pudgy fists.

"Who says?" asked the dwarf. "Been smoking all my life, ain't done me no harm."

"Maybe it stunted your growth," said the boy simply.

As he lit the pipe and took his first few long drags, the little man thought about this. "Maybe it did. Maybe I was supposed to be a six-foot-tall dwarf," he let out a quick, loud laugh as he took another puff. "Maybe, but maybe not."

"Yeah, maybe not," repeated Buddy.

"You planning to spend the night with me?" asked the man.

"Are you gonna chase me away?"

"Haven't decided."

Buddy started to cry again. "I have never been in the woods at night before."

"Don't start that blubbering. You can stay. You can stay."

The wolf growled softly. He would have to search elsewhere for his meal. Without a sound, he slipped between the gnarled roots and branches of the trees and headed off toward one of the farms nearer to town.

Sleeping in the woods can be a very enjoyable experience if you have all the necessary items and have planned well. Buddy had always been told that. But Buddy had none of the things that would make sleeping on the hard ground more comfortable, and he wasn't sure how he would make a place to sleep.

"Do you have an extra pillow?" he timidly asked the dwarf who was deep in thought puffing gently on his pipe.

"You want me to do magic, eh?" said the man. "That I only do for payment. What have you got? Gold ring, bracelet, coins?"

Buddy had no jewelry or money. He pulled the plastic army man from his pocket. "This?"

The crooked calloused fingers of the dwarf encircled the little green army man as he took it from Buddy to examine it.

"What's this made of? 'Tisn't wood nor metal nor stone."

"Some kind of plastic, I guess."

"Plas-tick huh? Never seen it before. Must be rare. Okay, youngster, you got a deal."

Suddenly Buddy had not only a pillow but a small bed had appeared with a soft mattress and thick duvet of goose down.

The boy's mouth dropped open. Magic! He had a magic bed to sleep on.

Suddenly he wanted to talk to the dwarf more, but he was too tired and it was very late. The magical bed looked so inviting, that he instead removed his shoes and socks and climbed between the sheets.

Buddy had no idea what time it was when he awoke suddenly the next morning to the loud cackle of a murder of crows, but the fire had burned away to just a small pile of dark ash, and the little man was not about.

He called in a different direction as he sat on the edge of the bed putting his shoes and socks on, but he heard no reply. He got up and walked about looking for the dwarf.

When he looked back, the bed had vanished. "I thought that might happen," he sighed as he continued to call for his new friend.

"I wish I knew his name." Buddy found it difficult to call someone when he didn't know his name. He yelled "Rumpa," but he knew that was only part of it.

"I wish I had some breakfast."

When it seemed certain that the little man wasn't coming back, Buddy decided to continue his search for his mother. As he glanced back one last time hoping to see the wrinkled squashed up face of his new friend he noticed instead a pile of apples and a small piece of paper where his bed had been. "Hey," he called out, wondering how long the apples had been there.

He collected the apples and started eating one immediately. He opened the paper. It was a map. He could not read the words printed there, but he could see a picture of a small fire and a dotted line through the woods that led to a town with a big castle. In a fine spidery handwriting it said at the bottom.

And if you don't find your mother in that town, follow the trail down the corner to my hollow. Sarah, I'm sure, would be glad to make your acquaintance. Be sure to bring plas-tick, if you got any, though as yet I can see little use for the stuff. R.

Although Buddy could not read the message, he understood that this map was left by his friend to help him find the town on the other side of the woods. He was sure he could follow it.

84

CHAPTER 10

—HARRY BAILEY...
  —Harry...
  —George you ole son of a gun.
  —Harry, Harry...
  —I got here a little too late.
  —I got him here from the airport just as quick as I could. The fool flew all the way up here in a blizzard.
  —Harry how about the banquet in New York?
  —Oh, I left right in the middle of it just as soon as I got Mary's telegram... Good Idea, Ernie, a toast... To my big brother, the richest man in town...

  Dear George—
  Remember no man is a failure who has friends.
  Thanks for the wings.
  Love, Clarence

  —What's that?
  —That's a Christmas present from a very dear friend.
  [jingle, jingle]

—Look, Daddy. Teacher says every time a bell rings an angel gets his wings.
—That's right. That's right. Attaboy, Clarence

THINGS HAD CERTAINLY CHANGED in the years since Charlie had been brought to this place. The former vision of some sort of Xanadu had been compromised everywhere. The India room had been converted to a rec-room with a pool table and a ping-pong table and permanent chess set-up and Chinese checkers—which would have made more sense in the China room, but the China room had been taken over by crafts. It looked like a kindergarten, with blocks and number stations and writing stations and big puffy numbers and letters everywhere and a weather/science station. Even here in the Persian room, which had stayed pristine the longest, they'd put in a gaudy wide-screen, plasma TV—right in front of the swords and scimitars and tapered helmets. If you looked for it, you could still see the vision behind the junk in most of the rooms, but it wasn't the same. How could you chill in a room where any one might come in any time and snap on a mammoth television set? Even now, someone had left it on. Here it was November and someone had popped in *It's a Wonderful Life* and just walked out on it. Breaking house rules.

Charlie stood in the middle of the room staring at the screen. George Bailey was hanging onto Zuzu with such joy, smiling as big as the moon. "Hell of a movie," said Charlie to himself as he trudged over and clicked it off. "Give up on your dreams and see how wonderful life is."

"Hey," said a voice, "I was watching that."

Charlie spun around to see a young boy he didn't know sunk so deep in Doug's leather recliner he was almost lost in it. He seemed not to have noticed Charlie until he turned off the movie and broke the spell. The boy had an open book in his hands and a Tootsie Pop in his mouth.

"How can you read a book and watch TV at the same time?" said Charlie.

"How can you walk and chew gum at the same time?" said the kid. A kindred spirit. Charlie smiled.

"It was over anyway," said Charlie.

"So?" And then, "How about you read this to me?" The boy rattled the candy over his teeth. He couldn't have been much more than seven. And it was a big book.

But Charlie had other things to do. Colin Fuller-Brinks had followed him into the house. What Colin had done after that Charlie didn't know. Charlie had ducked down the hallway and Colin had gone in another direction. That was over an hour ago. He must be long gone by now. It would be safe. Now that the caseworker suspected him, he'd have to pull the laptop out of its hiding place right away, find out what that carrot-brain was up to and find a way to get the thing back into his car—or bury it or get rid of it—before anyone could do more than suspect him. But he couldn't get to it with this little kid in the room.

"What's your name?" asked Charlie.

"Gwen was reading it to me before."

"Listen," Charlie began, not yet knowing where the sentence was to go from there.

The boy stood up in the chair as though to attempt to bring himself to Charlie's height. "Don't you know how to read?"

And then a voice from the doorway called, "Have you seen Morris?" Charlie turned around to see a little girl. "Morris," she yelled at the boy in the chair.

"Why don't you go play with this girl," said Charlie.

"That's Jenny. She's a girl," Morris explained. He called to Jenny. "Charlie was gonna read to me." Everyone seemed to know who Charlie was.

"Can I listen?" Jenny asked.

Morris handed the book to Charlie as he sat back down and scrunched over to make room for everyone. Jenny climbed in.

Marveling at how kids—especially OzHouse kids—managed to bully people so much larger than they, Charlie dropped himself between the two children and read from the open book:

"I was not always made of tin," began the Emperor, *"for in the beginning I was a man of flesh and blood and lived in the Munchkin Country of Oz..."*

"We already read that part," said Morris.

"No we didn't," said Jenny.

"Did too. Turn the page."

"You certainly are a bossy one," said Charlie. If Colin Fuller-Brinks was truly gone, perhaps Charlie could wait a little while to get the computer. He certainly wasn't going to be rid of these children any time soon.

"Turn the page," ordered Morris.

"Okay, okay. What page are you on?" asked Charlie.

"Tin Man's cuttin' his head off."

Charlie continued:

"Nimmie Amee still declared she would marry me, as she still loved me in spite of the Witch's evil deeds...."

"Is this the right place?" asked Charlie.

"Keep going," said Morris.

Just then another girl passed by the door and looked in. "Hey, are we reading?"

"That's Brittney," said Morris.

Before Charlie could answer her, Brittney yelled down the hallway, "Hey, Samantha, he started reading without us." Almost instantly the two girls were in the room. "Gwen's spose to be reading this," said Samantha.

"Is it night time already?" said Brittney. "I didn't get any supper."

Charlie looked around the circle of children who had pulled up little chairs and set them in a circle without being told to and sat quietly, staring up at him, several with their elbows on their knees and their hands on their chins. It was an amusing sight. He wondered why he hadn't done this when he'd lived here. There were always so many young children to entertain. He'd missed out on a lot of fun, he guessed. He'd missed out on a lot of things.

"Aren't you gonna read?" said Brittney.

He read:

"The girl declared I would make the brightest husband in all the world, which was quite true. However, the wicked witch was not yet defeated. When I returned to my work the axe slipped and cut off my head, which was the only meat part of me then remaining."

"Gross, huh," said Charlie.

"How come?" said Samantha.

"Just read," said Morris.

Charlie chuckled and read:

"Moreover, the old woman grabbed up my severed head and carried it away with her and hid it. But Nimmie Amee came into the forest and found me wandering helplessly, because I could not see where to go, and she led me to my friend the tinsmith. The faithful fellow at once set to work to make me a tin head."

As he read, Charlie did his best to act out, without getting up, the things he was reading. He had not intended to do so. But he found himself

88

pretending to carry his own head away, and they laughed. And he sat up straight and tall when the Tin Man was proud of his new head, and when several of the kids did the same, Charlie became even more animated.

"Being now completely formed of tin, I had no more fear of the wicked witch, for she was powerless to injure me."

"He sure is making the best of things," said Charlie.

"I wish I had a tin head," said Jenny as she moved her arm stiffly in a chopping motion.

"Just read," said Morris.

"The straightest route isn't always the best, Morris," Charlie advised.

"Just read," said Morris.

Charlie turned his head and noticed Gwen leaning in the doorway, listening. When his eyes met hers, she came in. "Don't let me stop you," she said. Charlie smiled at her.

"That was one of Suzy's favorite books," said Gwen for no apparent reason.

Charlie looked up at her again. Gwen reached over his shoulder and pushed the pages aside to reveal the page at the front. "She wrote her name in it." Charlie stared down at the printed bookplate:

This book belongs to Suzy Bishop.

"She wouldn't talk," said Gwen, "but she would read books."

Of course, thought Charlie. She'd have to have been interested in books.

"Just read," said Morris.

"Sorry," said Gwen, apologizing for her interruption of the story.

Charlie turned his eyes back to the book. But before he could start again, he heard his name from the doorway in Beth's distinctive accent. In a moment, Beth was in the room, shooing the children away. "You've heard enough. Gwen has a fun activity for you."

"But he was right in the middle of..." Morris began. But Beth picked him out of the recliner and aimed him at Gwen; Gwen stared back with round eyes and a wrinkled forehead. But Beth just stared and shifted her eyes at her until she gathered the children around her like little ducklings and shuffled them down the hall. She'd have to find out later what this was all about.

As soon as they were gone, Beth closed the door. Charlie looked up from the depths of the leather chair. As she marched toward him, he let all the emotion drain from his face.

"He's going for the police," she said.

"And?" said Charlie.

"Don't give me that, young man. Gary and I tried for a bloody hour to calm him down." She put her hands on her hips and stared straight in his eyes. "He wanted us to drag you into the kitchen 'If he's innocent,' he says 'let him prove it.'"

"Why didn't you?" Charlie looked Beth right back in the face, careful to keep the intensity from his gaze.

"Because you stole the computer."

"Did someone steal a computer?" Charlie picked up the remote, aimed it at the TV. It was all too much for Beth. She leaned forward, put her hands on the two arms of the chair, stared at Charlie as though she were talking to a little kid. With him sunk so deep in the recliner, she was just big and tall enough to bring off the gesture.

"I don't need this, Charlie. You know bloody well you stole it."

Showing still no sign of concern, Charlie put down the remote. "How would you know that—even if I had?"

"Let me remind you: You are a visitor at this house, a guest, not a resident. You are here at our discretion. Do you understand?"

He heard that. Get Beth emotional and she lets go with what's really going on, behind it all—the façade of interest, the pretense of caring, they fall away. He froze like a statue. *A guest?* No more than that, after all these years? Was that all he'd ever been? Had he just dreamed he'd become a part of this house—this rather oddball configuration of family? Had he deceived himself into thinking of this place as home? Could he have?—when all he'd ever been was a hardly tolerated guest.

Yes, he thought, and dope that he was, he'd come all this way to save them—to save a hotel he wasn't even registered in. He looked up at Beth, but now he couldn't meet her eyes, "So you're kicking me out?"

"I am asking you to deserve the years we have devoted to you," Beth was too angry to register the effect of her words. "We have been very kind to you, patient— and, yes, trusting of you for a long time..."

"Not you, Beth, not Doug, not Gwen." Charlie looked over at the door. "Just Gary." Then he looked back at Beth, and this time he managed to look into her eyes. "The rest of you, when Suzy left, you were looking for the body."

Beth's face went blank. Charlie filled the space with words, "Yeah, I've been a thief ever since I moved in here. Not even a guest, was

I? Just someone you couldn't get rid of. No wonder no one ever gets better around this place."

"Don't turn this into something it's not, young man. This is not about you or your troubles. It's about those lost kids and this house." She wasn't going to let him conceal stolen goods with that sentence.

"I'm here to help," Charlie shot back. "Why else would I..."

"I can think of plenty of reasons," Beth interrupted. "Are you going to give back that computer or not?"

Charlie sunk deeper into the thick leather and spoke quietly. "I haven't got the freakin' computer."

Beth stood up and turned as though to head for the door. But she didn't go anywhere. "That was just the last straw for him. Mr. Colin Fuller-Brinks is about to walk into the police station and tell them that the murderer of Suzy Bishop was at the house when Buddy Samson disappeared. It doesn't matter that you know you weren't here. It doesn't even matter that you can prove you weren't here. As soon as they go to the police, the reporters follow along like flies on a warthog's buttocks. Before you can tell anyone the truth we've got 'Alleged Killer Living at OzHouse at the Time of the Murder' all over the bloody news. If you really came back to help us out, you're not doing a very good job. If I could at least give him back the computer..."

"I haven't got it," said Charlie weakly. Beth left the room.

Why did he find it so hard to lie his way past her? He couldn't manage it. All he could do was hold the deception between them. It was like refusing to wipe the sauce from his face while he maintained to the death he hadn't eaten all day. He didn't like it. But how else could he do what he now decided he'd come all the way up from Rhode Island to do? This simple thing they could not—despite all their imagination and money—manage to do themselves.

Simple? No, it wasn't simple anymore. It was bad enough he had to lie to Beth. No sense lying to himself. But now at least he had a clue where she was—where Suzy was. Now, at last, it was possible he could find her. He couldn't let Beth stand in the way.

As soon as she was safely gone, Charlie climbed in behind the doorway to the passage no one was supposed to know about. It was a stairway and a series of hallways that led between the two halves of the house. The Oz book still in his hands, he picked up the laptop where he'd laid it on the bottom step and climbed stealthily up the long gradual slope.

"A guest," he muttered. Suddenly this whole rescue seemed a little less urgent. What difference did it make. A damn guest. Sure. Why hadn't he understood before? This place wasn't home. Kids came and left

91

too quickly for anyone to get attached while these four reclusive crazies performed their innocent good works with as little commitment as possible. He himself was a fluke— living here all these years. They didn't want the long-term commitment, did they? They'd never wanted him. They'd been stuck with him. They weren't his parents; they were people that gave him a bed and kept him distracted so he wouldn't kill anyone. OzHouse was no one's home—no one but the rich artists who built it. Maybe it deserved this trouble. Maybe he should just leave them to their good intentions and shoot himself back to school. Let them suffer; maybe they'd learn from it—if people like them can learn, which they probably could not. They didn't keep anything new around long enough for it to have an effect. Maybe instead of rescuing the place, he should just burn it down.

If not for Gary, perhaps he would. But he could hear Gary: "I'm paying for your school and you're burning down my house?" No tears, just confusion. But Gary had money. It was no trouble for him to pay Charlie's tuition. It didn't signify any huge commitment. Gary used his money to keep himself hidden in his fantasy.

So why save these kids? Why go through all this trouble?

Maybe just because they needed saving. Maybe to maintain his excuse for coming back. On the other hand, maybe he could just join them in fairyland.

Suzy had gone to Oz, he was almost certain. She'd been reading about the Tin Man when she disappeared. That meant she must have gone to Oz. And if she hadn't come back, she might still be there. He understood completely. There was always a temptation to stay behind. Even watching *The Wizard of Oz* on TV, he could never figure out why that little girl from Kansas was in such a murderous rush to get back home. To what? A sepia-toned farm and Miss Gulch's cat! And no reprieve for the dog.

He paused on a landing and looked up the dark stairway. The space was lit only by a skylight that had not been cleaned in years; he could not see the top, the secret door hidden in the wall.

Okay, he told himself, so maybe he wasn't sure why he was going, but he knew where he had to go. Still, all these years later, would he be able to find her? He needed to find Buddy and Jessica too, of course, but it would also be nice to find Suzy, clear his name, show her to Colin Fuller-Brinks and say, "So I'm a murderer am I?" That would be something to come back for. What would Beth think then?

The stairs seemed to take forever. He ran, and then, tired, he slowed down. A terrible thought hit him. Why would anyone believe, even if he found her, which was unlikely, really, even if he found her and brought her back and stuck her right in front of their eyes, who would believe that it was Suzy Bishop? All these years later—she'd be grown up by now.

He didn't know Oz that well, hadn't had much interest in the books in years. He'd arrived there more or less by accident any number of times—always in search of something else. Whenever it happened he came right back and tried over as soon as he'd figured out where he was.

Still, he told himself, he could try. He didn't know where Jessica was, or Buddy. He could try Suzy first. And maybe she could help him, somehow, with the others. It didn't seem likely, but at least it was a plan: he'd sneak into the Narnia room, check out the laptop, find out what Colin Fuller-Brinks was up to, find out if OzHouse was in any danger from that rat turd social worker, then throw himself through the wardrobe. It would have to work now. Didn't it always work better when you needed it to work? He could even take the laptop with him, bury it in some fairyland. No way Beth or anyone else could accuse him of stealing it then. Or, better yet, take the laptop through the wardrobe and open it up there where there was no way he could be caught with it in his possession.

He stopped on the second landing to take a breath. Resting against the wall, he looked back down the long corridor that disappeared in darkness. It was a pretty dismal part of the house smelling of dust and old wood.

Was he fooling himself? He hadn't made it to any fairyland in so many tries he'd given up even before he decided to go away to art school. The wardrobe no longer worked for him. He'd changed. He'd grown up, he guessed. It was clearer now that Gary never talked about the wardrobe because it had never let him through at all. He and Doug had got it for the children; Charlie had always thought they didn't want to interfere with the children's travels by talking about it—explaining it. It certainly was the kind of thing that could be destroyed if you knew it in the wrong way: like how it worked or where it came from. He needed to go now—but it wasn't as though the wardrobe was alive. It didn't know your need. It was a door. Like any door, it worked under certain conditions. The door didn't know him. It didn't *let* him through. It just worked or didn't work by rules it wasn't even aware of.

Charlie looked up the stairs, toward the door that led to the hall; he could almost make it out. "Confidence," he told himself. Doubt was more than anything what locked the door.

He kept climbing. It didn't really matter if he thought it would work or not, did it? There was no turning back. He had the laptop in his

93

hand. He crept up the narrow stairs to the top floor, moving more carefully now, listening for anyone who might be in the hall. He put his ear to the door. He heard nothing. He let himself slowly out into the hallway just across from the wardrobe. If Colin had it in for him or Gary or OzHouse, the evidence would be here on the laptop. He'd just need a minute to find it.

He looked both ways—and bolted through the wardrobe. He laid his hand over the gump sensor as he crossed into the room. He'd heard all that mechanical head had to say years ago.

Inside, the green-tinted light of the familiar room seemed friendly. He relaxed. It would be a while before anyone looked for him in here. He put his hand on the book where he'd signed his name so long ago that he hardly recognized his own signature. He ran his hand along the name, and as he did, he had the sudden feeling that something wasn't right. Something in this room.

Funny how you can sense these things. He looked up. He knew where the source of the awkward feeling was. He turned his eyes to the gump.

There in the center, surrounded with toys like a kid in an oversized bathtub sat Gary, staring at him, just staring, and frowning in disapproval.

THE EMPEROR OF CHINA, wrapped in his royal bathrobe, slouched in the big chair in his chamber and stared at the diamond-studded bird. The little mechanical bird was singing—singing beautifully. Jessica recognized the tone and the melody. Another nightingale, a real one, the very one she'd met in the forest, sat on the branch of a Bonsai tree and harmonized with the mechanical bird fastened to a perch beside the emperor.

"P," said the royal chamberlain when Jessica asked him what the emperor was doing.

"That's what he says to everyone," sang the nightingale without interrupting its song.

"Even the emperor?" asked Jessica.

"The emperor is not everyone," said the Chamberlain as though he were talking to himself.

The nightingale had brought her here to the emperor's palace. He'd followed her to the parade and found her in the melee. When a blind old man had bumped into her and yelled at her to get to work, the nightingale flew by and sang her the way to the palace.

"But you told me not to go there," Jessica had said to the bird.

"Bad then, good now," said he bird. "Do you sing?"

94

"Of course I sing. But why is it good now?"

"Do you sing as pretty as I do?" asked the bird. "No one sings as pretty as I do," he went on.

"Why is it good to go now?" she asked again. "Isn't he vain and…and…and…" she was trying to remember where she could be. Who wrote "The Emperor's New Clothes" and that other story about the nightingale? Was it Grimms'? Because if it was Grimms'—witches that ate children, hags that were forced to dance in red hot shoes… But then it might have been Hans Christian Andersen. But then there was that poor match girl, and the steadfast tin soldier. People met such horrible ends there too.

"Sad," said the bird.

"I almost remember a story with a bird that talked much better than you do," said Jessica.

"I almost remember a song that brought tears to the emperor's eyes," sang the bird.

She followed the nightingale. She had nowhere else to go. She got the idea that the bird wanted her to help cheer up the emperor after his embarrassment. This was not the sort of thing she did well, however. But she went—hoping something would happen. Something always did.

"P," said the chamberlain when he met her at the door. But seeing the bird who was with her, he led them both to the emperor. They found him in his most private chamber, oblivious to the world, staring raptly at the diamond-studded bird.

When the artificial bird stopped singing, the emperor wound him up again, and he played a different tune, a pretty, very regular tune. And the real nightingale sang along, danced his voice along with and against the voice of the artificial bird—ran ahead and fell carefully behind, and added life to the mechanical bird's enchanting song. Jessica thought it was beautiful. The real bird had not always had so much success singing with the mechanical bird. It had had to learn the other bird's song, and that had been somewhat humbling, until it learned how to use the mechanical bird's song to make its own seem even prettier—and then it was as vain as ever. And the emperor cried, and then his teary face looked ever sadder. The bird seemed to be trying hard to cheer him up, but it wasn't enough. Jessica did not know what she was to do.

"Sire," said the Chamberlain, "I hate to interrupt you in your moment of grief, but the tailors…"

But the emperor didn't seem to be listening.

"They're getting away."

"Let them go," said the emperor.

"Sire, they are criminals, they are thieves, con artists. Worse than that, sire, they have embarrassed you in front of your subjects. They must be captured. They must be executed publicly as a warning to all who contemplate…"

"Let them go," repeated the emperor.

"Sometimes you need to just sit and listen to music," said Jessica to the chamberlain. And the chamberlain's eyes grew wide, and he lifted his hand as though to strike this dirty foreigner—and a girl no less—who'd dared address the emperor's minion in such a tone. But the nightingale, singing louder than ever, flew loops around the man's head and arms, confusing him. And the chamberlain knew better than to swing at the emperor's favorite bird. "Get this girl out of here," yelled the chamberlain to one of the maids standing by the door. But Jessica ran toward the emperor, and the nightingale flew back to the Bonsai tree. When the emperor put his arm around Jessica, the maid who had been running toward her at the command of the chamberlain stopped still and bowed.

"Shall I relieve you of this, this unusual peasant child?" she said.

The emperor looked at the maid. He was no longer crying. He no longer had the blank look on his face that had been there when he had spoken to the chamberlain. He smiled at Jessica. "No," he said to the nurse, looking all the while at Jessica. "This odd, brown-haired, large-nosed peasant child seems to have some wisdom for us, from whatever distant land she hales." And as he said this, he turned his head toward a full-length mirror in an ornate frame that stood in the corner of the room.

Jessica pressed her fingers to her nose. No one had ever called it large before. Not her mother, not Bill, not even in their hottest anger. She wanted to complain: her nose wasn't large. There was plenty about her that her mother had found to criticize, but her nose?

"What did she say about music?" asked the emperor. But he answered the question himself: "Sometimes you have to listen to music. It is very soothing, isn't it?"

"Sometimes I go to my room and put on my headphones and I don't have to hear them fighting."

"But, sire—" said the Chamberlain.

"Headphones?" asked the emperor. Jessica knew he'd never heard of them.

"Sire, this is not the time for sitting and music. Not now, sire."

"Not now?" shouted the emperor rising from his chair. And he looked down at his royal slippers and along the length of his royal robe as though he were reminding himself which of the two of them was the emperor and which the servant. The real nightingale stopped his singing. The mechanical one soldiered on.

"They have publicly..."

"Embarrassed me? Yes, I heard you. Or shall we say instead they have taught me a lesson? Perhaps I owe them a reward." He walked over to his great big looking glass, a beautiful oval mirror framed in ornate gold in which images of birds had been wrought, parrots and peacocks, and inlaid with the brightest jewels. "I think they have taught me two lessons," the emperor went on. "They have shown me first the danger of vanity. Perhaps I shall destroy this beautiful looking glass—or better yet, melt down the frame and set it in the plain wooden frame that it came in so as to give it its humble and rightful place. And they showed me as well my vulnerability." The emperor turned to the chamberlain as he spoke. "A valuable lesson that will protect me far into the future."

"But if they are allowed to go free..." reasoned the chamberlain.

"If they are allowed to go free, the people will think I am weak? Others will try to repeat the con, having no fear of me. That is what you were going to say, isn't it?"

The chamberlain stuttered and stammered and did not reply.

"And so you would have me punish these clever tailors to pay for the crimes some unknown future charlatan might commit? Is it not the fundamental principle of my empire that everyone pays for his own crime? That a punishment meted out as a sign to hypothetical future thieves, is it not itself a crime against justice? Is this not what separates us from the barbarian people?"

"With all due respect, sire..."

"Let them go," yelled the emperor. "And woe to the thief emboldened by the fraud of these two tailors. We will be ready for him—more ready than ever before."

The chamberlain puffed out his chest, but knew better than speak. He bowed, turned on his heels, and marched from the room. He was followed by the maids. When they were gone, the emperor turned to Jessica and motioned her over to him and thanked her. "I've always found that a public garden or an unscheduled holiday did more to recover one's reputation among the people than a public execution anyway," he said. And he seemed much recovered, and he called the little nightingale to him. The nightingale flew to his finger. "Wonderful bird," he said. The mechanical bird had wound down and stopped. Now the nightingale sang alone and the song was so cheerful it almost made the emperor laugh. "But on to business," said the emperor. "Who are you, little girl, and how did you get here. And do you belong to those tailors?"

97

"Why would I belong to the tailors?"

"They're the only foreigners around here besides you. You can't tell me you walked all the way from Europe by yourself."

So Jessica told him her whole story, starting with Bill breaking her CD player.

"What's a CD player?" asked the emperor.

"It's a machine that plays music."

"Like my bird," said the emperor, motioning to the mechanical nightingale.

Then she told him about the disappearance of Buddy through the wardrobe—she didn't suppose the rules of the Narnia room applied inside a fairy world— and how she too found her way to his fairyland version of China.

At first the emperor didn't seem to understand. "You've been to other worlds?" he asked. He seemed much more interested in this magic than in the loss of an unknown little boy.

"Yes," said Jessica. And she told him she'd been to Oz once, for a few minutes, until an irate munchkin farmer had scared her away—just because she'd tried to take his scarecrow down from its stake. She'd been under the sea once in the world of the mermaids and the undersea folk she'd read about in a book called *Wet Magic*—a very old book that Beth was fond of. And she'd met Robin Hood once. And the Sheriff of Nottingham scared her out that world. That was the time she'd tried to meet Queen Gwenivere to warn her about Lancelot and Mordrid. But she'd ended up in the wrong world. And she'd once met a boy named Snythergen, which was a very funny name. He said he knew Santa Claus, but she'd never managed to meet Santa Claus. Or Alice, although she'd tried to get to Wonderland several times to warn Alice about the Queen of Hearts and to help her get home.

"Alice," said the emperor then. "You know about Alice?"

The question confused Jessica. Could the Emperor of China really know of Alice in Wonderland? "Everyone in America has heard of Alice in Wonderland," she said.

The emperor had never heard of America.

"But how do *you* know about her?" asked Jessica.

And then he brought her to the mirror. "This," he said, "is the looking glass of Alice. Do you know why these tailors managed to fool me so easily—such a wise and beautiful emperor as I?" The nightingale sang a note of caution in the pause that followed the question. The emperor cleared his throat. "It is because these same two men several years before brought me this very mirror. They said it was from a foreign land and that it was full of magic, that if I stared into it, I would see right before my eyes a story unfold—the story of a little golden-haired girl lost in a dream searching for home." Then the emperor paused and looked at the nightingale on the Bonsai tree. "You know, now I wonder: being mountebanks, perhaps they didn't know themselves that they were telling the truth with the mirror."

"Or perhaps you and your kingdom are all fools," sang the nightingale. And the emperor looked at the bird and laughed. And the nightingale sang to Jessica, "My, but his clothes were beautiful."

The emperor took Jessica to the mirror and had her stare into it. "I have never allowed another soul to peer into my mirror," said the emperor. "It is my solace alone. I come to watch the story of the little girl lost in the dreamwoods whenever the business of the empire seems overwhelming. It's as soothing in its way as the nightingale's song. And everyone needs to listen to music now and then. As a reward to you for your timely advice, I shall allow you to see—the vision."

But Jessica didn't hear the emperor. She was staring though the mirror at the image of a caterpillar curled up like a cat on a mushroom. It was like watching TV, only everything seemed so much more solid than it does on a TV. And she wondered, *was this really* the *looking glass?* She reached her hand out to touch the glass, and her hand disappeared. The astonished emperor looked at the bird. He had never suspected this quality of the magic himself. And he was about to grab Jessica and toss her aside so he too could stick his hand through the mirror. But before he could, Jessica—not knowing exactly why, except that she was sure she'd never find Buddy in the world she was in—leapt through the mirror. She nearly crushed the caterpillar and his mushroom as she landed.

CHAPTER 11

SIR? SIR, PLEASE. You will have to remain calm and speak more slowly.

Yes, yes. All right. I am out at the foster halfway house, you know, that Oz place up on Old Mountain Road.

Your name, sir?

Colin Fuller-Brinks, the last name is hyphenated. I work for the New Hampshire DCYF. I am here investigating the disappearance of a young boy, and now it seems a girl as well.

And you said something about a murder and a robbery?

Yes. There is a young man here who was implicated in the murder of a small child several years ago. Now he is back and more children are missing. Not to mention he stole my briefcase and laptop.

You saw him do this?

No, but I know he did. But more importantly, someone needs to get up here. This Charles Emerson character is skulking about and no one seems to even care that his arrival coincides with two more murders. You don't have to be a rocket scientist to...

Two more murders? I thought you said they were missing. Have bodies been found?

No, not yet. But anyone can see he's up to no good. He's a brooding gawky kinda kid. The type to wear a long black trench coat, you know like those kids in Columbine.

Am I to understand that you have reason to believe murders have been committed? I have been monitoring the scanners all day, and this is the first time I have heard the word "murder" in connection to the disappearances.

Well they didn't just walk off the face the earth! I need some police up here right away. This is not a matter to be dismissed! I know you record these calls and when they find these bodies and realize that I called it in and you ignored me and allowed this gangster to slip away you can bet the media will have a field day with your career!

OK, OK, I'm sending a patrol car and two officers up there. Please be waiting by the entrance to meet them when they arrive so you can give them all the details. They will do what they can.

Do what they can! They must arrest Charles Emerson and force him to tell where he has hidden the bodies...and my laptop as well.

A police officer will have to assess the situation, Mr. Brinks, and they will take appropriate action as indicated.

Politically correct buffoons, they are all afraid of their own shadows, they never commit to anything, muttered Colin as he squeezed the red button on his cell phone and disconnected the call.

BUDDY WAS STILL CLUTCHING the hand-drawn map that the dwarf had given him. As he moved among the trees, he imagined that he was following the dotted line that Rumpelstiltskin had marked down to show him the simplest route to the town. He had never really looked at a map before, and he didn't understand any of the spidery words that were written in different places on the paper. Still, he marched through the forest with his eyes carefully fixed to the page, changing direction at every turn of the thick black line just as if he were actually following the directions.

"These houses must be the town I am spose to go to." Maybe that was where his mommy went after she left the shoe. Buddy had decided that his mother had gone to the shoe in Mother Goose Land to look for him among all those children. When she hadn't found him there, she'd moved on. And he was still going to find her.

He looked down at the simple drawings on the map and decided that the words "Bandits and Brigands; stay away from here" were the name of a place.

Luckily for Buddy the path he was following wasn't really taking him in the direction of any bandits or brigands, but was instead leading him to a forester's cabin. Sometime after noon, the boy saw the simple log cabin snugly built between the tall trees, and he approached the building with a big smile on his face. Maybe his mother was in there.

He knocked on the rough-hewn door. No answer. He knocked again and even kicked the door when his knocking made so little noise. He called "hello." All was silent in the woods as Buddy's voice was carried among the trunks of the trees and returned after striking the side of a cliff.

Although he remembered that his mother told him not to open other people's doors, he turned the door handle and found the cabin to be unlocked.

He thought perhaps he could wait inside. "I won't touch anything, so they won't be mad at me." He entered the simple room and sat on a wooden chair. He looked around. The room had a small but comfortable-looking bed with a colorful patchwork quilt in one corner. In the center of the room was a rustic wooden table with two chairs. On the other side of the room was a cast-iron stove with a thick black pipe that ran up to the ceiling and out of the cabin through the roof. Against the back wall, just under two windows, was a long table filled with utensils many of which Buddy had never seen before. And propped up against the wall near to the door was a large shotgun. Hanging from the beams were drying herbs and vegetables. And some kind of colorful bird hung there too, by its feet.

Buddy took a chair and tried hard to sit still and wait. He sat so long on the chair by the table near the stove that he soon began to get hungry. He was all out of apples, and he thought of looking about the cabin for something to eat. But he knew that if he were caught taking food, he would not be offered a place to sleep, and his fear of being alone in the woods at night was greater than his hunger. He sat and waited, sometimes switching chairs, until the cabin began to grow chilly with the coming of the evening; he hoped the owner of the cabin would return, and more than once he got up and laid his map out on the table and imagined himself trying to find the town on his own.

Eventually he noticed a woodcarving of a fox on a windowsill. Buddy didn't know it was a fox; he thought it was a dog with a long bushy tail. He pretended it was Scnapsy, and he told it how he missed sleeping with his old friend. He patted its head and pretended to comb its fur.

"When mommy comes home we will all go back to our house, and we can play and I promise to always remember to feed you," he told the wooden fox. "I'll even bring you to OzHouse so you can meet Gary and Gwen. You'd like them, they are really nice and I know they like dogs 'cause they seem to like lots of animals. Mommy will like Beth and Doug too and they can visit us sometimes."

The door handle rattled; Buddy jumped. The wooden door creaked open on its ancient hinges.

Standing in the doorway was a large, bearded, burly man in a checked jacket, a fur cap upon his head. Buddy thought he was a monster or a bear when he first caught a glimpse of the creature looming up in the entrance to the cabin, the fading sun behind him. The man's eyes fell immediately on the little boy.

"Who are you?" boomed the man.

"I… I'm Buddy and I didn't touch anything, honest I didn't!" Buddy glanced over at the fox as he said this.

"But what are you doing here? I mean out here in the middle of the woods, not to mention in my hunting cabin?"

"I went in the door and mommy wasn't in the shoe, and so Dumpty Dumpty said go to here and then the little man with the nose gave me the map so I came. Is my mommy here?"

His anxious speech was rewarded with a bright toothy smile from the forester. "That's quite the tale you tell, little man." He leaned his gun against the wall and removed a large pack from his shoulders. "I can't say as I know your mother, didn't see anyone new in the woods today. But you won't be the first lost child to cross my threshold. Kind of quiet since Sanna left. Make yourself useful and fetch some water from the pump outside, and I'll get the fire started in the stove."

Buddy didn't know how to get water from a pump, but he was thirsty, so he grabbed the pail the man held out to him and rushed outside just as if he did.

"GARY, I... I WASN'T expecting you in here," Charlie stammered.

"Obviously." An amused smile fell from Gary's face as he put down his book and crossed his arms. The authoritative pose was so rare with Gary—he really couldn't pull it off in ordinary circumstances—that Charlie bit his lip while his thoughts charged in all directions in search of an exit.

Charlie glanced at the guest book. Gary still hadn't signed it. "You're here, come and sign the book," he said with what seemed to Gary misplaced anxiety.

"I think you should be more concerned about that object in your hand than with that ledger book. We have much more important things to talk about."

"No, we don't. Just sign it." The tone in the boy's voice made Gary cautiously rise and slowly approach the book, a befuddled expression on his face. "If this isn't the most asinine thing I have ever heard of." Gary picked up the fancy pen.

"Please."

He looked down at the short list: Suzy Bishop, Charles Emerson, Rhonda Thompson, Lindy Mullen, Francine Conners, Markus Honner, Thomas Bennis, Bradley Levine, Edward Bouchard, Jessica Holton. "If you're trying to distract me, you're not buying more than ten seconds here with this book." With a quick flourish he scribbled *Gary Robbins* on the next available line on the page, just above the crayon scribbles that served as Buddy's signature.

"Now," began Gary, "I think you have some 'splainin' to do."

With a deep sigh, Charlie sat on the silver chair. "Well?" asked Gary. Charlie seemed to have forgotten Gary was still in the room. The young man looked sideways at his mentor. Now that he'd regained his composure, he wasn't sure he was going to speak.

"Don't do this, Charlie. I signed your damn book, now tell me about the computer."

Charlie waited several seconds more, and then he laughed, one quick bubble of laughter. "I waited ten years for you sign that book so I could talk to you about it. Now I don't know if I want to."

Gary leaned back against the couch, crossed his arms, and waited.

"You really don't know about it, do you?" said Charlie at last. "This wasn't just a test to see if I would follow the rules."

"What on earth are you talking about? What rules? After my recent defense of you, I'm frankly a little disappointed to see you sneaking in here with *that*."

"You really don't? God," Charlie filled his lungs and then exhaled all the air, "I figured out you didn't, but I still can't believe it: you people created this place and you don't know about the doorway."

"Of course we know about the doorway. I found the doorway. I had it shipped from England." And then he paused. "Doug got Beth, I got a closet. How do you think I got in this room just now? But that isn't what we are talking about."

"Yes, it is."

"The laptop, Charlie."

"Forget the laptop." Charlie placed it beside him in the chair. He held *The Scarecrow of Oz* on his hand and used it to point: "That door, that's where you'll find Buddy and probably this Jessica girl, not to mention Suzy."

Gary's eyes widened.

"What? Why are you looking at me like that? How can you not know about the door?"

"Slow down, Charlie. What have Jessica and Buddy and certainly Suzy Bishop got to do with your stealing Colin's laptop? Could we just start with that, please?"

"We've got to forget about the computer, Gary."

"No. Listen, Charlie..."

"Okay, okay, I took it. I needed to see what that moron had written about me, us, OzHouse. He wants to close this place down. Surely, you know that. God only knows how he's twisted things. We can't defend ourselves unless we know what that jerk is up to. He wants me in jail, I can tell you that much. I never met the guy before today, but he has it in for me anyway."

"Well, maybe you hadn't done anything before, but now you have stolen his computer, and when he catches you, he'll definitely press charges, and he will do everything he can to use this against both you and all of OzHouse. For the guy who wants to protect us, you have handed your enemy a hell of weapon."

"Lecture over?" Charlie asked with a roll of his big green eyes.

Gary sighed. "I am just trying to explain to you what's really going on here."

"No, you are lecturing me as if I were a child. But I'm not. And if we use the wardrobe and find the missing children, you will not have to worry about that idiot Colin or his plans to trash the reputation of your little mansion."

Gary stared hard at Charlie. It occurred to him only at that moment that something else was going on here—much more than the stolen computer. "Charlie," he said deliberately. He was still trying to process the signals.

But Charlie didn't let him talk. "So maybe it wasn't such a great idea. I mean, who am I to protect your hotel? Maybe I should just let you protect it yourself. But you don't even know how. You don't even have the first clue what's really going on here."

Gary rubbed his hands over his head and face as if to brush away everything that was upsetting him. Placing his hands on the boy's shoulders—a gesture that made Charlie squirm—he looked into his eyes.

"Chuck," he began. "I don't think *you* know how serious all this is. If you are found with this laptop, Colin, overstuffed pompous ass that he is, will have the right to charge you with a serious crime."

"What do you care?"

"What?"

"I mean it. What the hell do you care? I'd be gone, right? That's what this place is for, keep people alive until they can find someplace else. It's a bus station, for God's sake. Who cares who's on the bus as long as the seats are full? I'll just get off at the next stop."

Gary took his hands from the boy's shoulders but kept his gaze directly on Charlie. "What do I care?" A smile was growing on his own face. "What do I care?" He laughed. "After ten years, you're asking me that? The mouse feeds the lion cheese year after year, and then the lion says, 'You're just fattening me up because you want to eat me.' Listen to yourself: *'What do you care?'* Gary rolled his eyes and held onto a supercilious grin. "Wouldn't Gwen be in tears to hear you say such a thing? Beth would cash in the whole enterprise to think we'd accomplished so little in all these years." Gary still held the grin, but it was becoming more posed. "My God, Charlie. Step out here and listen to yourself. I wish I had a camera."

"You can afford..."

"That's us, all right. All we ever do is throw money into other people's wounds. And that's all you've ever been. I confess," he mocked, "you're just a hole we all just enjoyed tossing money in. I ran down to RISD because..." Gary laughed again, "because I had all this spare cash I needed to dispose of."

Charlie waved his hands in front of his face as though to block the words. "Nobody wants me here, Gary. That contract's over—okay, maybe *you* do, a little. But Gwen, and Doug, and Beth, they thought they'd gotten rid of me. Just like you do every kid you ever take in. Patch 'em up and send 'em out."

"I'll grant you Doug. I mean, he's Doug. Nice friend, great brother, but he's still Doug. When you're here he'll sell his soul if you need it. But when you're gone, you're gone. If *I* moved away, he'd hardly notice. But never mind that. You can't say that about Gwen or Beth—or me."

"You should've heard Beth ten minutes ago."

"You'll never have the first idea all we've done for you. This place is your home. And you're going to be welcome here always. You can move back in as a little old man with a walker as far as I'm concerned."

Charlie rolled his eyes and exhaled dubiously.

"Fine. Forget it. Hang onto the self-pity as long as you want. That's yours too. Feel free to keep it if you want. For now, let's get back to the topic. If you get caught with that laptop...."

"I have no intention of being caught with the laptop. I'm just gonna look at it. Them I'm gonna bring it with me through the door and leave it somewhere." And then after a moment, he added, "What *did* they do for me?"

"They kept you out of jail for starters. Okay?" Then he put his hand on the computer, which was again in Charlie's lap. "We can't go peeking into another man's personal things. And if you take this thing outside this room, you may be caught with it before you can leave it anywhere. I'm probably in trouble now just for knowing about it."

"Where I plan to take it, no one will find it. We can bring it to the restaurant at the end of the universe if we want. That is," Charlie said as he closed his eyes for a moment, "that is if we can get through the door. I haven't been able to for a long time, and let's face it, Gary, you're a lot older than me."

Once again Gary was confused. The doorway was wide enough. It was made to swing in either direction on very silent hinges.

"They kept me out of jail?"

"Yes."

"But I wasn't even guilty."

"Innocent people go to jail sometimes. How about this: just give me the laptop, and I'll tell Colin I found it. He'll still say you stole it but there won't be any evidence. It's not a great plan, but it's all I can think of right now."

"I still can't believe you don't understand," Charlie declared. "This *is* your place, isn't it?"

"Don't understand what? Charlie, what are you talking about?"

"The door. The enchantment." Charlie looked directly at Gary.

"What?" said Gary.

"It's not that easy to say. You're gonna think I'm crazy. Especially if it doesn't work, which for you is so likely it's almost certain. And so far you're the only one that hasn't thought I was crazy."

"That's ridiculous on so many levels. I'm certainly not going to think you're crazy. So just say it."

"I wasn't guilty."

"How about now?"

"I needed this laptop."

"It's still a crime, Charlie. Tell me about the door."

Charlie closed his eyes tight. "If we go through the wardrobe..."

"Yes..."

"And think about, you know, Baum for example..."

"Okay..."

"It will take us to Oz. There. I said it."

"Are you nuts?"

Charlie threw up his hands. "See. I told you. You think I'm nuts. And in case you're wondering, *nuts* and *crazy* are the same thing."

"I don't think you're crazy, Charlie. Maybe I think you're joking. I know you think I'm gullible. But, come on. You're telling me the wardrobe is magic?"

"Yes. The wardrobe is magic. It can bring you places."

"Like Narnia?" said Gary with a mocking smile.

"Like anywhere," Charlie insisted. "Usually it's what you have been reading last. If you were reading Lewis Carroll you might end up in Wonderland. If you were reading C.S. Lewis, then, sure, you could end up in Narnia."

"You're serious?" Gary sat down.

"But it is only reliable when you are really young. The older you get the less control you have, and eventually one day it seems to stop working. But I still think you could get it to work again, somehow. I'm sure I can. I don't think it's simply a matter of belief; that seems too simple. I think there is a trick to it, but I was never able to discuss it with anyone but kids because none of you guys signed the book, but I'm sure if it worked once you could make it work again. I think it has something to do with how kids believe in things rather than how we believe when we grow up. It's either something very simple or something very complex is my guess."

Gary chuckled. "Why...." but he didn't know what to add. He tried again, "Why would you think I'd take that bait? I'm a grown man."

Charlie stood up; he left the Oz book on the chair and tucked the laptop under his arm. "As I said, that's the problem." He grabbed Gary's hand and pulled him toward he door. Thinking the boy would get caught with the evidence, Gary started to pull back.

"No, don't," he said. But Charlie grabbed him and pulled him through the doorway and into the wardrobe.

"Nothing's gonna happen," said Charlie. As they exited the other side through the fur coats and into the hallway, Gary could hear commotion downstairs: walking and voices. A deep-voiced man and an authoritative woman that he didn't recognize. Nothing very strange about that. But they were walking toward the stairs and the voice of Colin Fuller-Brinks was with them. The police must have arrived, and they were arguing with Colin.

"Damn," said Charlie when they set their feet into the hall. "I shouldn't have said that. Try again." Gary didn't understand how the boy could be so calm.

"Oh, my God." Gary pulled Charlie back through the wardrobe and into the Narnia room. "You can't be caught with this."

"We're gonna try the door again." Charlie had become as calm as a man without conscience. "We both have to be thinking of a place we want to end up at."

"Chuck, you are losing it, man." Gary looked deeply at the troubled boy.

"Just do it with me," Charlie said. "Do you really believe *this* is all there is?" And by "this" he seemed to mean not just the Narnia room or OzHouse but the whole world. "How could it be? There are more things in heaven and on earth than are dreamt of in your philosophy, Gary."

"Quoting Shakespeare doesn't make it real, Charlie."

"Maybe it does. This is the only thing that matters," he tapped the wardrobe door. "It'll save us. Just come with me."

"We can't go out into the hallway. The police will see you with the laptop."

"If we do it right, we won't be in the hallway. Just try it again."

"Please, Charlie, not now."

"Just have faith. Nothing bad will happen. We don't have to worry about some stupid cops. We haven't done anything."

Gary sighed again. The voices were in the hallway now. They must be searching the whole house. Why else would they be up here? "Listen," he whispered and pointed. "If they come in here, we'll be found with the laptop. Do you have any idea how bad that would be?"

"Then let's escape to fairyland. I've done it before. We'll do it together. Come on."

Closer by the second. "Let's hope they've never read the Chronicles of Narnia."

"I'm going through. Come with me, Gary. Just accept it. Believe in OzHouse. Think of munchkins. Isn't that what it's for?" Charlie grabbed Gary's arm and pulled him toward the doorway. "I'm not a murderer. You know that. I never hurt any of those kids. Do you think I'm lame enough to walk into Colin's hands with the evidence? I'm not a criminal. Not really." He held up the laptop, closed his eyes as he fell into thoughts of fairylands, and walked toward the doorway.

"If the shoe fits," Gary said as he began to rush toward Charlie to stop him from walking through.

Sensing Gary about to stop him, Charlie tucked the laptop under his arm and dashed into the doorway. Gary yelled, "Don't" and bolted after him.

In a moment Gary burst out of the wardrobe and collapsed on the rug, stubbing his foot on the doorframe. The two policemen who were a few feet down the hall turned at the sound.

"Hey, you all right?" one asked as he put out his hand to help him up.

"Oh, yeah, sorry. Hello, officer. Excuse me. I tripped. I…Uh…" Gary turned quickly around.

"Where's Charlie?"

"That's what *we* are trying to find out," came the high-pitched squeak of Colin Fuller-Brinks.

Gary looked up and down the hallway. Charlie had been right in front of him. He couldn't have left the room without being seen, and yet he wasn't in the doorway, nor was he in the wardrobe or in the hall.

"Where did *you* come from?" Colin asked. Gary was still twisting and turning to look about.

"I... I was looking for Charlie and thought he might be up here."

And before he could find a way to distract them from the Narnia room—but why did he want to hide the Narnia room from the police? Charlie could not possibly still be in there. No, he wanted to keep it hidden because it was for children, that's why, and because it was private and secret and because if everyone found out about it and it was in the papers and it became common knowledge, well there went the magic of course. The real magic of the room, the moment of discovery and the "wow" you said on seeing all these amazing things, and the feeling of being part of the club. Yes, that was it. Not some insane idea that it could

111

actually take you someplace. But before he could distract them, Colin was already reaching into the wardrobe with his spidery fingers and his beaky nose. And he found it. He peeked into the wardrobe door and one of the fur coats was stuck in the secret doorway in the back.

Gary heard the voice of the mechanical gump head issuing superfluous greeting as the door swung open.

"There's a whole room back here," Colin yelled as though all the mysteries of the missing children had suddenly come clear to him and he was going to find dead bodies entombed in the walls. And of course it suddenly looked to everyone like they were hiding something.

"Do you mind if we look in there, Mr. Robbins?"

What could he say? If he told them to stay out, that would look even worse. "Of course. Go ahead. It's just a playroom for children."

And they all went in and, of course, found nothing. And Doug showed up. Colin asked if there were any more secret rooms, and Gary said no, and Doug added, "Of course there is the stairway." And if Gary'd had a skipper's hat on he would have smacked his brother over the head with it.

So they had to open the secret panel to the stairs, where they also found nothing. Oh, but Colin kept making remarks as though all these secret places somehow proved that OzHouse was hell and Charlie was its devil.

"Come on," Colin ordered the policemen. "We have permission to search the house, so let's get a move on, and see if we can find the two children and Mr. Emerson as well."

Sometime later, the policemen and Colin emerged in the Persian room with the giant TV staring back from the wall. Gary was rubbing his shin. "It couldn't be," he muttered. "This just doesn't make sense."

"THIS DOESN'T MAKE ANY SENSE," Charlie said to himself as he stood before a fancy daub and waddle house on a cobblestone road. I was thinking about Oz, but this isn't Oz. How could I have ended up here?" Where was here?

Just then the door opened and out came two women. One was very tall and thin, the other short and fat. Both were dressed in fancy lace gowns with their hair piled high on their heads in ringlets and curls.

"Imagine. She thinks she can go to the ball. What a joke. We'd be the laughing stock of the kingdom if people saw her dressed in rags and stained with cinders."

The two women walked down the street ignoring Charlie who was still clutching his stolen laptop. "If the shoe fits," he muttered in disgust. "Nice going, Gary."

CHAPTER 12

THE SIGN AT THE ENTRANCE TO THE LABYRINTH:

天安門

Tien an men: the gate of heavenly peace. It was a beautiful sign, naturally. Gwen wouldn't make anything that wasn't: a placid blue background, a pool of water reflecting the sky, the characters suggesting light on waves. The three Chinese characters had come through to her at some point during her casual study of Buddhism. It wasn't any specific reference to any Buddhist idea that caught her attention. She liked the idea of a gate you could pass through from the life of worries and confusion to the place where such things don't matter. And she liked the idea that the way through the gate was itself a maze—and yet not really a maze, a winding path that didn't offer confusion or difficulties, that led you unerringly, without any rational cause for anxiety, through its many folds to the peaceful center, although at no point until the final turn home did it allow you any sense of how close you were: complexity with its perception of challenge winding inevitably to the simple center of peace. That was the beauty and the metaphor of the labyrinth. You know you'll get there. You wind in all the way and then all the way out again and again. You rub your shoulder on the center before you file back to the outer edge. But in the end, you arrive, you make it. You know that. You have no sense of how close you've come—and then there you are.

Gary rarely wandered into Gwen's labyrinth. The few times he'd tried, he'd given up at the very door. "I'm not that restless," he'd say. There were pictures to draw; furniture to make, repairs to be done to the house. But if ever he needed the peace it might offer, it was now.

Gwen had named the labyrinth some time before she'd realized that the three innocently chosen characters were the very ones used to name a certain violently contested square in China. Gary couldn't help but think as he entered the labyrinth that the gate of heavenly peace was a place of much strife. Gwen refused to change the name. Perhaps she was just too fond of her beautiful sign. He only hoped the characters would work better here than they had on that awful day in Beijing.

Gary brushed along the high cedar hedge, watching his feet, counting his breaths, unconsciously pulling at the soft evergreen needles. A fragrance rose from the bruised twigs, calming—maybe—invoking the memory of cedar closets and cedar chests from the old house he'd grown up in. His shoulder rubbed against the evergreen wall as he walked; although the paths were wide, the sides high—high enough to shield you from the sight of anyone else who might be in the labyrinth at the moment—and the hedges were thick enough to keep you from the sound of other walkers, he liked the feeling on his arm of the push and the give of the thin branches.

Gwen let anyone use the labyrinth who wanted to. But the idea of the labyrinth was solitude: to get centered, to get into yourself and to concentrate, to meditate. Gary didn't usually have a hard time shedding his troubles, but things were different this time. He'd first thought to go to his workshop. But the workshop was filled with the memories of all the time he'd spent there with Charlie, and right now he needed to clear his head from all distractions and think about what Charlie had said.

As soon as she'd found him after Charlie disappeared, Gwen had seen how agitated he was.

"Do you want to talk about it?" she'd asked.

"I don't know what to say." Did he finally have to admit Charlie was a little off in the head—after defending him all these years?

"Where's Charlie?" she asked. There was an innocent question.

"He's gone." What else could he say? He tried to go on, "But he told me..."

"I guess it's for the best," she interrupted. "He was making Beth awful nervous, and..." but the agitation in Gary's hands as he took a sip of tea made her pause. "What did he tell you?" she asked.

"I'm not sure I can say."

And of course the worst possibilities flitted through her mind. She suggested Gary try the labyrinth. They could talk afterwards. She left him at the door. He saw her walk into the house. He watched the police and Colin Fuller-Brinks pull away. In a light jacket, he wasn't dressed for the late-autumn cold. But he didn't bother to get his winter coat.

He walked the labyrinth, breathing slowly and deeply, counting.

Meeting others on the path would make him self-conscious, just knowing they might be there, sensing him, thinking of him, made it harder. An image shot through his mind of Gwen following his progress, looking down at him from the widow's walk, watching his balding head move like a steel ball through the maze. But he mustn't think of such things. He'd never get centered that way. He needed to deal with these troubles, focus on the moment. It wasn't a maze; it was a labyrinth. There was a difference. Be calm, he told himself. Take it slow.

But what the hell was Charlie talking about—Wonderland, Oz, Cloud Cuckooland? And where the hell was he? The truth was he had disappeared. Charlie was gone—like Jessica, like Buddy. Could it be as simple as Charlie knowing of the secret passage across the hall from the Narnia room? Even if he did, did he have time to get in it? And if he could have gotten in, wouldn't he have shown himself by now—stashed the computer where the police would not think to look and emerged like a Sneetch with no star on his belly?

He wasn't hiding; he was gone.

But where? Fairy worlds were stories. He knew there were grownups who still believed in the little people. But not him. He knew to leave those things behind. That's not something any rational mind retreats back into. He loved children and children's books—he wasn't ashamed to admit that to anyone—he would still read them even if he didn't also draw the pictures for them. He didn't use the excuse that this was research. He wasn't ashamed to say so. He loved them all the more because of the trauma he'd undergone when he'd been forced to face the fact that this stuff wasn't real. The trees did not grow because gods or fairies pushed them up through the ground. Jack Frost was not out painting the leaves; butterfly-winged fairies didn't ride them back to earth the way his imagination told him they must. The modern world had managed to kill all but the most tenacious of gods. But the imagination was still alive—the astonishing human power of fantasy. Was it possible to wonder, again, if, perhaps, somehow, some of that stuff was actually real, that there was, actually, magic in the world? Or did that thought mean he too was crazy? What had happened? Gary could only think that Charlie must have rushed into the secret hallway. But as far as Gary knew, that was the one part the house Charlie didn't know about. They'd used it mostly to entertain the kids throughout the years. The kids could walk out of the room with Beth or Gwen and then be brought back in on pretense of forgetting something, and there Santa Claus would be with his package of presents. It wouldn't make sense to let even Charlie in on that secret.

So where was he?

Gary went over it again and again: Charlie went through the wardrobe, Gary went right behind him. But when he was in the hallway, Charlie was gone.

And the police and that jelly brain Colin Brinks, Colin Fuller-Brinks, had been right there. Gary watched his feet pass over the smooth, round stones as he wound through the labyrinth; there had been no way for Charlie to go anywhere. But he was gone.

Okay, but no matter what Charlie said, fairyland was only in books.

He found nothing calming in this labyrinth. How come it worked so well for Gwen? He turned another corner, let the labyrinth lead him in its way, in its time. He slowed his pace. He felt the evergreen branches rub through his gloveless hand in the cold autumn air.

Did the police really accept the story of the briefcase or just pretend to? Colin found the briefcase, in the kitchen of all places, right out there in the open. Why would Charlie carefully hide the stolen computer and leave the stolen briefcase on the kitchen counter?

He knew why. Of course he did. That was an easy one. Charlie had decided he didn't need the briefcase after all, that the real incriminating stuff would be on the computer, and he'd left the briefcase where Colin could be convinced he'd forgotten it—or where others might be convinced that Colin had forgotten it. Which is just how it had worked.

"Now, if he stole it," Gary had said to Colin in front of the officers, "why would he have put it here, where anyone could see it?"

"But there was a laptop with it. Where's the laptop?"

"Wherever *you* left it," said Gary. "You drive off with your briefcase on our kitchen counter, who knows where you left the laptop."

"Do you have any proof that he took the laptop from your car, Mr. Brinks?" asked one of the officers.

"It's Fuller-Brinks. And he was the only one…"

"Did you actually see him do it?" asked the other.

"Well, no. But…"

Which story did the police prefer? It was hard to tell. They were trained to keep their observations to themselves, he supposed, let the criminals keep talking until they slip up. Had *he* slipped up?

Gary pulled into the space at the center of the labyrinth—at last. It wasn't working at all. He felt about as peaceful as a twig in a tornado. He stepped around the corner—and there was Gwen, sitting quietly on the stone bench beside the statue of the Minotaur, so deep in her own thoughts, she didn't seem to know he was there.

"What are *you*… How'd you get here?" He didn't know of any secret passages in the labyrinth, though apparently there was one. She looked up at him, but didn't explain. Every marriage needs its moments of surprise.

"Not that I want to make things worse," she said. "But I thought you ought to know. We got a phone call." Gary sat beside her on the bench. "You won't believe it. Apparently the woman has got a lawyer."

Gary looked back at the stone monster. Gwen had never liked it. Hardly conducive to the mood. But Gary had held out: "Think of it as a test of how firm the peace is; if you can maintain it in the shade of this— then, well, then you got it." This was before the hedge was high enough to block it. He turned back to Gwen. "She's probably been in trouble with the law before. I imagine it's not the first time she's tried to sue someone."

THIS TIME, JESSICA WAS REALLY LOST. She remembered coming through the mirror, brushing the side of a great mushroom and landing in a heap on the ground. And then there was that hookah-smoking caterpillar. And at one point she was pretty sure she ate the mushroom—she could still sense the dusty taste in her mouth. And then there was the boy with the vorpal blade complaining he had nothing to hunt. And now she was here, wherever *here* was, a gloomy path in a damp wood on a shivering cold day. Had a whole night passed? Had she slept? Or had the mushroom done something to her? Huge, dark leafless trees surrounded her. It was some part of Wonderland, of course, or Lookinglassland. But it didn't seem right.

She had to think about Alice. Now that she was actually here—all those times she tried to get here and couldn't make it—she had to try to remember what this world was like so she could be ready. In all those times she'd tried to get here, she'd never made it because, she decided, she had always been a little afraid of Alice's world: scary things came upon you so suddenly here, like a dream. Alice was always running into one ordeal after another—and all those strange creatures: the March Hare and the Mad Hatter and the Queen of Hearts and the Cheshire Cat. Everyone was a little bit crazy. But Jessica hadn't run into hardly anyone since the bigheaded old Caterpillar. Not the Walrus and the Carpenter or Tweedledum or Tweedledee or the White Knight. Oh, and wasn't she getting the two stories mixed up? She hated it when people got the stories mixed up. But now *she* was doing it. And wasn't that Caterpillar in Wonderland? And yet she'd seen him through the lookinglass, and she'd gone through the lookinglass to get here. But then, the worlds were connected. She'd always known that. It's no wonder they'd be jumbled in her experience if they were jumbled in her head. But maybe it wouldn't be scary now that she was in it. There was certainly going to be an adventure here somewhere. And maybe she'd get to meet Alice, who was such a thoughtful girl and needed a friend so badly.

Then she stopped right where she was and leaned her back against a huge brick wall she hadn't seen before. Each brick was as tall as she was. "Oh, no," she said. "There you go, Jess, letting your mind wander. I'm not doing my job. I need to fix things. I need to find Buddy so we can go home."

And where was Buddy? And was she any closer to him now than she was when she landed in the emperor's woods? And how would she get back to those woods if she couldn't remember where the Caterpillar was?

Her whole experience since she had crossed into this world, it was like she was waking up from a dream that she was rapidly losing. And what was this high wall she was standing beside with its great big bricks stuck out in the middle of the woods? And what were those huge dirty white cloudlike things floating—or rather, more like bouncing back and forth above her head?

The dirty white cloud-like things spread apart and in the space between appeared two gigantic eyes beneath which spread a huge, sinister grin. Jessica jumped back. Those cloud-like things were the bottoms of a pair of stockings! And there was a giant sitting on the wall staring down between his feet. She cringed and had to hold her ears at the sound of his strange, booming voice: "My," he said, "been to see the Caterpillar have you?" The voice almost knocked her over.

"How did you know that?" she yelled up.

"What?" he boomed back.

"I said, 'How did you know that?'"

"I'm afraid if you wish to talk, you'll have to grow first."

"How do I do that?" she yelled.

"What?" the figure yelled back.

"I said, 'How do I do that?'"

120

"Little—whatever you are—I won't say this again, if you want to talk to me, you'll have to eat the other side of the mushroom."

"Ah," said Jessica to herself. "Only, I don't have any mushrooms." And this was just as well, because she hated mushrooms. But then she remembered the story. And she put her hands in her pockets. Sure enough, there was a bit of mushroom in each one. She pulled the pieces out. It seemed the Caterpillar's routine hadn't changed much in all the years he'd been smoking that pipe. "I wonder if he'll ever turn into a butterfly," thought Jessica as she put the mushroom bits to her nose to see if she could find any clue which one to nibble. "I'd just as soon not have to nibble either side again," she said to herself. "Alice," she said, "licked one I think to see what it did. But Alice also was afraid she'd go out like a candle." As Jessica was thinking how unpleasant it would be to go out like a candle (although it certainly would save her a lot of trouble, she thought, and she almost laughed), she noticed that one of the two pieces had already been nibbled. She immediately and without thinking pinched her nose and took a good bite out of the other.

Next thing she knew she was staring Humpty Dumpty in the eye.

"Do you recall rule 42?" asked the egg man.

"Forty-two?" asked Jessica. "I believe that's the answer to the ultimate…"

"No, it is not," said the other sharply. "It means everyone more than a mile high must leave the courtroom."

Jessica was neither a mile high nor in a courtroom (as far as she could tell). But she was, she judged—as well as she could, having no reliable point of reference—quite a bit taller than she had ever been before. She was tall enough to put her hands on the wall whose bricks were now no longer than her finger and peer over the top into the strange configuration of paths on the other side.

"Back up," yelled the egg. "No one's allowed to look into the garden from that direction but me."

"And the birds," said Jessica, backing up.

"Nibble your mushroom or I will not utter another Word."

"Is that a labyrinth on the other side of the wall?" asked Jessica.

"The mush…" began Humpty, but he clamped his mouth together to keep himself from talking.

"Well now you've already said another word and a half, so you might as well keep talking," said Jessica, who wasn't entirely sure that the privilege of talking to Humpty Dumpty was worth the price of shrinking back to the size of little girl.

"And I suppose once you've broken one dish you're entitled to break them all," said the egg.

"I guess not," said Jessica.

Humpty Dumpty said no more, but stood staring, his eyebrows raised as though to remind the girl of what she needed to do if she wished to continue the conversation. "Oh, all right," said Jessica, trying to remember again which was the shrinking mushroom and which the growing, now that they were both nibbled. "Left for shrinking, I think," she said. Glancing again at the funny egg man's stern expression, she nibbled without holding her nose.

"Yuck," she said as with a whoosh of air and a roller-coaster feeling in her stomach, she compacted into her normal height. "I wish I had a pizza."

"I'm reminded of a rhyme," said Humpty Dumpty in an astonishingly friendly tone:

She asked me if I'd crash the plates
And take a bath in brine
I said I wouldn't hesitate
I do it all the time.

Eighty-four past six o'clock
I'm tilting into bed
I barely had the time to talk
Or climb into my head.

All the horses in the field
Are singing to my eye
Ga-lumph ga-lae the horsy pealed
Until her head was dry

I used to have another bat
Inside the circus tent
Until he burned the circus flat
And far away she went.

Will you learn me what I teach
Or teach me to lament?
I'd rather sing about the witch
Who swims in wet cement.

"There is also a chorus," said the egg man, approximating a bow without standing up.

"I'm sorry," Jessica interrupted as politely as she could, "I've read the books. And I don't have time for nonsense. I have to find Buddy."

"Nonsense?" yelled the egg. "Nonsense?" he repeated, pulling himself to his feet and pacing up and down the wall, his shell face growing so red Jessica was afraid his yoke might harden. "Nonsense!" he repeated as though that was all he could think of to say—and yet at the same time as though everything he needed to say had been said in that word: everything from "That certainly wasn't nonsense," to "You, child, have very little time for anything that isn't nonsense," to "How could anyone be such a fool as not to get it?" And he continued to pace up and down the wall, repeating the word to himself in every tone he could find to say it in, until he was finally just muttering. Jessica had to struggle against feeling foolish. She said to herself, "You can't swim in wet cement." She decided to leave him there muttering, and she would truly have done so if she'd had anywhere to go. "I'm sorry that I didn't like your poem. I did like it, really, but I have to find Buddy," she said. "Have you seen anyone like me pass by here?"

"Believe me there's no one like you since what's her name…"

"Alice?"

"Yes, Alice, and that was a hundred years ago if it was yesterday."

"I'm looking for a little boy," she said.

"Oh," said Humpty Dumpty, and he stopped pacing for a second. "Did you say Buddy?"

"Yes."

"Well if it's the same Buddy—you see visitors from Out There do come to this world. At least it's not unheard of. But he came to—" and then he whispered the name "—*M.G. Land*, which is not supposed to happen. I sent him with Tommy Tucker and—and whoever his girlfriend was that day. Nancy? Yes, Nancy. I'm sure of it."

"I knew it," said Jessica. "Can you get there from here?"

"*I* can. I do it all the time. But as for the more sensible question of whether *you* can, I greatly doubt it. You'd have to make your way through the maze just for starters—and it's not a labyrinth. A labyrinth is quite another thing. A maze isn't easy, not at all. And even if you do make it, there's only one chance in a thousand odd that you'd end up there. Only I know the true path."

"Will you show me?"

Humpty Dumpty laughed at this. "*Me* show *you* how to navigate the maze?" He laughed so hard he nearly tumbled.

"Why not?" asked Jessica, who had given up being polite entirely and was becoming boiling mad herself. But Humpty Dumpty just kept laughing. And he became as he laughed increasingly unbalanced, until he began wheeling his arms to stay atop the wall. But it didn't work. He leaned back over the wall, then one foot went up in the air, his arms spread as wide as they could go. Then the other foot too left the wall. And there was no recovering from that. He tumbled backwards, over the wall. And the fall was followed by a most disturbing SPLAT.

Jessica ran through the archway in the wall and then took several steps into the maze to see if she could help. But wherever she walked there was an impenetrable hedge between her and the place Humpty Dumpty had fallen.

"Are you all right," she yelled.

"Been better," came a thin voice through the foliage.

"Should I try to get to you?" Humpty Dumpty tried to laugh.

"Now you'll never be together again. And it's all my fault because I didn't like your poem."

"Never together?" And Humpty Dumpty managed a chuckle this time.

"All the king's horses and all the king's…."

"Never mind the kings," he said. "Ever known a king to fix anything? Don't think this is the first time this has happened. Happens all the time."

But Jessica didn't understand. "The rhyme says…"

"Yes, yes, yes. Feel guilty if you like. I'll be fine. As soon as someone turns the page." He didn't sound fine. He sounded like an egg whose yoke was seeping into the ground. The last sentence was as much groaned as spoken. She tried several more times to talk to him, but if he responded, she couldn't hear it. The harder she tried to get close to him in this infernal maze the farther away she seemed to get.

She decided to run back through the arch, which would be as close as she could imagine to turning back a page. But she was already lost, or perhaps the door had disappeared. How come you can never go back?

"I have to find him," she said to herself. "He needs help and it's my fault." Soon, however, she was so lost in the maze that finding neither Humpty Dumpty nor Mother Goose Land was a sensible or even a possible thing to do. All that she could hope to do was to find her way out. Any way at all.

Humpty Dumpty had not exaggerated the difficulty of the maze. She was hours and hours exploring the paths, constantly hitting dead ends and trying to remember her route, thinking clever ways to mark her progress, such as breaking off twigs as she had done in the emperor's woods. But still she half suspected that there was a power in the maze that cleaned up all footprints and debris. And as she grew hungrier and more tired, she was never sure she wasn't traveling around the same paths endlessly. At one point she tried turning left at every option. But that made her think she might well be traveling in a square. She tried alternating left and right, until she figured out that no maze maker would make a maze that easy to solve. She tried following the sun, but as soon as she did, the sky clouded over.

The maze was not, however, merely paths and hedges. And every once in a while she confirmed that if she had not made progress at least she'd gotten herself to a part of the thing she'd never been to before. At one point, she entered a square where she'd found a statue and a little garden, at another point a garden with a tree. At still another point the maze seemed to stop. She turned a corner and stood before a gaping open field. "I've come out, at last," she yelled. And she ran the way that Dorothy ran through the poppy field. But it turned out that this field was just another trick of the maze. On the other side, in fact on all sides, there were more hedges, more entrances, more zigzag hallways. Countless hours after she entered the maze she thought of the mushroom. "What an idiot you are, Jessica," she reprimanded herself. "All you have to do is eat the right mushroom and you'll be able to see over the top of the maze." That would make her way through very much easier. Unfortunately, she ate the left mushroom first in her haste and shrunk to the size of a bug. All the rest of the remaining right mushroom was only enough to get her back to her normal size.

It was a sad little girl who found a little grove of fruit trees in the maze as evening drew on. Not even the sight of all the ripe fruit she could possibly want made her feel any better. Still, she ate her fill and sat down to sleep until morning.

And then, just before she closed her eyes, suddenly there stood before her, without any sort of warning, a little girl, not quite as old as Jessica, a blonde-headed girl dressed in a fancy dress of several shades of green. Jessica was sure she must have been dreaming.

"Alice?" asked Jessica.

"Alice who?" asked the girl in a tone much more grown up than a little girl should use. "I'm sorry. I don't have time for this now. I promise I'll help you as soon as I can. But right now, I'm in the middle of—never mind, I can't even begin to tell you how complicated it is, and I don't have any idea how we'll get out of it. You're just lucky I was looking in the picture."

"Do you know the way out?"

"I know how to get you out. You can come with me. Stand up."

"I need to find Buddy," she said.

"Who's Buddy? Never mind. Look, I have to get right back now. I won't force you to come if you don't want to. But I have to get back now. You're pretty lucky I had the urge to look in on that place. I haven't told anyone, but I think they're mixed up in this somehow. Don't ask me how. That Gary—he's so much older now—walking through that labyrinth thing, talking to Gwen—and let me tell you she's older too—talking about someone named Jessica and how her mother's suing them. So I said, 'Show me Jessica,' and here you are in a worse mess than them."

"My mother is suing them? Is it because of me?"

"I'm sorry I don't have time. Are you coming with me?"

"Can you get me to Mother Goose Land?"

"That's what you'd prefer?"

"I have to. Then I have to go back. Can you get me back?"

"I could get you anywhere at all, if I had time. But I'm afraid I don't even have time for this. I'll do my best to keep an eye on you, if you like. I can't promise anything right now, unless this crisis has passed—assuming of course that it does pass. The picture itself isn't working the way it should. But I will do my best. Come on. We only have a minute."

And then the strange girl, who seemed so much older than her years, lifted her hand over her head as though she were signaling someone far away.

"What's your name?" asked Jessica.

"Suzy," she said. "Suzy Bishop." And then she disappeared.

Jessica had just time then to wonder if any of that had really happened before she blinked, and there in front of her was Humpty Dumpty; he was back together, sitting upon his wall, staring down at her. And it wasn't nighttime any more. It was bright day. And behind the egg was no maze, just a field and then a forest. Behind her was different too: a hill with a castle upon it. And in the distance stood houses of funny shapes and sizes—one she could clearly see was a giant shoe.

CHAPTER 13

ON MY WAY AGAIN up to that Wonderland on Old Mountain Road they call Oz House. Once we shut it down perhaps they'll turn it into an amusement park or a haunted mansion. It's half way there already. Problem with the culture these days: all these rich people paying their way out of trouble so they can continue their crimes. Call me an idealist. I'm going to stop it this time. This time, we'll shut them down for good. Keep them away from children.

Which would make me the hero.

Call it my instincts or a gut feeling, but I know they are hiding something. That Emerson boy is involved in this up to his pimply, redheaded scrawny neck. I would bet my 401K on it.

It cannot be a coincidence that he has been seen up there after all this time and more children are missing. From the reports I read everyone suspected this kid of being involved in the abduction and murder of the Bishop girl. Of course with no corpse there cannot be a prosecution.

Of course he killed her and God knows what else. Torture, and most probably rape.

"You friggin' pig!" Charlie yelled at the screen.

If those Robbins people won't work with me, I'll dig around under the guise of looking for this latest missing kid, Buddy Summers or something like that. Of course Mr. Samuels my administrative boss isn't going to close down Oz House because of a few missing kids. Hell there probably isn't a foster care program that hasn't lost kids... But murder! That's the trick! If I can prove that this Emerson kid murdered these two children, that will tip the scales. Maybe they've got enough money to beat even a murder rap. But they won't have any left when they're done!

All I will have to prove is that one or more of the Robbinses knew about the murder and helped cover it up.

Once I prove that little degenerate is a psychopath, I think pulling Gary Robbins or his brother into it will be easy. You publish a few books, sell a few pictures and you think you're God's gift to humanity. Yes, you know better than the administrative peon how to help troubled kids, don't you? Get yourself a little dough, a house out of a comic book and suddenly you know better than everyone about everything!

I heard that self-satisfied Brit Beth Robbins calling me a pompous stuffed shirt. When my theory is proven correct she'll sing a different tune. I'll get a good chapter of my book out of this kid, and I will not let the police's sloppy guesswork investigation screw it all up. But I need a body or both bodies would be better still. I'll have a chat with Charlie Emerson and let him blab on about things. People like him like to talk, they enjoy dropping hints they're sure you'll never pick up; it should be easy to trip him up. Then we'll have him! They all laughed at my theory at the meeting. We'll see who is laughing when I dig up the decomposed bodies of those kids with Charlie Emerson's fingerprints and DNA all over them.

"You jerk! I knew it." Charlie clicked the appropriate buttons and waited for the laptop to shut down. "Violent psychopath!"

Two small children walked by. They were carrying a water bucket between them, trying hard not to splash themselves. They slowed down further as they passed the bizarrely costumed figure sitting on the stone wall, a black box on his lap, muttering to himself.

"He thinks I'm a psychopath," he said. And the children must have wondered if he were talking to them. He looked right at them. And he was smiling like a jack-o-lantern. "If I were a psychopath, I'd crawl right back through the wardrobe and smash this computer over his head. I would've strewn Matt Frewer over the classroom and left his paints alone." The children smiled; their eyes grew big. Big waves spilled over the sides of their bucket as they hurried home.

Charlie removed the bootable floppy disc.

128

It might be amusing to give Brinks a good scare, carve crazy logos and pictures, skulls and bones into the body of this guy's laptop, find a still from *Friday the 13th* for his wallpaper then let him find his computer just where he found his briefcase. But, really, the only way to stop him was to find the kids.

Charlie folded the computer shut and tucked the disc into this pocket. It hadn't taken him long to break into Colin's computer. He had chuckled to himself as he quickly avoided dealing with all of Colin's passwords and simply turned on the laptop and allowed it to boot using his disc and then accessed the C-drive. They always made it look so difficult in the movies, trying to guess the person's password and all that hacking. A child could do it.

With the laptop tucked under his arm, Charlie returned to the cobblestone road. Cinderella's thatched cottage was just across the way. It seemed the wardrobe was not going to take him to Oz today. He could go back and try again. But on the other hand, he was here, and it had been hard enough getting anywhere. And if he went back now and stumbled onto Gary again or anyone in OzHouse for that matter, he'd have nothing to show. No, he might as well look around. The goal was still Oz. But there was no way to be sure Suzy was still there even if she had made it to her favorite country to begin with. Any of the three of them could just as well be here. It made sense. And if you are trying to find children, you have to get yourself to worlds that might appeal to them. Problem was, of course, those worlds did not particularly appeal to Charlie any more. This world was probably the youngest one he could still get into without too much difficulty. Little kids—little girls especially he supposed, even today with feminism in full flower—liked the idea of the poor princess meeting her rich prince. Charlie on the other hand was more in tune with the Freudian imagery, all those feet going in and out of that shoe. There was a girl in PY101 who was morbidly offended when their professor had pointed that out (she had her own Freudian issues no doubt). But, hey, something must keep us reading these same bizarre stories year after year.

He approached the simple wooden door in the plain white wall of the house and wondered if he should knock. This would be the servants' entrance. Did people knock at servants' entrances? Did people knock on other people's doors at all in this world, or was that just an our-world custom? Just then, the door swung open.

A very puzzled young woman dressed all in rags stood before him. He knew immediately it was she; it had to be—although she was far more ragged than he'd ever seen illustration of in any book, and it was certainly unusual to meet the most famous character of a story right off the

129

bat like this. Her dress was torn from hem to thigh in a dozen places. It looked a little like the shreds of a garment used in a gypsy dance except that the rags were stained and dirty. Her hands were darkened by soot and when she wiped her cheek, she left a line of soot there as well. The author must have done an awful lot of rewriting on this one. This young woman was not by any stretch beautiful. Her teeth weren't even straight. And her hair, long and something close to blonde, fell in knotted bunches from her simple bonnet; it needed more than a good brushing, it needed a strong shampoo and a bottle of conditioner as well. He thought of the way the auburn hair of Stacey, the life-drawing model, had framed her head and shoulders back at RISD. Princes must have pretty low standards in this part of the world, he thought. And there was a distinct odor of sweat and cooking grease that reminded him of the smell that clung to high school kids after a long shift at a fast food place. He hoped it was mostly just coming from the room, but of course it had to be coming from her.

No, she was not the vision of loveliness that was supposed to be so enchanting to Prince Charming, and that not too long from now, judging from her age. He wondered if maybe his part in the story should be to come back with a stylist and a clothing consultant.

Still there was one part of her that truly was enchanting, a part hard to hide or miss. It was her eyes. Yes. Large and green and very expressive, they stared mildly at him while the enigmatic twist of her mouth seemed to say, "What on earth is this strange creature standing outside my door?" Charlie stood across the threshold gawking at her eyes. You could put those eyes on anyone and they would do something to redeem any plainness in the rest.

"Hi," was all he muttered.

"High?" she said as if it were a question.

"You must be Cinderella, right?"

"I have been called such by some, but judging by your attire I should think you'd be more understanding."

"Oh, my God, I'm sorry."

Her eyes widened again and she gasped. Charlie realized he'd need to watch his language in this world. He apologized again, "I wasn't thinking. Of course that's not your real name," as Charlie stumbled through the words trying to apologize, he thought about his own torn jeans, his tie-dyed T-shirt and patched stonewashed denim jacket. What else could she think but that he was a poor peasant boy wandering homeless on the road?

"Really, it's all right. I'm used to the name by now. It's all anyone calls me since my father died. Have you some goods to offer?" She stared at the laptop hanging from his arm.

"Uh, ah, no, no, no. I'm here..." He really should have thought this out a little better before barging into the life of an other-worldly character.

"Then what is that black..." she paused, she could not come up with the word and had to settle at last on "thing," "that black thing that you carry? I am sorry to say if it is alms you seek, I have none to give, and as for my stepmother..."

"I'm sorry." He put the computer behind him. It probably would be best not to have to talk to her about technology. "I'm looking for some lost children."

The idea of lost children got her interest. She invited Charlie in and offered him tea. Without thinking, he laid the laptop on the table as she put some more kindling in the cast-iron stove and ladled water into the cast-iron pot. As she worked she sang, and her voice was even prettier than the voice of Lesley Ann Warren. Charlie was unfamiliar with the melody but the sweetness of the plain tune made him look again at the young woman putting wood in the stove. For all the hard work she'd been forced to do, her body under her loose fitting rags moved easily. He could detect the sweep of her shoulders and could imagine the shape of her legs when she scrunched down and then held herself with a fluid movement like that of a gymnast. He started to imagine her hair cleaned and flowing easily down her neck and shoulders, illuminating her face. It was long and thick and would no doubt be very pretty. He put in his artist eyes and thought of all the bodies he'd studied closely in life-drawing classes. He could see by how she moved exactly what she was like. This was a subject for an artist. If only he had a pen with him. Would it charm her to see him draw her?

Better start with her fully clothed.

The melody of her singing seemed to help his imagination clean the soot from her face. That face had a nice shape to it, really. And the irregularity in her teeth, the way the incisor tucked itself a little bit behind the canine, now that he looked again, it was kind of charming.

She broke off her song and walked back to the table. "And is this... box," yes, she decided it was a box, "is this box going to help you find the children?"

Charlie pulled the computer toward him. He should have put it on the stool or kept in on his lap where she couldn't ask about it. "You haven't seen any strange children, have you?" He tried to change the subject.

"Well..." she took a few moments to think. "There have been some strange things reported around here lately. But I don't remember any having to do with children." Then she reached out and touched the hard plastic of the computer case. "What is it made of?" she asked. "What's inside?"

"You wouldn't know the word," he told her. He was going to have a hard time getting her to ignore the thing. "It's really not important. I don't think polymers or silicone are ever likely to make it into fairyland."

"Oh," she said, sitting back into her chair with a kind of sad pout on her face.

"What?" he asked.

"I'm very tired of people assuming I am not to know what is what. 'Keep Cinder-Ella ignorant and happy.' Happy? Huh. Here? In the scullery? First, my mother dies. Did anyone tell me she was even sick? No. Why worry poor Ella. Back then my name was Ella. And as for the little brother or sister I was supposed to have, he doesn't show up either. No one tells me why. Then, my father comes home one day with a wife. I don't even know he's engaged, and all of a sudden, I'm the subject of an evil tyrant with delusions of grandeur. Then boom, dad dies. Same thing with my mother. No one even tells me he's sick. My stepmother must have known all about it. He must have been sick a long time. He's barely dead but the hearse shows up and off he goes. I don't even know where they buried the body. And then, just yesterday a message comes from the prince and he's throwing a ball for all the young maidens in the land. But do I get invited? No. They didn't even want me to know it was happening. And now you come in. You're poor like me. I thought maybe you would at least talk to me. And you bring this strange little box that's made out of some magic polygar silk cone and you won't tell me about that."

"Oh," he said, not knowing where to go with a speech like that one.

"You're not very talkative are you?"

Just Charlie's luck. The moment he starts to realize she really is kind of attractive, a woman he'd like to get to know, he finds he's been blowing it all along. "No," he said quickly. "It's not that at all. I love to talk. When I get going, people can't shut me up." He couldn't actually remember a lot of times when that had happened, but he hoped it was so. "It's a computer." He opened it up to reveal the keyboard and, what the heck, turned it on as well.

The screen sent shadows across her astonished face. She'd seen magic, he assumed. But nothing like this. The notes the system played on startup made her smile. So did the icons that moved across the screen. Even the innocuous background photo of a snow-covered hillside made her giggle. He looked for some picture files. But the file names in Colin Fuller-Brinks' picture folders (Janet.jpg, HelenStill.tif, PamA.bmp) made him think it might be awkward to go further in that direction. On a whim, he clicked on the internet browser icon. And to his astonishment, it seemed to work. Wi-fi in fairyland? No sense questioning it. He immediately went to a site where he'd stored scanned images of some of his own work. She'd never seen anything like that either. The non-representational pieces had no immediate appeal. But the vividly colored fantasy worlds made her big eyes grow even larger.

"Is that what your country is like?" she asked. And, "Do women wear such funny clothing there?" She had watched how his finger moved over the mousepad and reached over the table to try for herself. She clicked on a file named Fd06.jpg. Up popped a quick sketch from his life drawing class; it was Stacey, the very woman who had so recently rejected his advances. Oops. His jaw dropped. Would it be possible to explain to a woman from a children's story why he would have such a picture?

"You're married," she said.

"No," he said.

"You have to be. No woman is going to let you just do that to her if you're not married."

"It was a class," he said.

She got up to get the water for the tea. "I think we should talk about your lost children," she said. "Maybe I can help you." The sudden business-like turn of her speech startled him back to his senses.

Charlie fiddled with the silver ring that dangled from his left eyebrow. He wanted to think of a way to recover her interest. But of course he knew better. He had to find Buddy and Jessica. And this conversation he'd been having seemed wrong in other ways too. If there were anything like the prime directive in fairy world relations, certainly this went against it. This was not the sort of thing he'd ever worried about before. But there was perhaps a difference between having a conversation with a person from another world and having a romance with one. Her future included a prince and a very different scenario than he could offer her. Maybe that mattered. He'd certainly have to think about that before he took any chances. He closed the computer.

"The children I'm looking for passed through a magic doorway and I do not know where they may have ended up. I realized recently that

Suzy must have gone to Oz, but I can't be sure she's still there. She ran away years ago and this Buddy kid ran away just the other day. I think I may have a better chance of finding her, but I also hope I can find him. Problem is, she's been gone so long, she could be anywhere by now, and she'd be about your age. So that would make her even harder to find. I wouldn't even know what she would look like. Buddy is much younger, about five- or six- or seven-years old I guess. Not much chance Cinderella was his first fantasy land of choice, I imagine; no offense."

"This is hardly *my* world. It's not even my kitchen."

"But now I'm wondering if he or another girl, Jessica, might be in a place you could get to from here."

"If I understand you correctly, these children can pass from one world to another, without a fairy godmother?" All emotion had faded from her voice. "I've never heard that that was possible, although I heard from my stepmother just this morning that there have been rumors of strange things, as I told you. I haven't heard of foreign children. But I did hear that a woman was in the village claiming to be someone called Queen Zizi, or Zixi I think, from a country called Ix. My fairy godmother says she is a powerful sorceress who is hundreds of years old—and 'Ix' is certainly not a part of this land."

"I wouldn't know about that, but we do have a way of passing from one world to another, and that's how these two children were lost. I keep asking myself when I was his age where would I have gone? God, who can remember?" Cinderella brought Charlie his cup of tea. Charlie kept thinking out loud. "It was probably some old fairytale or nursery rhyme. It doesn't help that I never met this Buddy kid. Let me think, 'The Ugly Duckling'?"

"I've never heard of him," Cinderella tried to help.

"It was one of *my* favorites, but I was really messed up at that age. 'The Valiant Tailor'?"

"Who's he? I don't think lives in this village."

"I was older when I read that. Maybe he saw the Mickey Mouse version? But that's not a place to go."

Cinderella took a sip of tea and stared in confusion at Charlie. "Are you talking about places or people?"

"Same thing," he said. "Come on, Chuck, think! A little boy, I think Gary said his family died in a fire or something. Okay, logic! Think like a Vulcan. Where would a child that age go for comfort? I don't imagine he'd be looking up Mrs. Ladybug, that's for sure."

So much of what Charlie was saying made no sense to Cinderella. "My fairy godmother might be able to help you. She under-stands magic

134

more than I do. But I have no way to call her. She comes when she feels she is needed. This sad little boy who you said seems to have lost his family in a fire; where would he go for comfort?"

"Uh, kids? Safety? Mothers, home, safety? Did any of these children in fairytales have happy home lives? Snow White? The Tin Soldier? *You* certainly didn't."

"What do you mean, 'story'?"

"Hansel and Gretel?" Charlie continued, "Jeez, they are all miserable stories when you get right down to it."

She'd never heard of any of these people and certainly had no idea how to get to them.

"He's too young for *Alice in Wonderland*. Hey, wait! Dorothy! In the movie, life kinda sucked in Kansas with that Old Miss Gulch thing, but the book wasn't like that. She wanted to go home, and eventually had Aunt Em and Uncle Henry come to live in Oz."

"I think I have heard my fairy godmother mention Oz," Cinderella said with a smile.

"Yeah, it's a much later story than yours."

Cinderella contracted her eyebrows.

"Oz! I keep coming back to it. That's got to be it. Makes sense, really, OzHouse, after all. You can't get away from those stories. And Buddy, he'd think Oz would make everything better. Like I said, I already figured out Suzy probably started off in Oz. It always seems to come back to Oz. Who knows, maybe they're both there."

Cinderella took a sip of her tea and couldn't keep from smiling as she watched him, almost in a whisper. "You may be married in your world, but you're awfully cute," she told him, "even with that metal thing impaled in your eyebrow." And then she spoke to herself out loud, "Okay, Ella, that's enough."

Charlie had a hard time going on. "Okay. So assuming that Suzy went there years ago, and if she stayed there she might have met Buddy when he arrived. It's been so long; this is just a guess, she might still be there or if she moved on to another story, someone there might know where. But first I guess I need to get back to the wardrobe and then find a way into Oz. If Gary hadn't distracted me, I would have gone there right off." Charlie rubbed his hair back as he tried to think clearly. "Magic is a strange thing, isn't it?"

"Oh, it certainly is. I have never understood why my godmother's magic should be controlled by a manmade object like a clock. Do you think it's possible that the two children you seek really are in the Land of Oz?"

"There's no way to be sure, but it's a good enough guess that a kid with his problems might want to escape there."

"It is such a wonderful thing that you are trying to help these children," she said. He reluctantly said goodbye to her. He thanked her for the bitter tea, which he quickly gulped down. Tucking the laptop under his arm, he gave her a chaste hug.

"I'm sorry you have to leave so quickly," she said as she let him go.

"Ah," he said awkwardly, "me too."

"You never know, maybe my fairy godmother will show up. She would be of great help."

Charlie looked again at the beautiful girl with the sooty face and then looked at the door they'd just come out of and then in the direction of the wardrobe. Then he kissed her forehead. "Who knows; I may be back."

"I hope so," said Cinderella.

"It could happen." As he said it, he wondered if it might be true.

"SO WHERE EXACTLY do you come from?" asked the forester.

Buddy looked up from the table and made a small smile. "The other side of the doorway," was all he said.

"Was this doorway in the village or all the way to Bremen?" the forester sat on the wooden seat near where Buddy was resting.

"No," the boy paused. "It's in the house. It's really really far." And then he added, "It's in the hallway with the coats."

"Riddles eh? Okay, have it your way, most people's got secrets, not usually so young as you are, but we'll just say you got an early jump on putting a few skeletons in your closet."

"No skeletons. Just coats," said Buddy with a pout.

"You got skeletons, all right. Means you keep secrets. You got secrets don't you?"

"I can't tell anybody about the book," Buddy half muttered under his breath.

"I'm going to town tomorrow. Soon's I get back, we'll see if we can figure a way to find this Jessica or your momma."

"You could take me with you," said Buddy.

"You'd slow me down. You can't carry anything; you can't keep up. I'll leave you something to eat."

Buddy jumped from the chair and struggled to pick it up. "I'm strong," he said.

"Doesn't matter," the forester chuckled, "I don't have time. You'd slow me down."

136

"I'm fast," said Buddy, and he sprinted around the table to prove it.

"You're not afraid to be alone, are you?"

"Where's Fundaboga?" Buddy asked.

That made the forester pause. He crossed his arms over his chest and spoke slowly. "How do you know about Fundevogel?"

"Dumpty Dumpty told me."

"Strange things happening everywhere," said the forester to himself. "Grown and gone, I'm afraid. And that's too bad," he added. "There are strange things happening in the woods, I am told. With his magic, he would have been some help to me in finding out if the stories I hear are true. You're a clever boy," he went on. "Maybe I had better take you with me after all."

Buddy was imagining a car or van to drive to town, so he was quite surprised the next morning at sunrise when the forester woke him and handed him some goatskin pouches filled with water and a basket laden with bread and cheese.

He walked quietly behind the burly man who was pushing a wheelbarrow filled to overflowing with wooden objects. Buddy seemed to have a million questions and the man would just reply with a simple yes or no or sometimes an uh huh. When it seemed as though the boy might never stop chattering, the man changed his tactic and simply whistled a tune or sang an old folk song.

When they stopped for lunch, Buddy was so exhausted he could hardly eat. But he was too hungry not to. When the man got up and brushed the crumbs from his tunic, Buddy could not believe that the rest was over and they were going to walk again.

He wanted to complain, but was afraid of being left behind all alone, so he did not. "Are we there yet?" he finally asked

"What's the problem little boy, not used to a six hour walk? How'd you get to my cabin? You do have skeletons in that closet, that's for sure."

Buddy got to his feet with such effort—he was going to try his best to be a brave little boy—that the forester smiled through his bushy beard and moustache and told him he had a job to do before they could proceed. "I'll need to refill these skins anyway," he said. "You just wait here a minute. Guard my wheelbarrow."

The forester hadn't been gone very long when a large gray wolf approached the resting child.

When Buddy saw him approach he thought it was a big dog, like King, the Alsatian dog his neighbor back in Manchester used to have. When the wolf spoke, he used his softest, kindest voice.

"Have you found your mother yet?" asked the wolf.

Buddy sat up quickly. "I know you have been looking for her for such a long time," said the wolf as he looked at the boy with a sincere gaze.

"Do you know my mother?"

"Know her? Well, of course I do. She sent me to look for you!"

"Really?" Buddy was so happy he clapped his hands.

"Yes. She got lost and ended up here in the Grimms' Forest, but she misses you very much, and asked me to use my good sense of smell."

"You do have a very big nose," Buddy said.

"The better to follow your trail in the woods," smiled the wolf. "And lucky for you I do have such a large nose, because now I have found you, and I can bring you to your mother."

"You can? Oh, thank you! Now?" the child hugged the shaggy head of the wolf.

"Yes, right now. Come and follow me and I will take you right to her."

"The forester will be right back and maybe we could all go look for my mother."

The wolf looked about quickly fearing the man might be about to return. "We really should hurry," he said.

"The forester said he'll carry me for a while," fibbed the boy.

"Well, I could carry you," the wolf responded.

"I guess we could go." Buddy smiled.

And without another thought of the forester who had been so kind to him, or all the problems he had encountered since coming through the wardrobe, Buddy climbed the powerful back of the wolf as the creature nodded his head encouraging the action.

CHAPTER 14

BC NEWS Detroit, Sept. 27 - Child welfare authorities admit that thousands of children are missing from foster care programs nationwide.

LOS ANGELES (AP) - Hundreds of foster children who are part of the county's child-welfare system cannot be found. The nation's largest foster care system was unable to find 488 of them as of Aug. 30.

"This is yet another shocking revelation of a beleaguered child-welfare system that puts children at more risk in the system than if they had remained with their families," said Rodney Gomes, an attorney who represents the family of a child who ran away from foster care and was never found.

"Well, isn't that cheery," Doug mumbled to the big face of the stuffed Aslan peering over the shoulder of the gump in which he sat, legs stretched out before him, computer on his lap.

State Agencies Search for Foster Kids

Since August, officials in California, Tennessee and Michigan have disclosed that hundreds of children are missing from state and county foster care systems.

Scrutiny over missing foster children was spurred by the disappearance of a 5-year-old in Atherton who was reported missing in April after a foster care worker failed to check up on her for 16 months. An initial review of the state foster system turned up nearly 1,000 missing children.

In August, the body of 17-year-old was found in Collier County Florida. The San Matteo County Sheriff's Office told the San Jose Mercury News that she was murdered.

The Daily News of Los Angeles reported that at least eight children have been killed or died in accidents in the past few years after running away or being abducted from foster care.

Latimes.org

PERHAPS HE WAS JUST BEING STUPID—again. How was this depressing data supposed to calm anyone down? But with Beth so upset—thrusting tea at everyone who walked into the room—he couldn't think of anything else to do. He'd come here, to the privacy of the Narnia room, with his pumpkin-colored iBook to gather data to present to his wife in support of a rather simple proposition: there wasn't anything extraordinary going on here at OzHouse. Which was undoubtedly true. There wasn't. The data proved that. But now that he was actually facing the depressing state of normal, he could hardly imagine these numbers doing what he wanted them to do, which was to get her to see these crazy weeks as just another cloud that would pass, as the cloud passed when they lost Suzy.

But wasn't it just as likely the news reports would push her over the edge?

You'd think after all these years he could predict his wife better than this. But no. People are complex and they change. He'd rarely seen his usually very stable wife—how often had he teased her for being so thoroughly British?— quite so distressed, suddenly threatening to give up the whole project of OzHouse. He thought of the sad days before they'd converted their dream, of all the days they'd given to designing and building and decorating the huge home for the sons and daughters that never arrived.

No one knew how to handle this situation. Gwen was taking everything with her typical Buddhist indifference—it was good to see her convictions hold under such trying circumstances—; she was worried

140

more about the effect of this mess on Gary than about the threat to OzHouse. Doug himself wasn't worried about the threatened lawsuit; nothing official had yet arrived from any court or lawyer; it was almost certainly an empty threat, probably without legal merit anyway, although it offered just the sort of superficial drama the news media craved, just the sort of thing they'd glom onto if they ever got wind of it—which so far, thank God, they hadn't.

Doug slid his finger over the touch pad and added the latest quotation to his collection.

Poor Beth. "And I'm supposed to try to put on a jolly American Thanksgiving for all these children?" she'd almost yelled, a little earlier, in the kitchen, hauling the huge turkey out of the refrigerator, "while we've all got to go around in fear that some cow from Manchester chews on us like a bloody bone?"

She'd been talking to Gary.

So he gave her his theory of the lack of legal merit to the threatened suit. "It's just blackmail. She'll want us to give her some money to drop the case." At which point Beth had managed, unfortunately, to force him to admit that his theory was based on little more substantial than his opinion of Rebecca Holton, whom he'd never yet so much as laid eyes on.

"But still," he'd said, "who's ever heard of a birth parent suing a foster home? There's a certain credibility factor…"

And then she said, after handing him a steaming cup of Earl Grey, the first thing that had surprised him in a very long time: "Did it ever occur to you that we may actually be guilty?"

That stunned him. It hadn't occurred to him, of course. Nor had that question entered into his thinking of whether, if it came to it, they could win a legal battle. Wasn't law really just a complex strategy game in which winners and losers were decided based on their ability to negotiate the rules? But it did explain why Beth was more upset than he could have predicted. She was apparently more worried by the possibility that they had failed the children than by the threat this lawsuit might be to their resources and reputation.

If he could only convince her now that it wasn't their fault: it was the slip-shod, back-burner system that was to blame, and it was the nature of the enterprise itself. The trend was clear—they all knew it anyway, although they'd never sought out the numbers—thousands of children were missing from foster care houses all over the country. Runaways, abductees. It was a shame, it was a travesty as far as the state was concerned. What was happening to OzHouse was not in the least abnormal.

But that was almost worse. Beth wanted to believe that OzHouse was special, even within the damaged childcare system. Now what happens when she's forced to face the truth: that for all their resources, for all their compassion they were, after all, subject, like everyone else, to the same vagaries of a system that tried to find homes for so many emotionally damaged, so many downright broken kids—some of whom were going to get themselves lost or killed no matter how much money, no matter how much love was thrown at them.

They had to face the possibility that all their success through the years was just dumb luck. They'd lost three kids—two of them close together. What if all their successes and all their failures *were*, as the times suggested, just random events, statistically speaking?

What a diverse collection of people they'd come to be: Gary was afraid OzHouse would be taken from them and Beth was almost ready to give it up; Gwen would be willing to go with whatever happened—which left it up to level-headed Doug to save the day.

Doug kept firm to his belief that the cloud would pass. Things would get back to normal. They were improving already, really. The reporters were all gone. The grounds were no longer swarming with volunteers searching for the missing children. The state agency—Colin Fuller-Brinks notwithstanding—was putting no pressure on them. As soon as this lawsuit was dealt with, everything would be as it was. Perhaps they'd had their fantastic vision of happy skipping children stripped of its bright colors, but that was helpful too, about time, really.

Doug folded down the top of the iBook and leaned back in the tub-like depression of the gump. He looked around the room: a room stuffed with things for children to find: the books, the statues, the games, the quilts. Doug was surprised to realize that so few had managed to find any of it over the years. Of the countless number of children who'd come through the house, so few had ever signed the book.

Colored light filtered down through Gwen's stained-glass Oz window over his head. He heard the sound of a car pulling up outside. A door slammed.

He'd never let anyone know it, but he'd spent a good deal of time in this room during the years, mostly sitting here in the gump, thinking or reading. Whenever he was troubled, he came here. Gary went to his woodshop, but the problem with that was that anyone could find him any time they wanted to. No one ever thought to look for Doug here. The great advantage to living in such a big house is that you could get lost when you needed to. And if they asked where you'd been when they were looking for you, you just had to be a little vague about it and they'd never find your hiding place. Everyone needed a hiding place.

Doug's attention was drawn to a noise in the wardrobe. And before he could wonder what it was, Charlie tumbled into the room, a square, black object in his hand.

"Charlie," said Doug.

"Doug, can't talk," said Charlie, clambering to his feet.

"You see," said Doug, "I knew you were in the house all along. Gary thought..."

"Sorry, can't," said Charlie, and then he started mumbling to himself, "There's no place like Oz, there's no place like Oz, there's no place like..."

"You were egg-shpecting Hobbiton, maybe?" said Doug, adding a chuckle to his poor and irrelevant German accent. But before Doug could say any more, Charlie launched himself back through the wardrobe.

He's always been odd, thought Doug, only kid in the history of the house that never laughed at any of his jokes. He turned his attention back to the quest for information.

In 2000, 3 million referrals were received by CPS agencies regarding questions of child welfare and safety. Thirty-eight percent of those cases screened in were maltreated or at risk of maltreatment.

Data as reported to AFCARS indicate that in FY99, 1.2% of children were identified as "runaway." In FY00, 1.6% were reported. "Runaway" can include children that have run away as well as children who are missing by reason of the non-custodial parent or relative removing the child from placement, and any other manner of being missing as defined by the state.

— "National Data Available July 21, 2002," *Children's Bureau, ACYF, ACF, DHHS.*

In 1989 the GAO reported that 1.3 million children were living in the street each year.

The Children's Defense Fund estimates that 1,200 youth run away each day.

—APHSA, September 2002

Fantasy foster home threatened over disappearance
Lebanon, NH (AP)—A Cornish landmark that has established a reputation for helping troubled youth has been threatened with a lawsuit over missing children...

Well, so much for keeping it out of the news. This wasn't working at all.

Reality's possibilities are just too limited. And just as Doug came to this conclusion, he heard another rattle in the wardrobe—and then Charlie was back. And this time Doug recognized the black object.

Charlie shot a glance of unmistakable annoyance at Doug and he began mumbling again, "Oz, Tin Man, Cowardly Lion, Wogglebug, Emerald City, Glinda."

Doug looked over at the laptop. "Charlie," he said, "Maybe you'd better give me that computer."

"Can't talk, Doug."

"One rule about the Narnia room," said Doug, but he couldn't finish the sentence. He was going to remind Charlie that whatever was spoken in the Narnia room stayed in the Narnia room. It wasn't really a rule, but it made sense and might get Charlie to talk to him. He tried to pull himself out of the deep well of the gump, but Charlie was already gone.

No sense following him. Gary would take care of it. He looked back at his own computer screen, and as he did, once again he heard the rattling in the wardrobe and there, once again, was Charlie, with the laptop and, this time, something else—a white ball.

"What the hell are you up to?" said Doug.

As Charlie chucked his snowball at Doug, he said, excited but not angry, "Would you shut up for one second." And then he turned back to the wardrobe again and repeated the list of Oz items adding "you idiot" into the midst of the list. And then he dived through once again.

"Is it snowing?" said Doug aloud. But Charlie was already gone.

Doug hardly had time to scroll down when the sound of someone scrambling through the wardrobe came again.

"All right, Charlie. This is..." But it wasn't Charlie who stepped through the door. "Gary? You caught me. How'd you know I was here?"

"Beth said... Were you talking to Charlie?"

"Didn't you see him?" asked Doug, although what really interested him was how Beth knew where to find him.

Gary shook his head.

"You must have... He just... He threw this snowball at me."

144

Gary kept shaking his head. "It's not snowing," he said.

"Well, anyway, at least we know he's in the house somewhere."

Gary wrinkled his forehead at the logic of that remark. But as interested as he was in the news of Charlie, he had come to solicit Doug's help with an entirely different problem. "We have a guest," he said. "Rebecca Holton, Jessica's mother, is downstairs right now with Beth and Gwen. And she's drunk."

A minute later, they were all in the kitchen: Gwen, Gary, Doug, Beth, and Rebecca Holton. The smell of roast turkey pervaded the air. Young children, drawn by the smell and the congregation of grown-ups, were running in and out of the room. Rebecca Holton, a short, chubby woman with tight clothes and unnaturally blonde hair, was pacing the floor, arms in dramatic motion, colorfully lamenting the loss of her daughter. She paid no attention to any attempt to calm her as she ranted and paced and threatened.

"Don't think any one of you will get away with this one. My poor Jessica. I'll have your house and your garden and your swimming pool and your gym..."

Doug herded two little boys out of the room and called one of the older children, a young girl named Brittney, to take them away and guard the door.

"Mrs. Holton," said Beth, "We are just as concerned over Jessica..."

"What the hell is this place anyway. Some kind of cartoon. This place is a cartoon," she said it again as though to give the comment its full power to disarm and embarrass. "You think you're living in a movie or something, can't take care of the real world... Boy, you're gonna see reality after I'm through with you."

"Mrs. Holton, why is it you seem more concerned with how we live than with your missing daughter?" Gwen asked.

"My poor daughter." Jessica's mother seemed genuinely annoyed that she couldn't follow the exclamation with a convincing burst of tears.

Gary picked up the phone to call the number of the lawyer who'd sent them the letter, although he was not sure what he would say if the man answered the phone.

"That's right. Call the cops. Shows what kind of people you are. Kill my daughter...."

"Look here," Doug said, more loudly than he'd intended. "No one's dead." Then he looked around at the others to see if he had permission to speak frankly after all, and it was clear from the expression on everyone's faces that they were all tired of trying to appease the

145

woman. "We are doing everything we can to find your daughter— we care for Jessica just as much as..."

"A damn sight more than you do," said Beth. "You hateful lush. Who do you think you're fooling? You haven't so much as talked to your daughter on the phone since she arrived. You..."

"What did you call me?" Rebecca screamed. "You think I'm here because I'm... I haven't had a drink today, bitch. You steal my child, you lose my child, and then you..." But the fire had gone out. She stood still in the middle of the floor but seemed to have difficulty doing so. She reached for a chair and stumbled back, falling into it, her arm swinging onto the long table half laid out for Thanksgiving dinner, knocking over a goblet and a candlestick. She threw her head back. Just then a young child scampered into the room, a three-year old girl named Kate. She was holding a stuffed rabbit in her hand and giggling as she ran. Immediately Brittney appeared at the door. She flashed a guilty look at Gwen, ran into the kitchen, scooped up Kate, and ushered her off still struggling, still laughing.

Beth ceased her tirade the moment Rebecca fell into the chair. Putting down the phone without leaving a message, Gary glanced at Doug as though to say, "Looks like the booze is finally getting to her." Gwen interpreted the glance and laid a disapproving hand on Gary's arm. Rebecca's tears this time may have been genuine—though what lay behind the tears was impossible to tell. Gary surmised self-pity. Gwen seemed to think it was perhaps something more genuinely motherly. She went over to the woman and—in what Gary considered an extraordinary gesture, just the sort of gesture that periodically filled him with wonder at the capacity of his wife—she knelt down beside her and looked up at her tear-stained face and told her not to give up on Jessica.

Rebecca brushed Gwen away. But Gwen only moved to the chair beside her and leaned toward her and kept talking. Beth looked over at Doug and Gary and whispered, "Anything to get her out of here." And then she walked slowly over to Gwen and Rebecca and sat on a chair on the other side of their uninvited guest.

Gary shot another glance at Doug, this time to suggest that events had taken the sort of turn they should have expected but never would have, the kind that always seems to happen when women get together and one of them starts to cry, an event that renders the presence of males, at best, superfluous. Doug's return glance suggested he wasn't sure he liked what was happening but there was nothing he could do about it. "Better set another place at the table," said Doug as the two of them left the room.

146

"STILL LOOKING FOR BUDDY, I suppose," said Humpty Dumpty, sitting with his legs crossed, staring down from his wall.

"Yes, of course," said Jessica, although the question acted more like a reminder of what she was after. What she really wanted to know was how Humpty Dumpty had managed to pull himself back together, and how he had managed to get all the way over here to Mother Goose Land so quickly.

"And what have you learned my child that makes you worthy of the knowledge you seek?"

The question seemed just a little sarcastic, although Jessica could not be sure. She thought a moment and said, "There's no place like home."

"And thank God for that," said the egg man. And he peered down at her with his eyebrows raised and his eyes way up high as though he were trying to look over a pair of glasses and his mouth drawn back and puckered: it was an unmistakably ironic look.

Jessica didn't know what to say.

"You, my friend," continued the egg man, "are reading the wrong sorts of books. From what I've heard there are any number of places better than *your* home."

She wanted to say, "better to read the wrong sorts of books than live in them," but she knew that wouldn't be nice. Instead she said, "But I still want to go back there."

"Want to?" he challenged.

"Well, I have to. I have a sister, and a mother. It's just Bill…"

I've a cold in my nose
And a cramp in my toes
And a hole in my clothes
And the chills

But I don't complain
Of the cold and the pain
I only complain
Of the bills.

Humpty Dumpty huffed. "You're not the first person to complain about bills," he reminded her. He seemed to Jessica more interested in making puns than in helping anyone out.

"My mom's not so bad, you know. Before Bill came. Before she was drinking so much. She told me she wanted to be a doctor. But then I

147

was born, and she had to give that up. Then she was going to be a nurse instead. But then Izzy was born, so she didn't do that either. Now she just works at Wal-Mart. It's not her fault."

"I suppose it's *your* fault," said Humpty Dumpty.

Jessica was about to mention how it was because she'd been listening to the music when she should have been doing the dishes—but then she remembered the Emperor of China and his nightingale and thought that maybe that was one of the times when it should have been okay to listen to music. She was going to finish the dishes as soon as the fighting stopped.

"Maybe it wasn't *all* my fault," she said. "But maybe I can still make it better."

"Hmmpf," said Humpty Dumpty. And he swung around on the wall and put his back to her as though there were no longer any reason to speak to her at all if that was the sort of thing she was going to say.

"I want to see my mom," said Jessica.

"Well, that's different," said Humpty Dumpty, and suddenly he wasn't on the wall at all, but on the ground next to her.

"How did you…?"

"We all want to see our mothers," Humpty Dumpty interrupted, "even if they are a goose now and then,"

"But first I have to find Buddy."

"Because you lost him?"

"Yes, I showed him about the wardrobe and I…"

"Pretty determined little boy is my opinion. But feel free to blame yourself if you like. Could very well be your fault for all I know."

"That wasn't…"

"Very nice? Well why should I treat you any better than you treat yourself."

"But…"

"Enough of that. Over easy, as I say. This topic is easily got over." Humpty Dumpty started walking down the hill. Jessica assumed he was leaving her, but he kept talking to himself as he walked, and Jessica could hear the words: "Well I have it from Tom Tucker that your Buddy has indeed gone onto the Grimms' Forest." And then Humpty Dumpty, sensing there was no one beside him, turned around and said, "Are you coming or aren't you? I've things to do, you know. I've no obligation to help you. I do so out of the kindness of my heart."

"Things to do?" said Jessica so quietly Humpty could not hear her, "walls to fall off." She chuckled to herself as she quickly caught up to him.

148

"What are you finding so amusing. No, on second thought, I'd rather not know," said the egg man. "Listen carefully. I'm not going to tell you twice. And if you get lost it *will* be entirely your fault. You can blame yourself forever."

"Aren't you going with me?"

"Dangerous place. Never go there, myself. Wild animals, wild children. Lions, tigers and... and wolves. Actually, pretty much just wolves. Plenty of them. Savage, egg-sucking wolves."

"You sent Buddy..."

"Sent himself, I'm afraid. Tommy and Nancy tried to stop him. They told me themselves. No stopping him. Now listen, you take a left at the willow tree up ahead. You'll see a path through the leaves."

A trumpet sound shook the air around them before Humpty Dumpty could say more. They both turned in the direction of the sound. Approaching rapidly along the path on which they stood was a carriage pulled by a team of white horses. It was surrounded with a great number of horses upon which rode a great number of men, some of them holding long trumpets with streaming banners. These had paused some distance ahead of the carriage in order to herald the king's approach. The others were knights in full armor, draped in the king's colors—coal black and scarlet—long swords dangling from their sides, visors up to expose their faces. Jessica's attention was drawn to one knight among them, however, who was not dressed like the others. He was wearing white. His horse was white and his armor was bright silver, much brighter than the armor of the other knights. Sunlight bounced off it, leaving streaks across Jessica's eyes that made it hard to see. And he was weaving back and forth among the other knights as though he'd had far too much of the king's best ale. At first she thought he must be more important than all the others. But his weaving reminded Jessica of her mother trying to climb the stairs when she was drunk. His visor was down. And he was yelling something which, whether because the visor muffled his speech or because it was in a language Jessica did not recognize, she could not make out. The other knights were doing their best to ignore him. And he did not seem to have any purpose.

Jessica and Humpty Dumpty jumped aside to let the procession through, but as it came to them, it stopped. The old king stuck his head through the carriage window. "There's another one," he said. And he swung the door open with a flourish. "Name your rhyme," he said sternly to Jessica.

"My... excuse me?" she stumbled.

"Never heard of it," said the king. He hopped down the carriage steps to the ground. He was a short, round-bellied man who reminded Jessica a little of Humpty Dumpty himself. He was wearing a tall golden crown with knobs on the ends of the spikes and robes of scarlet and black that flowed to the ground. He had a marvelously wrinkled face—not really old-looking wrinkles, more like the skin of a hound, which he could push and pull into an enormous range of expressions. He looked over at Humpty Dumpty with a comically stern arrangement to his folds of skin.

"Well, I see you managed to reassemble our guardian egg. Very clever. In other circumstances I might actually reward you." Just then the chief of the horse guards came up to the king and dismounted. "You see, I told you," said the king to his knight, "we gave up too soon."

"And not a hoof mark on me," added Humpty Dumpty with a very slight deferential bow that had not an ounce of sincerity in it.

"Make a note of that," said the king, "next time, more men, fewer horses."

All the kings men had now stopped and gathered in a circle around Jessica and Humpty Dumpty—all but the one in white, who was still exclaiming unintelligible phrases as he continued circling around like a drunk, or like a man whose horse was accustomed to making all the decisions.

"Stop him," yelled the king. And one of his knights grabbed the rogue knight's bridle. As the animal clapped to a sudden halt, it was all the knight could do to stay upon his mount. With his forearm, he pressed his visor up—he was a grizzled old man with a huge mustache—and he looked around like a man who was in desperate need of glasses.

"Tsal ta Ecila dnouf evah uoy ees I," said the knight, squinting down at Jessica.

"You see that," exclaimed the king.

"She certainly *heard* it," said Humpty Dumpty, bowing ironically once again.

"The White Knight is talking backwards," yelled the king.

"Perhaps if you have him speak into a mirror," said Humpty Dumpty.

"Is this your doing?" inquired the king of Jessica.

"I... I... I..."

"Thought so, thought so. It is true you have recently arrived from Wonderland?" he continued.

"Yes," said Jessica. Humpty Dumpty, who might also have said "yes" to this, said nothing.

"And you brought him with you?" And the king pointed at the white knight who was doing his best to steady himself upon his horse.

"I didn't know," said Jessica.

"Didn't know," said the king, "as though that mattered. Look, something has gone very wrong in this land. He is one example. You are another. Things are getting in that should be staying out. I don't know who caused it, but I blame you. Arrest her," yelled the king. And the chief of the horse guards made a move to grab the girl. But she pulled back. As it was hard for the guard to run in full armor, Jessica managed to dodge him easily. She looked up at the battalion of knights, who threw down their visors as one and spurred their horses. Jessica turned and ran. The woods were not far away. She recognized what must be the willow tree Humpty Dumpty had mentioned, and she dived past it before any of the knights could reach her. For some reason she did not understand, no one followed.

"Merry old soul indeed."

CHAPTER 15

Dearest Elizabeth,

Assuming I can manage this befuddling contraption, I am going to try once again to send you an e-mail—or whatever it is you kids call this form of communication.

Your father and I have been very concerned after receiving your last letter. As you know, we have always felt that the foster home you and your brother-in-law started would likely be the sort of venture that might be over your heads.

We know you mean well, and have overcome many obstacles. I call to mind the incident of your local council refusing the planning commission back when you first started, and that time you had all that inside water damage due to, as you called it, "ice dams" on the roof backing up and you couldn't find a plumber to help put the problem right, and so you had to rely on Doug and Gary to give it a go. Why you didn't use slate on the roof as we suggested, I cannot imagine. Our home has never had such problems and it is over 200 years old!

I do hope that young man who went off to art school isn't involved in all this. Your father never cared for him, thought him a bit of a rabble-rouser. Naturally, you have never complained about the imposition Gary and Gwen put on you by allowing that boy to grow up there, but I imagine it must have taken its toll. These things always do.

I will try to call this weekend when the rates are better, and you can let me know if the little boy has been located. I'm sure it will all be sorted out by then, and this will simply be a tale to tell about how he got lost and wandered about in the woods. Is it very cold there this time of year? Would be dreadful if the child caught cold which can so easily turn into pneumonia. That is how Great Aunt Phoebe died last year, you know. It seemed like just the flu and within a week's time she was in hospital and died shortly thereafter.

Hearing about your Little White Horse room made me so nostalgic for the old days. How beautiful you were as a child. Such a pity you were not able to have any children of your own. Not a day goes by that your father and I do not comment on it.

Your sister Faye is still living in Birmingham with that Jake fellow. They are thinking of buying an old narrow boat and reconditioning it to live in. Better than the council housing, I'm sure, but where they will find the time, money and skill to renovate is beyond me. Your father is convinced they will expect us to help them again, but this time we will be steadfast in our decision to allow them to make of their life what they will without our assistance.

They certainly never come to us for advice, which we would be all too happy to give them. Dee is almost ten now, and no one has seen her father since he left 8 years ago. And it's not as if we didn't warn her about marrying that Welsh lay-about. But enough of family problems, you have enough of your own to deal with just now. Here's hoping your situation improves and all can be as it was.

Fondly,
Mum

"I SUPPOSE YOU CAN SEE why I had to escape England," Beth said with a laugh and a sip of tea. "Even from this distance, she can raise the old hackles." Beth brushed the back of her neck.

"I guess she was pretty upset by the news of the missing child," Gwen said with a shrug of her shoulders—although she suspected Beth's mother of using their misfortune as a pretext for running down their efforts on OzHouse or simply to show displeasure at Beth's choices in life.

"She only knows about Buddy; imagine if she knew about Jessica too. That would really fuel her fire. But it's good to know that whatever the crisis, my mother can find a way to make me feel even worse."

"That's a gift mothers have," Gwen said as she accepted a little more tea from Beth's pot.

"I love my mum, dearly. But isn't it funny you can hop the pond and you can't catch a break from her. Blessing of email. It's like she's right there in the kitchen, all the time, like when I was a kid."

"The last time my mom called, she practically had me in tears," Gwen added. "For a minute I actually believed that my brother's problems in school were somehow *my* fault. I don't know how they do it."

"There any more coffee?" asked Doug as he entered the kitchen.

"Just a drop of tea. Here take some of mine," Beth offered to pour some of her tea into Doug's White Castle mug. He was about to tell her not to, but then it was already done.

"Ah, tea. Caffeine for the weak at heart. Interesting bouquet, oh, and it tastes like you used the bottom of the mulch box," Doug laughed at his own joke. He had to duck to avoid the towel his wife hurled at him. "Oh by the way I came in here to tell you Rebecca Holton came back, but she's already leaving."

"Good," said Beth and Gwen at the same time.

Doug knitted his brow and pursed his lips as he gave them both a look of admonition. "One would think your response would be, 'what does she want? Is she still upset? Any progress in her attempt to sue us and take everything we've got?' Well, I think she's a bit settled down compared to how she was on Thanksgiving. Well, for her, anyway."

"He means sobered up, but just," Beth translated

"Cynics," sighed Doug as he surreptitiously poured his cup into the sink and turned to go.

"We have to have faith that things are getting better," said Gwen.

"Why?" asked Doug.

"Why what?" Gwen replied.

"Why must we have faith that things will get better?"

"It's good karma. If we expect good things to happen, they will."

"Can't argue with that kind of thinking, can we," said Doug as he placed the empty mug down on the counter.

"No, of course you can't," said Gwen.

"What did she want?" asked Beth at last. It was clear Doug was not going to say without an invitation.

"I have no idea," said Doug. "She wanted to see Jessica's room. And then she wanted a tour of the place where her daughter, in her words, 'spent her last days.'"

"Taking stock of her future property, I would imagine," said Gwen.

"You didn't give her the tour, did you?" said Beth.

"I, well.... she...."

"He did," said Beth to Gwen.

"Lovely tea, my dear," Doug said to Beth as he slunk from the room.

NOW THAT'S ODD, thought Jessica. She had been in such a hurry she had run head down straight through an old vine-covered door frame crossing the path like an arbor. What was it doing there? Had she hesitated, she never would have run through it. It was just the sort of door in the middle of nowhere that could have been a wardrobe, perhaps the very door that had dropped Buddy in Mother Goose Land. She shuddered to think how close she'd come to falling back into OzHouse.

"And after making it all the way here," she said to herself.

But after all, it was not a magic doorway. And yet... wasn't it suddenly colder? And hadn't it been morning when she was running from the king?

Through the doorway she heard Old King Cole and his men clomp away. She had to concentrate on looking for Buddy. Past the cluster of trees along the border a field opened brightly before her. Beyond it were more trees. Maybe that was the Forest of Grimm.

She headed through the field of tall grass and wild flowers. She hated walking in tall grass. But this was the shortest way to get there so she had to do it. Every few steps Jessica checked her socks and legs to see if she had picked up any nasty ticks. After a few minutes and several checks, during which she did not find any, she relaxed her guard and actually found herself enjoying the warm sunshine and thinking how nice it would be to get Buddy and get back to OzHouse and laugh about getting lost in the woods—because she could not of course tell people who hadn't signed the book where she'd really been (and she had, after all, really been lost in the woods, so it wouldn't be like it was a lie), and how everything would be all right, she told herself, happy to feel just a little bit optimistic. But then her foot slipped, and she slid down an unseen hill in the damp grass. Now her pants were wet and her shirt was stained with grass. "And there's another reason to hate tall grass," she said out loud. "It hides hills and rocks and who knows what else."

156

"Snakes," said a voice nearby.

Jessica leapt to her feet and looked over toward the sound. There she noticed a young boy sitting not far to her left. She turned and walked in his direction. He seemed about her age, maybe a little younger, and the girl tried to guess what story he came from.

"Snakes and bugs and things that bite," said the boy without looking at her.

"Excuse me," she began, and he turned and looked at her in surprise, as though he too had been talking to himself and not responding to her statement about the grass. "My name is Jessica Holton. Could you help me?"

The boy seemed nervous and didn't answer her right away.

"Did you hear me?" she asked as she approached him.

"I... I heard you. But I don't think I can help you. I'm lost."

"Really? What story are you from?" Jessica asked, suddenly more concerned for this boy's problem than her own.

"Not a story really, just some poems," he continued to look about as if trying to get his bearings.

"Well, most of these Mother Goose rhymes are just poems, I guess. In fact most don't even make sense really."

"Who is Mother Goose? And my poems make sense, at least they do to me," the boy explained.

"How can you not know Mother Goose? What is your name by the way?" Jessica fiddled with her hair.

"Willy," replied he boy. "And I am not from here. I come from a book of poems about boys and girls."

"Sounds like Mother Goose rhymes to me," said Jessica.

"Would you like to hear one of my poems?" Jessica was wondering if this might be Wee Willy Winkie; he was the only Willy she could think of.

In the family drinking well
Willy pushed his sister Nell.
She's there now because it kilt her,
Now we have to buy a filter.

And with that, he gave a small, nervous bow.

Jessica looked at him with horror. "What a disgusting poem. That's not Mother Goose!"

157

"You look a lot like my sister," said Willy with a malicious smile. Jessica decided she did not want to be talking to this boy any more, and started to back up.

Willy with a taste for gore
Nailed his sister to the door.
Mother said with humor quaint,
Now Willy dear don't scratch the paint.

And the boy began to laugh as Jessica continued to back up slowly so he wouldn't know she was trying to get away from him. This was not the kind of poetry she liked, and she could not imagine what he was doing anywhere near Mother Goose Land when he obviously did not belong there.

"I'm sorry. I am looking for a friend of mine and I really can't hang out with you right now. Maybe another time," she added for fear of hurting his feelings. She continued to back up—until she bumped into Humpty Dumpty.

"Oh, I am sorry," she said as the egg almost lost his balance. "Should be. Should be! Why aren't you looking where I am going?" And then he noticed Willy. "Who is this?" The egg stared hard at the boy.

"You don't want to know. He's a little creepy," Jessica whispered to the giant egg. "He says he's lost?"

"Lost?" Humpty Dumpty looked closely at the boy. "Beastly Boy?" he asked.

The wide, mischievous smile told the egg he was right.

"This is not your world. How did you get here?" he turned to Jessica.

"He's from a book of poems. But they are kinda gross and sick." Jessica was surprised to see Willy smile again that little malicious smile at her comment.

"That's not important." Humpty Dumpty began shouting as he waved his slender arms about. "This is impossible. Can't happen. Bad enough having the White Knight slipping in between the pages, but this boy has no business here at all."

"He said he was lost," Jessica said.

"Doesn't matter! Doesn't matter. If this is not his world—and it is clearly not his world—then he can't be here. And I do not mean he shouldn't be here or that it would be or better if he were not here. I mean he can't be here. It isn't possible. It can't happen. People do not stumble into each other's tales willy nilly."

"You do," said Jessica.

"I most certainly do not, you impertinent, insinuating child."

"You're here." Jessica was undaunted.

"That's different," the egg huffed.

Jessica didn't see how.

Willy finally spoke up. "I didn't ask to come here so stop yelling at everyone. I might just have a poem about a rotten egg if I can recall it."

"Rotten," shouted Humpty Dumpty. "You uncouth, incoherent scrap of acidified rag. You exhibit a reckless disregard for the laws of narrative, and yet you have the temerity to cast aspersions on the finest grade-A farm fresh, thick-shelled specimen ever to pass by the candle unscorched? I shall speak to the king about this, Beastly Boy."

"Just show me the way home," Willy said calmly.

Humpty Dumpty sputtered and started to say several things but nothing came out as menacing and rude as he wished, so he stopped. Then taking Jessica's hand, he led her away. Willy did not try to follow. It was, unfortunately, not at all easy to make a graceful and speedy exit. Large as he was, Humpty Dumpty's gait was not as long or as fast as the girl's. Nor did he act as though his shell were as thick as in his rant he had claimed. She had to be careful to walk at his speed so she would not topple him in the slippery grass.

"How did you find me?" asked Jessica once they had put a little space between themselves and Willy.

"Find you? I'm Humpty Dumpty," he said, as though that explained something. "I followed you." And then he added after a short pause, "a bit safer outside the range of Old Cole's temerarious eye, don't you think!"

"So we are still in Mother Goose Land?"

"You impertinent child. Does this look like Mother Goose Land to you?"

"Well, I went through the door. But the door always takes you back to OzHouse. And I didn't go to OzHouse. So I must still be in Mother Goose Land. But it doesn't feel like Mother Goose Land."

"Open your eyes, child," the egg man huffed.

"So this isn't Mother Goose Land?"

Humpty Dumpty simply huffed again.

"Never been much of a walker," he said, as though that were a topic of conversation.. He glanced back to make double sure that Willy was a safe distance behind. "But I'd rather crawl across this field than spend another minute with that trespasser."

"Technically I am a trespasser too, aren't I?" asked Jessica, keeping a close watch on her feet on the uneven ground.

"It's different," said the egg, stopping a moment to regain his balance.

"I don't see that it is. His poems were gross, but I guess he has as much right to be here as I do."

"No," blurted out Humpty Dumpty. "It's different. You are from the *outside* world. You folks have occasionally made it into one of our tales. But no one from one story can enter another story without some sort of link. Can't be done. Never done. Never can be done!"

"But you," Jessica began but was quickly cut off.

"Different. It is just different. I was placed in those stories. See, there's the link. I can go back and forth, often do in fact. Get tired of the juvenile nonsense of Mother Goose, I head for the dream-crazy world of Wonderland. Get tired of the nightmarish nonsense of adolescence, I head back to the cozy insanity of Mother Goose. See, there's the link. White Knight, crazy as he is, just must have followed me, or you, somehow, you see?" "No, I don't see," said Jessica. But the egg must not have heard her.

"Could be worse, I imagine," he said. "At least no incompatibles have gotten in."

"Would that be bad? And what's a...."

"Bad?" He did not give her time to finish her question. "It would be the end of everything."

"The end of everything?" Jessica wondered what he could possibly mean by "everything."

"Willy's not an incompatible?"

"Well, yes, of course he is. But he didn't happen, so it doesn't matter."

Jessica recalled all the times her mother had said to her, "Look, I've already explained it. If you don't get it, it's your own fault," and finished with, "so just quiet down and do what I say. No more questions!" But now she was more confused than ever. And when she was confused, although she'd often received a hard slap on the cheek for it, Jessica always asked another question. And every time, her face stinging, tears pooling in her eyes, she said "sorry, mom" and told herself to stop talking back. And now Humpty Dumpty was acting so much like her mother that she told herself she'd better just drop it. And as soon as she told herself to drop it, she said, "Are you an incompatible?"

Humpty Dumpty stopped and turned to look at Jessica with a serious scowl on his face. He lowered his eyebrows and raised an open hand toward the girl's head. "I'll only explain this once," he told her, his index finger pointing at the sky, "so if you don't pay attention, don't ask me to repeat it. There are rules, little lady. Not rules made up by some king or prince, or something or another that can be followed or ignored at the listener's pleasure. I am speaking of real rules. Like gravity or breathing."

"There's a rule for breathing?"

"Don't interrupt. Now, one of the most important rules is that each world is separate from any other. No one goes from one to another without a link. Now, if, like me, a character has been composed into multiple tales—not too many of us, of course—that will work. No one may find the passage for years, but it will be there. But if a story has always been a separate tale it will not have a…a…"

"Doorway?" suggested Jessica seeing the egg searching for a word.

"Yes, a doorway, if you will. That boy, Willy I think he called himself, could not be part of any other world. Every world has its borders. When someone goes from one world to another that person becomes bound by that world's rules. Do you understand? No don't answer; it will distract me.

"How come the new world doesn't become bound to his rules?"

"Some say it does. But not enough to notice. You'd need thousands of intruders for that. And that would be terrible. Think of this: if people from one world were to enter another, let's say if Dorothy Gale had gone to Narnia…"

"That would be a fun book," Jessica cut in. And then she thought of something else: "you said you weren't going to follow me."

"No, it wouldn't. And I changed my mind. If you don't mind, I think you would to better to keep to one conversation at a time. Clearly, you have more than enough trouble with that many. Now, listen: the rules of Oz are completely different from the Narnian rules. What would happen if Dorothy found herself in Narnia? Why, she would age. She might even die. That is never ever allowed to happen. Never has; never will."

Jessica wasn't so sure. "But what about Willy?" Jessica was truly confused.

"Willy never happened."

"But we both saw him and spoke to him. How can you say he isn't here?"

"More foolish questions. Willy can't be here because it just can't happen—positively cataclysmic! There is no sense in arguing or debating

161

the impossible. It doesn't matter that we have seen him and spoken to him, he is not here because he cannot be here. It is philosophical; you wouldn't understand." The egg started walking again being careful he wasn't going to slip on the hilly ground.

"I might understand," she paused a moment, "if you would explain it better for me."

"Then you won't understand," said Humpty Dumpty as he let go of her hand.

"Listen to me," Jessica was stern, like her mother. "Is this Mother Goose Land?"

"No," said the egg.

"Are you here?"

"Yes," said the egg.

"Do you belong here?"

"No." Humpty Dumpty was tolerant.

"Then how come you can be here if he can't?"

"Ah," said the egg. "That's different."

"How is it different?"

"Grimms' would be, yes, north of here, I'm sure of it." And off he trudged.

CHAPTER 16

Jillian's mom was a monster.
That was OK, thought Jillian, not her fault.
Monsters are creatures too.

Nothing had improved: Charlie and Jessica and Buddy were still missing. The lawsuit was still looming (despite the friendly overtures of Beth and Gwen to Rebecca Holton—a woman who craved sympathy but perhaps craved money even more—), and Colin Fuller-Brinks still wanted to close them down and throw them all in jail. But Gary was getting back to work. "Use it," he said to himself; "you're an artist."

He wasn't, however, a writer. That was Doug; Doug was a writer, and Gwen. But here he was, writing.

He looked back over his first sentence:

Jillian's mom was a monster.
That was OK, thought Jillian, not her fault.
Monsters are creatures too.

Well, that stunk. He tried again:

Jillian's mother was a monster. And being a monster, she did monster things—she threw plates at doors when salesmen came, she crushed bones between her teeth, she stomped through the cave in her underwear, and she growled at Jillian.
A lot.
And she left great big tufts of monster fur all over the house for Jillian to clean...

No, no, no, he thought. He started again.

Jillian's mother was a monster.
A chubby, short, bleach-blonde monster.
And it was Jillian's fault.

How did she know it was her fault?
Everything was her fault—the tiny cave in which they lived, her mother's fad diets, her sister's frizzy ~~hair~~ fur. ~~All those monsters her mother brought home after work. The funny grunting noises her mother made.~~ The fact that Jillian was not yet herself a monster.
It was all Jillian's fault.
Her mother told her so.

Perhaps he ought to just stick to the visual arts. Leave the writing for Doug and Gwen. But Doug and Gwen never wrote this sort of book. And didn't they always tell him writing is therapeutic? The woodwork hadn't helped. And the labyrinth was a bust. And painting—just illustration nowadays—that was mostly just work. He was tired of doing pictures for all those books the publishers sent him; it was all just a business nowadays. He never even met the authors of these things he was asked to illustrate. And he never had any say about the quality of the writing. He was asked to draw pictures for books he knew were awful: some of them by these celebrities who thought that reading the news or singing a pop song or marrying a prince turned them into Maurice Sendak. How could there be any art to it: it was just *children's stories*, right? He was tired of using the talent he used to think was considerable for what he used to think of as a rung on the ladder. He was a children's book illustrator. There had never been any doubt about that. Here he was, pushing middle age, and he still loved illustrated books, everything from *Where the Wild Things Are* to *Jumanji* to *Harold and the Purple Crayon*. He liked the prose; he loved the pictures—Barry Moser, Eric Shanower,

Maxfield Parrish, Tomie dePaola. And it was an old and esteemed form of art. The art of illumination was older than books; it went right back to the days of the Medieval monks. He'd studied the history in school, the lost and lesser-known artists as well as the ones everyone had heard of. But he knew how rarely the great art lasted when the books failed. No, you had to tie your pictures to the right prose. It wasn't enough that some editor in New York or Boston thought your work would boost sales of this or that mediocre narrative. You lived or died with the words. And lately, it had been mostly dying. He admired Charlie. Charlie had bigger dreams; he had a more personal control of his destiny. With him, the bets were all on the pictures alone, no words, no stories. Gary had never offered to get him into illustrating. It would be a dead end for someone like Charlie. Heck, his own talent was being wasted—with his own help and permission. No sense sending Charlie down the same road. It had become more of an addiction than a calling. Too bad it paid so darn well.

Forget the art, forget the wood, forget the Zen stuff, he thought; write your own book. In the midst of all this stress, maybe writing would help him with his present trouble and maybe, in the long run, the right words would help him create the book he'd always wanted to have his name on.

He felt a little odd turning Jessica's experiences into fiction. Not that he had not gotten numerous ideas in the past from the children of OzHouse—their poses and expressions had been so much the core of his book illustrations, he sometimes thought he ought to write them a check ("way to cry, Bob. Hang onto that wrinkle in your lip; here's fifty bucks")—he'd never taken a potential tragedy in the making and tried to turn it into material. Was it a good idea? Was he exploiting Jessica's sad life? Was he belittling it? He didn't think so, but he feared Gwen would think so. Or maybe even Doug. On the other hand, thinking over Jessica's problems, he saw a trait he'd seen before, one that he thought lots of children would benefit from exposure to.

He was—contrary to all practice—in the peaceful space of the Narnia room, lost in the foam cushion of the silver chair. Doug liked writing here (he thought no one knew): Gary had never worked here before. Why would he? His studio was the perfect place to work. But maybe a change of space would help make him feel less the pawn of such vast forces.

Besides, this was the last place he'd seen Charlie, and it was where he'd most likely show up.

He looked down at his screen:

165

Jillian's mother was a monster. A stubby, short, bleach-blonde monster. And being a monster, she did monster things—she threw plates at doors when strangers came, she crushed bones between her teeth, she stomped through the cave in her underwear, and she growled at Jillian.

A lot.

And she left great big tufts of monster fur all over the house for Jillian to clean...

And it was Jillian's fault.

Everything was her fault—the tiny cave in which they lived, her father's temper, her sister's frizzy fur.

The fact that Jillian was not yet herself a monster.

It was all Jillian's fault. Her mother told her so.

And she was right...

The trick to writing a children's book must be the same as the trick to illustrating them: put yourself back into your childhood. Concentrate. Lose yourself. Doug's advice: become a child. Shouldn't be too hard for Gary. Everyone always said he never grew up.

Bulululoop—

An email arrived. It was—he couldn't believe it—it was from Colin Fuller-Brinks. How did Colin Fuller-Brinks, the toad (yes, he would be a toad in Gary's next story) get his email address?

Better not open it. Better keep working on the story. He opened it. It turned out it wasn't from Colin Fuller-Brinks:

Gary, it's unbelievable. I'm here. I made it. I'm in Oz. Somewhere. I haven't met anyone you'd recognize. But they're all wearing yellow. Man, I gotta draw some of this stuff.

Okay, so here's the deal. You've gotta grab one of those books; use the one I left on the chair. I'm a long way from the wardrobe. Bring your laptop. We'll IM and find each other once you're here. Grab the book, read a chapter. Read a chapter about the Tin Man or about the Winkie country if you can. Think YELLOW. Get everything else out of your mind—go Zen if you have to—then pull yourself through the wardrobe. Get EVERYTHING ELSE out of your mind. If anyone can do it, you can. Once you're here, shoot me an IM. He calls himself "Brinksman." Can't believe wi-fi works even here. It's like magic—or Starbucks or something.

Hurry. We're wasting battery here. Chuck

Gary looked up from the screen, glanced around the room, stared through the green window.

It was ridiculous.

Bulululoop—

Another message, a single word:

Hurry!

He got up from the silver chair. He went over to the bookshelf.

"WOLVES GET BAD PRESS," said Glene, the wolf. "If I'd really wanted to eat her, why wouldn't I have done it as soon as I saw her? We were alone in the woods. I had a clear path back to my den. Strictly one-on-one."

"How come you ran to gramma's house?" asked Buddy.

"Ah, well, you see," his new friend explained, "I'd just received a letter from my relations in Russia. Seems my cousin Boris—terrible, terrible—he was taking his morning stroll when he came across a little boy. Wolves are by nature social creatures, you know. Pack animals you might say. Gregarious, really. We see a flock, we want to join. So Boris bumps into this little boy who's out with some of his other animal friends, a bird, a rabbit or something—I don't remember—anyway, he wants to join in the pack. Why not? He's an animal; they're animals. Cute little kid's got a little pop gun. They pretend one of my favorite games: hunter and hunted."

"Peter and the Wolf," Buddy exclaimed.

"Aah, you know the story: the grown-ups come... I think we should avoid grown-ups, don't you?"

"I want to find my mommy."

"—two shots later, no more Boris. You can understand; I really didn't want to be seen walking through the woods with Red after that. Much safer to run on ahead, meet her in the house."

"Are we there yet?" Buddy's rear end was starting to hurt; at every step the wolf's shoulder bones pressed into his thighs.

They seemed to have been going for a long time, deeper and deeper into the dark, pathless woods. The sun was almost entirely blocked by the tall pines. Orange needles strewed the ground.

"Soon," said the wolf.

"I'm hungry," said Buddy.

"Me too," said the wolf.

A large black bird looked down the long limb of a pine. It seemed almost to be watching them. The wolf looked up and cocked its head. "Shouldn't you be in the glass castle?" he asked the bird.

"Nevermore," said the bird.

"Very strange," said Glene. The wolf growled as though to scare it away. But it sat there and ignored him and repeated the word. "Very, very strange," said Glene.

"What?" asked Buddy.

"It's not one of our ravens." The wolf proceeded down the path. And although he wracked his brains to remember a bird that said "nevermore"—he could remember only the enchanted princess and other, ordinary ravens—and wondered where the strange bird had come from and what it meant. He did not share his thoughts with Buddy.

Eventually they passed within sight of something colorful—like something from Story Land, thought Buddy. A house perhaps, way out in the middle of the woods. He could just barely make it out through the trees. It faded quickly into shadows, but before it did, he thought he heard the sound of children.

"Who's that?" asked Buddy.

"No one," said the wolf, still lost in his own thought. "There's nothing there."

"But I saw…"

"Quiet," growled the wolf. And he turned his head to look at Buddy riding on his shoulders. And that was the first time the wolf had sounded like a grownup. "There's nothing there."

Buddy knew enough to be quiet when a grownup growled like that. And then the wolf howled. And in a moment a pack of wolves came running up. The wolves rubbed noses and ran in circles and growled and yipped.

"Who are they?" asked Buddy.

"Family," said Glene.

"What did you say to them?"

"I told them I'd brought someone for dinner."

"They seem awful happy," said Buddy. "Hey, wait a minute. We're spose to be goin' to find my mommy."

"Soon," said the wolf.

Buddy's mother was the same way—telling him they were going out for ice cream and then going shopping for hours and hours first.

When Glene's mate approached, he told her of the bird he had seen. She told him that she had seen on her hunt that morning a little human boy—no, it wasn't this boy but another; he was leading a parade of

168

monsters so strange, so wild, that she had run back to the den in fear and eaten nothing.

"I'm starving," said Buddy.

"Why don't you play with the little ones," he said, turning his attention to Buddy, motioning to a group of half-grown pups.

"What should we play?" asked Buddy.

"Hunter and hunted. You practice running. And they'll practice tracking you," said Glene.

The young wolves yipped all the louder. "But I'm hungry," said Buddy.

"No food unless you run," said Glene, although he seemed to be talking to the pups.

Buddy tried to pet one of the wolves, who reminded him a little bit of Scnapsy. But the wolf backed up and growled. Glene growled and yipped at the wolf, and then he turned to Buddy and growled at him. And now he didn't look friendly at all. His eyes squinted down and his bright red gums were all pulled back from his teeth. "Run," he snarled.

Buddy ran.

The young wolves didn't follow right away. Glene was holding them back. One little boy on foot could never outrun a pack of wolves, even young wolves. Glene knew that. He wasn't worried. He was just waiting until his prey was out of sight.

Buddy kept running. He didn't understand. But he didn't like the wolves any more, and he didn't think Glene was going to take him to his mommy, and he wished the forester would come and help him, or the little man with the nose. And then he thought of the colorful house. And he thought he remembered where it was. He changed direction and kept running. He ran over rocks and through the underbrush, as fast as his little legs would go. And then he heard the sound of yipping. It seemed to be far behind him. And then it wasn't very far away at all. And then he saw the colorful house. The yipping drew even closer. He ran toward the building. He could see that the door was closed. The young wolves were getting nearer. Glene was with them. Buddy heard the father wolf's howl. He looked behind him. Glene was ahead of the others now, running hard. Buddy ran harder, but it was no use. Glene's jaws were wide. Spit dripped from his teeth.

Buddy didn't see what happened next. There was a creaking sound—and then a shout. The world seemed to roll past him. Dead pine needles flew everywhere, and there was fire. Someone grabbed him. Someone else yelled. And then Buddy was inside the house. He was sitting on the floor. "Close the door," he yelled.

"Wait for Gretel," yelled the voice of a young boy.

Gretel ran in, a flaming stick in her hand. The door slammed. She threw the bolt. And then she turned to Buddy and smiled. "You're a lucky little boy," she said, walking over to the warm stove.

When she opened the door to throw her stick in, Buddy thought he saw a boot in among the coals.

Outside, the wolves howled.

CHAPTER 17

Dear Fairy Godmother,

I do not know if this letter will reach you. I am following the advice of two unusual children I met this morning. They suggested I write the letter, tear it up and place it in the fireplace. They assured me it would reach you. It sounded a bit ridiculous to me but with all the strange goings on these days I decided to trust the fates and do as they suggested.

The reason I am contacting you at all is that I am very much confused and need your wisdom and advice. As you know I have always dreamed of meeting the Prince and attending one of his magnificent balls at the Palace. The magical music, glittering gowns and the sparkling ballroom with its mirrored walls and alabaster floors have always seemed so wonderful to me. However, I met a young man who is about my age I suspect, although we didn't exchange such personal information. He was not dressed any less raggedy than I, but he wore unusual jewelry which hung from his eyebrow and the tops of his ears. He compelled me to think about my life in new ways. His concern for some lost children (not those I met today), children he had never even met, endeared him to me.

Now I wonder if perhaps I need not dream of a prince and the Palace to be happy. Perhaps I could find happiness at my own front door. Wearing beautiful clothes and attending a Royal Ball would surely be grand, but perhaps people like me need not strive for grandeur. Maybe a simple life with a simple husband who loves me would be enough. Besides it seems that setting my goals low would allow me a better chance of success and less occasion for disappointment. You know how horribly my "sisters" are working to ensure I am locked safely at home on the night of the ball. And I am not sure even you have the magic to change that.

Therefore rather than the coach, and gown, and a dance with the Prince, I think I might like to change my wish to a small cottage by the river with a young man rather like Charles. I do not think he would care for me in silk gowns or fur slippers. He seemed to be the kind of man who looks deeper and I think he liked me.

As you can see I am in a quandary; for so long I thought I knew what I wanted; now I am not so sure. Please help me sort things out; I really need someone to talk to. Perhaps you could send Charles back. If not, perhaps you could come yourself.

Love,
Ella

GARY SAT IN THE NARNIA ROOM preparing to read one of his favorite Oz books. He knew that Charlie had told him to read about the Tin Woodman, but if this was going to work—and he was amazed at himself to think he was actually taking this bizarre business seriously—he thought he should pick his favorite book.

He snuggled into the gump-body couches and adjusted the Victorian lamp that looked very much like an old gas lantern. He really wanted to believe in the possibility of things so strange as magic. All his life he wanted to believe such things were possible. But people have to grow up. He had long ago given up all such childish lunacy.

But for Charlie's sake, he hoped he did have a spark still smoldering somewhere. Although he would have sworn that it must have gone cold over the years, perhaps the incident of Charlie vanishing into the wardrobe had been like a hard breath on a cold, gray coal in a furnace. He thought of the snowball Charlie had allegedly thrown at Doug. That snowball had to have come from somewhere.

From nothing suddenly a glow, if ever so slight. So now here he was, Gary Robbins, professional artist, with his sneakers off, legs crossed and cuddling with this book from his childhood. He opened *The Magic of Oz* to his favorite chapter and started reading out loud. He paused and studied the Neill illustrations hoping to really feel like he was about to enter Oz. He had always been intrigued by the image of the Li-mon-eags, the large clumsy lion heads on the skinny agile monkey bodies. The wings

172

didn't look much like an eagle's wings, but they worked with the style of pen and ink drawing Neill favored. The brass balls on their tails never served any point except to make them more than just animals joined together.

He loved the part where the Cowardly Lion and Hungry Tiger got turned into a Fat Gillikin Lady and a bunny rabbit. He used to laugh at the drawing of the startled white bunny leaping ferociously at the Li-mon-eag! He read the dialog using different voices for each character and held the book close to his chest and tried to see the scene with his mind's eye.

Was that what he was supposed to do? He didn't really know. But he was going to give this his best shot, even if he ended up in the hallway feeling like an idiot. Does anyone ever learn anything real in life without risking feeling like an idiot?

He thought about the different characters in the Oz books. He wondered what exactly a man made of tin would look like. Not like Jack Haley, of that he was sure. Not such a human face. He looked at the Neill picture on page 246 and wondered about the drawing. Would a tin face have expression? Can tin bend to look sad or happy or frightened as a human or animal face can?

He started singing some of the songs from the movie. Having studied art in New York City, he was pretty good with the Cowardly Lion's parts.

Then he happened to look at the Aladdin's lamp on the small table across from his feet and his mind wandered to the Disney cartoon and Robin Williams' depiction of the genie.

"No, I must stay focused," he chided himself. He thought of everything Gwen had ever said to him about mindfulness. He looked at the large stuffed winged monkey that hung over his head and tried to imagine how big the monkeys probably were. The books were so vague on such things. Two carried Dorothy who was no more than six years old in the first book, well maybe seven— but definitely not a teenager as in the movie. Suddenly he was thinking of Judy Garland and how she almost lost the part to Shirley Temple who he thought was closer in age to the real Dorothy, but could she have ever pulled off the character as well?

"No, that's not right." He slammed the book shut. "Not movies or movie stars. I need to think about Oz—Oz as Baum wrote it." He opened the book and read more.

Finally he climbed off the sofa and stood facing the wardrobe. He had no idea whether he was ready to give this a try. There was no sign, no deep emotional connection to the world of Oz. The pictures were vivid in his mind, but there was no illusion of being there. This was working no better than the labyrinth for taking him out of his almost-middle-aged, mundane American self. He was here; he knew it, in the Narnia room of OzHouse on Old Mountain Road in Cornish, New Hampshire. He took deep breaths and placed the book on the back of one of the couches.

Taking even deeper breaths and closing his eyes (he had always thought magic like meditation would work best with your eyes closed) he took a few steps toward the wardrobe. With his hands out before him, he felt for the coats so he'd know when to step up into the doorway. As his fingers touched the old fur coats he stopped, opened his eyes, and turned back into the room.

"I have always thought people didn't think things through carefully enough in books when they were about to attempt some sort of a magic spell," he said out loud as if there were an unseen audience watching his actions.

Leaning toward the book of names, he grabbed the feather pen in the old brass lion inkwell in order to jot his wife a quick message.

But what could he say? "Gone to Oz, don't wait up?" Besides, he thought, telling about the magic spoiled it, right? After all, Gwen hadn't signed the book. Though hadn't he himself added that part just to keep the kids from talking about the room? Still, better not risk it. Gwen was Buddhist, after all. She'd be fine.

Laying down the pen, he noticed another name written below his in the book: Janey Philips. "Do you suppose we've lost another one?"

He grabbed his sneakers and—he almost forgot it—his iBook —and as he walked toward the wardrobe he thought about the *Magic of Oz*, about Munchkins and Gillikins and Nome Kings and the Wizard of Oz himself. While he did so, he started singing, "Somewhere Over the Rainbow," thinking of Judy Garland in the farmyard and trying not to make himself laugh: reading, concentration, meditation, song. If you try enough tricks, who knows, one might work.

His eyes were closed as he started to feel a second time for the fur coats in front of him. He stepped up into the wardrobe and hoped he wasn't going to feel very foolish in two seconds when he exited the other side of the apple-wood box.

He still felt the soft fur between his fingers and then the fur felt rougher and he smelled something musky and wild.

"We need more mothballs in here," he said with a grin.

"Who's there?"

At the sound of a voice, Gary opened his eyes. Was he caught? Was he in the hallway looking drunk or foolish? He was still in the

174

wardrobe. He saw only the black fur coats in front of him. Then he felt cool air all around him and he stepped back.

The fur coats also moved. One big black fur turned around and flashed black eyes in his face.

Gary held onto the computer, but he dropped his sneakers as he realized he was standing beside a very large black bear who had just asked him a question.

"HOW LONG DO YOU THINK IT WILL TAKE?" asked the in Emperor of the Winkies.

"I don't know," sighed Charlie. "Really it's a lot to hope he'll make it at all. He's never done this before, you know. It might not work, assuming he even tries. Plus, we can't even be sure he was on line when I sent the message. And then if all works out and he tries but doesn't make it, he might just give up." And then Charlie paused a moment. "No," he said on second thought, "Doug might give up, but not Gary. If any adult can make it, he'll be here." He was aware how big that "if" was. "What do you say we give him till the battery runs out?"

"If what Ozma's messenger has said is true, we do not have much time. We should start for the Emerald City immediately. This is not a short trip."

The Tin Man swiveled his tin head as he scanned the area looking for Charlie's friend. "Is that him?" he asked so suddenly it startled Charlie.

Charlie leapt to his feet to see better. Rushing up the road was a man in old-fashioned clothes: a green tunic and brown trousers; no, it was a boy. He could be no more than ten-years old.

"That's not Gary. He's a lot older," Charlie said, disappointed.

"Then who is it?" asked the Tin Woodman.

"How should I know? It's your country."

"Yes, but," the Tin Man stopped speaking for a moment. "This is not a native of Oz, green and brown, and a red cap? No, he must be from outside our borders, although how he crossed the Deadly Desert is a mystery." The boy rushed up to them and between deep breaths he said, "Thank goodness. I came down and everything was changed. Please I need your axe if you will be so kind, sir knight."

The Tin Man smiled a little. "I am not a knight. But you may borrow my axe if you have need of it."

"Oh, I do, I do. The giant is coming right behind me. I have only a few minutes to spare before he reaches the bottom of the bean pole."

"You're Jack?" said Charlie.

"Yes. May I have the axe, sir? I keep mine in the garden next to where the beanpole grew, but as I said, when I descended I wasn't in my garden at all. I do not know where I am."

"This is the Land of Oz," explained the Tin Man. "But why do you need my axe? What do you plan to do with it?"

"Chop the bean pole of course," Charlie answered for Jack, who pointed a short distance away to a huge bean plant reaching into the clouds.

"I did not notice that there a moment ago," the Tin Man observed. He was sure he would have seen it.

"That doesn't seem very Baum-like, does it?" asked Charlie, still looking at the beanstalk.

They could see no giant yet, but high above the ground the plant was shaking and huge strings of beans were raining down.

"If I chop it, that will kill the giant for sure," smiled Jack.

"You plan to kill someone?" asked the horrified Tin Woodman.

"Not someone, a giant. He's evil." Jack made a grab for the axe. "Please may I borrow this?"

"Of course not," replied the Tin Man as he pulled the axe from Jack's grip. "Even though a fall from a beanstalk would probably not kill anyone in Oz, he would suffer greatly, and I cannot permit that."

"But it will kill him," assured Jack. "He is supposed to die. He is very mean and cruel." The boy made a grab for the axe again.

"If you are so sure it will kill him, then I certainly will not loan you my axe," the Tin Man said sternly. "Why don't you talk to the giant and find out what he wants? Most problems can be solved with understanding far better than with violence."

"I know what he wants," shouted Jack, "to grind my bones to make his bread."

"Could have something to do with your stealing his treasure and his hen that lays golden eggs and his talking harp," Charlie suggested. "I always thought you had your nerve accusing the giant of evil when you are just a common thief yourself."

Jack stopped and looked at Charlie with anger in his face. "I haven't taken anything that wasn't my father's in the first place. The giant killed my father and stole all his possessions."

"Did he?" mused Charlie. He never realized. "Must have read a bad translation."

"But you still cannot justify killing the giant," the Tin Man shook his head.

"Well, he will certainly not have a problem justifying killing any of us," Jack yelled. "Please let me have the axe."

"Certainly not," insisted the Tin Man. "I have dealt with a giantess once, and my friend the Scarecrow had dealings with her husband as well, but we never resorted to such violence. I shall speak to your giant when he gets here."

"That will be soon enough," Jack called to them as he rushed off. "I for one do not plan to be here when he does arrive."

Charlie ran through what he knew of *Jack and the Beanstalk.* Then they looked at the beanstalk still shaking and raining beans. He thought he could see the big boots of the giant climbing down from the other side. "You know," he said to the Tin Man, "I'm not so sure that's such a good idea."

"PLEASE STOP CRYING," Gretel said as she wiped Buddy's face with a cloth napkin.

"Can't stop crying," the terrified child replied.

"Let him cry," Hansel said. "Sometimes it's the only thing you can do. I cried quite a bit when the witch first put me in her cage."

"I never had the time to cry," said the girl. She went back to the window as she spoke. "That wicked creature put me to work immediately, and beat me if I so much as stopped to take a breath."

"Are they...."

"Yes," Gretel interrupted. "They're still circling." Glene and the cubs had been circling the house ever since they'd recovered from the shock of the fire.

Buddy wiped his eyes on his dirty sleeves and rubbed his nose. He still felt like crying, but his eyes seemed to have dried up enough for him to simply rub them while he made little hiccupping noises

"I thought you'd be done soon enough," said Hansel. "You looked like a brave boy to me."

Buddy didn't feel very brave, but he liked this older boy thinking that he was. "I thought that mean old wolf was my friend, and then he tried to bite me; he has very big teeth."

Gretel showed Buddy to a chair and told him she knew all about bad people who pretended to be good. "The old woman who lived in this house seemed like the nicest lady we had ever met."

"Gave us all the sweets we could eat, and fresh gingerbread," added her brother.

"But she was even more horrible than that old wolf and its cubs. She locked us up and beat me and she tried to fatten up Hansel so she could cook him and eat him in a stew."

Buddy's eyes opened very wide. He had never heard of anyone cooking a child let alone making a dinner out of him or her. He had never heard the tale of Hansel and Gretel, so he did not know all the horrors these two children had been through.

"Ever since momma died," sighed Gretel, "life for us has been ever so terrible."

"Your mommy died too?" asked Buddy his eyes starting to fill with tears again.

"Yes," answered her brother. "Then poppa remarried and for some reason our new stepmother hated us, and did terrible things to us when poppa was away."

"Didn't you tell your daddy what she was doing?" asked Buddy.

"No. He worked so hard cutting wood all day and didn't come home till it was very dark. We hated to make him even sadder than he was."

"We always thought as things got better, our new stepmother would get nicer. But things didn't get better, and she got meaner and meaner," Hansel explained.

"Did you wish your mommy would come back and make things right again?" asked Buddy innocently.

"Momma was dead. Dead means she's not coming back," Gretel explained.

"But maybe if you wished real hard," Buddy began.

"No. Not even if you wish real hard. Dead is gone, forever," Gretel repeated.

Suddenly Buddy was crying again in earnest. The wall that held back all his emotions had finally given way, and he could not control his sadness any longer.

"Mommy's not coming back?" he sobbed. "I thought if I was really good or if I wished real hard."

"No. No, you didn't," said Gretel. "Don't say that. You knew she was gone. No use pretending. You know you did. You always know." And Gretel seemed as though she might cry as well.

"Everyone told me, but I didn't believe them. I hate that fire." And he continued to cry and put his head on the small table.

Hansel patted Buddy on the back to comfort him while Gretel, still peeking out the window, gathered some food on a large earthenware plate and placed it on the table. When he was done crying this time, she suspected he might be very hungry.

CHAPTER 18

OzWood: OK, SO I'M HERE, NOW WHAT?
    Brinksman: What else...?

OzWood: Follow the yellow brick road?

Brinksman: You got it. I can't believe you managed the doorway the first time; it's really acting crazy....

OzWood: Hey, give me some credit.

Brinksman: Ok, credit. But—first time? I'm blown away. Now, assuming you're in the land of the Winkies, as you're supposed to be, head West.

OzWood: Are you sure, because the map, as I recall from the end papers of *Tik-Tok,* is backward. East in on the left and West is on the....
    Brinksman: Head West.

OzWood: OK, west. As soon as I find it. Am I gonna run into any witches?

Brinksman: Well, I wasn't gonna say… But remember, first of all, we're supposedly past that. Witches are outlawed. Ozma is firmly in control. Only thing is, things aren't quite what they're supposed to be. It seems we're not quite sure Ozma's control is as firm as it's supposed to be. Something's going on in Emerald City. Nick isn't clear on the details. And we've got a little bit of a problem of our own. See there's this giant trying to sniff us out. Nick, that's the tin woodman, he doesn't smell too bad to this giant, but apparently, I…

OzWood: I know that. I know Nick's the Tin Woodman.

Brinksman: …apparently, I don't smell exactly like an Englishman, but the giant is still… Right. Of course you do.

OzWood: Low battery.

Brinksman: You're kidding me.

But Gary didn't get the last message. His screen went blank. He cursed. He tucked the iBook under his arm and kept his eyes out for the Yellow Brick Road.

He'd been in Oz for some time already, having started out in the purple country of the Gillikins. He'd realized soon after arriving what a mistake he'd made not following Charlie's suggestion more closely, which would have landed him in the same part of the country Charlie was in. Fortunately, as the daft bear had pointed out to him soon after he'd arrived, he had not landed all that far from the yellow country of the Winkies. It was a matter of about an hour's walk to get himself from the fields of lilacs, lupines, and loosestrife to the fields of buttercups and goldenrod.

He was awfully glad the bear had been friendly. But then this was Oz, the land where animals had not only voices but, generally, consciences. And this bear had been particularly good natured, if a little distracted, occupied with ripe blueberries—certainly reluctant to skip along the yellow brick road with a stranger who'd dropped out of the sky—or, anyway, plopped out of a doorway.

No problem, thought Gary when the bear nodded and left. Gary knew Oz well enough to find his way. He headed south.

He knew that he'd crossed into the Winkie country; he knew the moment the purple fields changed to yellow. As he crossed the border from the land of the Gillikins, he noticed not only sunflowers and goldenrod, but blooming forsythia, ripe corn and wheat as well. How was it, he wondered, all these things were ripe or in bloom at the same time? And there were yellow butterflies and yellow finches and golden eagles. Not everything was yellow, brown, or gold, but the many hues of that family were everywhere. It was so amazing, so amazingly beautiful. Just the sort of landscaping that they worked so hard to create at OzHouse; here, where even flowers were so reluctant to die, it was sprouting naturally or, more properly, magically. But then, was there a difference between magical and natural in this world? Even the leaves on the trees were many shades of yellow. As soon as he was safely over the border, he'd contacted Charlie.

As he walked along through the ochre fields, he thought perhaps he'd meet a Winkie farmer and he could ask directions. Men, do, sometimes, ask directions, he thought. But he saw no houses or people in the area. The sun was warm and bright. It made everything that much more golden. And although it was high overhead, the sun was not as hot as it seemed it should be. Indeed, there was a cooling breeze around. The sun probably never did get too hot in Oz. That was the thing that had always impressed him about the Oz books, though he knew that others criticized them for it: they were always comfortable. They were delightfully free of any real danger. Things hardly ever died. (Certainly, there was your occasional wicked witch, but that sort of creature had become less and less common as the annual sequels came into being. No one grew terribly old. Armies never fought real battles. Bad guys were punished by slaps and loss of privileges—as when Tik-Tok hit the wheelers with his lunch pails or as when the Nome King lost his magic belt or his reign It wasn't as though Gary thought all children's books should be like Oz books. Sure, kids needed to imaginatively confront dangers in their books to prepare them for the trials and dangers of life—sometimes. But there should also be Oz books, safe places of pure, unsophisticated fun.

More and more of the books came back to him as he walked along. Didn't Glinda have a magic book that told her everything that was going on in the world—or was it just in Oz? If so, she must know he was here, and Charlie as well. Maybe she was already sending someone to help. But then, he couldn't believe L. Frank Baum could have got that detail quite right. If the book told everything that was going on everywhere in Oz as it happened, how would you have time to read it? A description of every one of thousands of individuals getting up in the morning, making their toast, planning their day, a description too of every single winged monkey scratching every flea on every monkey butt in Oz? Why that book would even have to include a description of Glinda reading the book, and reading just that part alone would take 100% of your time. What a labyrinth that would be! Postmodern Oz? Hard to fathom. It was too much. And too invasive too. No—Oz was nothing Orwellian.

Book, or no book, Glinda or no Glinda, Wicked Witch or no Wicked Witch, he'd have to find the road and Charlie and, while he was at it, if at all possible, Jessica and Buddy, and even Suzy, sure. Wouldn't that be something? If they were all here, and not in some other fairyland.

Something in the sky ahead caught Gary's attention.

Something floating, or rather flying at great speed far away in the northwest. It was heading south, not quite toward him, but still getting closer. The way that it moved on the air, rippling on the bottom with a kind of lump in the middle, Gary could only think of a flying carpet. That did not seem appropriate to Oz, but he could not get the idea out of his head during the whole long time it took for the object to pass from sight. Before it was entirely gone, Gary felt the ground seem to rumble beneath his feet. He looked down to see the ground beneath the wheat boiling with—what was it? Mice? Yes, mice; thousands and thousands of them running as fast as they could. In Oz, of course, mice talk.

"Excuse me," he yelled down.

"Don't step on us," a small voice squeaked up.

"Am I going toward the Emerald City?"

"Unless you're an absolute cheesebrain. What else would you be doing?" This was another voice. The first was long gone.

"I mean is this the right direction?"

"Would we be going in the wrong direction?", "You are a cheesebrain," said two different voices.

"What's the rush?" yelled Gary, who had picked up one foot to step forward but was now afraid to put it down; the ground was so absolutely awash with mice.

"Ozma's in trouble," called a more sensible mouse.

"Nome King," yelled another. "Queen of Hearts," said another. And still more thin, squeaky voices called up, "Jabberwok," "forty thieves," "Mome raths," "Jub jub birds, thousands of them," "Bandersnatches," "witches" "and wicked step mothers too" "goblins and orcs..."

"Aren't they the same thing?" Gary asked.

"An abominable snow monster."

184

"I get the idea," said Gary. "You mean to tell me an army led by the Nome King is attacking the Emerald City?"

"Not a cheesebrain," said a voice.

"Something like that," said a second.

"We're a little fuzzy still on the details," said a third.

"I'd really like to put my foot down," said Gary.

"Tough luck, cheesebrain."

Gary lowered his foot slowly, and though he had to put up with a few more insults, or rather the same insult in various mousey voices, he managed to get the load off his tired left leg without hurting anyone.

He was certainly confused, however. Was this or was this not Oz? There were no Bandersnatches in Oz. At the same time, if any of those evil things had somehow made it into this story—what chance did all the forces of Oz have against them? The army of Oz, if he remembered right, consisted of a bevy of cowering generals and a single private with a popgun that had never been fired in anger. Had he managed to arrive in fairyland in the last days of all stories?

But what were the chances of that? Some coincidence that would be.

In the late afternoon, after hours of tiresome trudging, and plenty more worries, he at last found the road. He'd seen so many more strange things as the day progressed: a flock (if that's what you'd call it) of Winged Monkeys following the path of the flying carpet. Two witches— so they were not gone after all—on broomsticks, a conglomeration of dragons. Even now on the far edges of the wide prairie, he could make out different groups of creatures, armies he supposed of beings he could not make out, many moving, he assumed, toward the Emerald City, others perhaps merely wandering in confusion. Any traveling toward Ozma would likely cross paths with him eventually on the way, unless he got to the City first, which he was not sure at all he could do. Although he became more and more fatigued, he moved faster and faster, alternating between a jog and a walk. He dropped the iBook in the tall grass because it was only slowing him down. He could always buy another.

The sun was standing at the top of the distant mountains when he spotted the giant.

"YOU MEAN TO TELL ME, as nice as we were to that witch, she's still suing us?" said Beth.

Gwen passed her the *Lebanon Gazette*, pointed at the article in question. "You don't really find that so surprising do you?"

Beth put down her cup of tea. "I suppose the prudent thing to do would be to settle," she said, although it wasn't certain to Gwen that Beth was convinced prudence ought to be the guiding principle in this situation.

Doug came into the kitchen, switched on the small TV he'd recently added to the room's décor (against the objections of Gwen and Beth) so that he could track the growing infamy of his life's work. He turned up the volume higher than necessary. He took out a large bag of potatoes to start on supper. "How come the one who makes the menu every week is never the same person whose turn it is to do the cooking?" he asked for what must have been the four hundredth time since the system was drawn up.

"Don't get your knickers in a wad," said his wife.

"Because," Gwen explained with the patience and effectiveness of a help menu, "if *you* were planning your own menu it would be five nights of Mac and Cheese."

"And that would be bad because…?"

"State officials refuse to remove children from the foster care facility in Cornish despite the disappearance of at least three children, including two in recent weeks…" said the TV. *"The mother of one of the missing children has threatened to file suit in district court against both the state and the facility. Rebecca Holton alleges the facility has willfully created an environment of abuse and neglect."*

And there was Jessica's pathetic parent on the little screen well dressed and just perceptibly drunk, babbling into the camera, "They stole my baby and then they lost her. Those Wonderlanders. When are they gonna grow up? They play this little game with other people's children. And then they have the hypocrisy to call a hard-working mother like me negligent."

"Son of a…" Doug began.

"Beth disagrees with me; she thinks we should settle," said Gwen placidly.

"I didn't say that," Beth interjected. "I said, it might be prudent. We know the harpy is only interested in cash."

"Gary thinks we should just string her along until we find Jessica. By the way, where is Gary? Isn't he supposed to be helping with supper?"

Gwen looked puzzled. Beth asked her why. *"'Wonderlanders'? 'When are they gonna grow up?'* When did she start sounding like Colin Fuller-Brinks?"

"Now that you mention it—that is the sort of thing he'd say."

"Do you suppose he's been coaching her?"

"And isn't it funny she's started showing up here all of a sudden?" Gary observed.

The doorbell rang and a moment later, as though to confirm their suspicions, Colin Fuller-Brinks and Rebecca Holton were standing in the kitchen, led by Brittney, who had, since the loss of Jessica, made herself very useful around the house. Colin had a new laptop in his hand. The appearance of Rebecca Holton in person, so soon after her drunken image had faded from the small screen, was too much for Doug.

"Greetings, Mrs. Holton," he called out with dripping insincerity. "Lovely to see you continuing your visits to our Wonderland. Just saw you on TV; wonderful show. Noticed you slurring your words a little there…"

"Doug," said Gwen, hoping against hope that his name uttered in that tone would shut him up.

"Notice, guys," Doug went on, "this is, what, the third time the caring Mrs. Holton has shown her droopy face at OzHouse since the disappearance of her daughter. But how many times did she come to visit said daughter when she was actually here? Is this a woman who can smell money, or what?"

"Is this the behavior you model for the children?" asked Colin Fuller-Brinks, drawing Rebecca Holton to him in a friendly embrace. "As for Rebecca, she is here at my request. I have certain things to say that I think she would do well to hear."

"So what, are you two dating now?" said Beth.

"My personal life is none of your concern," said Colin, letting go Rebecca's shoulder.

"Just tell them why we're here," said Rebecca, putting her hand on the caseworker's arm.

Doug and Beth could not quite suppress a snicker.

"Fair warning," said Colin. "I've come to give you fair warning. We have solid evidence you are harboring a criminal so audacious that even in the atmosphere of suspicion under which this fantasy house of yours has been operating for months he was willing to steal a valuable piece of state property, namely my laptop. A criminal so reckless would not limit himself to petty thievery, I am sure…"

"Get to the point, doughhead," said Doug.

"The point? The point? The point is, we'll be closing this place down. Moreover, we'll be taking this matter before a grand jury. I fully expect criminal charges in the near future."

"Owwwwch," yelled Doug. Everyone looked over to see him grab his finger and run it to the faucet.

"He's cut himself," said Beth, rushing to his side, but he shrugged her off.

As he wrapped the finger in paper towel and held it tight in his right hand, he looked straight at Colin Fuller-Brinks. His face was contorted with the sting of the cut as he spoke, "Listen to me, Brinksy..."

"Relax," said Gwen, who had not moved from her seat. "Do you really think the police or the DCYF would send him here to tell us this? Do you think they would let him come if they knew he was going to spread this manure? As usual, he's just spouting off. Would you even be telling us this if it were actually so, Colin?"

"Oh, it's so, all right," said Colin.

"He's got proof," said Rebecca.

"As soon as I take this to the police, there's gonna be hell to pay." And as he spoke, he opened a new laptop on the table. "He stole my computer all right. And what's more, Gary knows about it. He and that sociopath protégé of his have been passing instant messages to one another on *my* account. Oh, it's hilarious. There I was turning on my account and this screen pops up, and I get the whole thing right in front of me. Some little fantasy about visiting the Land of Oz. It's so childish. A couple grown-up men pretending themselves into fairyland. Oh, I know he writes children's books, but a man that age indulging in make-believe... The man is sick. You're all sick."

Doug felt an impulse to inform Colin that he, not Gary, was the writer, that Gary only illustrated children's books. But the fact hardly seemed relevant. Holding his throbbing finger, he peered over Colin's shoulder at the screen. There it was, in colorful block letters: a short discussion between OzWood and Brinksman. Doug recognized Gary's username. Colin acknowledged the other.

"A," said Beth, who was now peering at the screen as well, "so what if they are playing a game? Maybe you don't approve it. Maybe I don't... I'm sorry Gwen, but I've always thought your husband was a little eccentric. Harmless of course, but..."

"And B," Doug broke in, "the fact that he figured out your username does not prove he stole your computer."

"And my password?"

"It has been done before, probably a common..."

"Studmuffin12? S-T-U-D-M-F-N-1-2. You think he just figured that out? Oh, don't snicker," he said to Beth, "Oh, and I'm sure the police will..."

"Well, just get him in here. Brittney, go find Gary, please. Tell him he's supposed to be making dinner anyway."

188

"He's not here," she said.

"What do you mean, he's not here? How would you know?"

"I know where he is."

"Where is he?"

"I can't say," she said. "But I'll go get him. I'll go get them all."
And with that the little girl disappeared.

"Just send him an instant message," said Gwen.

"He's not on line anymore," said Colin, looking at his buddy list.

"Then send one to Charlie," said Doug.

"I can't send an IM to myself."

"Of course you can." And Doug pushed Colin out of the way and
typed a message to Brinksman: "Charlie, where are you?" And the words
showed up in a new box on Colin's new laptop. But whether they popped
up on some other screen wherever Charlie was there was no way to know.

"DON'T YOU UNDERSTAND, little girl, if I cross that line, something
dreadful is bound to happen. And it will be your fault." Humpty Dumpty
crossed his arms and refused to take another step. Jessica looked down at
his huge face which had on it such an immovable expression of defiance
that it seemed to be painted on.

The line to which he referred was the border of the Forest of
Grimm. It was marked by two things. The first was a long, white picket
fence. The second was snow. It was true, on the side upon which they
stood, it was autumn, just beyond the fence, winter. It was snowing even
now, not heavily. Nor had it been snowing long. There was hardly more
than a dusting on the ground. But it was clear that the snow was respecting
the border. In front of them was an open gate.

"No, it won't," said Jessica.

"Won't what," said Humpty Dumpty, "won't happen or won't be
your fault?"

"Won't neither probably. Whatever bad thing happened to mix up
the fairy worlds, that has already happened, even if you don't believe it.
And you've already been in this world, so you might as well go to another
one. And if something bad happens after that, it will not be my fault. I'm
just trying to save Buddy."

"I thought you liked being to blame?"

A huge black bird crossed over their heads from the Grimms'
Forest. It made a harrowing sound like that of an ominous bird but which,
at the same time, sounded like "nevermore, nevermore, nevermore."

"I can't be to blame for *everything,*" said Jessica. "And I can't fix
everything." And with that she took a step over onto the snow. She was

glad to discover that despite the snow, it wasn't especially cold in Grimms' Forest, at least not here at the border.

"Well if you aren't to blame, why are you even going after the little brat? Grimms' Forest isn't exactly a place of fun and happiness," said Humpty Dumpty without changing worlds, "People do actually get eaten by witches there, and wolves, and God knows what else. I cannot guarantee your safety."

"Buddy is in there, and he needs me. And we're going." And with that she grabbed the egg man's skinny arm and hauled him through the gateway.

"Careful," yelled Humpty. "Fragile shell."

"Sorry. But you're here now. And nothing dreadful has happened."

"Yet!"

"So let's go."

And so they did. The woods stretched before them in the snow without the hint of a path to direct them. They had no idea how to find anyone lost in such a place.

"I'm sure," said Humpty Dumpty, "we'll come across some dreadful creature happy to give us directions…"

"That would be nice," said Jessica.

"…into his stomach," the egg man continued, "straight down the esophagus, left at the lungs."

"I thought you knew everything," said Jessica. "You should know how to get us through this."

"I've read everything," said Humpty. "There's a difference. Our situation is untenable, young lady. Our options are, our hopes are, few and all equally tenebrific."

"Tenebrific?"

"Oh yes, perhaps we'll find a path of breadcrumbs and follow it to the candy house of a witch prepared to fatten you for later and fry me up for lunch."

"But don't you always come back when they turn the page?"

"That doesn't make it fun. Or perhaps we'll follow it the other way and I can be cracked open by an evil stepmother. Or perhaps we'll encounter wolves, or…"

"Shhhhhh," said Jessica, who had just noticed something moving in the trees ahead of them. They hid themselves behind a huge rock and tried to peer around to see more clearly. "It's just bears," said Jessica. "Probably the three bears."

But it wasn't just bears. Behind the bears—and there were far more than three bears to begin with—in a kind of parade, came a troop of centaurs with bows in their hands and quivers on their backs. And behind the centaurs came some rather stern looking fauns carrying warclubs. They were followed by creatures Jessica could not even name: tall, gangly, tree-like creatures who were followed in turn by a team of reindeer pulling a sleigh driven by a dwarf and upon which sat a very tall pale woman dressed all in white.

"Happening already," Humpty Dumpty whispered.

"What's happening?" Jessica whispered back.

"Something dark and dreadful. Those are not Grimms' creatures."

"And it's my fault; I get it. But we're going to find Buddy anyway."

The army passed without seeming to notice Jessica or Humpty Dumpty. "They don't belong here," said Humpty when they were gone. "*I* don't belong here. Stay if you like. Something unprecedented is happening in all the world of stories. And I don't wish to be part of it. I think I know what it is, and if I'm right, I can do nothing about it. And therefore, I am going home, to my nice comfortable wall in Mother Goose Land. Cats to witches, Old Cole's over his little royal snit by now."

And then they heard a crunching in the snow and looked to see a large, bearded man with an axe approach: "What would that be?" he asked them.

"What would what be?" said Humpty Dumpty, trembling.

"The cause of the unprecedented happening. I hear report from the crows of three children trapped in that old witch's candy house, and a pack of wolves trying to eat their way through to get at them. Already rescued one little girl and a grandmother from a wolf this week, lost a little boy to a wolf as well. Now three more? And then these creatures walking through like an army. If you know what is going on, tell me. But do it as we walk. I don't know how long those children can hold out."

191

CHAPTER 19

...is another man from outside of Oz, Gary Robbins, who has just left the Winkie Country and is trying to find the Emerald City. A boy named Jack has escaped a giant who has smashed two homes of Winkie farmers looking for him. Nick Chopper is hiding Charles Emerson in a cave in the Gillikin country; Princess Dorothy is returning to the Emerald City, riding in the red wagon. Trot and Cap'n Bill are waking up after a nap in the mountains of the Quadling Country. Ozma is meeting with her councillors in the throne room. The Shaggy Man has reached the base of Mount Munch. Suzy Bishop is trying to make the magic picture work. A boy on a flying carpet has appeared over a wheat field in the Winkie Country. Polychrome and Ojo the Lucky have left Oz and have almost completed their journey to meet with Queen Zixi of Ix, who has been missing for several days. Button Bright is lost in the Forest of Gugu...again. Betsy Bobbin is asking for directions from a woman in the Munchkin Country. The wizard is knocking on Glinda's front door.

GLINDA THE GOOD AROSE in the middle of the night from a dream disturbed sleep and spent ten hours reading from her magic book. The dreams had been a sign to her of further troubles in this peaceable kingdom. It was not the content of the dreams that told her so—although they were full of the kind of monsters that had hardly been seen in Oz since the days of King Pastoria. It was the fact of the dreams. One does not get nightmares in the easy land of Oz. And now, despite hours and hours of reading, she had yet to find the information that would tell her exactly what was going on.

Still, she had her suspicions.

The Red Sorceress stopped reading and asked Rosamond, one of her servants, to answer the door.

"But, I haven't heard anyone knock," said the maid as she placed down the rose quartz vase she was dusting.

"You will," replied Glinda with a tired smile.

A knock was heard. With a nod of understanding, the girl went and let the wizard in. Breathing heavily, the little man wiped his forehead with his handkerchief. Despite the fatigue of long hours spent poring over her magic book, Glinda rose in proper form to meet her guest. The wizard's leather bag had hardly touched the floor when the exhausted man asked what the sorceress had learned.

"Again this book proves far too cryptic to be a good source of information in this case," sighed Glinda, inconspicuously stretching her limbs beneath her long robes. She invited the emotional wizard to sit as she moved to her grand, red velvet chair. "It doesn't tell us much of anything about the doings of animals, as you know. I can discern that the Cowardly Lion and Hungry Tiger have been sent to fight a thing called a Jabberwock, but I cannot learn whether they have prevailed. Nor can I find out if Toto has reached General Jinjur's farm or if the Glass Cat has roused the great army of Oogaboo. Moreover, the book makes little distinction between the meaningful and the trivial. Mentioning only unusual circumstances or the actions of very important personages, it leaves large gaps in the information. If only it were as complete as the Royal Historian often said it was."

The wizard, still standing, gave a wry smile.

"By reading between the lines all morning I have come to suspect that this land is full of alien creatures. A great number that may perhaps be an organized group seems to be heading toward the Emerald City, but as far as I can tell, the greater part are oozing all over the map. Exactly who they all are, where they are from or how many, I can't even guess. But I have deduced this much: the dangers we are encountering seem somehow to be related to the arrival of two human strangers. One seems to be named Gary Robbins and the other is Charles Emerson. The book keeps coming back to them."

194

"But if it doesn't distinguish between the trivial and the important...."

"I said it makes *little* distinction. Now, the book tends to favor the unusual over the common. And yet these two have done nothing at all unusual that I can tell, and still the book won't stop mentioning their every step. That must mean something."

"I see," said the wizard, who was just starting to breathe more easily. "This is what you mean by 'reading between the lines'?"

"Unless the book too is suffering from the general breakdown or transformation that seems to have infected the magic of Oz."

The wizard did not seem to have heard this last remark. "So you think these men are important?" he asked.

"I'm grasping for anything at this point. But they are the only beings of their kind. That is certain."

"Did they come from America?" The wizard fidgeted himself onto an ebony and velvet chair.

"The book did not say. They did not arrive together; and the name of the one meant nothing to me: Gary Robbins. But Charles Emerson, his name sounded familiar." The wizard nodded and Glinda went on. "So I asked the book for all references on Charles Emerson. Not only has he been to Oz before, a number of times in fact, never staying for long, but he has been to a great number of other fairylands as well."

The wizard was having some trouble following her thinking. "Why would that matter?"

"I cannot be sure that it does. But something has connected these worlds in improper ways. This is certain. Something has brought foreign magic into our peaceful land. And this Charles Emerson seems to have been to all the lands of incompatible foreign magic now invading us. I have been wary of visitors for a long time, as you know. And this tells me I was right to be so. The real trouble may well be traced to the time when people such as yourself started finding our peaceful country."

"My dear Glinda," the wizard sounded defensive. "I'm sure my presence here cannot be the..."

"You have proven your worth," said Glinda, putting the wizard at ease. "The point is that if good can get in, so can evil. This is why we came up with the Deadly Desert and the spell of invisibility that was supposed to make it impossible to see or get to us from outside. We have always been entirely separate from most of these places and their creatures. Now something with which I am not familiar has disturbed the balance of magic and allowed all these other intruders to find their way across our borders. The desert and my spell seem to be useless."

195

The wizard began to understand.

"Think of it. Everything we know of magic could change in an instant."

"Has anything changed yet? Is your magic still working?"

"So far."

Glinda closed her tired eyes just a moment. The wizard felt the great fatigue that must be upon her. He felt an impulse to tiptoe out of the room and let her rest, despite the grave danger. But in a moment, the great sorceress' eyes shot open, and she clapped her hands.

Three of her serving maids rushed into the room. "Prepare my swan chariot," she commanded them.

Then looking at the wizard she added, "We must find this outsider that the Tin Woodman is harboring and discover where he actually comes from and how he has brought all these dangers to our world."

"And then?" asked the wizard, afraid of the answer.

"At all costs he must be expelled—and hope that will be enough to undo the damage."

"And if it isn't?"

"We must hope that it is."

"I STILL HAVEN'T FOUND GARY... or Charlie for that matter," sighed Gwen.

"They may be out searching in the woods," Doug replied in his off-handed manner.

"Their coats are still on the hooks in the front hall," added Beth. "Charlie might go traipsing about in the woods in just a cardigan, but that doesn't sound like Gary to me."

"Me either," said Gwen as she pushed back her hair from her face and fell onto a stool in the corner of the kitchen. "When Colin and Rebecca Holton left, they seemed convinced that we were hiding Charlie from the authorities."

"But they are so paranoid," said Doug. "I know. We mustn't let them upset us."

"Charlie may have stolen his laptop, but even if he did, it is hardly proof that he committed any crimes against the children," Beth added.

"If Gary knows anything, I'm sure he'd tell us." Doug placed his half-empty cup of cold coffee in the sink. "That's it!" Doug announced with his finger in the air. "Gary knew too much, so Charlie disposed of him along with the bodies of the missing children."

"Oh God," Beth cut him off. "Not even in jest. All we need is someone to overhear a statement like that and we'll have a whole bloody Stephen King novel forming around our ears."

"Sorry, Beth. Didn't mean to upset you. My way of dealing with the stress, I guess."

"I know. I know. We can't start imagining that every person who is late for dinner has mysteriously vanished."

"Maybe they just went through the wardrobe and flew off to Narnia," Doug lightened the mood; Beth snickered, and even Gwen chuckled.

"But seriously," said Beth, "Gary and Charlie are probably concocting a plan to find the missing kids. Maybe they are in the basement."

Beth helped her husband prepare dinner while Gwen went down the wooden stairs into the unfinished cellar. In order to make the Oz house seem like a Cornish landmark from the days of Maxfield Parrish and St. Gaudins, they had designed it with a cellar much like many old farmhouses in New England have. Rather than knotty pine walls and a shag carpet, it had large granite stones for walls and a dirt floor. It stayed dry, but could get pretty chilly in the winter. It was a large, dark, empty room, lit by two lines of bare bulbs. Among the storage containers, hot water heater, and furnace, she saw little more than cobwebs and two mice. In one spot, she noticed the dirt floor looked disturbed; images from terrible movies flashed through her mind. She closed her eyes tightly and when she looked back, she could see the spot was simply where a wooden box filled with old boots had been moved. No shallow grave.

Only as she was inspecting the box did she recall that someone had suggested that very possibility when Suzy vanished years ago. They'd gone through the cellar from one end to the other looking for a body.

As she started back up the stairs, her head was swimming. She sat on the cold cellar stairs and pulled her hair in frustration: she knew it was irrational to be imagining all manner of horrors simply because her husband wasn't in his workshop or wandering about in the cellar.

"Darn that Colin Fuller-Brinks and that pain-in-the-ass Holton woman." As if their lives weren't complicated enough, now they had to worry about nonsense. For a moment, all those years of meditation and contemplation seemed to go right out the window. She took a deep breath and headed up the stairs.

Beth was placing the stoneware plates on the long wooden table as Gwen entered the dining room. Without asking, Gwen started putting napkins and cutlery next to the dishes.

197

"Find Gary?" asked Beth after a minute or so.

"He must be outside somewhere. Maybe in the labyrinth or in the woods." When Beth looked back confused, she added, "He has other coats."

Beth smiled dubiously, as if to say, "Not ones he wears." But what she actually said was, "Want me to ask one of the kids to go take a look?"

"What? Oh no. He'll be in for dinner. It will be dark soon anyway; I can't imagine him staying out after the sun goes down, too cold for him this time of year."

"You sure?" Beth asked.

Before she could answer, into the room stormed Janey who had been crying.

"What's wrong, honey?" asked Beth as she put down the remaining glasses and placed a hand on the side of the girl's head.

"I…well I, it's not working now. It worked the other day, and I did the same thing, but… Oh, I shouldn't be telling you any of this should I?" the girl wiped her freckled nose.

"Telling me what? Why can't you tell me something?" Beth placed both hands on either side of the little girl's face.

"The rules. You know. In the special room." She looked around the room to be sure no other children were there.

Gwen approached the two. "Special room? We have lots of special rooms. Do you mean the Little White Horse Room?"

The girl swallowed hard and licked her lips. Her eyes flashed from Beth to Gwen and back again.

"You didn't sign the book. I can't talk to you unless you signed the book."

"The book? Oh, you mean the hidden room. You found that, did you?" Gwen smiled.

"Am I allowed to talk to you about the room? Are the rules only for kids?"

Beth relaxed a little. She had thought this was something relating to the missing children, but it was just a game. She wasn't in the mood for any games just then, but she knew better than to spoil the magic for the child.

"No, honey, you can talk to any of us—me, Gwen, Gary, Doug."

"Just not with the children—or with people that don't live here," said Doug.

For the moment, Gwen's mind stopped cataloguing all the problems they were dealing with and reveled in the simplicity of a child's world. How marvelous it was to be able to put so much importance into a game. No fear of lawyers or police, no life-and-death decisions or worries of state laws or court cases. She leaned over and kissed the child's forehead.

"No. You didn't do anything wrong. The Narnia Room was made to be found, and you seem to be just the kind of girl to enjoy the secret."

"But, then," Janey stopped, "I mean, if I didn't do anything wrong... then why won't it work now?"

"What won't work now? Is the light burnt out?" Beth asked.

Janey laughed, "No, not the light. The magic. I couldn't get it to work this time."

"The magic is always going to be there. It's just that sometimes when we are upset or sad or frightened, we have trouble seeing it. But it's always there," Gwen comforted.

"So then it will work next time?" Janey asked.

"Of course. You must be patient, and not expect too much."

"Oh, good," Janey said as she clapped her hands. "I was really scared that I did something wrong and that that was why the magic was gone."

With another kiss on the forehead, Janey was told she could go play for a little longer while dinner was cooking. The child rushed off happy that a grown-up had solved her problem.

"What would you give to have our problems solved so easily?" Gwen asked Beth.

"God, for the simple faith of a child. Even kids like these who have suffered so much in their short lives can lose themselves in play and just be at peace sometimes," Beth said as she pushed the swinging door into the kitchen and prepared to gather up the salad bowl and dressings.

"IF YOU CANNOT SLOW DOWN, I shall simply sit here and wait for you to return," said Humpty Dumpty with a huff.

"Didn't you hear what the forester said?" asked Jessica. "There are wolves attacking the gingerbread house of the evil witch."

"That's not how the story goes. He must be mistaken. Besides, I refuse to risk my shell rushing off to save some witch, and an evil one at that."

"He said there are three children inside," Jessica made a grab at the egg's tiny hand.

"That story has two children," said Humpty Dumpty as he rolled his large eyes.

"No," cut in the forester. "The crows said three children. And if the house is only made of gingerbread, the wolves will not be long eating a way through it."

"Two children," insisted the egg. "And I wouldn't worry too much about those gingerbread walls. Probably so stale they'd be as hard as wood by now."

"Have you seen it?" asked Jessica.

"Well, no," admitted Humpty Dumpty. "But I read that story over a hundred years ago. Not much chance the cake is still fresh is it?"

"Would you like me to carry you?" asked the forester.

"I should say not. I am perfectly capable of getting about. Been doing so since before you were born, I'd wager."

"Then get a move on, or I'll leave you behind," growled the man, and he began taking longer strides with his great legs.

"Please, please," said Humpty Dumpty, "no one likes a runny egg."

"Why is all this happening?" asked Jessica as she held up a prickly vine for Humpty Dumpty to pass under.

"Can't say. Won't say. Shouldn't say."

"Why not?" asked the girl angrily.

"Because I don't know," said the egg with a sigh.

"If you two can't move any faster, I'll go ahead. If those wolves get a hold of those three,"

"Two," cut in Humpty Dumpty.

"Stubborn egg," the man grumbled. "Hurry up, or there won't be enough left to know if it was two or three of them, not that it would matter much at that point."

But it was clear there was no way Jessica and Humpty Dumpty could keep up with forester. And he soon left them behind. Within a few minutes the man had walked so far he was lost to their sight. Jessica tried to keep Humpty Dumpty walking quickly, but his tiny feet found it hard to keep their balance on the rough ground covered with twisted roots.

"I refuse to end my days on these dreadful Grimms' Forest trails. I am well aware of the need to make haste, so you need not remind me again, but until you are a large egg with spindly legs and feet too small to be of much use, you will not understand my difficulty. I was composed for sitting, not traveling"

Jessica felt sorry for Humpty Dumpty and tried to make an effort to clear his path for him. "It must be really hard for you in the woods."

200

"Give me a conundrum to ponder and I can hold my own with the best of them. But unless you make proper accommodations for me, this kind of travel is truly out of the question."

Jessica stopped a moment to allow the egg to find purchase for his feet in the slippery leaves that lined the slope. When they finally came to the bottom of the ravine, the girl asked, "Now which way?"

Humpty Dumpty looked at her in amazement. "Well?" she asked again.

"My dear girl," began the egg, "this is not my story. I have never ventured into the Grimms' Forest. How would I know the correct path to take me to a place I have never been?"

"You said you read the book," Jessica exclaimed.

"Yes, I read the book. It didn't have a map or directions though did it? This is as far as I can discern your quest, young lady, not mine."

"This isn't my quest. My quest is finding Buddy. I was just trying to help those children trapped in the gingerbread house."

"Nonsense. None of our business. Those two…"

"The forester said three."

"Those two brats got themselves into this trouble in the first place, and besides they always get out of trouble on their own. Although I do concede, this story about wolves is disturbing. Shouldn't be any wolves in this story, you know."

"I do know that," said Jessica.

"So, do you want to rescue your friend Buddy or these two children trapped by wolves?"

Jessica didn't know what to do. She hated feeling like this. It didn't take her long to realize that they had lost their way trying to follow the forester. Reluctantly she decided they should try to find Buddy rather than the gingerbread house.

"Bravo," exclaimed the egg. "Making a decision is the first step in solving a problem."

"I don't feel any closer to solving my problem," sighed Jessica. "Out here in the woods I have no idea which way to go to find Buddy. There isn't even anyone to ask directions."

"Trust me, kiddo, that never really helps," chuckled Humpty Dumpty.

The two travelers continued through the woods. Jessica continued to feel frustrated by the slowness of the egg, but she could see he was trying to make haste so she did her best to remain patient. If Humpty Dumpty saw any look of frustration on the girl's face, he did not comment on it.

The snow had stopped, but not before completely obscuring their tracks. Jessica recalled again the importance of marking your trail when you're wandering in the wood. When she thought she saw a broken branch or footstep she would adjust their journey accordingly. After about a half hour or so the little girl realized that her tracking skills had been unsuccessful.

"Why do you keep breaking sticks like that and placing them on the ground?" asked the egg. He had been watching her do this for some time.

"I'm making a trail so we don't get lost."

"As I thought," said the egg. "And I am sure you realize that if we followed your masterful trail, it would lead us.... Well, where would it lead us?"

"To another spot in the middle of the woods," Jessica admitted.

"Exactly. And one random and indistinguishable spot in the infinite woods is no better than another, is it?"

"I guess not," said Jessica.

"You see you have to start your tracking from a known point of..."

"I get it," said Jessica.

"I hope you do."

She did. Neither she nor Humpty Dumpty was any closer to knowing where they or anything else was.

"And when it gets dark, who will protect us?" asked the egg after several minutes of silence.

"I'm doing the best I can," replied Jessica. "It's not my fault we're lost."

"It's always your fault," muttered the egg as he pulled his foot free of a root.

"What's that supposed to mean?"

"You know full well, young lady. Everything is your fault. Since you seem to be convinced it is somehow your job to set all wrongs right, naturally I assumed you also took responsibility for their having gone wrong to start with," Humpty Dumpty gave her an odd look that she could not read. Was he serious or was he just making fun of her? Was this his way of helping her, or was he just grumpy?

"I was just trying to help. Buddy is lost because of me and..."

"Just as you surmised those children trapped inside the gingerbread house were your responsibility too? Why?"

"I was just trying to help."

202

"You said that. But let's be truthful. We're lost and going to be in terrible danger and then no one will be around to rescue your friend Buddy, all because you didn't follow my advice."

"Is that what this is all about? You have to be right? Okay. Fine! You were right. Does that make you feel better?" Jessica started to cry.

"Yes, in fact it does," said Humpty smiling. "I may be eaten or lost forever but at least I will die knowing you know I was right."

Jessica was suddenly too angry to cry. "You are a horrible, rotten egg," she yelled as she started to walk off.

"Hey, hey. Wait up. Don't leave me," cried Humpty Dumpty.

"Why not? You won't help me and you're really mean."

"You can't leave me stranded here in the Grimms' Forest. I only came here because you dragged me here. I knew better."

"I...? You....? You followed me, remember?"

"This is a dangerous place for a man with a shell. Since you made me come, it's your responsibility to take care of me." The egg didn't sound haughty or smug now.

"Well, since taking responsibility is something I do so well, I guess I will stay with you." Humpty Dumpty looked instantly relieved. "But you've got to be nice," the girl added.

"Goes without saying," said the egg. "I now know on which side the bread is buttered. Now, since Mother Goose Land is south of here, and we are trying to get deeper into the Grimms' Forest, that is, to find Buddy... We are trying to do that, are we not?"

Jessica nodded.

"Then I suggest we go south."

"But..."

"No, no, no. Mother Goose Land happens to be beyond the deepest part of Grimms' Forest. I know this for a fact. That means if we go that way, we cover the most ground. And the more ground we cover, the better the chance of finding little Buddy. Now, doesn't that make sense?"

Jessica had no way to argue. "Okay. So which way is south?"

"That way," the egg spun himself around and pointed with his tiny hand.

Jessica started to walk that way and then asked, "How do you know?"

"Oh, easy," Humpty Dumpty replied. "Moss grows on the north side of a tree," for one thing, "and fiddle head ferns always curl in a southerly direction."

"But there's snow on the ground," said Jessica.

"And I saw a bird flying overhead, and it was heading due west," her companion continued as though she had not spoken.

"I didn't see any bird," said Jessica.

"And the slant of the light through the trees at this time of day definitely says that that is east," Humpty Dumpty pointed in the direction he'd determined.

"I can't see the sun." The forest was dim and evenly lit. The day was heavy with clouds.

"Clearly, we have no choice. We want to go this way." He pointed.

Having no better notion of her own, Jessica was willing to let the egg man take the lead. But after a moment she asked, "You wouldn't be just trying to lead us toward Mother Goose Land just so you could get back there would you?"

"Of course not, child. I'm insulted you would ask such a thing."

They hadn't walked long at all, before they saw a structure of some sort through the trees.

CHAPTER 20

The wizard eats Wogglebug poop!
                    The Scarecrow is a stupid bag of hay!
The Cowardly Lion rules.
                    The Hungry Tiger ate my baby sister.

            The Woozy is a Blockhead!

The Shaggy Man has split ends
                    Toto's a dumb dog
Uncle Henry is more henpecked than Billlna

            Scraps: it ain't just the quilt, you are crazy!

Jack IS a pumpkinhead

            The Sawhorse's bark is worse than his bite.

Long Live the Wicked Witch.

"THIS WHAT PASSES FOR GRAFFITI in Oz?"
            "Seems more than nasty enough to me," said the Tin Man.

205

"More like bathroom stall stuff. Take a bus through New York some time."

"I don't think I would care to do that."

"I notice there's nothing here about Ozma."

"It's bad enough they insulted the beloved Scarecrow. But not even a rebellious child could be so callous as to insult our Ozma, the gentle and just. We simply do not raise children that way in Oz. Mombi herself could hardly bring herself to do it. And she was an evil witch."

"Nothing about you either, is there," said Charlie.

"I can't read this one," said the Tin Man, one hand pointing at the cave wall, the other resting on the front of his barrel body where his stomach would be if he had one.

Outside, the pounding of the giant continued without rest and so regularly that the sound reminded the Tin Man of the Nome King's mechanical giant with its hammer. Clearly this giant had some sort of club with which to beat away at the boulder that was partially blocking the cave mouth and which so far had kept Nick and Charlie safe. Charlie had mentioned that, as he recalled, the giant in Jack and the Beanstalk was not very smart and would probably not realize for some time that he could not move that boulder by hitting it with a club and would likely never think of using the club as a lever. Still, they did not feel safe.

"What's it say down there?" said Charlie.

"I'm hungry," said the Tin Man.

"All those words to say, 'I'm hungry'?"

"No," said Nick, rubbing the place where his stomach would be. "I'm hungry. I used to be meat, like you, you know. I know what it feels like. Should have asked Oz for a stomach."

"Maybe you could eat your heart out," joked Charlie. The comment earned the young man a stern, reproachful look from the usually mild Nick Chopper.

"That one says, 'Oz is a prison! We are oppressed by the tyranny of love, the hypocrisy of kindness. Revolt in the name of Elphaba.' Can you imagine that?" The Tin Man sounded particularly sad as he said it. "The tyranny of love? The hypocrisy of kindness?"

"You were lucky," said Charlie, walking over to read the odd bit of graffiti, "most people if they don't have a heart don't ever realize they need one." And then he added, "who's Elphaba?"

"Never heard of her," said Nick.

"The tyranny of love," Charlie repeated the words again. "And they thought *I* was strange."

"Do you suppose whoever wrote that thinks we put the Deadly Desert in place to lock ourselves in?" said Nick, straightening himself up. "It makes me sad to read such things." Nick didn't wish to read any more.

"Graffiti in Oz," said Charlie as though he were thinking up a book title.

"Must be some secret meeting place for disgruntled youngsters," said Nick. And then he rubbed his stomach again, "I'm really hungry," he said. "I'm dying of hunger."

"You can't die; this is Oz."

"I can't get hungry either. But I am."

Nick and Charlie turned their heads toward the cave mouth. The thumping had stopped. In the next moment there was a booming voice of the giant, "Fe, fie, foe, fix, turn around and no more tricks."

"He's not much of a poet," said Charlie.

"Most giants won't even try," said Nick.

And then commotion: a jumble of voices, the deep voice of the giant, a higher female voice, the voice of a man—of two men, the voices running together, a growl, "watch out," "hey," "wow," "that's it; fall in," and some relieved hoorays. And then the woman's voice said, "at least that worked." And then standing in the cave with Charlie were Glinda and the wizard—Charlie recognized them immediately, John R. Neill's illustrations come to life—and, amazingly enough, behind them, in strolled, of all people, Gary. Charlie went right up to him and held out his hand; Gary pulled him in with a hug.

"How'd you get rid of the giant?" asked Charlie.

Gary explained: Glinda opened what looked like a hole, as though she'd made a rip in the fabric of the world. They could see another place, another world inside the tear. And when he'd gone for them, the giant had stumbled into it.

Glinda and the wizard ran over to the Tin Man. He was sitting, doubled over, with both hands on his stomach. Charlie and Gary looked over.

"I'm very hungry," the Tin Man mildly said. He put both hands on the floor, but he was too weak to move. It was as though all the hunger of all the years since he had lost his flesh and blood body were catching up to him.

Glinda stared hard at the two foreigners. "You two, follow me." She rose and marched toward the far side of the cave. Without a word, they followed. Glinda looked back over at the Tin Man then up at Charlie, a glimmer of accusation in her eyes.

"Hey, I didn't do anything. He was standing up just a second ago."

"For whatever the word of a stranger might be worth, I'm sure Charlie would have done nothing..." Gary began. But Charlie cut him off.

"We've just got to get him some food." The young man fumbled through his pockets.

"He hasn't got a stomach," said Glinda.

"The wizard gave him a heart," said Charlie letting the obvious implication sit out on the air for the sorceress to grasp.

"The wizard gave him a silk pillow," she said. "He gave himself a heart."

And they all wondered at once if a man made of tin could die. The Tin Man looked over at the entrance to the cave and raised an arm as though he were going to try again to get up. The wizard rifled through his bag of magic as though to find something there that might help, knowing full well it was helpless. The Tin Man's joints did not have the strength to support his weight. Glinda led Charlie and Gary outside the cave. "I don't have time to explain this," she said. "In fact I don't understand it myself. You two have to leave, now. I have firm suspicions that one or both of you are the reason why that good man who hasn't felt hunger in 100 years may now be starving."

"Hey," said Charlie, pulling away from the light grip Glinda held on his arm.

"I'm not saying you did anything deliberately, young man."

"Even in freaking Oz," he exclaimed, "one thing goes wrong and everyone turns on oddball Charles Emerson."

Gary put his arm on Charlie's shoulder to try to calm him down, but Charlie shrugged it away. Glinda raised her wand. She felt the temptation to inform them both that Oz was not a fit place for anyone's psychopathologies. She wished to tell them she'd like to help them if she could. She wanted them to know that she felt deeply whatever personal demons the two of them were wrestling with and that she hoped very much that they would eventually defeat them. But she was working on very little sleep, and something frightening was happening to the good Tin Man, and Oz itself was acting crazy. She'd pushed the giant through a hole in the fabric, back—she hoped—into his own world. But he was not the real problem: this pair, one or both of them was very likely the real problem. It was their magic, or their lack of magic—it was some quality about them, or it was something they had done that had brought this calamity on Oz. Once they were back, everything would become normal again. But there was no time to say any of this. She held out her wand. The wizard stepped out of the cave just in time to see.

"Where do you come from?" she said.

Charlie tried to get her to understand how important it was that they stay in Oz. They had something very important to do before they left. But she would not hear of it. She cut him off: "Tell me where you came from," she said. And it was clear she would not be giving them an option or asking their permission. Their quest, whatever it was, meant nothing to her against the safety and happiness of her people and her land.

"I understand," said Gary, "but…"

"Tell me," she said.

Gary was about to speak again, but Charlie interrupted.

"No," he said. "I'm not telling. I came here to…"

But Glinda holding her wand like a weapon would not let him finish. "If you do not tell me where you are from, I will send you somewhere else. You must leave Oz. I would like to send you home, but if you do not tell me, I will have to send you somewhere."

"'You don't have to go home, but you can't stay here,' How many times have I heard that at closing time," Charlie quipped.

"How much time do you spend in bars?" asked Gary.

"*You may not stay,*" Glinda interrupted. And with that she raised her wand higher. Gary recognized the motion that had caused the rip in the air when the giant disappeared. "America," he said, "New Hampshire, Cornish…" He did not want to end up somewhere in China, or, worse, some other fairyland he might never get out of. He was just about to blurt out the street address when Glinda lowered her wand, a look of disappointment on her face.

She scowled. "It's not working." And the tone in her voice had more of helplessness in it than anyone in Oz had ever heard from the mighty sorceress. "It's getting worse by the moment." But she would not dwell on this.

"It's not my fault," said Charlie.

"Well we won't be sure about that until you're gone," said Glinda, calmly.

And then the sorceress ordered Gary and Charlie to help the wizard move Nick to her swan chariot, still afloat in the river. "We must get him to the Emerald City," she said.

But what they would do there to save the Tin Man or Oz itself, no one knew.

"HE'S NOT IN the Narnia Room," Doug announced.

"Not in the workshop neither," said Beth coming in the other door.

"Well then perhaps the labyrinth," said Gwen doubtfully.

Outdoors, the air was cold. Early snowflakes could be seen like last bits of ticker tape hanging in the air. The dark sun sat on the treetops. "Not exactly contemplation weather," said Doug.

"Have we got to walk through this whole bloody thing to find out if Gary's in there?" Beth asked.

"Just shout," said Doug who put his hands to his mouth. Gwen grabbed them.

"No," she said. "No shouting in the labyrinth."

"Your husband's missing," Doug pointed out. "I think this might be a good time to break the rules a little."

"A little broken is all broken," said Gwen. And then she added, "and he's not missing. And we don't have to take the whole path. There's a short cut through the back."

"All these years, I never knew this," said Doug, kneeling down to get his body through a small opening in the hedge. He awkwardly maneuvered himself through the space that was not quite large enough.

"Careful," said Gwen. She had cut this space meticulously, just big enough for her own small body. It was cleverly disguised. Built on the principle of a simple optical illusion, you could not see it when you were standing up. The green of the surrounding hedge seemed to fill the space. "This way," she directed them, once Beth had made it through. And she took them through diagonal cut outs carefully maintained in the hedge, cut outs you would only be able to see if you took the labyrinth backwards, which was something you were not allowed to do. The cuts made it possible to follow a straight path to the center.

"Cool," said Doug. But Gwen asked him again to be careful with her delicate labyrinth. He was too big for the space and also a little clumsy; he was bending the branches out of line. Beth was not much better.

"They're evergreens for God's sake," she said to worried Gwen. "Self-repairing."

But what if the bent branches distracted the walker from contemplation? What if the trimming of them left a scar that made the short cut visible? That would violate the whole project of the labyrinth. "Just be careful," she said.

"We've got to worry about a lawsuit and a bunch of missing people; I'm not going to fuss about evergreens," said Beth. And Doug agreed.

210

"But that's what it's for. You don't burn down a house to get a mouse out of the walls," said Gwen. "Just be careful."

Doug grumbled, but he tried. The space was just too tight. When he broke a stiff cedar branch Gwen grabbed hold of his arm and pulled him back. "O.K.," she said, "tell you what. We really don't need three people to see if Gary's there. You two stay here. I'll check."

"But I want..." said Doug.

"Then take the path," said Gwen with that quiet authority in her voice that usually managed to get her orders followed. She disappeared into the hedge.

For some reason Gwen felt there was someone in the labyrinth. Perhaps Gary. But she couldn't say for sure. It was odd enough he'd given the thing a chance once. Perhaps it really was working for him, and if so, he might have Charlie with him, and that would be one mystery solved. Then again, who knew, it could have been Colin and Rebecca Holton plotting the destruction of all they'd worked for—or perhaps just making out like teenagers. Perhaps she should make a little noise before passing through the last line of hedge.

She was about to clear her throat when she heard a voice. Not Gary's, nor Charlie's—nor Colin's, nor Rebecca Holton's for that matter. A small voice, the voice of a girl. "It didn't work," said the voice. "It isn't working."

"Brittney?" Gwen called, although it did not sound like Brittney's voice.

"The picture, the belt."

"Brit?" said Gwen as she started through the last hedge.

"Oh, my stars," said the voice.

But when Gwen crossed into the center, there was no one there.

She went quickly to the path leading out of the labyrinth, and just barely saw a little girl's swinging blonde hair turn a corner. None of the children at OzHouse had long blonde hair.

"Please, stop," Gwen called.

"I can't believe I'm here," said the voice. "How could I be here?"

Gwen approached the voice, but it kept moving ahead of her, not running, keeping pace with Gwen. "Bring me back, bring me back."

"Who are you?" Gwen called. "I don't recognize your voice."

"You've never heard my voice." And then she added, after a short pause, as though she were thinking about whether to say it, "Gwen."

"But how..."

"It doesn't matter. I can't stay here. I have to get back. She needs to pull me back. I wasn't supposed to be here. This is the wrong maze. I should never have left. I was looking for the other girl."

"The other girl?"

"But I ended up here. Nothing's working."

Though she rifled through her memory, Gwen could not think of who this could be. Was it the child of a friend who had come to walk the labyrinth? But in this weather, and so late at night? And then where was the friend? And she sounded so much older than the small girl she'd caught a glimpse of running away, almost as though she were playing with Gwen.

"Are your parents here?" Gwen shouted, picking up her pace.

But the girl picked up her pace as well.

"I have no parents. You know that."

"Do I know you? What girl are you looking for?" asked Gwen.

"Yes," said the voice. "You do, or did. But never mind that. I'm looking for Jessica."

"Jessica," said Gwen, jogging now. "Are you a friend of Jessica?" Maybe it was Jessica's sister. But Gwen didn't know Jessica's sister. And how did she get here? "Why do you think Jessica is out here?"

"She's not here. I just thought she was in trouble. I had a feeling. I thought maybe she didn't make it out after all. I thought she might still be in the other maze. Not this one. The picture wasn't working. I wanted to look. I don't know why I was sent here. It didn't work."

"What didn't work? Who are you?" said Gwen, still unable to catch the girl or even see her face.

"Of course. Wait. Is the room still there?"

"Room?"

"You still don't know? Still?"

"Know what? Would you please slow down." They were approaching the exit to the labyrinth. The girl did seem to slow. She and Gwen spoke from across the hedge. Gwen would be able to see her as soon as they both left the labyrinth.

"All these years, and you still don't know. Then it has to be there."

"What's your name?" asked Gwen.

"Suzy," she said—and then after a pause she added, "Bishop." And then the hedge rustled and the girl began to run again. Gwen ran too. But when she finally made it to the exit, Gwen was breathing hard and there was no sign of the little girl. Doug and Beth ran over from the other side.

"What were you shouting about?" asked Beth.

"And in the labyrinth," added Doug.

"Did either of you see her?"

But they'd been stuck in what Beth called "this infernal maze," and hadn't been able to see anything. Nor had they heard the girl's soft voice.

"Something weird's going on here," said Gwen. And she was half-hysterical. "A little girl who said she was Suzy Bishop."

"Suzy Bishop?" said Doug.

"Suzy would be all grown up by now," said Beth.

"Maybe it was a ghost," said Doug.

The frantic look on Gwen's face caused Beth to reach out to comfort her. Gwen grabbed Beth's outstretched hand and squeezed it, then pushed it away, "She's gone to the house. The room. The room. She said something about a room. What room? What room would she be going to?"

"But Suzy?" Doug began.

"All right, it's not Suzy," said Gwen. "It can't be Suzy. But whoever it is knows Suzy."

Doug wanted to believe Colin was trying to play a trick on them as some part of his plot to sue them or close them down. Maybe he thought if he planted a little girl to pretend to be Suzy they would somehow reveal hidden gravesites to him. But the theory didn't hold up. Beth wanted to know how Colin would know they were on their way to the labyrinth, for one thing. "And then," she added, "what are we supposed to do, dig up her bones to make sure she's still dead?"

"Maybe he's just trying to drive us crazy," said Doug, no more helpfully.

"Maybe he's not that smart," said Beth.

"She went to the house. We've got to find her." Gwen took a deep breath and ran.

THE STARS GLITTERED in the dark, moonless sky. Hansel, Gretel, Buddy, Jessica, and the forester sat around a campfire. Humpty Dumpty was asleep in the doorway. They still held in their hands the sticks they'd used to roast their dinner of wolf meat. Now and then one of them poked the fire to keep it going. The forester pulled his stick back. Then he pointed up to the sky.

"That one," he said, continuing the conversation and indicating a star that had just emerged from the only wisp of cloud in the sky on this beautiful night, "that one is new."

"New?" said Hansel. "Is that possible?" Nothing new ever seemed to happen in Grimms' Forest. Everything fit right into the stories, what the stories made possible. Not even the witch or the attack of the wolves had any sense of newness to them. Maybe there was a Grimms' story in which new stars appeared. Or maybe it was some other story.

"Been looking at this sky every night of my life," said the forester. "I know it like I know the trees of the forest. Never saw that one before."

They all felt pretty lucky to be sitting around the fire this night, still alive. The forester had arrived just as the wolves had eaten their way through the walls of the candy house. The three children inside had been able to man the opening with burning sticks at first. But soon there were more wolves and more holes than there were burning sticks to harry them with, and one of the younger wolves had just made it into the cottage when a shout from the forester diverted the wolves' attention. It was clear immediately that his angry human shouts had startled but not scared off the wolves. From inside the house the three children had heard him. For the wolves, this forester was no more than an additional dish for their feast and an obstacle that must be dealt with before they could finish the children. Any one of them he could handle, but the whole family would require more than a strong man with an axe. He knew this as well as they did.

Inside the cabin, the children turned their attention to the one young wolf growling at their waving sticks of fire. Though they'd heard shouts, they did not know why none of the other wolves came in through the newly chewed openings. As they held the young wolf at bay, Buddy and the other children listened from inside.

"The very one," said Glene, "the very man who has protected Red from the whole pack all these years."

And then the children in the cottage realized the mother wolf had shown up as well. "And what can he do against four wolves at once?" said her taunting voice.

About that time Buddy's weapon had burned down to a warm stick of smoking black. He let Hansel and Gretel take care of the half-grown cub who had made it into the cottage and ran to the window. He saw the forester standing in the midst the family of circling wolves. It seemed they were trying to make him dizzy.

"Go ahead, forester," said the daddy wolf, "attack the leader. As soon as you do, the others will be on you." And just then one of the young wolves lunged at the forester's leg. She managed to get a hold of the forester's thick leather boot. But the forester swung at her with his axe.

214

The father wolf growled, and the whelp just barely managed to let go and back away before getting cut in two.

A conspiracy of ravens arrived from nowhere and sat in the branches of the trees all around, making a horrible din.

In the stories, the forester always won. But this forester looked as though he might not win. "We've got to help him," said Buddy. But Hansel and Gretel, their flaming sticks just charred wood now, were busy with chairs and a broomstick, keeping the young wolf away.

The forester didn't look scared to Buddy. He stood with his arms wide open, his axe in one hand, ready to defend himself, waiting for them to attack. "Oh, but I was scared," said the forester when it was all over. "I was worried for myself. But I was also worried that Jessica and Mr. Eggman would arrive before the fight was over. A pack of hungry wolves would make short order of them..."

"Please," said Humpty Dumpty, "no puns." And then he yawned, "I am so tired of puns."

"He only likes puns when they're his," said Jessica.

The forester politely apologized, although he was unaware of any punning.

Rumpelstiltskin approached the fire.

"Decided to join us, then," said the forester to the dwarf. The little man looked around suspiciously, "think I've earned my share of the bounty, don't you?"

"More than earned it, my friend." And the forester handed him the whole hunk of wolf he'd just roasted for himself.

"Still say the girl's mine," Rumpelstiltskin said, meaning Jessica.

"What?" exclaimed Jessica as she looked from Rumpelstiltskin to the forester.

"And I say again, she's not mine to give," said the forester.

"What did I save you for?"

Buddy had seen it all. The wolves getting more bold, darting in toward the quick axe, jumping back just in time. The taunting failed to get the forester to attack any one of them, but it didn't much matter. It was clear they were hoping to tire the forester and thus minimize the likelihood of injury to themselves. Against so many, it wouldn't be hard to insure he would tire first. It would have been clear to anyone older than Buddy that the forester had arrived in haste and without a plan. Had Rumpelstiltskin not shown up, it would have been the wolves and not the people who had enjoyed a meal this evening. But the little man did show up—he would not explain how—high in a tree among the ravens. He called down to the man.

"What would you give to be up here with me instead of down there with them?"

The forester, who had been looking over his shoulder for Jessica and Humpty Dumpty, glanced up at the dwarf in the tree.

"If you can get me there and rescue those children in the house, you can set your own price," yelled the forester.

"I've recently lost a bet with a conniving human," said Rumpelstiltskin, "and I'm not at all happy about it. I'll make the same deal with you I made with her, your first born child."

"Deal," yelled the forester. "I felt a little bad about making that deal," said the man later, "My only child's grown and gone. I've produced no more since Fundevogel and Lina left and have no intention of ever producing more. I don't even have a wife."

"What about that girl right there?" said Rumpelstiltskin.

"She's not mine," the forester reiterated.

"I have a mother," said Jessica.

"You do?" said Buddy. He thought everyone who came to OzHouse must have lost their parents.

"Oh?" said Rumpelstiltskin.

"She's coming to get me as soon as Bill leaves," said Jessica, squeezing tighter the little boy whom she had not let go of for a moment since she'd run into the house and thrown her arms around him.

"Will she take me too?" asked Buddy.

"Tricked me. All you humans, you're nothing but conniving tricksters."

"Hey," said Hansel.

"Look who's talking," said Gretel.

"I know what I know," Rumpelstiltskin challenged, and then he added, as though it were a point of particular pride, "and I never tricked anyone."

"If you're so anxious to have a child, why did you leave this one behind," Humpty Dumpty pointed to Buddy, "when you had a chance to just take him?"

"Told me he had a mother," said Rumpelstiltskin. "No one to give him to me. I'm no thief. I hadn't made any deal for him." And then he looked long at Buddy. "But you say you don't have a mother?"

"You can't have him, either," said Jessica. "He belongs at OzHouse."

"Got rid of the wolves, didn't I?"

That he did. "Hey, Mr. Wolf," he'd called down from his branch in the tree, "catch." With some sort of magic the nature of which he did not disclose, he had stunned the ravens who'd flown over in hopes of a meal of wolf or forester pickings, and they fell like rocks to the ground. The untrained young wolves lunged for the falling birds, leaving only the adult pair to deal with the forester. The wolf parents, seeing what was up, yelled at the children to stop. This distracted them from the forester just long enough for his axe to fall first on one then the other. The young wolves ran off in fear, each with a bird in its mouth. The one in the house must have heard what was afoot a well. He bolted through the hole in the wall and followed his siblings back to the family cave. And that was all there was to it. Humpty Dumpty and Jessica arrived just after the commotion was over and learned the whole story.

CHAPTER 21

GWEN, GARY, BETH, DOUG,

I do not have time to explain everything. I can't stay. But something dreadful has happened, and no one knows who is causing it or how to fix it. Everything tells me that OzHouse is mixed up in it somehow. You may know that already. And knowing you, you'll do your best to fix things.

Don't!

Please do not attempt to help. Undoubtedly you will do more harm than good no matter how good your intentions.

I did not mean to come here today. I do hope I have not caused any trouble. You must not take this personally (you were all very nice to me years ago), but I have no desire to come back to OzHouse or any other part of this world; it would grieve me to do so. If I'd ever doubted it, ten minutes back here has been long enough to convince me it is not for me.

I wish there were time to explain.

Now, I pray the room is still where it used to be, and that it is unaffected by all this trouble.

My love to you all,
Suzy Bishop

"W...WHAT THE HELL?" sputtered Doug as he showed the paper he had found on the kitchen table to Gwen and Beth.

"Is this some kind of sick joke?" Beth said aloud to herself as she dropped into the chair.

"So that little girl did mean she was Suzy Bishop," Gwen muttered as she rubbed her forehead trying to forestall a migraine.

"Suzy would be almost 20 years old by now," Doug insisted waving the note around like a semaphore flag. "If someone is trying to claim to be Suzy, she would hardly still be a child. Didn't you say it was a kid that was in the labyrinth?"

Gwen paced around the kitchen; she got a glass and filled it with water from the tap. Without taking a sip, she dumped the water back into the sink. "I didn't see her very well. She seemed to be a child, maybe six, seven years old—well, no, I mean she sounded older, but certainly not an adult."

"Unless she grew up to be a midget or something," said Doug.

"Little person," Beth instinctively corrected.

"The person I was chasing could not have been four-foot tall. Oh, I don't know; I didn't see her clearly; she was always around the next corner."

"I didn't see anyone outside," said Beth.

"Why would I lie about this?"

"Relax, Gwen. I wasn't implying you're lying. Someone wrote this letter. I meant whoever it was must still be in the house somewhere. She mentioned a room, right?"

Gwen took a breath. The girl had mentioned a room; she'd called it a special room. But what help was that? All the rooms were special in some way. So many rooms. But there were three adults to search around. Maybe they could find this mysterious child who left the note.

"And maybe she can teach me how to do this calligraphy," laughed Beth. "She must have scribbled this down awfully quick and look at it."

They had all noticed how neat the lettering was. It looked more like writing they had seen from the late 1800s when people cared about such things as penmanship.

Doug took off for the east wing. Beth took off for the west. And Gwen, once she was sure no one was hiding in the kitchen or pantry, went upstairs.

Because each room was so filled with furniture and knickknacks of every size, it was no easy chore to be sure a small child wasn't hiding in them. At one point Doug, sure he had caught the child, grabbed Samantha, who was reading a comic book behind the large treasure chest in the Pirate Room. The little girl was so startled she started crying, and Doug had to waste precious time calming her down.

Beth stopped each child she found and had them join in the search.

"What's this girl look like?" asked Sarah as she fidgeted with her ill-fitting overalls.

"She's a little smaller than you, I think, and has blonde hair. That's all we know," Beth explained hastily.

"Not much to go on," said Sarah with a pout.

"It will be someone you have never met. In fact if you see anyone you don't know, call out." And Beth hurried past the girl and started looking in the Arabian Nights Room.

By this time Gwen had reached the upstairs and had checked two storage closets and the newly created Harry Potter play room. Then she had a thought. "Room? Yes. The special room. Just what Janey had called it. Did she mean the Narnia room?" And she rushed out of the room she was in leaving two small children perplexed as they read their books on a couch that looked like a turquoise back seat of an old car.

At that moment Suzy was in fact in the Narnia room. She had flipped though a few Oz books but found the illustrations distracted her and made it hard to concentrate. "The Wogglebug looks nothing like that silly picture," sighed the little girl. She decided she would be better off to rely on her own memory and not use the books at all.

The first two attempts failed, and Suzy had found herself half in the wardrobe and half in the hallway outside the room. She didn't panic, however. She knew it might not work right away. And she'd been through too much in her years in Oz to panic so easily. She just kept at it.

Gwen was about to turn down the hallway—and would have seen the child slipping back into the wardrobe had she not heard someone downstairs yelling.

"I found her. I found her."

Turning instantly, she rushed back down the long staircase and headed toward the room that contained the yelling child. Beth and Doug reached the room at the same time. They opened the door to see Sarah holding the sleeve of Samantha's sweater.

"I came in here so I wouldn't be scared again," sobbed Samantha. "Why did you say you found her?" Beth asked Sarah again.

"I did find her. See." And she pulled on her sleeve

221

"But you know Samantha. I told you to look for someone you *don't* know."

"Oh yeah, I forgot," smiled Sarah.

"False alarm," said Doug. Beth patted Sarah on the head and they all returned to their searches.

On Suzy's third attempt she walked through the wardrobe and into the Emerald City.

"I SHOULD NEVER HAVE TOLD YOU about the room," Jessica said for the tenth time. "I knew the rules, and I disobeyed them, and look at all the trouble I caused. Just like when I told at school about Bill. I knew I wasn't supposed to tell, but I did it anyway. I was sure they'd come and take him away. Then things could be like they used to be, but instead they took me and my sister away."

"The whole world is that girl's fault," said Humpty Dumpty to the forester.

"Maybe not the whole world," said Jessica, "but some things really are."

"Pieces of them may well be," said the forester.

"But you still have a mommy," Buddy told her as if that made everything all right.

"It's more complicated when you get older," Jessica explained. "When I was your age everything was great."

"Life has never been very good for Hansel or me," Gretel cut in. "Our mother died when we were very young, and our stepmother has never taken to us."

"When things got bad for father, she seemed to like us even less, as if it were our fault," added her brother.

Buddy's eyes were filling with new tears. The more he listened to the other children talk about their parents, the farther away his mother seemed to be. He had no memory of his father. His sisters, Donna and Ellen, he seemed to recall fairly well, but maybe that was from the photo he had of them from the newspaper.

"I think it's time for you children to get to sleep." The forester stopped looking at the new star he had spotted, stood up and brushed the bits of wood shavings and twigs from his heavy pants.

"Tomorrow we will find our way home," Jessica said in her I'm-a-little-girl-who-thinks-she-knows-everything voice.

"Doubt that," sighed Humpty Dumpty in his I'm-a-great-big-egg-and-I-do-know-everything voice.

The forester looked up at Jessica and saw her smile fade.

"Why do you say things like that?" the forester asked Humpty Dumpty with a frown.

"I say things that need to be said," the egg replied with a harrumph. "We have no idea how to get these two children back to their world, let alone get me out of this filthy forest and back to my unsullied wall."

The forester scratched his beard and looked up into the trees for a moment. The firelight flickering on the underside of the leaves was in sharp contrast to the darkness and gloom of the forest. Then he looked across the campfire at the little gnarled man who sat licking his fingers after eating his portion of the cooked meat.

"How about you?" he asked suddenly.

"How 'bout me what?" asked Rumpelstiltskin with his usual jerky motion.

"Could you help these two children get home?"

Rumpelstiltskin pulled Buddy's plastic soldier from his pocket and twisted it in his hands. "What would you offer me in return?" He squinted his small eyes so tightly that his bushy eyebrows just about touched each other. "And no tricks. I've had it with humans and their tricks."

Buddy's face was tight, trying not to cry.

"Could I have the boy?"

The forester sat up straighter. "He's not mine to give, any more than the girl is."

The dwarf went over to Buddy and put his hand on the boy's shoulder. Then he kneeled down and looked him in the eye. He looked at the soldier in his hand, and he handed it back to Buddy. Buddy smiled and took the toy in both hands. "Fine," replied the dwarf as if a small gun had been fired. Jessica and Buddy looked intently at the dwarf. "Doesn't matter what you would offer me," he admitted. "I don't know how to help them, and unlike some creatures in the forest, I do not make bargains I cannot keep."

"What about the way you tricked that princess out of her first born child."

"I did no such thing. I made a deal fair and square. Was it my fault that greedy liar of a miller made promises he couldn't keep? Or that miserable excuse for a king was willing to murder the miller's daughter if she couldn't fulfill her part of that impossible bargain? I merely stepped in and helped her out. She agreed to give me her first born child of her own free will. But did she ever plan to honor her word? I think not. My wife practically kicked me out of the house for not getting her a child. I

223

could've stole one, easy. You know it. I could've used magic to take one from any human in the forest. I didn't. This seemed like as fair a way as I could find to get me one. No one can say I ever failed to keep my word. It's these duplicitous humans who cheat me of my rightful rewards—every time."

"What about us?" asked Hansel.

"Hansel," Gretel scolded.

"We need a good home," said Hansel.

"Gotta be free and clear," said the dwarf.

"Tomorrow, we *will* find you the road home," said the forester, looking over at the grumpy egg. "For now, you four children go into the witch's house and sleep. Mr. Egg and I will guard you while you rest."

"I'm surprised father hasn't found us yet," sighed Gretel as she started walking back into the gingerbread house. "Perhaps he will arrive at sunrise to take us home."

"No one's gonna be here to take you home," said the dwarf to Buddy. "So why go back?"

"We have to go back." Jessica hugged Buddy close.

"Why?" asked the dwarf.

"Because it is where we belong," Jessica explained, ignoring Rumpelstiltskin's stares. "We can't live here in the Grimms' Forest. We're not fairytale characters."

"Don't know about that," said the dwarf as he cleared his gravelly throat. "Little Buddy doesn't seem to have a home to go back to."

"But people cannot trade children for favors. That's just not right," Jessica said, pulling Buddy a little closer.

"That's it exactly," cut in the forester. "You may have been cheated little man, but you shouldn't have expected a mother to part with her child."

"Our mother was happy enough to part with us," sighed Hansel.

"*Step*mother," corrected Gretel.

"I want my mommy," Buddy started to whine.

"Stay here and you can have a mommy and a daddy," the dwarf suggested.

Buddy stopped whining and his big blue eyes stared at Rumpelstiltskin as if he was actually considering his offer.

"I DON'T KNOW. I remember in the books it always seemed like everyone could hop aboard the chariot and get whisked away to wherever they wished," Charlie muttered as he and Gary and the wizard walked along the road to the Emerald City.

"Not true. Not true at all," the wizard corrected the visitor to Oz. "Very few people ever get to ride in Glinda's chariot. Those swans are large and powerful, but they are still birds. It would be a bit too much to ask of those poor creatures after all. The Tin Woodman must weigh quite a bit more than they are used to lifting. And someone had to go with him. You didn't expect Glinda to walk all the way from here in her silk slippers."

"But why was her chariot in the river? Would have made loading the Tin Woodman into it a lot easier if we didn't have to also worry about getting him wet." Charlie seemed more annoyed than curious.

"Swans can only land or take off in water. Didn't you know that?" the wizard explained.

"Never read anything about that in the books," Gary said scratching his head.

"Can't say about that. But even in Oz we follow the laws of nature, at least most of the time. That's why Glinda's chariot has no wheels."

"Never noticed that in the pictures either," Gary said. And he thought he'd studied the pictures in great detail. "I also didn't realize what a long walk it is to the Emerald City from the Tin Woodman's castle." Gary stopped and wiped his forehead with his shirtsleeve. "Adventures seem so much easier if you are only reading about them."

The three men walked along under the hot Winkie sun not really knowing exactly how much further their journey would be. Each of them was hoping that the crest of the next hill on the yellow brick road would reveal a line of shade trees. The wizard of course had lived in Oz for most of his life, but he usually spent his days in the Emerald City studying his books of magic or meeting with visiting dignitaries not traipsing along brick roads without so much as a wooden sawhorse to ride upon. After some time, Gary saw a small yellow-domed house and a stand of trees on the left side of the road. Recalling his days as a child reading Oz books, he suspected they might find a cool drink and a comfortable seat to rest upon.

The woman in the house, all dressed in traditional Winkie garb with her bright yellow skirts and sun bonnet, was happy to supply each of them with fresh lemonade, and they all sat on wooden benches amid the small grove of citrus trees.

"Have you heard any news from the capital?" asked the wizard.

"Just rumors," replied the woman as she refilled everyone's glasses. All were encouraged to realize that the magical anomalies had not yet touched the simple rural parts of the Winkie country. The woman went on: "Something has gone wrong with the magic, I hear. Not like it's gone, but that it's changed. I've even heard tell that some people believe they are growing older."

"Nonsense," the wizard rebuffed her. "The trouble has only been observed for a few days at most. Who could tell they had aged three or four days?" He laughed and took a small sip of his lemonade.

"Flies or mosquitoes maybe," Charlie suggested. "They usually only live a few days, if everyone is aging in Oz, they might have noticed."

The wizard stopped chuckling and looked grave. Then he laughed again. "Just a rumor, I'm sure."

"I wonder," said Charlie, putting Colin's laptop on the table beside him, "I'll bet with magic all strange, we could find some story..." He booted it. "I know this'll sound weird, but a story whose magic might work here."

"You too have brought magic?" asked the Winkie woman when she noticed the black box open and play music. "And is it working?"

"What an idiot," said Gary.

"Well, I never," said the Winkie woman.

"It might work," said Charlie.

"I'm sorry, ma'am, not you. You've been wonderfully helpful. And not you, either, Charlie. Me. You've still got that thing. You can send an email to Gwen."

"What? Why? We gonna try to get the whole world here? You think that'll help?"

"She could be worried."

"Oh, she must have stopped worrying by now," said Charlie.

"It's only been a few hours," said the wizard. "Are you sure this Gwen has even noticed that you are missing?"

Gary smiled. "Just tell her we're OK," he said, "you know, 'finishing up some business, home soon, will explain later.'"

"Wait, wait, wait.... Ah....crap." Charlie looked up from the keyboard. "Battery's dead."

"So your magic's not working either," said the woman of the house.

All three travelers would have enjoyed a longer rest from their walk in the Winkie sun, but they knew they had to reach the Emerald City as soon as possible. Handing them three cheese sandwiches wrapped in wax paper the woman wished them safe travels.

"I wish we could give you something for your kindness," said Gary.

"Nonsense," said the woman. "This is Oz."

"Yes, yes," said the wizard. "It would be considered insulting to pay for hospitality in this country."

"Where we come from, it would be insulting not to…"

"Would a bit of broken American magic be of any use to you," said Charlie, holding up the laptop in its finely monogrammed case. "A curiosity to show friends?"

"But, you see," said the woman, with some embarrassment holding her hands in front of her.

"Ah, yes," said Gary, "You see, to us it's worthless, now that it's broken. But being rare in Oz, you might find some function for it. A conversation piece."

"Well," said the woman, "it is rather plain. But that zippered cover, I could use that, I suppose. If you are sure it is useless to you."

"You would be disposing of it for us," said Gary. "Well, thank you then, very much."

As soon as Gary, Charlie, and the Wizard were out of earshot, Gary wished aloud that all cultural differences could be so easily managed.

"Do you have a theory about what exactly is wrong with the magic of Oz?" Gary said to the wizard after some time of contemplative silence. "Glinda seemed rather upset. She's not as approachable as I always imagined. I didn't dare ask her to explain anything."

"But leave out the jumping to conclusions that Charlie Emerson is responsible for all your problems and just give us the facts," Charlie added. "If I wanted that kind of treatment, I could have stayed home."

The wizard removed his top hat and wiped his bald head with a fancy silk hanky. He even loosened his old-fashioned tie as he limped along the road.

"Not used to long travels, I'm afraid, running around in the hot sun."

"Sure you're not feeling your age?" asked Gary."

The wizard looked quizzically over to the American, unsure whether he was joking. "No, no," he said at last. "I do, however, perhaps, have a possible answer to your question. It is, as you suggest, just theory, of course. Now, where should I begin?"

"It's always best to start at the beginning," Gary said with a smile.

"True, true," began the wizard. "We cannot say for sure. But the speculation is this: as far as we know someone or something has opened a portal into Oz. Now as you both know, people from the outside have often found their way into Oz, dozens in fact. But no one from a world not in our domain and not from your world has ever found a portal in. I can't say

227

for sure, but it seems to me some one must have broken a fundamental rule—put things together that were never meant to be, you know like eye of newt and pixie dust. Big explosion. And whoever did it not only opened a door that was never supposed to be opened, they left it open. Now creatures such as the giant that had you all trapped in that cave are roaming all over the Land of Oz."

"I'm sorry," said Gary. "I don't see the problem. I remember several giants in the Oz books. Since you have giants in Oz, what's the difference if another one slips in from 'Jack and the Beanstalk'?"

Charlie shrugged his shoulders and added, "Yeah, I don't see what you are all upset about either. I remember a big, scary giant in a cave somewhere, right here in Oz."

The wizard stopped for a minute to catch his breath, and then tried again to explain. "Magic is a funny thing. It isn't exactly a science, but here in Oz it almost is. You must be referring to Mr. Yoop; see, he is an Oz giant. That means for all his bellowing and grabbing, he hasn't ever eaten anyone and most likely never will. Nor would we or could we kill him. It simply isn't the Oz way."

Gary and Charlie nodded as they heard this. It resonated with their recollection of the Oz books.

"Do either of you know the fate of the giant we just expelled from Oz—in the original story I mean?"

Charlie's face dimmed. "He dies when Jack cuts down the beanstalk."

"Exactly right. Most Oz people of course would not even know the story he is from. No Oz mother would read such a horror to her child. But I'm originally from Nebraska and that was a tame story in my day back in the late 1800s."

Gary recalled having read some very old fairytales while doing research for OzHouse and he nodded as he recalled some of the more gruesome scenes.

"There's only so much interaction that a magical world can have with a nonmagical world, or that one magical world can have with another. I've some reason to think I may be under some suspicion myself." The old wizard seemed suddenly distracted. "After all these years." But then he came to himself, "I'm sure as well read, responsible adults, you would not deliberately have done anything that would have fundamentally changed the relationship between your world and the magical worlds. This giant however would not be so careful. When he came, he brought his own magic with him. He can die."

"But we also can die," said Gary.

"We are beginning to wonder if that matters. You may have your own magic, after all. See, until now, you couldn't die, not here. A little of your "magic" had no effect on the great supply of the stuff in Oz. Now it appears there are quite a number of creatures in Oz who can die. Perhaps now we can all die. Someone has opened a door and he has stepped through it. And he's brought death with him. He or someone like him must have brought a kind of magic into Oz that has affected the Tin Man. Normally non-meat people do not get hungry or thirsty, but he claims to be starving. If we do not find out who is opening these doors and close them, Oz knows what will happen next."

"So why not blame him instead of us? The sorceress thinks one of us is responsible," Gary frowned.

"More than likely one of you *is* responsible. He could not have created the door he stepped through. You are the ones hopping around from world to world. We just don't know exactly what you have done or how to undo it, but…"

"Allegedly done," Charlie said quickly.

"Huh?"

"Never mind," said Charlie.

"So Glinda seems to think if she can only get rid of whoever opened the door, the rest will just, as they say, 'poof.'"

"And if she does and they don't 'poof'?" asked Gary.

CHAPTER 22

DEADLY.DESERT.NO.HELP.STOP.EMERALD.CITY.
UNDER.ATTACK.STOP.MAGIC.FAILING.STOP.
OZMA.WORRIED.STOP.ARMY.DEFEATED.STOP.

"ANYTHING ELSE?" ASKED DOROTHY.
"Let me think a minute," said Ozma, pacing.
"Takes you a whole minute to think?" Scraps was amazed. "Why I don't generally take ten seconds for that."
"And that would be out of a whole day," observed Professor H. M. Wogglebug.
"And my friend the Scarecrow takes even less," said Scraps.
"I myself never stop," remarked the Wogglebug as though to himself.
"No, you don't," observed the Patchwork Girl. "I noticed that."
Dorothy sat at the wireless, a box of mechanical magic that the Shaggy Man had taught her to use so long ago, ready to enter any additional information forthcoming from the group while the princess and

the Wogglebug paced the dusty room and Scraps spun herself in circles around them all.

"I assure you there is precedent for such a circumstance, though little in Oz since the foiled attack of the Nome King in the early years of your reign."

"Funny old Ruggedo," said Dorothy.

"Roquat," muttered Ozma, correcting her.

"Whoever," said Scraps.

"Take heart, my princess. The benign magic of Oz has always prevailed against all malign forces that have endeavored to subdue the realm." The Wogglebug's pacing had slowed considerably. Indeed, he looked tired. Sighing deeply, he put one arm on his hip and pointed a feeler pontificatingly in the air. "I dare presume…" he began before Ozma cut him off.

"But the magic's not working properly," she said.

"That does place us in a somewhat novel position," admitted the Wogglebug, "rendering precedent somewhat less certain. Still, I must maintain the wisdom of an ample defensive fortification for just such cases, composed of, say, mortar and stone to a width of…"

"Why are they attacking us?" asked Scraps. She uttered the question while standing upon her head, her two cotton-filled legs arcing forward and backward like the drooping stems of twin tulips. Professor Wogglebug, who had a hard time taking the crazy quilt seriously in any circumstance, found it particularly difficult to do so just then.

"I beg your pardon?" he said.

"Well, why? Wouldn't it be easier to get them to stop if we knew why they were doing it in the first place?"

"Well, yes, of course, but," said the Wogglebug.

"Save a bundle in mortar too I think," said Scraps.

"Why *are* they attacking us?" asked Dorothy as she inspected and oiled the various parts of the wireless that had lain idle for so long that there was great doubt that it could still function.

Now that Dorothy had asked the question, the Wogglebug felt more at ease in addressing himself to it: "Certainly," he said, "a more pertinent question than your earlier one, to wit: 'Who are they?' Idle curiosity that one, not to be indulged in in a moment as urgent as this. Indeed why are they attacking?" Professor H. M. Wogglebug put two arms to the small of his aching back as though he were trying to push himself erect.

"Don'cha think we oughta be asking, How we gonna stop 'em?" Scraps cut in. Her quilted skirts flowed out as she twirled in place.

"On the contrary, I must maintain, my ragged friend, that...."

"That's what we're doing," Ozma interrupted. "We're trying to get help. They have already refused to talk with us."

"Did they refuse?" asked Dorothy. From what she had heard the Wogglebug and the Soldier with the Green Whiskers, who had been sent as emissaries, had simply bolted to the safety of the city gates the moment they'd stepped outside and seen their company of snarling faces. The soldier was in such a hurry, he'd banged his head on the closing door.

"They have devastated all our defenses," Ozma went on, "—except for the door that some of them are now pounding on with all their might." Ozma stared at the dusty box of the old wireless transmitter. "I wonder if he's still there," she said. They wondered if they even remembered correctly how its magic worked.

"You think?" Dorothy replied, trying to add up the years she'd been away from Kansas. Were they enough for a grown man to get old and die? People simply did not count years here, in Oz—or months or weeks or days for that matter—at least not in normal times. This failure to account the passing of time made for a pretty blissful life mostly. But it also made it difficult to get a sense of the outside world. "I'm sure it can't have been *that* long," said Dorothy. "I'm sure Mr. Baum is still there."

"If the Royal Historian *is* still there," said the Wogglebug, "then why has he not contacted us since the war with the Skeezers and the Flatheads?"

"Don't you 'member," said Dorothy. "He kept saying he wanted to make books about other places, you know, made up stuff. I think he just got tired of being just a reporter. He wanted to be a writer."

The Wogglebug resumed his labored pacing of the room as he spoke, each of his several appendages brushing cobwebs out of the way of his freshly cleaned top hat, waistcoat, and trousers.

"Well, I don't see how he can help us anyway," said the Wogglebug. "No matter what anyone says, I for one do not believe there is any magic in the pen of any human being in some far off land. I know there are otherwise-respectable philosophers even in Oz who tell us that everything that happens here is just the effect of some flowing ink in another world. I find the proposition absurd. Your Royal Historian could write it a thousand times: *'And then the evil creatures from foreign lands suddenly disappeared, leaving everything as it was before.'* And they would still be pounding on the walls. And Jellia Jamb would still be bleeding on her bed, and the Royal Army of Oz would still be walking around with an ice pack on his skull, and Tik-Tok would still be missing."

"We understand," said Ozma.

The door to this room had been shut so long now that until today most of the Emerald City had all but forgotten those odd years of steady contact with the outside world. It was not normal for Oz to contact or even to think about any world beyond the Deadly Desert. They remembered now: that period of contact with Mr. Baum had coincided with the time the wizard first had shown up, and Dorothy, too. That contact had continued for several years—and then had stopped, suddenly, like a rock to a padded wall. There had been no meaningful contact with that mysterious world of America between then and—and the time Suzy Bishop had shown up, when another such episode of contact in the mostly unchanging history of Oz had, apparently, begun. Since Suzy's arrival, Glinda had reported that a few others had entered Oz from some unknown source, had had brief adventures, and then vanished as mysteriously as they had come. No one had thought much of it—until just a few days ago, when unheard-of creatures invaded from worlds unknown. Glinda had seen them in her magic book. Ozma had watched them in her magic picture. These events had put them in mind of the Royal Historian, and that brought them back now to the long-closed room.

"I'm sorry," continued the Wogglebug, "you simply cannot change things with a pen. No Royal Historian or anyone can do it."

"If I had a pen, and I twisted it around those thingys under your nose and that long curly chin of yours, you would stop talking," said Scraps, "and that would be a big change."

The Wogglebug shot a derisive glance at the Patchwork Girl—a glance that cart-wheeling Scraps took no notice of.

"They have airplanes," said Dorothy.

"CAN YOU SEND AIRPLANES?" Dorothy tapped into the wireless. "TELL US IF YOU ARE THERE?"

"It makes sense," said Ozma, repeating something she'd said earlier. "The last time we were invaded like this, there was a man behind it with a pen. And maybe that pen is magic. Maybe instead of just recording things, he was able to make things happen. This time there must also be a pen somewhere." And then she looked at Dorothy. "Ask him if he can use his magic pen."

"Why can't you just find him in your magic picture?" said the Wogglebug, "or bring him here with your belt."

"Because they have stopped working," said Ozma. "The belt hasn't worked since I drew you back to the Emerald City and sent Suzy to the labyrinth to find that other girl—what was her name?, the one she said might know something that could help us? Well, anyway, Suzy disappeared and neither the belt nor the picture has worked since."

"Then perhaps the magic of the wireless will not work either," said the Wogglebug, sitting down upon a packing crate. "Mechanical magic is awfully prone to failure. Just look at Tik-Tok."

"That's dusty," said Ozma. It was certainly not like the meticulous Wogglebug to sit upon a dusty crate. The Wogglebug just sighed.

"Are you all right?" asked Ozma.

"I don't know," said the Wogglebug. "I'm tired. All day, I've been so tired. More tired than I ever remember."

"I'm sure it's just the army outside trying to knock in the walls," said Dorothy.

"We're all tired," said Ozma.

"If I didn't know better, I'd say I was getting old," said the Wogglebug. "You know before the magic that made us all immortal, wogglebugs lived only a few days, even in Oz," he continued, citing an extraordinary fact he'd picked up from his copious reading. "Hardly long enough to learn anything."

Just then the door creaked open. A streak of light from the bright outside shot into the dim room. In rushed Suzy Bishop. Suzy had been hunting for Ozma from the moment she returned to the Emerald City. She wanted to tell her what had happened when she'd tried to find Jessica. She'd run around the whole city in her search for the girl princess. Asking everyone where Ozma was, she met nothing but scared citizens eager to tell her what they knew about the current attack. She picked up news everywhere she went. As soon as she'd found someone who could tell her what Ozma was up to, she ran all the faster to keep her from wasting her time. She wanted to inform her that it would do no good to contact the Royal Historian. Mr. Baum had, of course, been dead for more than 60 years. But she didn't say this. Something else had happened while she was running to the room where the wireless was kept. The whole city had seen it: Glinda's swan chariot gliding over the battlements: "Glinda's here," she panted, "with the Tin Man. And he's dying."

"NO, NO, NO," SAID BRITTNEY. "It's not like that. Once you're here you can never go back."

"That's not true," said Samantha. "Kids leave all the time. Just since I've been here, there's been Derek, he went home, and Jamison, he got adopted, and Meagan…"

"Would you guys just shut up," called Morris. "I'm playing a game here." On the screen, Link was attacking Ganon. Morris held the tip of his tongue between his teeth as he mashed the buttons on the controller.

"No," said Brittney, ignoring the boy, "they just must've ran away and got kidnapped. That's the only way you can leave."

"I'm not talking to you any more if you're gonna be so stupid," said Samantha. "I saw it."

"Well I'm not gonna talk to you if *you're* gonna be so stupid," said Brittney.

"Good," said Morris. "Could you not talk to each other someplace else?"

Samantha turned on her heels and left the room. Morris let out a groan. Link had died—again.

"They don't ever leave," said Brittney, "they run away or get kidnapped."

"You're right," Morris said. "Kids just disappear here all the time. Only it's worse than that. There's a room upstairs where kids go in and they never come out."

"No, there isn't," said Brittney. "Where?"

"Upstairs. At the end of the secret passage." Morris hit *continue.*

"What secret passage? There's no secret passage. Where?"

"It's a secret. I can't tell you."

"There's no such place," said Brittney.

"Suit yourself," said Morris, his hands writhing as he re-engaged his evil nemesis, "but I'll bet Samantha's on her way up there right now. I'll bet she knows where it is. I'll bet you got her so mad, she's going right in there, and you'll never see her again."

"Will too," said Brittney.

"Just like Buddy," said Morris. "Just like Jessica. One day they're here, next day, poof..."

"How do you know?"

"You're never gonna see Samantha again," he said. "Too bad the last thing you ever did was fight with her."

Brittney stared at Morris. Morris wrinkled his face and showed his teeth. Then he let out another groan, relaxed his hands and looked over at Brittney. "Bye-bye, Samantha," he said.

Brittney turned and ran out the door. Morris heard the yelled name of Samantha fade down the hallway.

Things were pretty good nowadays. The grownups were all distracted. At times, like now, no one even knew where they were. That was just fine with Morris. He's was getting in a lot more quality time with the television.

BETH AND DOUG AND GWEN were in the Narnia room. Doug found that fact amazing. How rarely they'd been in this room over the years, he thought, and how often of late. This room was meant for children. He and the other adults were not supposed to gather in it, make noise. He suddenly thought how lucky he'd been that no child had ever wandered in when he himself had found refuge here over the years. It would ruin the magic if a child wandered in to find an adult there. But then, what were the chances? So few children had ever wandered into this room. He marveled that he was here again, looking about this room, as though there were some connection between this room and all the troubles they'd had these past few days with the lost children and the DCYF. Gwen and Beth were on opposite sides of the room, scanning for an unlikely clue.

"You said you saw Gary here," said Beth.

"What was Gary doing here by the way?" asked Gwen.

"Looking for me."

"And what were you doing here?" asked Beth as though she didn't know.

"Looking for Charlie," he fibbed.

"And we know Charlie loved this room. He used to come here to read—and hardly be seen for days. And we know Jessica found this room and showed it to Buddy just before they left."

"What did Suzy mean when she said we shouldn't get involved, that we'd just make trouble?" asked Doug.

"First of all, that wasn't Suzy," said Beth.

"But what did she mean?"

"Even if we knew what she meant, do you think we'd just sit around and do nothing while everything fell down around us?" asked Beth.

"Pretty arrogant, don't you think," Gwen observed, "a little girl telling us to butt out because we might screw things up?"

"I think it's spunky," said Doug. Beth threw a pillow at him.

"I could just kill Gary." Gwen ran her finger down a display of stuffed toys, knick-knacks, and statuary commemorating the great villainesses of literary history: the White Witch, Snow White's stepmother, Maleficent, Morgan le Fay, the hag sisters: Adelaide, Castigetta, and Whiggamora, as well as Mombi, and the Wicked Witches of the East and West. "Running off like this, not even telling anyone where he was going."

"Nice Buddhist sentiment," said Beth.

"I'm sure he's with Charlie somewhere," said Doug.

"As though that makes it better."

237

"I don't know what you expect to find in here," said Doug. "Do you know what would happen if one of the kids found us in here? There's no door out of here except the wardrobe."

"Are you sure of that?" Beth asked, pulling books aside as though searching for a secret passage. "Gwen and I are still turning up little surprises you two designed into this house."

"Well I'd know, wouldn't I?"

"Yeah, but would you tell?" asked Beth.

"Or would you even remember?" asked Gwen. Doug wished Gary were here to back him up. "Isn't it astonishing that so few kids have found this room?" Doug ran his eyes over to the names in the guest book.

No one replied. Taking her cue from Beth, Gwen began pulling back books from the other side of the room and peering behind them.

"That's weird," said Doug pausing over the page. Still staring at the book, he called out more loudly, "Oh, that's even weirder." When this sentence too elicited no response, he announced, "Gary signed the book."

"Why would Gary sign the book?" said Gwen.

"It's for children," Beth added.

"And you know what's even weirder?" he continued. "Suzy signed it." Doug's finger was pointing to the open book.

"We know that," said Gwen.

"Gary signed this book just before he disappeared," said Doug. "And, and Suzy signed it, too," he sputtered.

"We *know* Suzy signed it," said exasperated Beth

"The very first signature," said Gwen.

"No," said Doug quite loudly. "She signed it *again*. Today."

Gwen and Beth went over to the book, and there, under Doug's pointing finger, was the elegant flow of ink registering Suzy Bishop's name, so beautiful it was nearly illegible—so different from the little girl's printing of the same name so many years before at the top of the still unturned first page of the book.

"So she *did* come to this room," said Beth, realizing how close she may have come to catching her. "I'll bet she's still in the house."

"Creepy," said Doug. But he didn't believe they could find her. Either she'd already left or was so well hidden—and she must know the house very well, somehow, to have found this room so easily when so many children had not found it in the course of years—that it may not be worth the time to look for her.

"Creepy?" Beth repeated. "Maybe so, but that's all it is, creepy. It doesn't mean anything."

"Oh?" said Gwen. "I don't care how she got here, to OzHouse. How did she know this room existed, and why would she come to it?"

"That's easy," said Doug with sudden illumination, and still talking more loudly than the situation called for. "That just proves that Brinks sent her. He's been in this room."

"But why? Why would Suzy come here? And why would she sign her name?"

"Hello?" came a voice from the hall. "Where are you?"

Beth and Gwen clapped their hands to their mouths.

"In here," yelled Doug without thinking. Gwen quickly slapped him on the arm. "You're not supposed to tell them," she whispered.

"Where's here?" yelled the voice. "Have you seen Samantha?"

"Now you've done it," said Beth, reaching through the wardrobe and opening the door to motion the little wild-eyed girl inside.

"Cool," she exclaimed when she found herself in the middle of the magical room. "You've got a playroom up here the whole time. I have *got* to tell the others. This is great." She jumped up and down in the middle of the gump.

"Better not," said Beth.

"You see this is a special room," said Gwen.

"We just found it ourselves," said Doug. Beth shot him a disapproving glance for the fib.

"It's true," said Doug, "our names aren't even in the book."

He drew Brittney's attention to the guest book. "See, it says when you find the room, you're supposed to sign your name in here and not tell anyone whose name isn't in the book."

"Cool," she said again. "Like a secret club. I gotta tell Samantha."

"You can't tell Samantha," said Doug.

Brittney grabbed the pen to print her name, her letters large and wobbly. "Then I'll just bring her here," she said.

"She doesn't get it," said Doug.

"You see, Brittney," Gwen began.

And all of a sudden the little girl looked worried. "Wait a minute. Is this is where they all disappear?"

"What are you talking about?"

"Morris said kids come here and disappear and never come back."

"That's silly," said Doug. He ran his eye down the pages of the guest book to see if Morris had found the room. His name was not there.

"I told him," said Brittney, fully satisfied.

"Tell me again. What did Morris say?" said Gwen, momentarily wondering whether the boy might really know something.

239

"Morris said kids go into the secret room and disappear," Brittney repeated in a tone that suggested that grown-ups were almost too dense sometimes to bother talking to.

"He's just making up stories again," Beth reassured her. "Children do not just disappear."

"Yeah, I told him." Brittney flipped through the pages of an open book, pausing over the enlarged colorful reproductions of the artwork. "I gotta show this to Samantha," she said again and ran to the wardrobe.

"Wait," yelled Doug, almost lunging toward her. He didn't want her to tell everyone about the room. Even as he determined to stop her, he thought it odd how much he cared about this little room at this worrisome time, but he did. It still mattered—a lot. Brittney stopped and turned around. Doug breathed more easily.

"Remember," he said, "you can only talk about the room to people who have signed the book."

"Okay," she said, still implying that the games of grownups made little sense.

"Now, can I go?"

"Yes," said Gwen, "but remember...."

"I signed the book," she said, putting her foot down. And then she turned again as she entered the wardrobe. "Oh, yeah. Morris is playing video games again even though it's not TV time." And then she ducked into the wardrobe. The name "Samantha," came back through the wardrobe. But it was oddly clipped. Everyone noticed it, as though someone had covered the little girl's mouth with a hand in the middle of her yell. For a split second, they all assumed she'd finally understood that she wasn't supposed to tell Samantha about the room. But in the second that followed—when there was no sound of a door closing or footsteps in the hallway, they all dashed toward the wardrobe. Doug leaped through first.

"My, she's fast," he said to Gwen once they were both in the hall. They looked up and down the empty hallway.

RUMPELSTILTSKIN PUT DOWN THE BOOK. "That's it?" he asked. The children were huddled in blankets on the floor of the witch's candy house. "That's all a father does in your world to get you little humans to sleep at night?"

"I would usually get a glass of water," said Buddy.

"Doesn't that make you have to pee?" said the dwarf.

"Wow," said Hansel.

"No one ever read to us," said Gretel. "I wish I lived in your world."

"Yeah, well no one ever read to me either," said Jessica. She couldn't imagine her mother or Bill sitting down and reading a story to anyone. The only books in the whole house were the ones she or her sister brought home from the school library. "I had to do my own reading. I think Buddy's the last human to get a bedtime story in the entire universe."

"What about Gwen and Beth and Gary and Doug?" asked Buddy.

Jessica recalled the four of them taking turns reading to all the kids in the evening in the Middle Earth Reading Room just off the Library of Alexandria. Older kids and younger kids together. They didn't ever call it bedtime reading. Late-Night Book Club, that's what it was. Jessica hadn't realized she'd actually been getting a bedtime story. "That was just a book," she said. "Anyway, those people at OzHouse are different." She missed them.

"See, being a father to a little human's not so hard," said Rumpelstiltskin. "I do hope you will be reconsidering my offer, boy."

"I think it would be okay," said Buddy.

"No," said Jessica. "He can't live with you."

"I think he can speak for himself."

"He can't stay here because the whole reason I came out here was to find him and fix everything. He's got to come back."

"The boy wants a home. I got a good one. Listen to me, Missy."

"I'm tired," said Buddy.

"Oh," said Rumpelstiltskin, calming down at once. "Of course you are." And he leaned over and patted the little boy on the head. "We'll talk about it in the morning."

"No, we won't," said Jessica, "because he's coming back with me."

And she rolled over onto her back and crossed her arms and locked her teeth shut.

Rumpelstiltskin sat back on the twig-built rocking chair. A tallow candle burned on the little side table.

"Should I put out the candle?" he asked.

"Excuse me, mister," said Buddy.

"Yes, boy?"

"Do you think that happy families are all alike?"

Rumpelstiltskin put his hand on the fat book by the candle. "I think that witch had pretty strange taste in stories," he said. And he squeezed the candle wick between his calloused fingers. He rocked

241

slowly in the dark until he heard the rhythmic breathing of the children, telling him they were all asleep, and then he rocked some more. The forester and Humpty Dumpty were outside waiting to talk with him about what was to be done tomorrow with the children. Buddy and Jessica were easy: Over the objections of Rumpelstiltskin, Humpty Dumpty was going to lead them back to Mother Goose Land, and from there, home by whatever means they'd arrived. But the other two were not so easy. They had to decide whether Hansel and Gretel could be returned to the wicked stepmother who'd tried to lose them in the woods and the desperate father who'd let her do it. By what authority could they keep them? But how could they let them return to such a house?

"It all turns out well, in that one," Humpty Dumpty had said when the topic came up earlier. "I know the story."

"Well, I don't," said the forester.

"And I don't think I'd trust the memory of a short-tempered, self-serving softshell even if the world were turning the way it always had before," added Rumpelstiltskin. But that's where the conversation ended. Humpty Dumpty was boiling. But the forester had suggested they not pass such words in front of the children.

And now Rumpelstiltskin, rocking back and forth in the peaceful night among the sweet smell of the confectionary house, wasn't sure he wanted to continue the conversation at all. It would be more peaceful to rock off to sleep.

He closed his eyes. He heard a knock on the door. "Shhhh" he whispered. "The kids are asleep." And then, "dopey egg," he muttered to himself. But the egg wouldn't have knocked. He decided he'd only imagined the sound. And then he heard it again, another knock, more desperate this time. "Shhhhhhh," he said again, more loudly. And then he was sure he heard footsteps crossing the floor upstairs. But there was no floor upstairs! His eyes bolted open. The rosy sky through the window told him the sun was coming up. Had he slept for hours? (And that miserable egg hadn't come to get him.) The dark outlines on the floor told him the kids were still asleep. All was quiet. Had he imagined or dreamed the knock on the door? Steps on the second floor of a one-story cottage?

But then he heard a voice: "No one lives here," it said. And it came from above. "Everyone is dead?"

And then a voice came through the door: "Won't you please open the door for me?"

And then the voice from above—he would have said "upstairs" but there were no stairs—called down in great fatigue: "But I too am dead."

242

That at least made sense. Only a ghost could live on a floor that did not exist. One of the children stirred.

Rumpelstiltskin felt an urge to quiet the voices: "Shhhhh" he almost yelled, "the children."

"Dead?" asked the voice at the door. "Then what are you doing at the window?"

"I am waiting for the undertaker to take me away." And then the "upstairs" footsteps walked back across the floor—or the roof, the dwarf supposed.

"Oh, lovely Maiden with Azure Hair," cried the voice at the door, louder than ever.

Rumpelstiltskin could not imagine who this was or why that dopey egg outside or the forester wasn't helping him give these children a good night's rest. "Please open," the voice continued. "Take pity on a poor boy who is being chased by two Assass—"

Rumpelstiltskin threw open the door. "Would you shut up, you little..." and then he paused, "little...."

"Who are you?" asked the one who had knocked on the door. "You're not the maiden with the azure hair." He was a small boy, not any taller than Buddy, though much louder and more sure of himself, clearly. He seemed to be much older than that little boy. And he was made entirely of wood.

Rumpelstiltskin squinted. He looked down at the new boy; he looked left and right. Before he'd opened the door, he'd been rocking in the rose-colored pre-dawn light. But now it was full day. The sun was bright. How could the sun outside the cottage be bright when it was early dawn inside? And then—odder still, if that were possible—there was this living, wooden child in front of him: And he seemed nervous, turning, darting his eyes. "They're right behind me," he said.

Rumpelstiltskin turned around to see that the children were still asleep on the floor. There they were—beginning to stir. The sudden light from the door seemed to have awakened them.

"Who were you talking to?" said Rumpelstiltskin to the little wooden boy. And then he added before the wooden boy could answer, "Did you see the egg?"

"Can I please come in?"

"No."

The wooden boy turned around and yelled at the top of his wooden lungs: "Assassins." He really seemed to see someone behind him. Rumpelstiltskin stared back into the woods—which were not the same woods of the day before—but he saw no one. Behind him the children all awoke. The dwarf pulled the boy into the house and closed the door.

"Something is not right," said the wooden boy, no longer the least bit distressed. By now the sun was streaming in through the windows. Had it cleared the horizon just now, or had dawn turned suddenly to midday everywhere?

"Pinocchio," yelled Jessica, running over to the little boy.

"You know him?"

"You're not a real boy, yet," said the girl.

"Why would I want to be that? Marionettes have much more fun. Real boys have to go to school, and do chores, and learn a trade."

And then another new voice entered the conversation. "Pinocchio?" it said. And they all turned to the figure in the corner of the room: a pretty blue-haired girl. "This is wrong."

By this time Buddy and Hansel and Gretel were wide awake. The children from the Grimms' Forest merely looked at one another in confusion. But Buddy understood. He looked at the blue-haired girl: "You don't look like the blue fairy," he said. He knew the story only as a cartoon.

"But I am." And then before their eyes, she grew larger, from a little girl into a young woman. And she started pacing the floor.

"You're supposed to have a blue dress and a magic wand and come down from the sky," Jessica explained.

The blue fairy just smiled at the children. "How would I get into the sky?" But she didn't wait for an answer. "Something is wrong, all right," she said to the room. She went over to the four children, asking their names. Jessica and Buddy meant nothing to her. But Hansel and Gretel— she knew their names.

"The worlds are melting into one another." She looked at Rumpelstiltskin. "The borders are dissolving," she said, and then in a commanding voice: "Keep them here. I'll be right back." And then she seemed to walk a set of invisible stairs and disappear.

"All right, children, outside," said Rumpelstiltskin as soon as she was gone.

"But the blue fairy," said Jessica.

"I don't take orders from eggs, and I don't take orders from fairies."

"I'd like to order some eggs," said Hansel.

"Outside," the dwarf commanded.

And they all preceded Rumpelstiltskin through the door.

244

Outside, the world had indeed changed. Rumpelstiltskin did not recognize the landscape. Nor was there any sign of Humpty Dumpty or the forester. He was entirely lost. The children, all but Pinocchio, understood at once. "What will we do?" asked Jessica.

"I don't suppose you two left a path of breadcrumbs?" Rumpelstiltskin asked Hansel and Gretel.

"Are you really going to help us?" asked Jessica.

Rumpelstiltskin held his hand out in front of him as though he were arresting a thought that was trying to invade. "Well," he said. "I, ah... Do you think I'd just leave you here?"

"You left me at the fire," said Buddy.

"Different," said the dwarf. "That was not the same."

"Why?" asked the little boy.

"Just was." He put his hands on his hips and puffed up his chest.

"What are you getting out of this?" asked Jessica. "You said you don't do anything unless you get paid."

Buddy was standing right beside the dwarf; Rumpelstiltskin reached over and rubbed the little boy's head. "Nothing," he said. Then he thought a moment and corrected himself, "Satisfaction, maybe." And then he took another moment and looked around and said, "No. Nothing. This one's on me."

The comment did not satisfy Jessica. "Then why are you doing it?"

But the dwarf did not explain himself further.

Jessica looked from the dwarf to the boy. She thought maybe she better get Buddy out of fairyland altogether and as soon as she possibly could. But she also thought she'd need the dwarf to do it. And she said no more on the subject of payment. "If we could just find the wardrobe door," she said, "I'm sure we can go home. I know just where I left it. I marked the trail."

"Where was that?" Rumpelstiltskin asked.

"China."

"China!"

"I left it in Mother Goose Land," said Buddy.

That was much better. There were, apparently, roads from the Grimms' Forest there—if this still was the Grimms' Forest.

"Maybe we should just wait for the Blue Fairy," said Hansel.

Rumpelstiltskin harrumphed.

"Mother Goose Land is south of the Grimms' Forest; that's what Humpty Dumpty said," Jessica said.

"South, huh? How hard could that be? He can wait for the fairy if he wants," pointing to Pinocchio. "That's his story."

Just then a rabbit scurried by close enough to touch. Pausing at the feet of Pinocchio it said, "little boys who ignore good advice and wander in unknown lands always come into trouble."

"Ahh, whadda you know?" the marionette replied. And as he prepared to give the little creature a kick, the rabbit scurried off into the underbrush.

"Well, that's funny," said Gretel, to whom no animal had ever spoken.

"Happens all the time," said the wooden boy. "Birds, crickets, donkeys, weasels. Really annoying." And then he turned to Rumpelstiltskin, "Why should I wait? There have to be better adventures in a goose land than here."

Rumpelstiltskin glanced from one child to another. "These crazy days, spitting on a campfire is an adventure."

CHAPTER 23

THINGS AS THEY HAPPENED

1 Buddy turned up missing before dinner.

2. DCYF was notified, as were the police.

3. Locals arrived to search.

4. Colin Fullofhimself-Brinks arrived.

5. Charlie showed up.

6. Jessica disappeared searching for Buddy.

7. Charlie stole Brinks' laptop.

8. Brinks accused Charlie of stealing his laptop and intimated his involvement with the missing children.

9. Rebecca Holton threatened lawsuit.

10. The Police arrived via Brinks' call.

11. Gary and Charlie went missing.

12. Some little girl claiming to be Suzy Bishop was seen on the property.

13. This "Suzy" went in the Narnia Room.

14. Brittney didn't show up for Dinner after being with us all in the Narnia room just an hour before.

"IS THAT ALL?" ASKED DOUG as he put his fine-point behind his ear.

"Let me think a minute," sighed Beth. "Did Charlie get back from school before or after Jessica ran off to look for Buddy?"

"And did we notify the police before we called Rebecca Holton, and when did Colin and Rebecca show up the first time? You didn't even include that," Gwen said as she ran her fingers roughly though her hair.

"And then they showed up on Thanksgiving. And Rebecca was drunk and... no... that was the day before Thanksgiving."

"No that was Thanksgiving morning, because we were still cooking and we invited her to stay for the meal."

"I didn't invite her," Beth cut in.

"Forget it," Doug exploded and crumpled up the paper. "This isn't helping. We can't even decide what to put down let alone when." Tossing the ball of paper into the wastebasket, Doug slid his chair back and put his hands behind his head. He couldn't quite recall why he'd thought making a list would help. But then again, sitting around doing nothing was worse than doing nothing productive. With all the children in bed, there weren't even any immediate children's needs to occupy the time. Everyone was tense. Doug and Beth had had a rousing argument when he refused to call the authorities over Brittney's disappearance. Gwen was on the verge of panic.

"There has to be a connection," Doug said. "This is simply too coincidental. And I don't care if Brinks was behind the Suzy Bishop girl showing up or not. Five people are missing and I for one don't believe they are all runaways. If that were the simple truth of it, why would Gary and Charlie also be missing? I can't imagine Gary running away from home!" He forced a small laugh.

Beth had a few gruesome possibilities running about in her head, but with Gwen in the room she didn't feel right about sharing any of them.

"Let's keep searching the house for Brittney. Gwen, you go try Morris and Samantha again if they're not yet asleep. Especially Morris. He might know more than he's saying." Doug stood up.

"If we don't find her soon, and I mean real soon, we have to call the police," Beth said to herself but certainly loud enough for Doug to know her mind was made up.

When Gwen reached the corridor where Morris' room was, she noticed wet spots on the hallway floor. With all the distractions, no one had insisted any of the children take their baths, and she could hardly imagine Morris DeFalco taking his bath without being made to. She

248

followed the puddles. They didn't go into Morris' room, after all, but across the hall to Samantha and Brittney's room.

Opening the door quietly, she saw the night light was still on— and there was Brittney. She was standing in the room half undressed and soaking wet. Samantha was sitting on her bed; the two had obviously been talking while Brittney changed her clothes.

"Uh oh," Samantha said, "now they caught you."

"It wasn't my fault, Mrs. Robbins. I fell in and got wet by accident."

"What? Did you sneak into the pool? You couldn't. Do you know how dangerous that is?"

"No, no, no, honest," said Brittney.

Gwen was relieved. Sneaking into the pool should certainly not have been possible. There were ample safeguards. And she herself had checked the door. "You wandered outside and fell into the big fountain, then, didn't you?" She gave Brittney no time to respond. She almost laughed at the thought. "That was very bad of you," she said unconvincingly. "It's freezing out there." She should have been more stern, she knew, but she smiled with a great sigh as she realized that the terrible mystery was innocently solved. Gary too would show up any minute with just as simple a story.

"I went to Bikini Bottom and met Sponge Bob and Patrick," Brittney corrected her. And then she added, "Morris was playing the game with Xbox. But I didn't want to go there."

"With all the tension in this house these days, it's nice that some of you can still take time to be silly and have some fun," Gwen said. Children, they always managed to amaze her—even now. "If only we adults could find a way to recapture some of that. Now you wait right here, don't move a muscle. I have to get Beth and Doug and tell them you are all right." As Gwen turned to leave the room, a dozen movie plots ran through her head and she stopped. "No, I am not going to make that mistake. I think it best you come with me, my little Sponge Bob fan."

"But I'm still wet."

But Gwen was not going to let the girl out of her sight until everyone knew she was safe. She picked her up, wet as she was, and carried her out of the room as Brittney tried to reach down and pull off her wet socks.

A minute later Gwen stood her up on a wooden chair in the kitchen and helped pull the wet socks off the little girl's feet. She called Doug and Beth, and as they entered the room she was saying to Brittney, "We were very worried about you when you didn't show up for dinner,"

"Sponge Bob and Patrick and I ate at the Krusty Crab," explained the little girl. "Mr. Crabs allowed me to put it on my tab if I promised to come back and pay him later. He was much nicer than he is on the show. Even Squidward was nice."

Doug stifled a laugh. Beth and Gwen were so glad to have the little girl back they decided not to pursue the conversation and allowed the childish flight of fancy. Picking the sodden clothes off the hardwood floor, Gwen wrapped a large towel around Brittney and passed her to Doug who carried her back to bed.

As he shut off the nightlight, he whispered, "I'm sure crabby patties are good, but if you are still hungry, let me know, and I'll bring you a peanut butter and jelly sandwich. Otherwise you two girls get to sleep." He glanced over at Samantha who was squeezing her eyes shut.

Brittney made no mention of being hungry, so Doug left the room and headed back to Gwen and Beth, relieved at least that no new mystery would confuse their minds tonight.

"WHO ARE THEY?" Gary pointed down toward the main gates of the Emerald City. He, Charlie, and the wizard had just reached the top of a hill.

"Oh my," breathed the wizard as he slumped down and peered through his pocket telescope. "We certainly are being invaded. I do not know who those creatures are, but they are not from Oz, of that I am sure."

Gary helped the wizard up and tried to assess the situation. Several dozen creatures at the very least were camped outside the large wooden gates. "Would you look at that," said the wizard, looking again through his telescope. "The Wogglebug—he's just.... And the soldier with the... Oh, dear. Oh, my."

"What," and "What is it," said Gary and Charlie together.

"Oh, thank goodness," said the wizard, breathing hard as he lowering the instrument. It seems the Wogglebug and the Soldier with the Green Whiskers came through the gates just now. They didn't make it more than a step or two out in the open—with a while flag in their hands mind you—when those evil creatures raised their weapons and stormed after them. My friends barely made it back behind the gates with their souls intact."

Gary took the wizard's telescope and peered down at the scene. A small army of evil creatures had begun pounding on the gates. They could hear the reverberation clear up the hill. "I recognize some of them. Those are orcs with those big sharp spears and that looks like an ifrit from *The*

250

Arabian Nights. Those furry things look like Scandinavian trolls...and who's that?" Gary pointed to a large green man with a battle ax. "The Jolly Green Giant?"

"Oh, I don't think so," said Charlie, taking the telescope. "Who's next, Boo Berry the ghost? Count Chocula? Lucky the Leprechaun? The Trix Rabbit?" Charlie scanned the field of incompatible bad guys from all sorts of stories. Impossible. They represented so many ways of being bad. And these would have to be what was interfering with the magic of Oz. But something of Oz would probably be interfering with their powers as well. He found the huge green creature Gary had seen. He stared hard. The man was green from head to toe, and burly. His clothing green as grass, a green fur coat, and green belt. Charlie lowered the telescope, smiling. "You know who that is? It's the Green Knight—remember, from *Sir Gawain.*" He raised the telescope again. "Is that a children's story?" That would be one to visit, for sure. "And someone else. It looks like the Big Friendly Giant, though he hardly seems very friendly pounding on the door with his fists."

The wizard did not seem to have heard him. "I don't see any orks," he said as he took back his telescope and scanned the crowd. "Besides wouldn't they just fly over the top? And why would they attack us? We've always been friendly with any orks that arrived to Oz."

Gary paused a moment and then smiled "No, not Oz orks, the four legged bird-like creatures, but Middle-Earth orcs. Evil creatures created by Morgoth the Enemy during the War of the Great Jewels."

"Wow," said Charlie. "You do know your Tolkien." Charlie shook his head as he took another turn with the wizard's telescope.

Gary was starting to understand just how dangerous it was to mix up the tales this way. Oz was never created to house such horrific creatures. The things they were capable of could devastate the nearly defenseless country. How could Ozma or Glinda or anyone here ever know how to deal with them?

"What the..." Charlie exclaimed.

"What do you see?" asked Gary.

"A wardrobe," said Charlie, handing the telescope to Gary and pointing. "It just appeared out of nowhere."

"Really? How has that..."

"It's not like the wardrobe to show up outside the walls of a city," said Charlie.

"Nothing is like what it's like as far as I can see," said the wizard.

"Has someone else come?" asked Gary as he struggled with the telescope to find the brown box Charlie had directed him to.

"And what is the significance of this wardrobe anyway?" asked the wizard.

"It's how we came," said Charlie. "It's like a portal."

"No," said Gary, "it *is* a portal. And if another has shown up, then someone must have arrived from OzHouse." Beth? Gwen? Doug? Or was it one of the children? But who else even knew about the wardrobe?

"I didn't see anyone come through," said Charlie.

"Would you look at that," said Gary, handing the telescope back to Charlie.

Charlie focused again on the wardrobe. The doors opened and closed. But no one emerged. A number of the creatures besieging the city gates had gathered around to inspect the suddenly appearing magic portal. Whoever was in there had better retreat fast, Charlie thought.

"The magic is really going crazy," said the wizard, taking the telescope from Charlie and returning it to his little black bag. But they couldn't think of that right now. They had to get to the city to offer what help they could, with or without magic.

Gary wondered if he were killed here in Oz by some lunatic orc would he really be dead or would he reappear back home waking up as if from a dream.

The wizard inspected the contents of his black bag, still hoping it might offer some help. With sighs of frustration, he pulled them out one by one and then placed them back into the leather satchel.

"None of my magic is working," he wiped his face with a white silk cloth.

"That's the first bit of good news all day," said Charlie with a start. "If none of your magic is working then we can assume none of their magic is working either."

"Doesn't take too much magic for a spear to kill you," Gary reminded him.

The wizard was about to say people don't die from a spear wound in Oz, but he thought better of it and said nothing.

EVERYWHERE INSIDE THE WALLS, the inhabitants of the Emerald City were pacing and wringing their hands. And when they saw how concerned Ozma and Glinda were, they paced and wrung all the more.

The swan chariot had landed in the large pool outside the palace doors and several servants had rushed out to assist Glinda in carrying the Tin Woodman's heavy body to Ozma's throne room where Ozma, Dorothy and the others rushed upon hearing Suzy's report.

"I... I do not understand how I can feel this way," moaned the man of tin. "I am so weak and hungry and yet I cannot eat and have not eaten since I became tin."

"Just relax old friend," Dorothy said as she patted his hard, metal face. "We have been through many adventures together and have always prevailed."

"Are *you* feeling hungry?" Ozma asked Scraps as she spun around the flight of marble steps.

"Don't know," smiled the crazy quilted woman. "I have never eaten or been hungry so I do not know what it feels like."

"If what I think has happened has happened," began Glinda with a nod to Suzy, "then each of us may respond differently as the magic is altered."

"Altered, not gone?" asked Dorothy. They were just entering the throne room.

"Altered. But that may be even worse than having it leave us completely," explained Glinda. "As creatures enter Oz from other fantasy worlds they are bringing their own magic, and it seems to be mixing with Oz magic and creating some kind of new or hybrid power."

"If what you say is true, then what magic has failed before might suddenly start to work again or what has been constant might suddenly change. We just don't know." Ozma was about to say more when several people rushed through the garden crying that the doors to the city were starting to crack from the pounding of the creatures outside.

Hardly had the door been closed when it opened again, and in came Jellia Jamb, a bandage on her head, with news for the Princess Ozma. She had received word from mice, still arriving from all over the kingdom, that still more magical creatures were arriving. Most, it seemed, meant no harm. Many were converging on the Emerald City however. There would likely be a steady stream for days if something were not done.

"Surely the doors will not hold against so many," Jellia Jamb concluded.

"I think I will go speak to the people at the gate," Scraps said as she stopped spinning. "You gather your magic bits and bobs, but I think someone should just go talk to them."

"We tried that when they first arrived," explained Dorothy.

"You sent a diplomat and a dullard," the Patchwork Girl gave a glance at the Wogglebug. "This needs a woman's touch."

"They'll do more than touch you, woman," the professor scoffed. "They'll tear you to pieces and toss you back over the wall in bits."

"Then Auntie Em can sew me back together," said Scraps. "Can't say anyone will notice a few more seams." Her pearl teeth shown as she smiled back at her friends.

"I don't recommend that action," Ozma told her, "but I won't forbid it since we have no other plan just now. But please be careful, for all we know it might hurt to be ripped apart with the magic altered."

"Pshaw, I'll be fine. I always am. You know me. Finest fabric; can't be ruffled. Let's just see if I can find out what these folks really want." And Scraps headed, imperturbable, to the front gate where many of the Emerald City folk were crowding about trying to devise ways to bolster their defenses and reinforce the great doors.

"I still suspect the problem lies somehow not with these creatures, but with the human." Glinda paced.

"Plenty of humans have found their way to Oz," Suzy noted.

"I have nothing against humans, as you know. I have met these two who came today, and they seem like good people. But it's their actions that might have started all this, not their intentions." The sorceress rubbed her back.

"I see," said the Wogglebug.

"I don't," said Suzy.

"If I may," the professor began with halting breath; he was clearly too tired for this conversation but could not resist the opportunity to display his acumen. "Pandora's Box," he panted. And then he closed his eyes and leaned his head back without further explanation.

"I can't be certain that his strange course of entry is not an effect rather than a cause of this mixed-up magic," Glinda explained. "What troubles me is that those creatures outside our walls did not come from any one world. They have never been to Oz before; he has. This Charles Emerson seems to have been the weak stick in the dam. Waves of creatures came flooding in somehow when the weak stick broke."

"But these are just guesses, I assume?" Ozma asked.

"For the moment," the sorceress returned.

"MAYBE WE SHOULD HAVE WAITED with Hansel and Gretel," said Jessica, apparently sensing their leader's confusion. Hansel and Gretel had chosen not to continue with them on their quest for the wardrobe. "Humpty Dumpty seemed to know the way."

"*Seems* is right. I say we waited too long as it was," grumbled Rumpelstiltskin. "That arrogant egg and the forester are gone. Can't say I'll miss the egg."

"He was gonna get us back to the door," said Buddy.

254

"If we'd wasted the whole day hoping he might return, it would be dark before we got out of Grimms' Forest—if this even is Grimms' Forest, which I more and more don't think it is—and that would bring with it a whole new set of problems."

"Follow me, if you want adventures," declared the wooden puppet.

Rumpelstiltskin rubbed his neck as though to take the stiffness out. He looked over to the puppet. "I get the feeling you're gonna stick with us no matter what."

"I like Pinocchio," said Buddy.

"On the other hand," Rumpelstiltskin continued, "it's not impossible you will be of some use before this is all over. Just don't make a nuisance of yourself." And then he smiled the biggest, ugliest smile of warning Jessica had ever seen.

"I think I remember part of the way back," said Jessica.

"But this is different," said Buddy.

"Maybe it only looks different," said Jessica. She wasn't exactly sure why she was saying so. But the dwarf was clearly stuck, and she wanted to help.

"Good enough, I suppose," said Rumpelstiltskin, who had no better plan. "Then you shall lead us until we are permanently lost." He still held a crooked smile.

Jessica didn't like the way that sounded.

"I think we came from this way." She imagined she'd found something familiar in the landscape.

"Is that south?" said Buddy.

Rumpelstiltskin patted the boy on the head. "West, young man," he told him. "Rising sun is behind us."

"Because Dumpty Dumpty said Goose Land is south."

"We came from this direction," said Jessica pointing emphatically.

The dwarf looked over at the girl. "Think that one over, miss. Trees look an awful lot alike."

"Not to me," said the puppet. "But then I am related to some of them."

"Do they tell you anything about how to travel?" Jessica asked.

Pinocchio frowned as only a wooden face can. "How silly are you, girl? Trees don't talk."

"Neither do puppets," Jessica quickly replied, "unless someone pulls their strings."

Without another word, the wooden boy kicked Jessica on the ankle.

"Ow!" she cried. "That's not funny. It hurt!"

"Wasn't meant to be funny; it was meant to hurt," laughed Pinocchio.

"You recall what I told you before we left?" Rumpelstiltskin said as he grabbed the wooden boy by the neck and easily raised him off the ground. "If you cause trouble we will leave you to the assassins and murderers you came to us crying about. Is that clear?"

Fighting an impulse to kick out in all directions, Pinocchio instead went completely limp in the dwarf's large hand. He didn't like this gnarled little man with all his rules, but he was afraid to be left alone in the woods, so, with head drooped and eyes raised, he pretended to be sorry and forced a big smile on his wooden face.

"Now, which is it?" asked the dwarf as he set Pinocchio behind him. "West or south? We don't want anyone taking us in the wrong direction just for stubbornness." He looked at Jessica. "Who knows what trouble that would lead us to?"

"He said south," said Buddy. And for the first time since she'd found Buddy, Jessica felt the impulse to hit him.

"South," Jessica repeated.

"Very good," said the dwarf. "And well done."

On and on the small group trudged. Eventually the woods thinned out and turned to tree-spotted fields of wild grasses. Buddy tired faster than the rest and the little man was sorry he wasn't big enough to carry the boy as the forester had done.

"Can we at least stop and eat?" asked Buddy.

"Yes, yes," added Pinocchio. "I'm starving."

Rumpelstiltskin wasn't happy about a break so soon, but agreed for the little boy's sake. He tried his magical powers, as he had before they'd left the gingerbread house, with much grumbling and, again, no luck. He could not produce any food that way. They pulled out what they'd taken off the house before leaving.

"Do you eat?" Jessica asked as Pinocchio grabbed a large hunk of gingerbread and icing.

"Sure," replied the puppet. "I prefer candy and sweets to all other foods."

The girl watched as Pinocchio gobbled down the lion's share of the food. She didn't understand why a wooden boy would need to eat. He couldn't explain it himself, except to say he thought it had something to do with the magic of the Blue Fairy.

"Speaking of her," began Jessica as she popped a gumdrop window decoration in her mouth. "I'm starting to think we should have found out why she told us to wait."

"Did I already tell you," thundered Rumpelstiltskin, "I don't take no orders from no fairies, blue or otherwise?"

Buddy cowered up to Jessica at the sound. He was not used to grownups yelling.

"I just want to get us home," Jessica ignored Buddy and yelled right back. Buddy looked from Jessica to Rumpelstiltskin Buddy scrunched himself up into a ball and bit the cloth on the knees of his pants.

"Now, now, now," said the dwarf. "You're disturbing the little guy, yelling like that." And he gathered Buddy to him and patted his head.

Rumpelstiltskin was not anxious to let Buddy leave, but he would be happy to rid himself of the little girl who was a constant reminder to Buddy that there was another place to which he belonged.

"That's not fair," said Jessica. But the dwarf said no more.

"Come on," said Pinocchio, "keep fighting. I want to see who wins."

Rumpelstiltskin glanced hard at the puppet. Pinocchio put both hands over his mouth and raised his eyebrows in apology.

"This is boring," said Pinocchio when they had walked for some hours and encountered nothing more than trees and grass and insects and a few small animals, none of whom said a word. "I might have stayed in school for all the fun I'm having."

"Isn't that someone behind the tree?" asked Buddy as he held Rumpelstiltskin's hand and stared.

"He look familiar to anyone?" asked the dwarf.

At about the same moment, the boy they had spotted seemed to have seen them also, for he started running toward them and shouted, "Wolf! Wolf! It's the Wolf!"

Rumpelstiltskin's eyes widened as he quickly took in the scene. Jessica pulled Buddy away from the dwarf.

Pinocchio grabbed a willow branch to defend himself, though it didn't seem like much of a weapon to Buddy.

As the shepherd boy stumbled between the trees and into the clearing beside Rumpelstiltskin, Jessica, Buddy, and the puppet, he was still crying, "It's the Wolf! Help, help!"

"Where is he?" asked the little man as he began digging through his pouch looking for a magic spell. "Tell me boy! I cannot see the beast. Which way is he coming from?"

Suddenly the boy started laughing in such a scornful way that Jessica instantly knew who he was.

"Fooled you! Ha ha!" laughed the boy. "There is no wolf. Haven't seen one for days! Ha ha!"

Rumpelstiltskin's old eyes flashed. "What kind of joke is this? You ignorant imp! See how you frightened the children?"

"He doesn't care," said Jessica. "He always thinks it's funny to lie and fool people. I think you are a dreadful little boy."

"I don't even know you."

"But I know you. I read your story lots of times when I was little."

"I don't know what you're talking about, but I must say you looked very funny when you were scared and the little kid was practically crying. Ha, ha!"

Before Rumpelstiltskin could do anything or say another word, Pinocchio used the willow branch and began whipping the boy across the arms and legs. "Laugh that off, real boy."

"Hey, people don't hit children for making a mistake. No one has ever hit me before. Ow ow! Stop it, that hurts," the boy said as he rubbed the red marks where the willow branch had struck him.

"Meant to hurt," said the marionette.

"It was long overdue, I'm sure," Rumpelstiltskin grumbled.

"Where I come from you'd have gotten far worse for such a prank. Not that I ever did such things, but I've heard tell," Pinocchio said as he raised his whip again.

"Then I do not ever want to go where you are from," said the boy as he rushed off back between the trees still rubbing the welts on his leg.

"Let's move on," Rumpelstiltskin said with a slightly new opinion of the wooden puppet.

"But what about that boy?" Buddy asked. "He's all alone."

"He'll learn his lesson one day," sighed Jessica. "But as I recall it will be a little too late for him."

"He probly belongs with those Cautiony Tales," Buddy added. "That means we're close to Goose Land." And Buddy smiled happily for the first time in a long time.

"And that means we'll be home soon," Jessica added.

CHAPTER 24

Dear Santa,

I ben a vary good girl this year. So you can foreget what Morris said. I did'nt not lie about where I went. I did go to Bakeeni botom and I did see Spung Bob and Im not crazy. And I went to anuther place to. But its not a lie if you do'nt tell them somthing they do'nt ask abowt. Like I do'n't tell everywun evry time I go to the bathroom do I? So Morris is beeing bad, not me. And you can give me all the stuff he put on his Chrismis list to if its not junky because he shood'n't get anything for writting that letter to you that was'nt not very nice. I went to the other place furst but then I wen't back in the closit and I just ended up in spuonge Bob when I thought I was coming home. So I stayed their till super time. OK maybe latter then suprtime. I did'nt tell them about the first place becuse it was scarey. And I thot maybe I wus bein bad for goin there. But nobody wood get mad at me for goin to Spung Bob. I mean its spoug Bob rigt? Isnt it? I didn't even get out of the closit in the furst place becoz it was just like wickid loud and dusty. And then a big guy with all this hair and all these teeth that rored like a lieun came runing rite at me and I screamed and he wus gonna eat me like when my mother said she was gona feed me to the kanniballs and I don't want to think abowt it so I doved back into the secrit room and fell right on spung bob like a mattriss.

259

So I did'nt not lie. And I still want the Amerikin girl named Kaya. Plese let me have it.
I Love u.

SAMANTHA PUT DOWN THE PEN. "Is that all you want me to write?"

"Well, yeah, because I already said, 'I love you,' so I have to stop."

"Okay. Then just write your name."

Brittney printed her name with the red Sharpie that Santa was certain to like. "We'll write the address in green," she said.

"So you really went to this place where you were almost eaten?" asked Samantha.

"No," said Brittney, slamming down the pen.

"So you're lying to Santa Claus?"

"No," said Brittney, staring hard at Samantha.

"Well did you go or didn't you?"

"I just remembered I can't tell you. Anyway, I didn't tell you. You just wrote the letter because I don't know how and it was an emergency."

Samantha looked at Brittney very seriously. "But you just told me."

"No I didn't. You just wrote the letter. I didn't tell you. And I didn't tell Mr. Brinks either. Not on purpose. I just forgot."

"You told Mr. Fuller-Brinks?"

"He just asked me where I'd been, and I just told him. But I know it's okay because he told me once he has to keep my file private."

"What file?"

"It's private, okay. And that means I can't tell you. I can tell him whatever he asks me. He said so. But it's a secret. I shouldn't even of told you about it."

"What has your file got to do with you visiting Sponge Bob?"

"It just does. Don't talk about things you don't know about." And then after a thoughtful moment, she added, "but I think I wasn't suppose to tell him too. I have to fix that, I guess."

"Can we go back?" asked Samantha, ignoring Brittney's last remark. "Can I go with you? I want to see Sponge Bob too."

"But we might end up where they eat you," said Brittney. And then she threw both hands over her mouth. "Stop making me talk about it," she said.

"That would be better than here," said Samantha.

"But OzHouse is fun," said Brittney through her hands.

"It's not home," said Samantha. "You can't put enough games and toys and books in a house to make it be like home. It's like the candy house in Hansel and Gretel. There's always a witch in it."

"There's no witches in OzHouse," said Brittney.

"It's not home," said Samantha. And then she said, "I wonder if that's what happened to all the others—who was it?—Jessica and Buddy and Gary."

"And Charlie."

"We should tell them. We figured it out. We should tell Gwen and Beth and Doug."

"They probly know. But maybe not Mr. Brinks."

"He's downstairs, you know," said Samantha.

They could hear people talking loudly downstairs, not really yelling, the way they both remembered people yelling before the DCYF people took them away, but not in a happy way either.

"FRANKLY," SAID COLIN FULLER-BRINKS, "I am disturbed by the stories."

"I really don't think that you should let a child's imagination...." Doug began.

"Imagination is all good and well," said Colin. "But when a child who has been taken from an unsuitable home—from violence in the case of so many of these children—and she cannot distinguish between truth and fantasy, well, on the one hand it's perfectly understandable, of course: there are repressed feelings of anger; there's unresolved issues, ambivalent feelings of hatred and love, guilt, often very intense feelings of guilt, as though they, the children themselves, suppose they must have somehow been the cause..."

"We understand," said Gwen. "We've been at this a long time. We've read all the books."

"My point is that you seem to positively encourage these children's attempts to confuse imagination with reality. With you, imagination is not a temporary refuge; it's not a buffer from painful memories; rather, it seems to be the goal."

Beth jumped in, "That's absurd."

"We all know you have the right to see these children," said Doug. "You are their caseworker."

"We have not tried to keep you away from them or from doing your job," said Gwen.

"I would think this house is in enough trouble without trying to obstruct the state's work," said Colin.

"But when you accuse us of..."

261

"That girl honestly believes she has been in the presence of a cartoon. Who is trying to tell her this isn't true?"

"Just as soon as we 86 Jolly Old St. Nick," said Doug, "I'm on it."

"We happen to believe that this period of identification with an imaginary world is an important step for many of these children," said Gwen. "We've seen it over and over again. They make up these adventures, and..."

Beth picked up on the narrative, "They don't usually tell them to us. Often just to one another when they don't know we're listening."

"And these are the very ones that improve the most rapidly," said Doug. "Charlie, for instance..."

"Yes, Charlie," said Gwen. But she too was cut off.

"Come on, people. Do you honestly expect me to see Charles Emerson as one of your more stellar successes? A young man with perhaps two more homicides on his—I would say conscience but it's clear that is one thing the young man lacks utterly..."

"That is false and offensive." Doug no longer felt the need to contain his anger. "Charlie has never hurt a soul."

"And I suppose the recent incident at the Rhode Island School of Design is included in that," Colin hurled back.

"How do you know about what happened to Charlie in school?" Beth asked with more anger than she had intended.

"That is not the point," said Colin. "His devolvement into fantasy is the topic here, isn't it? It doesn't surprise me a bit to hear this from you. This house has a terrible influence on the inhabitants. And it's no wonder, this ornament to your reclusive perversion... You honestly believe his is the outcome by which you model your.... Oh, you're insane. That's right. You're crazy. What's more, I'm telling you you're a damn cult. Yes, the Branch Davidians of Western New Hampshire. And I'll be saying just this in my next report."

"Well we'll see who looks more foolish when that report is read."

"Do you remember what Brittney was like when she arrived here?" said Beth, ignoring with great effort the wandering sermon of the caseworker.

"She would hardly eat; wouldn't associate with any of the other children," said Gwen.

"She suffered nightmares, bedwetting," added Beth.

"That's my point," said Colin "She's improved much. And if you undermine all the work I've done with that child by allowing her to..."

"*You've* done," Doug exploded from his chair. Gwen was in front of him in a flash.

"We don't need that fight, Doug."

"Not now," Beth joined in with her sister-in-law.

"I should think not," said Colin. "This house is hanging on by a thread. You'll be fortunate to end up merely with a lost license. May I remind you that both criminal and civil action is pending on this operation? The sooner we can get these children out of here altogether..."

"I think the sooner you get out of OzHouse altogether, the safer we'll all sleep," Doug raged.

Colin smiled. "Perhaps if your brother were here to calm you down, you'd... By the way, where *is* your brother?"

"He's out," said Gwen.

"Still wandering about in the Land of Oz with Charles Emerson is he?" asked Colin.

"That does not fall within the compass of your job," Beth added.

"Nothing will get accomplished if we are not civil," Gwen admonished.

Brittney entered the Persian room, breaking the irate silence that followed this exchange. "Mr. Brinks," she said, "I forgot to tell you, all that stuff about Sponge Bob, it was just a joke."

"YOU'VE BEEN HERE BEFORE," said Glinda to Charlie as they and Suzy Bishop walked back and forth along the ramparts that ran the length of the high wall surrounding the Emerald City. Glinda was right. Charlie had been to Oz before, more than once, but he had never visited with any of the people made famous in the stories, had never seen Glinda before, even from afar. She surprised him. He'd of course read all about her; like everyone, he'd seen the movie. This strong woman was nothing like that frilly, giggling airhead from the movie. Nor was she exactly like the calmly controlling, gentle voice of adulthood, the quasi-parent he recalled from his reading. This woman was more direct and powerful; she maintained control, when trouble arose, she quickly intervened. Things were fixed immediately. The Glinda from the books was never confused. He thought the same was probably true in most cases with the woman before him. But if that was so in general, today was different. Today her power was not quite serving its accustomed function. Today, for the first time in who knew how long—perhaps ever—she really did not know what was going on. She exuded all the confidence anyone could muster, but Charlie could tell it was mostly out of habit. She really was afraid she'd make the wrong choice. Close up right now she seemed so—so real, so human. Wisps of auburn hair which had come loose under her headdress blew across her face in the cool wind. The great volume of material in her robes caught the wind too. She walked away from him to get a better look at the confusing scene in the field below. And her step was tense and uncomfortable. The long dress impeded her easy movement. When she looked at him her face was both stern and puzzled, if that were possible,— and something else too, something hard to read. Was she young or old? The skin was young, but the eyes were old and hard. The immortality the Land of Oz had granted her could not keep her mind from aging, and the mind was revealed in the eyes.

"Now, don't try to deny it," she went on, crossing back to him. "I've studied the magic book daily for years. Your name has come up in it now and again. Still, I know that you have not only been here before, but you have been to a great number of fairylands."

"Why would I deny it?" He looked straight at her, calm and easy. He understood that she'd pulled him aside as the one in the group with the best chance to give her the information she might need in order to understand what was going on, and also because she still suspected that he more than anyone else was responsible for the whole mess. Why she'd asked Suzy along, he could not tell. Perhaps she thought the girl could help her to understand Charlie or could feed her some information she could use to get him to talk. The sorceress seemed to expect he'd be less forthcoming, less frank, and more in awe of her power.

"And I believe you have gotten to know one or more of the inhabitants very well."

Charlie immediately thought of Cinderella. "How much information does that book of yours include?"

"Enough," she said sternly. "*You* did this." And she waved her arms out as if to include the whole land of Oz in her gesture. Charlie recalled how the police interrogated him years ago. They told him they knew—they had evidence enough to put him away—they knew what he'd done to Suzy. They did it so well; if he had done something he was sure he'd have cracked.

"*I* did this?" he chuckled.

"Charlie?" said Suzy, surprised. "All he did was visit." If Charlie was involved, if innocent visiting could do this, was Suzy on trial here too?

"Whether alone or not, I cannot say." Glinda looked down at Suzy. "But the more I contemplate the whole thing, the more it comes down to him."

"If only you could send me home," Charlie lightly mocked.

"I no longer think that sending you home by itself would do it. The doors are wide open." She looked again at the array of creatures surrounding the city.

Charlie too gazed over the ramparts. So many creatures were down there, so many kinds of evil. And so disorganized. Whatever good creatures may have crossed into Oz they had not made it to the Emerald City. No heroes among them. And perhaps that was just as well. Oz was no fit place for the final battle of good against evil. The forces amassed around the city had no leaders at the moment: the orcs did not seek help from the giants, the giants did not look to the witches. The powerless ifrit sat alone. The Nome King and a few of his nomes—old Ruggedo after all these failed attempts finally at the gates of the city—they huddled in what must have been fear behind all the others. But there were indications that the dynamics were changing. A bevy of harpies were parlaying with a shipload of pirates. Two men who may have been Shahryar and Shah Zaman were conferring with the Queen of Hearts and an evil stepmother. Was the evil organizing? Would it break into mutual destruction or would it unify and sack the helpless city?

There was no telling. For now, at least, the disorderly siege had been halted. The newly reinforced doors were proving difficult to shatter. Another group of the evil ones was now gathered around the seemingly abandoned wardrobe that stood outside the walls. The door of that wardrobe, which, on the hill, Charlie had seen open and quickly close, was now open again. But if anyone was coming through, Charlie could not tell. As usually happened, the wardrobe came into this world back first: with its back doors exposed and its front opening in some other world. Charlie saw two or three of the magical creatures climb in through the door—and disappear.

"You don't know that I caused this," said Charlie, looking back at Glinda.

"You used to make quite regular trips through the portal, did you not?"

He certainly had. Sometimes for an hour, sometimes for days at a time. Hardly a day went by for years when he didn't travel somewhere.

"Restless boy," said Glinda. "You've littered these portals all over."

"Is that what you think happened?"

"You invade one world after another, leaving your open doors behind you. Your visits have broken the walls." And then she looked at Suzy. "That is what happens, isn't it? You too have some experience with the magical doorway."

265

"Pinocchio did not come through a portal." Suzy did not know what else to say.

"I don't know that I'm taking credit for this," Charlie began.

"Blame," said Glinda.

"Look," Charlie continued, "even if I am responsible in some way, I don't see why travel between the worlds is such a bad thing."

"Not a bad thing?" exclaimed Suzy, standing on her tip toes, looking down over the wall. She turned to Charlie, "You can't say that. Look at what is happening!"

Charlie kept his eyes on Glinda. "If you hadn't put all your power into holding everything else out all these years, maybe they wouldn't be beating down the doors."

Glinda rolled her eyes. "Okay. Let's just ignore the fact that the Emerald City is under attack. Just look: the Wogglebug is dying. The Tin Man too—he's actually starving to death. Worlds change when they mix."

"Pinocchio thinks he can help the Tin Man," said Charlie.

So he had said soon after he arrived and heard of the problem. No one had any idea how the living marionette had gotten into Oz. He himself did not know. He and his whole company had just appeared at the gates of the Emerald City at the same time that Gary and Charlie and the wizard had made a run for the entrance. Seeing the evil creatures distracted by the wardrobe, they'd had a pretty easy time sneaking down to the entrance, where, to their good luck, Scraps was just opening the gate in order to slip out to talk with the evil creatures. (The wizard easily forced her light body back behind the gates but had a far more difficult job keeping the determined and fearless crazy quilt from charging back out as soon as he had set her down: "No need to endanger yourself right now; they're not attacking," he'd told her. "But I must find out what they want," Scraps replied. Charlie had finally dissuaded her by saying, "But once they see your tremendous beauty, we'll never get them out of Oz."

"That's beside the point," Glinda went on, "healing Nick would not take care of the Wogglebug. Nor would it alter the fact that the mixture of the worlds is the worst possible event in a magical world like Oz."

But Charlie was not convinced. "If the Wogglebug dies, I'm sorry," he said. "Death happens everywhere else in the world. I think you find it a little more horrible than we do. It has its advantages. You still may in the end be better off in contact with other places than without it. If you don't make contact with other peoples, if you don't visit other places or read other people's stories, you stagnate. That's what I think. And I

266

think there are ways of dying much worse than what the Wogglebug is going through."

"I do not believe he would agree with that." And then in a moment she added, "What a strange young man. I suppose you think the loss of all our power is a gift as well? I can see we will need to get you out of here as fast as we may."

"The transformation of your powers, the adaptation…"

"Oz needs to stay as it was," said Suzy, wondering what side that put her on. Was she condemning herself to return—and Dorothy too, and the wizard and the Shaggy Man, and anyone else who was from outside? Or was she just helping Glinda clean the realm of all the trouble Charlie had caused?

"It can't," said Charlie.

But Glinda had heard all she cared to of the headstrong youth from another world. She pointed her wand directly at him, and he knew she wanted him quiet. And though few adults had ever had the power to still Charlie's tongue when he was in a mood, and although at this moment Glinda had no magic at all to support the gesture, he quieted as suddenly as if Glinda's magic were fully working and she had cast a spell on his mouth.

"I did not bring you here to debate Oz policy. That is set by Ozma with my advice and that of her most trusted Oz subjects. Unnaturalized foreigners have not been consulted since the disastrous days of the wizard's rule. I still think the problem is greater than this wardrobe portal. But if that thing is involved in any way, I wonder if you two can tell me any more about it."

Smiling, Charlie obediently and calmly repeated what he understood: that the wardrobe originated in his world, served as a portal to and from fairylands and that it could not—as a rule—be used by adults, himself and Gary notwithstanding. "I didn't realize until just now that the things remained behind after we went back," he said.

"The backside always works," Suzy added. "You can never be sure the front side will take you out of your own world, but the backside always takes you home."

Glinda looked down at the wardrobe and the hordes of foreign creatures surrounding it. "There goes another one," she said as, at just that moment, a very large orc leaped in through the door and disappeared.

"Then the first thing we need to do is get them all through the door, and then you and your friends and those almost Oz-like creatures who showed up with you—Pinocchio and the one who was so reluctant to tell us his name."

Just then a loud reverberation like the sound of an explosion caused Charlie and Suzy to start and dive down to safety behind the wall. Unused to personal danger, Glinda stood erect and did not flinch, but turned her head toward the sound to see the second blow of a giant's club and the splintered wardrobe spread out like a blanket on the grass. Up rose the shouting and laughter of the hordes fighting or singing or dancing around the mess.

AFTER INTERROGATING SUZY and the oddly dressed young man from Dorothy's country, Glinda, Suzy and Charlie met Ozma and the others in the princess's throne room. Ozma refused to leave the side of her dear friend, the Tin Woodman. The evil creatures had, for now, stopped pounding at the gate. But probably they would resume their barrage before long. Even so, Ozma could not leave her friend. Too weak to talk, too weak even to move, he lay on a couch in her throne room. Big drops of oil dripped from his joints. Not even a siege on the Emerald City could draw her away at such a time. She watched anxiously as Pinocchio leaned over the couch and spoke carefully into his ear. It was hard to understand how he could be so weak only hours since he had felt the first hunger pang.

"All those years of not eating," said Dorothy to those in the room who were not hovering over their sick friend: Scraps, Rumpelstiltskin, Jessica, Buddy, Gary, and the wizard. The Wogglebug seemed to be asleep on the throne.

"Yes, that's very likely," said the wizard. "But what makes Pinocchio think he can help?"

"He always thinks he can do anything," said Jessica.

"And why is the Tin Man the only one who is having this problem: not you, Scraps, or the Scarecrow?" asked the little wizard. "None of you have ever eaten. But you're not hungry."

"Well, that's just it," said the Wogglebug, never opening his eyes. "You've *never* eaten. But he, as Nick Chopper, ate every day until he was transformed. I imagine elsewhere in Oz any creature who was once made of meat and now is not is suffering just like poor Nick."

"Pinocchio was never real," said Dorothy.

"Yes, but he does eat," said Jessica. And then she added, "a lot. And he will be real, some day." She wasn't sure whether that last part was relevant.

"What?" said Pinocchio, "Would everyone please speak up!" yelled the little wooden puppet. "Why is everyone whispering?"

"No one is whispering, little boy," said Ozma.

"What? What did you say?" Pinocchio shouted, shaking his head back and forth.

"She said no one is whispering," Charlie repeated more loudly.

"If you're in the habit of moving you lips, I would think you'd let some sound out," said Pinocchio.

"Why can't he hear us?" asked Gary. "He could hear just fine a moment ago.

"I've seen rabbits with better tricks," yelled Pinocchio, "birds, snakes, rats with practical jokes funnier than this. Why isn't anyone talking? This is no time for jokes. Do you want me to fix your friend or not?"

"I hear *him* just fine," Charlie said.

Pinocchio looked around the room at the curtains flapping in the wind, at the people talking among themselves in corners. The puppet knocked on the Tin Man's hollow chest. Nothing was making any noise. "Well that's something," he said out loud. He put both hands on his head and spun it all the way round. Then he lifted it up and down on the peg of his neck as though he were trying to get the sound to work its way through. "Can you guys hear?" And then, "What have you done to me?"

"I see the problem," said Glinda calmly. "Someone get me a pencil please."

On Glinda's orders, Charlie and Gary held the struggling wooden puppet as still as they could as sorceress drew a small, uneven ear on the side of his head.

"Can you hear us now?" asked Charlie.

"Stop shouting at me," Pinocchio yelled.

"Sorry, I was too close to your ear."

"I don't have ears," replied the puppet.

"You do now," Glinda explained. "One anyway. I just drew it on. In Oz you need ears to hear."

"But he didn't need ears before," said Jessica.

"Draw me another one," said Pinocchio, turning his head to Glinda. "And make it neat, please. Gepetto should've carved me some. It has never been a problem before. Oz magic is strange."

"The magic is changing," said Glinda. "Turning on and off."

"Like a loose wire," said Gary.

"Needing ears to hear doesn't seem so strange to me, sort of makes sense really," Charlie remarked more to Gary as the puppet turned his attention once again to the Tin Man.

"What are you going to do?" asked Dorothy.

"I'm going to remind him how to eat," said Pinocchio. "Look, I'm made of wood, and I eat all the time. I even go to the bathroom."

"Don't be vulgar," said Jessica.

"Why?" asked Pinocchio. But he didn't wait for an answer. "It's not that he *can't* eat. He's just forgotten how. It's been ages and ages since he last ate." And with that Pinocchio took a piece of cake from a tray recently ordered by Ozma (and dutifully delivered by Jellia Jamb) and put it a little piece at a time into the Tin Man's mouth while Ozma worked the jaw.

"More precisely," said the Wogglebug, who seemed still to be speaking from the depths of sleep, "now that Pinocchio is in Oz the magic that allows him to eat is here as well. Until he arrived, the Tin Man could not eat—not cake or carrots or anything at all. Now that that magic is here, he can."

"How *did* you get here?" Dorothy asked Jessica.

"I don't know."

"We were just walking, and here we were," said Pinocchio, who seemed to have a remarkable ability to concentrate on what he was doing while listening very closely to all that was being said around him.

"That's impossible," said the wizard. "There had to be magic involved, a belt, or one of those portals or something."

"Yes," Dorothy confirmed, "you don't just walk across the Deadly Desert without knowing it."

"The worlds are mixing badly," said Glinda.

"Well I don't know anything about that," said Rumpelstiltskin, who, until now had taken no interest in any of the proceedings. He had in fact been walking around the large green room, hand in hand with Buddy, admiring all the elegant furniture, artwork, and artfully arranged decor. "That's just what we did," the dwarf continued, "walked and walked and then here we were. None of us has had the slightest idea since yesterday where on earth we were."

"Hey, a gump head," yelled Buddy, "just like in the secret room."

And as soon as he said this—pointing as he spoke at the trophied head of the deer-like creature mounted on the wall—the head moved. From the time they'd entered the room until now it had not moved so much as an eyelash—and if the truth be known, not for many years prior to that, being a rather unfriendly, indeed grumpy creature who preferred to talk to no one and to whom no one wished to talk. But now the gump head looked directly down at Buddy and brought its eyes forward and narrowed them, "Just like?" it mocked. "There is not another mounted gump head *just like* mine in this vast universe. And you, little foreign child," it went on, "are the very definition of impertinence."

The Wogglebug sighed deeply but determined not to waste energy in arguing semantics.

Buddy jumped back in fright. And while Rumpelstiltskin patted the boy's head in hope of comforting him, Jessica ran over to Buddy and hugged him—as the gump, now that the sluice of his vocal chords had been unclotted, went on and on about his own uniqueness, the ignorance of every being in the room—not excepting even the Wogglebug whose theories could not account for his own lack of hunger and....

"That's enough," yelled Jessica to the gump head.

"Oh, and I suppose little foreign head number two is going to tie shut the defenseless gump's mouth," laughed the gump. "Can't hear the truth, eh?"

"The truth," said Ozma without looking up from her task of moving Nick Chopper's jaw—into which the food was, somehow, disappearing, despite the lack of throat or stomach—"the truth is that you will stop talking now on the order of the Princess Ozma."

"And if I don't?" said the gump.

"There is no 'if I don't,' gump. You know that."

And the gump, as though it were an imitation of the electric version of itself mounted in the Narnia room, turned itself off.

"My theory," said the Wogglebug, again without raising his head, "is that once the worlds have started to mix, they may cross one another in any number of ways. Coming from Ev or Mo or any country contiguous to our own, you would have to cross the Deadly Desert, but coming from any other world..."

"Hey, the Tin Man moved," yelled Pinocchio. "He's chewing on his own."

"He did," said Ozma, smiling down at her friend

"And the banging has resumed at the city gates," said Gary.

And they all heard the sound.

CHAPTER 25

Sarahstiltskin
Grimms' Forest, South West

My Sarah:
You were right, my dear: everything gets strange when you're away from home too long. But I think some of the strangeness has come from the disruption in magic too. Can you feel it? Have your adventures these past few days been as outlandish as mine?

I'm sure you have wondered if this crazy time is what's kept me away so long. You're right about that too.

Where am I? you ask.

I am trying to find my way home from a land with the peculiar name of "Oz." (No, it's not an abbreviation. That's the whole of it.) You will want the whole story, but I am afraid I can't tell you more than this. It is all I know.

But that is not the main reason I am writing this letter. You will never believe our great fortune. Your Rumple, your honest and clever and hard-working Rumple, has accomplished what all the gold in Grimms' could never have managed. I have found us a child! At last. And not any child, a human—yes, human, as you always wanted. He calls himself

Buddy (I know it's a queer name, but we can change it). It is time for you to start making the bed.

I know what you will say, but don't worry. This time I am not relying on the promises of any one. And as for the guessing of my name— my one mistake with that rogue of a miller's daughter (who would have believed a woman with so little shrewdness could have found out my name!)—I will not be so swaggering this time. No deals! No deals!

The boy I have found has no mother to spoil our plans—or to lie or to cheat us. He seems a bright lad and is still young enough. Just as you hoped. Now, as soon as the magic is made right—I am certain the magic will soon be righted; these things always come around in time—as soon as the magic works, I will bear our new son home.

I have just one other obstacle: Buddy has a young guardian who seems determined to keep him away from us. She has the misguided idea that he "belongs" in her world. Whatever that means. But she is no blood relation. And I will not allow her to spoil our happiness.

I am sending this letter via dove. I found one here from our world; it tells me it knows a way back. I hope it reaches you quickly. If you do not get this in a day or so, send me a reply so I can try again.

Your devoted husband,
Rumple

"GWEN, PLEASE RELAX or you will make yourself ill. Can I get you a cup of tea?" Beth tried for the third time that night to calm her sister-in-law.

"No, thank you, and I went past making myself ill hours ago." Gwen dropped onto the painted chair in the noisy kitchen. A child rushed in and out of the brightly lit room oblivious to the plight of the adults. Gwen continued putting words to her fears. "Where could they be? Gary would never take off without telling me. He must know how on edge I've been since this whole fiasco started. He wouldn't just take off. I know he wouldn't."

"But he did," Beth said in as soothing a voice as she could manage. "And, let's face it, he can be a little oblivious about such things. Nor are you the quickest to reveal your feelings. Let's be honest. He left without saying a word. We know this. Question is, why? He and Charlie must be up to something. Maybe they have found some clues and they are simply following them up."

"If they were simply following some scheme of his, he would have told me he wouldn't be back. Or he would have called... unless..." She paused as too many terrible thoughts rushed through her mind.

"Unless he planned to be right back and something has happened to prevent him from getting home."

"Maybe his car broke down. He never takes a cell phone with him."

"None of the cars is missing. That's the first thing I checked. Could they have gone trekking in the woods and gotten lost? I doubt it. He and Charlie could map this whole area of trails and dirt roads. If one of them fell and got hurt, the other would have come back to get help. Could they both have gotten hurt and neither be able to come back for help?" Gwen rubbed her face as if to erase all the awful possibilities.

"We could imagine positive and wonderful things that might have happened as easily as terrible ones," Beth said, sounding more like her sister-in-law than her usual self. "Maybe they located Buddy and Jessica and the trip back was too long for the small children so they decided to camp out in the woods, and they'll be here early tomorrow." Beth saw the look of disbelief on Gwen's face and tried to quickly think of a more likely scenario. After a few stammering false starts she admitted it wasn't *as* easy to imagine good things, but the rewards were far greater and worth the trouble. Gwen nodded her agreement without any conviction.

"Any news about Gary or Charlie?" asked a seemingly cheerful Doug as he entered the kitchen.

"Why do people always ask questions like that?" sighed Gwen mostly to herself. "If there had been any news, wouldn't we be sitting in a room filled with positive energy and glowing with relief? Do we look like we are glowing with relief?"

Doug almost replied with his usual candor that they would only be glowing with relief if the news were good, but this wasn't the time for levity.

"We are falling behind schedule," Beth said. "It's half past nine. The children should all be in bed by now. I'll take the girls from the first floor and. "

"I just put Brittney and Samantha to bed," said Doug. "I found them poking around the wardrobe. I suppose Brittney couldn't keep it secret enough. It was a bit like herding cats getting them and Lauren and Sarah from the Lookinglass Room to bed, but it's way past their bedtimes, so I used my stern voice."

"Worked like a charm, I'm sure," said Beth.

"I'll see to Morris and Roland," Gwen said with no emotion as she stood up. Beth was about to offer to do it, but then realized it might be good for her to keep busy and have other things on her mind.

275

As Gwen left the kitchen, Doug whispered to Beth, "Neither of them is a minor, so we do not have to report them missing unless we want to. I think it best to not complicate things right now. When this mystery is all sorted out, I'm sure we'll laugh about all the horrors we imagined."

"You think?"

"Sure. We'll pull the rubber mask off Colin and reveal who is really behind all these mysteries and Shaggy and Scooby will make an inane joke. The canned laughter will be deafening."

As usual, Beth only half understood her American husband's humor, but his seeming lack of worry encouraged her.

"THANK YOU FOR THE RIDE HOME Mr. Brinks, oh, I mean Colin, dear; I hope it wasn't too far out of your way."

"Not at all, Becky, not at all. I appreciate your stopping by the office to go over these papers. I will be meeting tomorrow with your attorney to help with the charges against the Robbinses and their absurd half-way house."

"Are you sure I shouldn't be there also?" the woman asked as she closed the shiny Volvo door.

"I know how busy you are. With these signed papers and your power of attorney I will have no trouble taking care of these matters; you can be sure."

"But *I* get the money?" she cut in.

"Of course. Of course. As Jennifer's social worker, it would be a conflict of interest for me to pursue the Robbinses in my own name. The money will be all yours. The satisfaction on the other hand will be all mine."

"And Jessica?" said the woman with extra emphasis on the name.

"What? Oh, yes, of course, Jessica. I meant Jessica; she'll be back home, too. Goes without saying. I do hope you enjoyed the dinner."

"Never had that fancy ethnic food before, but it was pretty good once you got used to it. What was it I had?"

"Pork Egg Foo Young. I'm surprised you've never eaten Chinese."

"We don't usually go to places we don't know. Money's kinda tight, you know. But not for long, eh, Brinksy?"

Colin cringed at the nickname. "I'll know more tomorrow. Good night, Rebecca. Would you like me to walk you to your door?"

"Nah, I'm still sober. Those fruity drinks with the rude names had hardly any kick. Talk to you soon."

276

Colin Fuller-Brinks pulled away from the curb happy to be rid of his evening companion but surprised she hadn't invited him in.

As Rebecca Holton fumbled with her keys to open the weather-worn door to her duplex, it suddenly popped open and she scurried inside.

"Careful, Bill. Don't let that Brinks idiot see you. You're not supposed to be within 100 yards of me, my kids, or this house."

"Yeah, yeah, I know," Bill slammed the door. He grabbed Rebecca's shoulders in a not-too-delicate grip and asked, "So? When do we get the money?"

"We'll know tomorrow," she replied pulling herself free and removing her coat.

"You sure this social worker's not screwing us over? If he is...."

"Patience, Billy." She gave him a kiss. "He meets with a lawyer tomorrow. It won't be long."

"LET GO OF MY ARM OR I'LL CLOCK YOU ONE," Scraps said through gritted pearl teeth.

"If I let you go, you'll rush straight into the crowd of ruffians and evil-doers and we won't be able to protect you," the wizard explained as he continued to hold tight to the cotton-filled arm.

"Don't say I didn't warn you," smiled Scraps as she grabbed a large book from a table and slammed it against the wizard's head, knocking his top hat across the room.

Before anyone could even help the little man up, the Patchwork Girl had cartwheeled out of the room and down the hallway. Sliding down the banister, she looked more like a child at an amusement park than a woman on a perilous mission. The hoard of evil creatures had finally succeeded in smashing through the emerald-studded wooden doors of the city and was marching toward the palace.

"Someone please stop her," the wizard cried as Jellia Jamb helped him up. "She has no idea what she is getting herself into."

Gary and Charlie rushed out of the room after Scraps; they were immediately joined by a group of creatures so strange the two humans almost stopped running to look at them. From an adjourning room came the Scarecrow of Oz in his blue, faded, straw-filled clothes. He stumbled along, knocking over a small end table, scattering the little bottles and vases that had been decoratively placed upon it and tripping on the edge of a fancy scatter rug. Behind him came Jack Pumpkinhead; his lanky limbs made from pegged willow branches clicking and clacking as he rushed along. A square, blue, dog-like creature that Gary remembered was called the Woozy passed all the rest and was halfway down the long alabaster hallway before Scraps had reached the bottom of the staircase. There was even a tall frog-like man dressed in fine golden silks and velvets who, had he hopped, could have easily caught up to Scraps. However he seemed to prefer moving in the more cumbersome manner of a gentleman, swinging a gold-tipped cane and carefully balancing a silk top hat between his bulging eyes. He had little chance of reaching the crazy quilt woman before she left the building.

"Jeremy Fisher?" asked Charlie.

"I don't think so. Ozite," Gary puffed, "Frogman, I think he's called."

The look of amazement that Gary gave Charlie as the motley crew joined them made the young man smirk and say, "Toto, I have a feeling we're not in Kansas anymore."

"You got that right." Gary rounded the corridor, grabbed the banister, and started down the stairs.

By the time they were half way down, Scraps had left the palace and was outside rushing along the marble inlay path toward the ferocious crowd now marching on the building.

There were muscular giants and hairy horned trolls. There were snarling orcs carrying spears and there were screeching harpies. Werelions were growling and jumping about on the balls of their feet. Pig-faced ogres banged their heavy cudgels on the ground and pawed at the dust with their cloven feet. Right into the midst of these creatures ran Scraps, waving her arms and calling to them to stop and listen to her.

"No one here is to blame," she yelled. "We are in just as much danger and confusion as you."

The whole procession stopped. They gripped tight their weapons and turned in on the gaily smiling rag doll.

"We feared as much," snarled one of the trolls. "Won't Ozma or Glinda help us?" added a giant.

"W…what?" asked Scraps.

"They seem to want to know if Ozma or Glinda can help them," repeated Charlie as he, Gary, and the Woozy came to a stop next to the Patchwork Girl.

"I heard them. I just wasn't expecting them to say anything like that," Scraps said, pulling on her brown yarn hair.

"Even in our far-away lands we have heard rumor of the powerful sorceress. We came here to ask for help. Surely Glinda holds no prejudice against us. And with all the magic at her command she can surely undo these terrible things," a harpy screeched as she landed on the shoulder of a red-bearded giant.

"They thought you were attacking," Gary explained as Charlie nodded.

"Please," said an orc. "Give us a little credit. Ozma has never been a threat to us, nor have we ever meant her any harm. We are not ignorant savages who blame innocent people when misfortune befalls us. Well, perhaps some of the giants are a bit impetuous and may have caused a little damage."

"I think an ogre burned down a farmer's home in the Quadling country," added the harpy.

"Okay, yes, they did that, but for the most part we came here for help. With such a diverse population, one must expect a few mishaps," the orc explained.

"I think Oz has gotten to them," whispered Gary. "Something in the air."

"Not much like I pictured them," Charlie whispered back. "He has a better vocabulary than you."

"It seems some of us have jumped to conclusions and treated these people with great disrespect," Scraps announced as she flopped to the dusty ground. "Granted, their manners when pounding on the doors and terrorizing the locals may leave a little to be desired, but who am I to criticize when someone does things her own way?"

"Very philosophical of you Scraps," smiled the Woozy as the Scarecrow, Jack, and the Frogman arrived.

"We demand to see Ozma," said an ogre sternly as he waved his heavy club.

"No! Glinda," added several shaggy headed giants. A skirmish broke out as ogres, orcs and giants yelled and swung at each other.

"I don't know if either of them can actually help you, but why don't a bunch of you come with us and you can talk to them both," shouted Gary stopping the argument before any one got hurt and before the Ozites could even speak.

"So that's the magic of Oz?" said Charlie.

"Where else in all of fairyland would these guys act like this?" said Gary. "Not to mention paying attention to you when you shout at them. Half the time we can't even get the kids at OzHouse to pay attention."

Deciding who would accompany them to meet with Ozma and Glinda was done with not a few more arguments and physical attacks. Two ogres were knocked to the ground and bleeding, and a werelion jumped on the back of a harpy and bit her head. But eventually, with the help of Gary, Charlie, Scraps and the Woozy a group of ten was chosen.

"I'll show you the way," declared Scraps who was not quite as disturbed as the other Ozites by the violence. The Scarecrow was speechless. Jack Pumpkinhead had pulled back in fear and was holding his delicate pumpkin to protect it. The Frogman had ducked behind a small fruit tree as the fighting became more violent. The brave Woozy had held his ground, ready to protect anyone that might have needed it.

The Patchwork Girl marched back to the palace leading the way swinging her cotton-filled arms, spinning around and occasionally hopping on one foot.

"Didn't we have a kid at OzHouse who acted like her?" Charlie asked Gary as they followed Scraps toward the marble staircase. The Woozy, The Scarecrow, Jack, and the Frogman stayed with the group, hoping to keep them from getting violent again or at least to keep them out of the flowerbeds.

"You mean Raymond? The little boy with autism?" Gary frowned at Charlie.

"He used to spin all around the *Cinderella Ballroom*. Kinda drove some of us nuts."

With a good-natured smack Gary said, "Remind me to sign you up for more of Gwen's *Appreciating Diversity* classes."

"Oh, please, no. I'll be good. Those classes are killers. Maybe we'll get lucky and never find the way home. Then, at least, I won't have to deal with Brinks, those morons in my painting class, or Gwen's sensitivity classes."

"Oh, we'll get home; don't you worry about that. No one is going to stay here in fairyland once we fix things up," Gary said as they walked down the hallway toward Ozma's throne room.

Charlie considered calling Gary on his childish faith in happy endings, but they had far too many other things to consider as they hurried through the palace.

The ten delegates had already gone in, and the Soldier with the Green Whiskers closed the door just as Charlie and Gary reached it.

"Guess we're not invited," laughed Charlie.

"Ozma is limiting the number of people in the room so the visitors won't feel overwhelmed," explained a young girl sitting on the window seat. "She asked Jessica and Buddy and the little man with them to take a tour of one of the gardens, and only a few councilors were asked to remain."

"Thank you for explaining that," smiled Gary. "I was starting to feel like the Oz folk aren't too keen on us mere mortals. In the books they seemed to welcome people with open arms, but Chuck and I didn't exactly get the red-carpet treatment."

"Try not to judge them too harshly," said the girl. "Things are pretty scary right now. Once we get things under control, I'm sure they'll treat you a lot nicer."

"I suppose," sighed Charlie.

"Are you a native Ozite?" Something in her voice made Gary ask.

"Don't you recognize her," said Charlie. "It's Suzy Bishop."

"Don't be crazy," Gary said. "Suzy would be a teenager by now at least and..."

"It's her. It's Suzy. We've already met. Glinda brought her along for the interrogation."

"You do look familiar..." Gary looked hard at the girl.

"I am Suzy," she told him flatly. "It's Oz." It was all the explanation she was going to give him. The "my how you haven't grown" surprise was clearly wearing off.

"Oh, right. People don't age here."

"I didn't get to say this before, Charlie, but you look a lot different. Are rings in your eyebrow the fashion these days back in New Hampshire?"

"Not much is ever in *fashion* in New Hampshire," laughed Charlie. "But in the rest of the country and at RISD, this would be considered quite tame."

"I can't believe it's you after all this time," Gary added. "I see you're talking more."

"After Charlie yelled at me, that pretty much got the words flowing for good."

"Sorry about that." Charlie took a breath. "But..."

"It's okay. I mean, it could've gone either way. You scared the bejeepers out of me, for sure. Almost shut me up for good. But it turned out okay."

"So why didn't you come back?" asked Gary. "We were worried sick about you. They tried to put Charlie in jail." Gary found looking at little Suzy Bishop as bizarre as looking at a pumpkin-headed man or a giant frog wearing human clothes.

"Why didn't I come back? Hmmm? Let's see. I could return to a violent world where the few living members of my family couldn't be bothered with me, where horrible men who drink too much plough their trucks into innocent families and kill most of the passengers in their cars and then don't even get punished, *or* I could stay in a land of beauty and kindness, where no one dies or gets sick and where I was made to feel not

281

just welcome but desired. Shouldn't take a rocket scientist. And I had no idea about Charlie."

"But we were worried about you," repeated Gary. "People thought you had been killed or kidnapped or God knows what."

"Pretty selfish of me, I guess, but I was eight years old. Besides, the problems I might have temporarily caused you really couldn't compare to the joy I have experienced all these years." But she didn't sound terribly joyful.

"Yes, and..." said Charlie.

"Well, you heard her. I don't know how well you've read the books, but Glinda can be kind of aloof and mysterious. She doesn't just talk to anyone anytime they want to see her. She kind of hobnobs with the wizard and Ozma—that sort."

Charlie didn't understand; neither did Gary.

"You heard her," Suzy repeated. "I think she's trying to find a way of sending me back." And when Charlie looked dumbfounded, she added. "I got here the same way you did."

Gary found it fascinating to hear such words from a child who still looked no more than nine-years old. "But wouldn't that be for the best, really? I know it's hard. But that's where you're from, your own world. Isn't that really where you belong?"

"Not everyone gets to live in OzHouse, Gary," Charlie pointed out.

"I don't want to leave," Suzy insisted. "I belong here now."

Gary remained doubtful.

"That doesn't mean it's always easy. There was the time I was captured by the Hammerheads for a day and the time Trot and I got lost in the Blue Forest for almost a week and had to subsist on nuts. Those times I was a little frightened. But, overall, it's been truly wonderful. In fact it has been pretty much years of pure joy. Of all the worlds I found, Oz is best suited to supplying me with everything your world had seemed determined to make sure I never experienced." Suzy looked directly at Gary. "When you figure out where you belong, I think you should stay there." Then she hopped off the window seat and approached Gary and Charlie.

"You were very young," said Gary. "You didn't give our world much of a chance."

"All I had seen of life was death and horror, and misery, and I just didn't want to see any more of that. Here in Oz I found peace and acceptance. That's the magic here, you know."

"Yeah," Charlie said. "I think that's why I never really took to the books"

"Oh, you'd like it here, Charlie, once you got used to it. Here being unique isn't just okay; it's preferred. You can't be too unique." And then she paused. "Well, maybe Scraps, but she revels in being the oddball among oddballs. I tried to live in other worlds at first. They're all just like OzHouse..."

Gary started to defend what they did at OzHouse, but Suzy stood on tiptoes and placed her little fingers on his mouth and said. "No, don't do that. You were preparing people to live in your world. And you all did it with love and caring. But I had decided not to live there, so it didn't apply to me. I think what you and Gwen and Beth and Doug do is great. The way you helped Darren, the little boy who had been burned in the fire, or the way you worked with Cynthia, the little girl who had that large port wine stain on her face, was perfect—in your world."

"Darren?" Gary had to think a moment to recall the boy. Cynthia too. Darren had left them to be adopted almost six years ago, and Cynthia had been put into a foster home and eventually her new family had moved to California.

"So you left your own world for this perfect place but you kept tabs on all of us?" Charlie smiled.

"You guys were the only family I remembered, at least the only ones still alive. I didn't want to live there, but I sorta felt like I needed to have some ties to my own world. Sounds stupid, huh?"

Gary didn't think it sounded stupid exactly.

"It sounds perfectly logical to me," said Charlie.

Gary thought it was mostly just running away.

"Would you ever want to come and visit?"

"I was just there." Suzy rolled her eyes.

JESSICA WATCHED A WHITE BIRD that seemed to have something in its beak circle around the head of Rumpelstiltskin and then take off for the sky. The dwarf was sitting on the edge of an ornate fountain with a statue of Ozma in the center. Buddy was in front of him, playing with a legion of little mice.

"What was that?" she asked curiously, pointing to the dove as she approached the dwarf.

The dwarf didn't seem to hear her. "The mice are waiting for word from their queen," he said as though she'd asked him why Buddy was being permitted to frolic with rodents. "Not much like the mice in your world—or mine for that matter."

Buddy was talking to the mice and laughing at their jokes, and one of the mice parents was warning the boy to play carefully and not to crush the children.

"Do you think we can we go back inside now?" Jessica asked.

"How should I know? Seems like we was just dumped like a bunch of old trash."

"I'm not trash," shouted Buddy louder than he needed to.

"No, you are not," exclaimed Rumpelstiltskin. "You are a fine young man. These Oz folk don't seem to know how to treat a visitor."

"You might be being a bit too hard on them, you know," said Jessica. "They have a lot on their minds right now."

"Or he might not be being hard enough," came a familiar voice from the green marble wall that surrounded the garden.

Jessica looked up and smiled. A familiar face sat tottering atop the wall, his thin legs hanging uselessly over the edge. "Humpty Dumpty," she shouted as she ran to the spot at the wall just under the egg.

Rumpelstiltskin was not as pleased to see this new arrival for he feared the forester might be with him, and the forester seemed like another rival for guardianship of Buddy. "Are you alone?" asked the grizzled little man.

The egg looked around in an exaggerated mock search of the area and then replied, "It would seem so."

"Can you get down?" Jessica asked.

"A question the answer to which it would not be worth it for me to suffer as I have neither need nor desire, nor, indeed, intention in that direction. I like this wall very much. It gives me a grand view of the garden and I never feel quite as safe as when I can see all sides. By the way you have some rather nasty looking characters amassed down in the direction of—well, pretty much everywhere outside."

"You are never quite safe up on a wall either," Jessica reminded him.

"Never claimed to be, then, did I? I said I don't feel safe down there, which I don't. Can't see that I left myself open to any criticism on that point."

"Pompous as ever," sighed Rumpelstiltskin. "Let's leave him and go back inside."

"Do you want us to leave you alone?" asked Jessica sadly.

"Never said I did," the egg replied. "However, if people are going to stuff my mouth with words, then I think I might prefer to be alone."

"I'm not putting words in your mouth," explained Jessica as Buddy, having played all he cared to with the mice, started to walk off with Rumpelstiltskin. "I only asked a question."

"Never been too keen on answering questions either." As the egg said this, he noticed Jessica starting to follow Buddy and the dwarf. He quickly amended his tone. "I am very much alone in this world. This place is nothing like Wonderland, you know. Except for you mortals from the outside world, no one here likes a good banter. Oz people are so matter of fact it is hard to find anything they say to take offence at."

"You said that like it was a bad thing." Jessica walked slowly back to the wall.

"Mental stimulation is requisite, especially when one is mostly a head."

Jessica almost mentioned that she thought of him as mostly a body, but she could imagine that leading into a drawn out discussion that would have pleased the egg but that she didn't have time for just then.

Buddy and Rumpelstiltskin reached the side door to the palace, and as they reached for the shiny knob, the door suddenly opened out and startled them.

Gary and Charlie had followed Suzy's directions hoping to find Jessica and Buddy and herded everyone back into the garden.

CHAPTER 26

Sarahstiltskin
Grimms' Forest, South West

My Sarah:
You were right, my dear: everything gets strange when you're
away from home too long...

Blah, blah, blah...

You will never believe our great fortune. Your Rumple, your
honest and clever and hard-working Rumple, has accomplished what all
the gold in Grimms' could never have managed. I have found us a child!
At last. And not any child, a human—yes, human, as you always wanted.
He calls himself Buddy (I know it's a queer name, but we can change it).

"'Change it?'" said Jessica out loud. "'We can change it?'"
Rumpelstiltskin tried to steal a baby from a princess before. Now he was
going to steal Buddy. Just thank God that dove brought this note to her—
although why it brought it to her, she had no idea.
"Reading other people's mail?" asked Humpty Dumpty, looking
down from his wall.

"What?" asked Jessica.

"I heard that dove as well as you did."

"It gave me the note." The bird had reminded her of the nightingale that she'd met—it seemed a long time ago—in the land of the Chinese emperor. She had no idea why she'd be attractive to birds.

"It was not your name it was calling."

That was true. It had circled her head making a sound that she now realized must have been "Sarahstiltskin, Sarahstiltskin" before it landed on her shoulder and she'd seen the letter in its beak and realized that this was the bird she'd seen flying away from the dwarf.

"You know as well as I do that you are not Sarahstiltskin," said Humpty Dumpty.

"I didn't know what it was saying?"

"Oh, yes. Now I see. As 'Sarahstiltskin' sounds so much like 'Meddlesomejessica' that you just naturally...."

"I didn't know it was a name," Jessica shouted. "And I'm glad I did it, anyway. He wants to steal Buddy."

"Tut, tut, tut," said the egg man putting his hands to his ears. I don't need to know the contents of other people's private letters. And then he lowered his hands and mumbled, "I wonder how he plans to do that."

And then Jessica thought of something. If they were trying to get to Rumpelstiltskin's house through the wardrobe, they'd have to go to OzHouse first. Because that's where it always took you. It's the middle of the wheel.

"Did these creatures all come through your front door?" asked Humpty Dumpty when she told him her thought. "Perhaps it only seems the center to you because whenever you use it, that's how it works. I would ask if you have a wheel with many hubs."

Perhaps that was true. Did it mean she was wrong about the wardrobe or that the wardrobe was broken? She didn't know. She did know she'd have to make sure that dwarf didn't get Buddy.

In the next moment, Jessica noticed the huge swan running toward her; it was one of a half dozen she had seen earlier grazing like cows on the lawn, then lifting their heads and hissing at one another as though they were talking. They had been there ever since Jessica had arrived in the garden.

The swan bolted toward her, or rather toward the letter in her hand; it stuck its long beak around the paper as though it were stealing a bite from a sandwich—and it pulled.

"Stop it," said Jessica angrily, "that's not food." The girl pulled the letter back, just managing to free it from the uncertain grasp of the fowl.

"I will not stop it," said the swan once its beak was free of the paper. "That's not your letter."

"Whose letter is it?" said Gary. Jessica turned to see Gary and Charlie walking calmly toward her.

"Rumpelstiltskin is planning to steal Buddy," said Jessica frantically. "I have to find him."

"Hang on, hang on, hang on," said Gary, putting his hand on Jessica's shoulder. "Even if that's so, there's hardly any place he could take him just now. Let me see that letter."

As Jessica handed the letter to Gary, the swan at her side lunged again. "That's not her letter," said the swan, just before the large bird grabbed it out of the air.

"Hey," yelled Jessica, almost falling over as she swiped at the air where the swan had been. Gary too grabbed for the letter. Charlie grabbed for the swan. They all missed, and the swan ran down the grassy incline, hopped into a pond at the bottom of the hill then spread its wings and took off over their heads. The bird was so large it seemed an awfully clumsy, lumbering process, getting into the air, as though it happened in slow motion. It rose like a lump that might come crashing down at any second. Yet with a few strained flaps of its wings, it gained speed and height and become suddenly out of reach and graceful. It flew close enough to Humpty Dumpty for him to touch it, but the egg man got himself out of the bird's way as dexterously as his rolly body allowed. Jessica looked up at him in disgust.

"Do you really imagine I would let a great big swan throw my fragile body off this high wall?"

"You'd be all right as soon as someone turned the page," Jessica called up.

"Less and less page turning every day as far as I can tell." And the egg man paced back and forth with his hands behind him.

Just then in a white whoosh a second swan darted past Jessica, down the slope, into the pond, and up into the sky. By the time it cleared Humpty Dumpty, it was able to gain speed with astonishing quickness for a bird so big—almost as large as an ostrich as far as Jessica could tell. It hurled itself toward its partner and, swift as could be—Jessica was more than astonished at the sight— plucked the letter out of the other swan's beak. Then it pivoted as if its wingtip were tied to a piece of sky and dived back down to the ground where the humans stood open mouthed. The first swan turned just as quick and charged after.

The second swan handed the letter to Gary as she plunked herself down. "Pardon my partner," she said, "quite the legalist."

"That is just like you, Ceeloh," the first swan said as soon as his feet touched the ground, "delivering a letter to someone to whom it was not addressed." Ceeloh's partner paced as he spoke in a way that somehow reminded Gary of Groucho Marx.

"Whatever made that dwarf think he could mail a letter between the worlds?" said Gary as he scanned the contents.

"Yes, Brayna, it *is* just like me," Ceeloh bantered back to her partner. "I do think saving a child from a kidnapping overrides the little question of a proper address."

"And I suppose it's up to you to decide what is and what is not a kidnapping," said Brayna.

"I suppose it is my job to use my God-given brains when the occasion arrives," said Ceeloh.

"She's right," said Gary, handing the letter to Charlie. "He wants to steal Buddy."

"So what are we going to do about it?" asked Jessica, nearly frantic.

"When the time comes, we will stop it from happening, of course," said Gary.

"When the time comes?"

"There's nothing we can do right now," said Charlie. "And it's not as though Buddy is unsafe in his company. And frankly, what's the big deal anyway? Buddy needs a father."

"But Rumpelstiltskin is a lying, kidnapping..." said Jessica.

"Don't worry, Jessica," said Gary. "We can't let him take Buddy."

"Don't you think we should think about that a little first?" Charlie asked. "The boy needs a family..."

"We can't abandon a human child in a fairy world. It's out of the question, Charlie."

"Perhaps we should ask Suzy's opinion before we decide that."

Jessica was unable to believe her ears. "We have to save Buddy. That was the whole point of the whole adventure."

"Think about it, Jessica," said Charlie. "What if he's better off..."

"Never mind that," said Gary. "And don't you worry, Jessica. We'll save Buddy. But for right now, it's probably best if we don't alert Rumpelstiltskin that we know what he's up to. That will only make him scheme all the harder. We've all read the story. We know how clever he is."

Humpty Dumpty paced back and forth between the turrets on the wall.

"Our job," said Brayna to Ceeloh, still ignoring the conversation playing among the humans, "is to do nothing more or less than what Glinda orders."

"Oh, and I suppose Glinda ordered you to rescue this letter from the nefarious fingers of these innocent humans?" Ceeloh charged right back.

Humpty Dumpty had to speak: "How can *innocent* humans have *nefarious* fingers?" he yelled.

"Shut up, yoke brains," yelled Brayna.

"Yeah, respect your elders," added Ceeloh.

"My elders?" questioned Humpty Dumpty.

"We're full grown swans," said Brayna.

"You're just an egg," added Ceeloh.

"Can you imagine what's going to hatch out of that thing?" asked Brayna.

"Twin Rocs from the look of him," Ceeloh replied.

"That will be enough," Humpty Dumpty huffed. "Not all eggs require hatching."

"True," remarked Brayna. "Some get fried up and buttered."

"We've got to rescue him right now," said Jessica.

"He'd feed half the Emerald City," Brayna said to Ceeloh.

"We weren't really going to eat him," said Ceeloh to Jessica.

"I meant, Buddy," said Jessica.

"How?" Gary asked.

"Ozma could help."

"Not likely. Even if she had the power or authority in this matter, I'm sure she has more urgent concerns at hand right now," said Charlie.

"If only there were someone who'd been to Oz before, someone who knew where a door was," said Humpty Dumpty as though no pair of swans had ever suggested he shut up.

"How would that help?" asked Jessica.

"They stay behind," Charlie told her. "When you go back through, the wardrobe door is still there. But they usually end up in such out of the way places. The ones we came through, it took most of the day just to get here..."

"And if someone wanted to take a little human boy with her before the evil dwarf..."

291

"Oh my, God," said Jessica, cutting Humpty Dumpty off. She looked at Ceeloh, "Can you help me?"

"At your service." And then Ceeloh looked appeasingly at Brayna. "At least until Glinda tells me otherwise."

Ignoring Gary, Jessica hopped onto Ceeloh's back.

"Where are you going?" yelled Brayna as Ceeloh ran down the hill into the pond and leapt into the air.

"Wherever she says," said Ceeloh.

"To get Buddy," yelled Jessica. "I've been here before. I think I know where a wardrobe is."

"You can't do that," yelled Brayna, leaping.

"Jessica, get back here," yelled Gary.

"This oughta be fun," said Charlie.

JACK PUMPKINHEAD'S PUMPKIN HEAD felt, he seemed to think, prematurely soft. It was difficult to be sure, however, because whenever it began to get soft, his thoughts started getting a little mushy. And then, he knew, or at least he usually knew, he had just a little while to get the head replaced while he still had seeds enough—or rather seeds fresh enough—to do the job of competently picking and carving himself a new one. It wasn't such an emergency, generally. True, once or twice it had happened that he had waited too long. Once he left his old head on so long that when he did manage to carve a new one his thoughts were so mushy that the face came out with the most uneven, most unpleasing expression: the eyes out of round, the nose like a poorly executed arrow tip, the mouth an awkward, crooked slash lost between silly and sinister. Just wearing it had made him look, feel, and see funny. He'd of course discarded it as soon as he'd managed to get a second one carved. But this had been a matter of days; he'd had to wait for a new head-pumpkin to ripen. And he'd had to spend those days locked away in his house, because, although he was not usually a vain creature, he was unwilling to be seen sporting such a disreputable countenance. Another time it had been even worse: he'd waited until his head was so far gone, he could not at first remember what it was he was supposed to be doing—standing like a bulb-headed scarecrow in the middle of his pumpkin patch—and then he couldn't remember anything at all. That time Ozma had found him planted in the mud like a dead tree; realizing with the swiftness for which she was so rightly renowned exactly what was wrong, she had herself chosen and carved for Jack a new head. He was of course grateful—once he'd come around and understood what had happened. But the head she'd chosen and the face she'd put on it, they were not what he would have chosen for

292

himself—nothing like the original head she had carved him back when she was Tip and he was just a prop designed to scare a witch. And because he knew it would seem unappreciative of him not to wear it for a period, he'd forced himself to wear Ozma's head some weeks before he could reasonably claim it was getting soft.

In the old days, that was the worst sort of thing that could happen; the worst case was always something he could pretty easily handle. Oz was beautiful that way. No harm could come to him. So, in normal times, finding just the right head in time was important, but it was not an emergency.

Now, having learned his lesson, Jack, without a moments' worry, habitually changed his head at the first sign of mushiness. But today, when the magic of Oz itself had grown mushy, everything was uncertain. Would a mushy old head outperform a new, ripe one?

Perhaps. But he wasn't going to wait to find out. No. He thought of those bad heads he'd been stuck with, or stuck to, in the past, and he resisted the temptation to wait until the magic of Oz was working as it should. He just had to hope. Yes, indeed, he had to; he did not want to wait for his thoughts to get mushy; he did not want to end up with a head he had to hide away. He did not want the kind of head that would give him thoughts that were green or half-baked. Whatever the risk, it was essential that he choose his own head, and that he do it while he still had one that worked.

And that was why he was on his way to Ozma's chambers where the magic picture hung. His head felt a little mushy.

Or was it because Glinda had said, "If you were Tik-Tok I'd say your thoughts need rewinding" when he'd suggested she could solve everyone's problem if she would just get out her magic book and read it backwards.

He had a vague memory of someone telling him the picture had suffered, like everything else, from the recent injury to the magic of Oz. But was that right? Everything was fuzzy today. The picture had always worked before.

And he needed it, he thought, for... for something. Yes, for something—to look for... something. To look—he remembered, how wonderful that he remembered—at his pumpkin patch to see if there was anything ready.

He found himself in front of the long picture in the ornate frame— what a pretty radium frame inlaid with scenes from the history of Oz.

But he mustn't waste time looking at frames! The picture itself in its neutral state revealed a plain enough view of the Emerald City; he asked it to show him his pumpkin patch.

Nothing happened. Did he remember how it worked? Or maybe it didn't work because he'd only thought of asking to see the pumpkin patch without actually asking. Or could it read his mind?

He could not remember. He asked again.

And the picture flickered. It did. And the moment it did, his head felt clear. And he touched his head, and it wasn't so terribly mushy. It should easily last another week or two. The mushiness was not in his head after all; *it was all in his thinking*—as though the general damage to the magic were affecting the power of the seeds in his magical brain. Oh, a lot of creatures would suffer if the effects of the powder of life that had brought them to consciousness wore off.

And he stood there wondering how he could have been so foolish as to think the broken picture would work at all. Yes, he was thinking much more clearly now, as though a little magic were getting fixed. But what had brought it back?

He asked again to see his pumpkin patch. The picture again sprang to life. But it showed him things he had not asked to see: a giant or an ogre or something evil smashing that wardrobe thing outside the city, and, at the same time, a giant egg with a face on it appearing—just poofing there by magic—upon the high wall of the city.

Something odd was happening. The picture was showing him things more urgent than ripe pumpkins. And his thinking remained clear long enough for him to understand that he needed to tell Ozma.

OZMA WAS IN THE THRONE ROOM when Jack Pumpkinhead lumbered in. Several others were there with her in the large hall, most of whom stood out for their oddness: the orcs and harpies and the evil-looking creatures he could not name; not the sort of thing one usually found in Oz. Jack was not delayed a moment by the guard however: He was Jack and Ozma was his father. That was that, and in he ran. Jack ignored everyone else and went straight for the throne.

The Princess of Oz was keeping the Tin Man close to her even though old Nick Chopper was doing so much better now that he'd learned or remembered how to eat. Ozma was also staying close to the Wogglebug. In fact, she had given the Wogglebug her throne, the most comfortable chair in the room. *He* was not doing at all well. His eyes were closed and he was emitting a low groan that suggested pain had invaded his unconscious body. He would not speak or open his eyes or even turn his head for anyone.

"Father," said Jack as he creaked his awkward body through the room. "Father, it worked. The picture worked—a little."

"Oh?" said Ozma, "and did you find any likely heads?"

"No pumpkin heads," said Jack, "but I did see a giant egg head."

"You would not look good in an egg head, Jack," said Nick.

"It showed up just at the same time that wardrobe portal thing broke," said Jack.

Nearby, Glinda stood consulting with an orc and a harpy and some other ugly foreigners. Having seen Jack arrive and having overheard his conversation, "Oh?" she said, in order to make herself a part of it.

"That would be Humpty Dumpty," said Ozma. "I have been told he arrived."

"But did he really arrive at the very moment the doorway was destroyed?" asked Glinda, half turning away from the foreigners. And then she flicked her magic wand in the direction of the Wogglebug—and he stirred, yawned, and then went back to sleep.

"You think this matters?" said the orc at Glinda's side.

"Yes, I think this matters very much. The destruction of the doorways increases the magic."

"So breaking the wardrobe is like closing a door to keep the wind out," said Jack.

"Jack's brains are much better all of a sudden," said Glinda. "Nick is also feeling better."

"That's because I've eaten," said the Tin Man reaching for a piece of mean apple pie from a tray as it passed.

"Maybe," said Glinda. "Or perhaps we just assumed that was why."

"So all we have to do is find all the wardrobes in Oz," said Ozma.

"And destroy them," added Jack.

"After sending everyone back through them," said Glinda.

"And our problem will be solved."

"Well, that's easy," said Jack.

"Providing the magic of the portals does not fail along with all the other magic, and providing we can find them," said Glinda. "And assuming that that *is* the whole problem. We have no idea where they are or how many there may be."

"But all that would be in your book," said Jack.

"Perhaps," said Glinda, but she was not sure that information had all been recorded. People would have to have noticed them at the very least. And if they were in the deep wilderness, the book may not have marked even that.

"If we could find just one," said Ozma. And looking out the window she saw the strangest thing: the human girl Jessica on the back of one of Glinda's swans—and Buddy with her. And then, behind her, another swan, with Rumpelstiltskin on his back. They seemed to be racing in the direction of Munchkin Land.

"GWEN," DOUG YELLED, "Beth; Gwen, Beth," he repeated their names as though the iteration would push the sound further or more quickly down the long hallway. He hit the record button on the TIVO. "Bethy, Gwen."

There it was on the screen. He was amazed, and yet he wasn't amazed. It changed everything—but then again, it changed nothing. "Beth. Gwen."

Tiny footsteps beat a quick tattoo on the floor over his head, small feet racing over to the heating grate. Doug looked up; a little face looked down into the room.

"Did Charlie come home?" said a girl's voice.

"No, Brittney," Doug called up. Then he put his finger to his lips. "Quiet. You'll wake up the others."

"Yeah, right," said Brittney.

"What does that mean?"

"Well, here comes Sam. I can hear her," said Brittney. "Where's Charlie?"

"He's not here," said Doug. "Go back to sleep. Nothing's changed."

"But I thought because you were yelling…" and then more footsteps and Sam's face could be seen through the grate.

"What do you want, Doug?"

"Nothing, Samantha. Girls, it's way past your bedtime."

"Then why are you yelling?" asked Sam.

"I just wanted Beth and Gwen. Beth, Gwen," he yelled again, yet more loudly.

He heard Samantha's muffled voice through the grate. She was talking to some new, unseen presence upstairs: "I don't know what he wants." Then her voice came down more clearly, "Morris wants to know what you want."

"I just saw something on TV, I wanted to… Just go back to bed, kids. We can talk about it in the morning."

There was nothing to talk about in the morning—not to the children anyway. But Doug assumed, or anyway hoped, they'd forget by morning and not ask. And then Morris's voice came distinctly down, although his face was nowhere near the grate. "Of course it's important; what is he yelling like that for if it's not important?"

Then Morris' face was at the grate. "What is it, some kind of grown-up TV show? I'll bet it's *Girls Gone Wild.* Did you get a unscrambler?"

"Why would he yell to Gwen for that?" asked Samantha.

"My dad used to watch that stuff all the time. There's these women…"

"Morris, that's enough," yelled Doug. "They got these big…"

"I don't want to hear it," said Brittney.

"Morris, I said that's enough."

Morris mumbled something Doug was just as happy not to hear. Then Doug breathed a sigh of relief as Morris' footsteps left the hallway upstairs. But a moment later the heavy footsteps of a pre-pubescent toughy could be heard charging down the hall outside the Persian room.

"Gwen," Doug yelled. "Beth."

And then Morris was in the doorway in his bare feet and Winnie-the-Pooh pajamas.

"They got the coolest stuff on TV at night," said Morris. "These women with frizzy hair that read your fortune, tell you if you're gonna get lucky."

"Morris, I really think you need to go…"

"No really. You just dial this number."

And then Beth's voice could be heard down the hallway. "Young man, it is way past your bedtime."

"Don't look at me," Morris said back, "he's the one waking everybody up."

"Just get back to bed, Morris. Someone will be up to tuck you back in," said Gwen. Doug thought she put a little too much emphasis on the word "back."

"Next time you want to watch some late night TV, just use the intercom," said Morris, looking in at Doug. "I'm on it."

Doug never thought to use the intercom.

Beth gave Morris a little push back toward his room while Gwen eyed Doug. "What is so important you needed to wake a houseful of sleeping children for it?"

"The intercom is way over on the other side of the room," said Doug.

"Well?" said Beth.

"Look at this." And Doug hit play.

297

"How can you watch TV at a time like this?" asked Gwen.

"What other chance do I have?"

Gwen became interested as the picture of an ambulance appeared on the screen behind the words, "... was taken to the hospital by ambulance. Meanwhile..."

"Who?" yelled Gwen. "Who was rushed to the hospital?"

Doug hit "pause."

"Just a second, you'll see." And he hit play again. "William Simmons, the alleged perpetrator was taken into custody." The TV showed a man being led away in handcuffs.

"There," said Doug. "What do you think of that?"

"What do I think of what?" said Beth. "Who the bloody hell is William Simmons?"

"Who did he send to the hospital?" said Gwen walking up to the TV.

Doug hit play: "Simmons reportedly was the subject of a restraining order," the TV went on. "In other News, a bomb went off in Tel Aviv..."

"Turn that off," said Beth.

"I'm calling the hospital," said Gwen.

"Why would you call the hospital?" asked Doug.

"To find out about Gary."

"Is Gary in the hospital?" asked Doug.

"Isn't that what this is all about?" Gwen yelled.

"No. Shhhhh. No." Doug prepared to play back the scene. "Rebecca. Mrs. Holton. Jessica's mother. Apparently that guy she was living with beat her up. She's in the hospital. He's in jail."

"Oh," said Gwen, collapsing into a chair.

Beth stared at her husband for several seconds before she said, "What the hell is the matter with you?"

"I thought you'd want to know."

CHAPTER 27

Hear Ye Hear Ye

By order of her Majesty Ozma of Oz all peoples under her rule
must read and obey this edict!

In order to protect and preserve our Marvellous Land of Oz
all subjects are required to search their local domain for signs of intrusion
by alien visitors!

All outsiders MUST be forced through any magic portals found
ANYWHERE IN THE LAND OF OZ, and then
the portals must be
Dismantled AND DESTROYED!

All other work in the Land of Oz will cease until every portal has been
found, every outsider has been forced back through, and every portal HAS
BEEN PHYSICALLY destroyed!
This edict must be obeyed by every man, woman, child, animal, insect, and
magical being capable of understanding its meaning.

Do not delay! our world is in danger! Respond Immediately!

Signed this day in November by The Sovereign Ruler of all of Oz,

Ozma

Queen by right of succession by the faerie band of Lurline

"RATHER XENOPHOBIC of her isn't it?" Gary muttered after he read the notice that some mice had just posted on the tree.

"Yes," Charlie agreed. "Sounds more like something *our* government would do. Next they'll be enlisting civilians to guard the borders. Wouldn't want any stray cards from Wonderland shuffling across during the night."

They were on the ground, all of them: Gary, Charlie, Jessica, Buddy, Rumpelstiltskin and Glinda's swans; they were, they believed, somewhere near the wardrobe that Jessica was trying to find. At least they hoped they were. The swans and all the crew they carried had circled and circled but finally had been forced to land. The weight of all those people had been too much for the great birds. And so Rumpelstiltskin had met up with Buddy again. No one had told the dwarf where they were heading, or why. But he was staying very close to the boy.

Having heard Charlie's remarks, Brayna snorted her annoyance.

"What was that for?" asked Charlie.

"Oz has never been a world where we encouraged outsiders to immigrate. We have always cherished our seclusion and have done what we can to hide from the outside world."

"Lucky for you Dorothy found her way here despite your efforts. Otherwise you'd be overrun with wicked witches and false monarchs."

"Point made, human," the swan replied. "But when Glinda turned all of Oz invisible to outsiders, we had hoped to protect ourselves from just such a problem as we now have."

"Very sudden changes do bring such trauma," said Charlie. "You put up a wall, and then all that pressure builds and lets go all at once."

"Not to mention we've had no really good Oz stories in about 100 years," said Gary.

"Stories fun to read are not always fun to live," Ceeloh joined in the conversation.

"We do not exist for the amusement of the outside world," Brayna huffed.

"It's *never* a good idea to isolate yourselves," said Charlie. "And it doesn't work, either."

"It was for our protection, our identity. Our way of life."

"I don't buy it when our government says things like that, why should I buy it here? We expected a nicer welcome when we came to Oz. Maybe we just read too many children's books," Charlie huffed.

Jessica emerged from behind some bushes and ran up to Gary.

"Did you find them?" Gary asked.

"I found Buddy sitting by himself by the stream, just over there." She pointed. "So I told him what we planned to do. But Rumpelstiltskin must have been behind a tree. When he heard me tell Buddy we were going to find a wardrobe to get him home, he grabbed his hand and rushed off. He must have seen me chasing them, and now he must be hiding. I haven't been able to find them again," Jessica said with a huff. "We have to find them."

Jessica led them back to the stream.

"That's why I didn't want us to go off halfcocked like this," said Gary. "Now that Rumpelstiltskin knows we are trying to separate him from Buddy, he must also realize that we know of his plans to kidnap the boy."

"He was gonna try to take Buddy anyway. I just wanted to warn Buddy before he did it so he wouldn't trust him."

"Are you telling us it's *not* your fault?" asked Charlie.

"It isn't," and then she hesitated a moment before adding, "is it?"

"Look, no matter what happened, this was going to be difficult. I don't think she made anything that much harder," Charlie was quick to add.

Gary saw plenty of room to argue the point, but realizing that this was the first time he'd ever heard Jessica refuse blame, he just said, "You're right. You're both right. Let's just get Buddy and go home." Gary gave Jessica a smile and a hug.

"So you're on our side now?" said Jessica to Charlie as they walked.

"Just making observations." Nothing he had seen in any fairy world, not even the xenophobia of Oz, had yet convinced him that the outside world was better. He had not stopped thinking since he left how easily he could be tempted to stay in Cinderella's world and live a simple life as an artisan.

"Maybe we can spot them from the air," said Gary as he looked at Ceeloh.

"I realize we are larger than your average swan, and that we are expected to help humans in travel, but a full grown man is very heavy, and I and my friends need some time to rest after carrying you so far so quickly."

"But Rumpelstiltskin will get away," whined Jessica.

"We'd do just as well to find the wardrobe you left behind," Gary observed. "That would be their only way out of Oz."

But Jessica couldn't say exactly where the portal would be.

"I didn't stay long. I got out. I walked around. I found a farm. And then there was this scarecrow in the field. And I went up to talk to it. But it didn't say anything. So I thought maybe this wasn't Oz. Or maybe it wouldn't talk until I took it down. I haven't read all the books. But I still thought it must be Munchkin Land because the trees were bluish, and all the flowers were blue. And then this farmer started chasing me with a pitchfork."

"Farmers do not chase children with pitchforks in Oz," said Brayna.

"Maybe you were in *Seed of Chucky* or *Texas Pitchfork Massacre,*" joked Charlie.

"It was Oz. And he had a pitchfork," Jessica insisted.

"Farmers do carry pitchforks," said Gary.

"So I ran. And I crossed the yellow brick road looking for the wardrobe."

"That doesn't narrow it down a whole lot," said Gary. "Blue house, blue flowers, near the road."

"But I crossed this place where three rivers came together. I told Ceeloh."

"There's no such place," said Brayna.

"True enough," said Ceeloh. "But there is a place where the Munchkin River divides into two, half going east, half west. Right over there to the right. Close as we can get, I'd say."

"I'll look around," said a voice near Jessica's head. A robin bluebreast landed on a branch near the girl's head. "I haven't noticed any magical portals in this part of the woods, but since Ozma has ordered everyone to look anyway, and you seem so upset about it, I can fly about and see if I can help."

"You see, that sort of thing never happens in our world. A bird overhears you, and solves your problem," said Charlie.

"Seems to happen to me all the time," said Jessica.

"Well, he hasn't solved anything yet," Gary pointed out, "And I think you'd find it a little disturbing, like having a microphone and surveillance camera on every corner."

"You people from the outside world think in very very strange ways," said Ceeloh almost to herself.

"Have any of you mice seen any magic portals about while you were putting up posters?" Brayna asked a large mouse that was carrying a bag of brads.

"Too busy following Ozma's orders. Got to get these signs up. But we'll keep eyes open."

"Rumpelstiltskin can't know the exact location of the portal," said Gary. "He wasn't with you when you came here the first time."

Jessica shook her head.

"Still, that little guy is very clever, and he is no stranger to magic."

"CAN WE REST A MINUTE, I have a pebble in my shoe," Buddy asked the little man.

"Rest? Well, I... I... Of course. Let me see your shoe. Can't have a pebble in there hurting your foot." Rumpelstiltskin pulled Buddy's sneaker off and shook out a small blue stone. Then he removed the boy's dirty sock and made sure all other dust and debris was out. Then he pulled the sock back on and smoothed out the wrinkles.

"Are we hiding?" Buddy asked as the dwarf retied his sneaker using a knot the boy had never seen.

"It's like a game."

"Like hide and go seek?" asked Buddy.

"Not familiar with that game, but the name sounds right. The others are looking for us in the woods, so we are trying to hide while we search for a portal back, uh, back home," Rumpelstiltskin explained.

"I don't have a home," said Buddy.

Back and forth the gnarled man paced. He seemed anxious about something but didn't say a word to Buddy. Once he stopped and waved his hands and, to his own surprise, created a small apple for the boy to nibble on. "Ha," he called out, more loudly than he would have liked. "It's back," he said. "Things just keep getting better," he said. "Just like I told Sarah." He almost asked Buddy what he would trade for the snack but caught himself before he did.

"Okay, I can walk now," smiled Buddy. "Let's keep looking for that porty thing. What does it look like?"

The dwarf admitted he wasn't exactly sure, but he suspected it would look something like that closet they saw outside of the Emerald City. "Don't you worry about finding the portal; that's my job. You just make sure that Jessica or the others don't see you."

"I'm a great hide-and-go-seek player," bragged Buddy. "They'll never catch me."

"But we must keep moving," Rumpelstiltskin explained. "To win the game we must find the portal first."

"That's gools," said Buddy.

Holding the little man's calloused hand Buddy kept pace. Rumpelstiltskin made sure he stopped from time to time to let the boy take a breather even though he himself was not tired. Walking in the woods was hard for a boy of Buddy's age. To avoid being seen, they were not following any path. When it got too hard for Buddy to manage over roots and through briars, Rumpelstiltskin waved his stumpy arms in a mystic way, and the brambles vanished and the walking became easier. "Coming back," he mumbled again. And then he looked to Buddy.

"Walking with you is a lot more fun than walking alone," Buddy said as he rested his head against the man's rough tunic.

"Doing anything together is better than being alone," said Rumpelstiltskin.

They had been walking about an hour when the little man saw exactly what he was looking for, not, as it turned out, a wardrobe like the one that had appeared at the city gates, but a simple door frame, blue, rudely supported. "I don't suppose they'd all be exactly the same," said Rumpelstiltskin. But a doorframe in the middle of the woods could hardly be anything other than a portal.

"Maybe it's broke," said Buddy.

"Not today," said Rumpelstiltskin. "Luck's been running hot. We're good as home, I think."

And then Buddy laughed and smiled and pointed to the top of the door. There, suddenly, sat a large egg with a scowl on his face.

"Oh, not so hot," said the dwarf.

"Everyone always looking for things. You'd think they'd ask me first," said Humpty Dumpty. "I know what you're thinking: 'but you had such trouble getting home from the Grimms' Forest.' It's true. Couldn't get my bearings. But come now, here, Oz, big rectangle with four triangles inside. Piece of cake."

Suddenly a piece of cake appeared at Buddy's feet. "Hah!" laughed the egg man. "I see they've smashed themselves some portals.

"You are nothing but trouble," rumbled the dwarf. "Always showing up where you're not wanted. Do you know what we do with bad eggs in the Grimms' Forest?"

"Riddles?" said the egg, unperturbed. "Trick question? You forget; I've read all the books. There are no bad eggs in Grimm. And why do you assume that I am for them and not for you, anyway?"

"Don't trust no one," said the little man with a challenge in his voice.

"Good advice, I suppose, if one is a devious dwarf. In fact, I have not said whom I support, if indeed I support any one, so there was no reason for you to assume. And so I now, at last, thus declare myself." He stood up on the doorframe and raised his right hand, his index finger pointed at the clouds. "I am on," and then he looked down his nose at the dwarf and lowered his voice and finished, "my own side." He sat back down.

"I'd like to see you sunny side," growled the dwarf. Humpty Dumpty scrunched up his mouth.

"Another egg joke," he sighed. "How clever. I know what you want, and I know what the others want. I even have a good idea what I want. But has anyone asked the boy what he wants?"

"What are you talking about?" asked Buddy.

"Ignore him, he's cracked. Spoiled no doubt. A poison egg if I ever saw one." Buddy giggled.

"I know what is best for the boy. You don't; you're only an egg."

"Only an egg. Hah! I laugh at the insinuation. An epithet hurled from a lumpy bag of flesh such as yourself could not effect the least crack in the smooth shell of an egg's ego. Soft skin and rigid bones. You creatures will never understand: eggs are the epitome of creation. And I am the epitome of an egg. I have seen more than any of you, and I am more well traveled and better read."

"Don't forget your great modesty," added Charlie as he and Gary and Jessica approached the group being led by a small robin.

"Oh! You double-crossing son of a brood," screamed Rumpelstiltskin as he slammed his foot down and got it stuck in the soft earth.

"SEE, OVER THERE. I told you I saw it," Pinocchio called to the group following him. The wooden boy scampered across the grass of the garden to the green wooden frame of a doorway from what once must have been a wardrobe. There was no door in the opening, but looking though the opening, they could all see a white light glowing from within. Suzy had

305

directed them here. It was the very portal she had used on her first trip to Oz.

The Scarecrow led a group of orcs as they stomped across the grounds. Relations among what they were now calling "the visitors" being what they were, Ozma had decided to divide them by kind and send different groups to different portals. At this portal, Jack Pumpkinhead was upset to see the flowers and plants trampled under the heavy feet of these brutes, but there were too many to control as they stormed past. Suzy too was upset, though it had nothing to do with the flowers.

"If you think of home and walk through, you'll return to where you belong. I'm sure of it. Glinda said so," Suzy explained.

"If Glinda promised it, we'll take her at her word," grumbled an orc. "If she has lied to us, we'll find a way back, and someone will pay."

"She would never lie," said Jack with his ever-present smile, "though she might be mistaken from time to time," he added under his breath.

"And remember," said the Scarecrow, "locate all the foreigners who may have invaded your lands, send them through any portals you find, and then destroy those portals as well."

"Do you really think we'll get them all that way?" asked Jack.

"If we get most of them, we will have solved most of the problem," said the Scarecrow.

With a great amount of pushing and shoving the brutes pressed their way through the doorway, each thinking of home. And when they had all gone, Pinocchio himself said an eager goodbye—no adventures left in this land for him—and ducked through. And then there was only Suzy, the Scarecrow, and Jack Pumpkinhead by the open door.

"Am I next?" said Suzy. "I saw you talking to Glinda before you left. The edict says 'all outsiders.' Is that what she said? I have to go? You have to force me through, it says. But you don't have to. I would hate to make you do that. I'll just... I'll just go." She looked sadly at the door but made no move to enter it. She was trying not to cry. "I just... I don't have any idea where it's gonna take me."

The Scarecrow and Jack Pumpkinhead startled her when they broke out in the strangest laughter Suzy had ever heard, the great windy guffaws of straw and pumpkin.

"The brains of that sorceress are nearly a match for my own," said the Scarecrow.

"She told us you might think that," said Jack. "We didn't believe her, of course."

"She gave us this paper," said the Scarecrow, "just in case." And as soon as he handed it to Suzy, he and Jack pulled out their hammers and set to dismantling the doorway.

Suzy read the paper and laughed. It was her citizenship papers. There had never been any such thing in Oz as citizenship papers. They'd had to make them up from scratch. But here they were, signed by Ozma herself, witnessed and attested by Glinda and the Wogglebug.

"And Dorothy?" asked Suzy.

"And her little dog, too," laughed Jack.

"Dorothy does not need papers," said the Scarecrow.

THE SOLDIER WITH THE GREEN WHISKERS entered the throne room announcing Rodaina, the Queen of the field mice.

"Sister mouse, how is the job going?" asked Ozma.

Rodaina scampered up onto to the small table as she said, "How fortunate that we have come to you. My people have spread out all over Oz putting up the broadsides. Many others have pitched in, some birds and even winged monkeys have assisted them from all reports. Before nightfall every Ozite will have seen the notice."

The Wogglebug, still sitting on Ozma's throne, leaned forward and muttered that that was an exaggeration. He added that an educated guess, which was the only kind he ever made, would suppose that *many* people would have seen the proclamation by this time. It might easily take a week for those living in the furthermost regions of Oz to know of the decree.

Queen Rodaina sniffed her rejection of the giant insect's comment and then approached Ozma. Meanwhile the Patchwork Girl had seemed to lose interest in the goings on and was twirling around the room like a colorful top.

"I realize it will take time," Rodaina gave a glance at the Wogglebug, "but already I can feel the magic of Oz returning. Many people must already have escorted the outsiders through the portals and dismantled them. The wooden puppet, Pinocchio, found a portal hidden among the morning glory in the western garden outside the walls of the Emerald City, and all of the orcs went right through and returned home. Then the Scarecrow and Jack Pumpkinhead and Suzy Bishop used hammers and garden tools and turned the doorframe into kindling. I think we all felt a surge of magic return to the land after that. The other evil ones are now being escorted, one group at a time, to the wardrobe lately used by Suzy within the walls of the City itself. And all over the kingdom, wherever outsiders are found, they are being led to other portals."

307

"She's correct," added Glinda who entered the room unannounced accompanied by Dorothy Gale and Toto. "The people of America used a portal in Munchkin Land. I saw it in the magic picture. Now that we know what we're looking for, the portals have been easy for the magic picture to find. I was amazed to find how many there were."

"Once people were told how they could help fix things, most of 'em rushed through the portals to get home," Dorothy said.

"Most people do seem to think there's no place like home," sang Scraps as she continued to spin about.

"The magic picture seems to be working just fine, and no new cases of magic failure have occurred. I think this disaster will soon be undone," Glinda explained ignoring the antics of the Patchwork Girl as best she could.

"I know I feel better," the Tin Woodman said, "though to be honest, I enjoyed remembering the experience of eating. I think I will miss that."

"I too am starting to feel stronger," agreed the Wogglebug. "In just the last few minutes I have started to feel like my old self. Or should I say my young self? None of my elbows hurt." And he moved his arms back and forth as though to prove it was so. And yet he had a little bit of strain in his smile, as though some of the aging may turn out to permanent.

"I feel the same," said Scraps from the other side of the room.

"Be that as it may, it would seem that we have found the solution to the problem. If my loyal subjects follow the decree, we will soon have all these problems behind us." Ozma smiled.

"But what about the doorway in America?" Dorothy asked. "How do we destroy that?"

"I've taken care of it," said Glinda.

"That portal helped Suzy. And there are other children," said Dorothy. "And it's much easier to use than a cyclone."

"THE SCHOOL BUS will be here any minute, so eat up," Gwen said as she spooned some scrambled eggs onto Morris' plate.

"I'm too tired to eat," whined the boy as he fidgeted in his seat, sliding his breakfast across the dish with no intention of actually eating it.

"Comes from staying up all night listening in to other people's conversations," Beth explained.

"I'm a little tired myself," Gwen smiled. But the little boy could not tell that Gwen had not slept at all. Beth, who knew, was still amazed that her sister in law had prepared all the children's breakfasts as though nothing had happened. She poured Gwen a cup of coffee.

It wasn't long before the children of school age were on the bus, and the few remaining children were in Gepetto's Toy Shop playing with puppets and dolls.

Morris had almost managed to convince Gwen to let him stay home, but in the end Beth intervened and ushered the boy out the door with the others. The phone rang, Beth went to the hall to get it, though there was a phone in the kitchen, and Gwen sat alone at the table, sipping coffee. She closed her eyes. When Gary left to see Charlie, she wrote in her journal. She felt no temptation to write now. She no longer felt sick, now just a little numb, beyond confused, because wherever Gary was there was no logic to it, no way to figure it out. It was as though he'd vaporized, as though God had reached down and pulled him out of the world.

And then it occurred to her why Beth had chosen the hallway phone: What if someone was calling with news of Gary? She rose and headed down the hallway that connected the kitchen to the mudroom where she could hear Beth murmuring.

"Who was that on the phone?" Gwen asked as she saw Beth hanging up the receiver.

"You will never believe this. First I got a call from some lawyer claiming he was representing Rebecca Holton regarding a lawsuit against us for the care of her daughter and her subsequent vanishing."

"I believe that," Gwen said, "just what we've all been waiting for."

"That's not all. While I was speaking to the lawyer I got buzzed on the call waiting, and it was a Mrs. Johnston."

"Who is...?" asked Gwen as she sat down in anticipation that she might need to.

"Mrs. Johnston is a foster parent who is caring for Isabelle Holton, you know, Jessica's sister. She just got a call that Rebecca has vanished from the hospital, and she and her boyfriend Bill Simmons, who was out on bail already, if you can believe that, were seen in a pickup truck leaving the state on I-89. The DCYF was afraid she was going to try to abduct the daughter and skip town, but it seems she wasn't interested in the child, just the skipping town, and with the man who beat her up last night."

Gwen shook her head hoping the act would help make all these things make sense. "Sadly, I believe that too." They were walking back to the kitchen.

The phone rang again, and before either woman could answer it, Doug entered the room from the other side and picked up the receiver.

"Yes. Yes. No, I didn't know that. Are you sure? But I just saw last night that... Okay, I understand. Of course, but what should we do? For how long? Right. Okay. Thank you." Doug hung up the phone. Beth and Gwen entered the room to see Doug staring at the receiver in confusion.

"Apparently Rebecca Holton has enlisted the aid of Colin Fuller-Brinks in her lawsuit. He's such a helpful man, but now she has run off with..."

"Bill Simmons, the boyfriend who beat her up last night," Gwen finished his sentence.

"Yeah, you knew that? And now Simmons has broken his parole, and is wanted, and her credibility has kind of gone down the tubes at this point, I'd think. That was her lawyer; he has decided not to take the case on her behalf."

Gwen decided to go to Gepetto's Toy Shop to oversee the small children playing while Doug and Beth continued trying to make sense of the happenings of the last few days.

Gwen found it hard to think about all these new developments while Gary was still missing. Watching the little ones helped her stay calm.

It was almost lunchtime when she heard thumps and bangs coming from upstairs and then the familiar call of her name.

"Gary?" she cried as she started running up the stairs.

"Gwen," called Gary as he took her in an embrace at the top of the winding staircase.

"I could kill you," she cried.

"I missed you too."

CHAPTER 28

CHAPTER ONE: They built it for children. There were certainly going to be children. There was no doubt about that. They had always planned on children. Lots of children. They were artists and writers, and their favorite books were the classics: Alice in Wonderland, The Chronicles of Narnia, *the Oz books, Middle Earth, Hans Christian Anderson,* The Arabian Nights, Mother Goose, The Little White Horse, *and the Brothers Grimm; and their favorite artists were the great illustrators: John R. Neil and Sir John Tenniel and N.C. Wyeth, and Maxfield Parrish, and Tasha Tudor, and Aubrey Beardsley, and W. W. Denslow.*

Yes, they planned on children. But life had other plans.

THAT WASN'T BAD, he thought. Probably have to change it before the final draft. But a good start.

This adventure had been so strange, it would make a heck of a book. He'd have to change the names of course. But that was all. The rest would be exactly as everyone remembered it. Let them believe it if they wanted to. So what if it they filed it on the fiction shelf at the store. He'd

311

change his own name too. But they could still find him if they really wanted to. He'd even let his brother, Gary, seem like he was the protagonist now and then. Gary would like that. He was a sucker for the spotlight. That would be a small price, anyway, since he had to get the greatest part of his information from Gary.

Now that everything had calmed down, and everything was back to something very like normal, it was easier to look back and smile at all that had happened. They'd lost Buddy, of course, and that was sad. But they'd lost children before, not quite the way they lost Buddy and Suzy, but children were always leaving—going back to their families, going on to other foster homes. Jessica was gone too, after all this. She and Isabelle had been placed together in a foster home north of Lebanon. It wasn't so far away, and yet, he knew they'd receive no more than a letter or two from the girl, to which they would lovingly reply, but after which they would almost certainly never hear from or about her again. You could not keep track of so many children. After a while, not even Gwen continued to try. You could hug them when they left; you could wish them well, and you could hope for the best. And that was all. Everyone wishes he could do more.

Gary assured them that Buddy was safe and happy. And even Jessica seemed reconciled after he and Charlie explained it all to her. When she realized Buddy had not come through the wardrobe with them, she ran, of course, right back to the Narnia room. She was prepared to go back again and find him—start all over. She tried to hurl herself through the portal, but Charlie caught her, and Gary called after her to stop.

"He was in my hand," she said. "I lost him. I had him." That's how it happened. There was a big argument with Rumpelstiltskin and then Jessica just grabbed Buddy's hand and dived into the wardrobe. Everyone else, of course, dived in right after: Gary, Charlie, Rumpelstiltskin. The little robin bluebreast flew in as well, but she went right through without leaving Munchkin Land. Jessica, Gary, and Charlie tumbled into the Narnia room. "I had him," Jessica repeated.

"We have to seal it up," Gary told her.

"But what if he comes back? He won't be able to get out."

"We won't destroy it," said Gary. "And we'll give him some time first, to make sure. But as soon as it's clear he's not coming, we have to seal it up. And you have to promise me you're not going back in there."

"We have to go get him," she pleaded. "It was my fault."

"Jessica, listen to me," said Charlie. He was crouched down to her height, looking her in the eye: "This was his choice. I figured it out when I ended up here. I should have known all along. It was his choice after all—not yours, not Rumpelstiltskin's."

"He's just a little kid."

"Sometimes even little kids get choices," said Charlie, his hands loosely holding Jessica's arms. "Think about it, Jess. You know it's true. It doesn't matter whose hand he was holding when he went into the wardrobe. The wardrobe took him where his heart wanted to be. That's how it works."

Jessica knew it was true.

"It takes you where you need to go. Then it brings you home," said Gary.

"But you don't always come back to the same place you left," said Charlie. "Buddy found himself a home and a family. That's what we all want, isn't it?"

And then Gary added, "And you made it possible."

"But I wasn't supposed to tell him," she said.

"Okay. You made a mistake. You know that. That's fine. But that mistake turned out for the best for him. Isn't it funny how that happens sometimes? We can control our actions, but we can't control what happens afterwards."

"But we don't have to seal it up. Just because Glinda said…"

"Maybe not forever. But for now. Let's agree to live in this world for a little while; let's at least let the fairy world settle down before we invade it again." No one laughed at Gary's joke, so he said, "We can't just keep having children disappear."

Charlie looked as though he wanted to argue, but he didn't. Jessica knew it was true.

It was not more than an hour later, Colin Fuller-Brinks was at the door, intent on his lawsuit. Gwen informed him that Rebecca had fled the state with her parole-breaking boyfriend

"You're lying," the social worker proclaimed.

"You'll find out for yourself," said Gwen. Beth and Doug were steaming by then, the conversation being, already, several minutes old. But Gwen—now that everyone was under her roof again—had recovered all her Buddhist calm.

"Why would a woman flee the state with a felon when she's on the verge of a huge payoff like this?" the social worker yelled, and his gesture at the word "this" took in unambiguously the whole operation of OzHouse, the structure, the lands, the means that had created them.

"You expected Rebecca Holton to make sense?" scoffed Beth.

"Well, frankly, that doesn't even matter," said Colin, opening his brief case. "I have a signed document here allowing me full rights to sue on her behalf. You have acted with demonstrable, culpable, legal negligence," he proclaimed, mustering all the redundance that years of bureaucratic service had put at his disposal. "You have lost her child."

Just then Gary walked in the room. "Hey," he said, "I didn't know you'd hired a clown; what'd I miss?"

Jessica came in beside him. "Hello, Mr. Brinks," she said.

"Who are you?" asked the stunned social worker.

"It's me, Jessica. Don't you remember me?"

Colin Fuller-Brinks pulled her file out of his briefcase and glanced at her picture. Then he stared at the young girl as though to find some way to deny that this was she.

"Do you have any idea the trouble you've caused, little lady?"

Jessica looked up at Gary, who gave her a shrug, then back at Colin. "I was just listening to music. It was Bill that caused all the trouble."

"That's not what I meant... Oh, forget it," yelled Colin as he grabbed his briefcase and stormed out the door.

"I think we've heard the last of Mr. Colin Fuller-Brinks," said Gary.

"What are you, nuts?" said Doug. "He'll be back twice a month for the rest of our lives. Some people never go away."

AS SOON AS JESSICA LEFT to be with her sister, Doug and Gary sealed the wardrobe. Gary put handles on the backside of the door so that anyone, even someone as young as Buddy, could easily pull the door open from inside the Narnia room. From inside the wardrobe, however, behind the fur coats, the back was sealed tight. Gwen painted a lamppost on the wall that had been a door.

Charlie objected right to the very end.

"You have to understand," said Gary, standing in the hall among a pile of fur coats as Gwen painted the Narnian scene.

"I do understand," said Charlie. "I just disagree. Everyone needs that room. And some of us need it very badly."

They discussed the question the whole time Gwen painted. (How she could concentrate on painting with that going on behind her, Doug would never understand. She painted; she heard every word, and she made not the slightest offer to join in or correct anyone.) Gary too stayed uncharacteristically calm. He said afterwards, "I was just so thrilled that Charlie could discuss something that mattered so much to him without any trace of violence in his voice. I spent the whole time thinking, 'He's going away. And he's gonna be fine.'"

Charlie said, "If this is what grownups do, I think I'd rather not." And he explained to Gary that as far as he was concerned, sealing up the wardrobe would disqualify him from ever using it again.

"I suppose you're right," said Gary.

Charlie looked away at that. That was what he was afraid of. Charlie did not explain, but perhaps Gary understood anyway: he had hoped that his last trip through the wardrobe would lead him back to Cinderella's kitchen. But the wardrobe always takes you home. It doesn't have a front or a back. From wherever you are it sends you out, and then it brings you home. Now he understood. Still, it was not easy for him to accept that more of his heart was here.

Charlie returned to the Rhode Island School of Design the next day.

On the bus from White River Junction, Vermont, Charlie looked across the border as the New Hampshire countryside rolled past. He opened his journal to write, but didn't know what to say. So he started to draw. The pictures he drew of Cinderella and Oz didn't explain anything. But drawing them helped.

Everything seemed, for a moment, to be quieting down. So many people leaving, so many little stories ending. But the quieting down was just a momentary illusion. The night before Charlie left, a little girl arrived at the door. Her arm was in a cast, and she was crying. Gwen took her up to the Little White Horse room with the pink geraniums and the view of the hills and the giant Wonderland chess set. Another child came the next day. And there would be more tomorrow.

EPILOGUE

Dear Gary, Gwen, Doug, and Beth Robbins:
Remember I promised to write to you and tell you how things are going for my sister and me in this new foster home? I meant to write this sooner, but my new school gives a lot of homework, and I have so much to catch up on that I just didn't have time.

Today is a teacher's conference day so I have time, and Mr. Bonnels, who is my new foster dad, said I could use this computer, so I am using his super deluxe HP Pavilion, and he said I could even use his printer to print it with any typeface I want.

This is really a very nice place, and until my Mom comes for us I know we will be safe and happy here. Not that I wasn't safe and happy at OzHouse, but you know what I mean.

I will be trying out for the school play next week. They are doing Babes in Toyland, which is going to feel very funny for me since I know who those people really are.

Of course I haven't told anyone about what happened in the secret room, not even my sister. This time you can count on me to keep my word.

The Bonnels are surprised that I will not eat eggs because it doesn't mention that in my files, but after knowing Humpty Dumpty for so long I just can't bring myself to eat an egg any more.

One thing though, and this is probably very important! I found this note under my pillow this morning. I am sending it to you so no one else sees it. Perhaps you can keep it in the secret room, or something. I don't know how it got here because you told me you closed the portal, but I guess Sarahstiltskin knows some tricks about getting around that even Glinda doesn't know about.

I am so glad that Buddy is really happy, I guess Gary and Charlie were right, though maybe you shouldn't tell Charlie I said that, because he might get a swell head! :) See that smiley face? Mrs. Bonnels taught me how to make that so people would know I was telling a joke.

I promise to keep in touch. My love to all, even Charlie! :)
Jessica Holton

Dearest Jessica,

My husband has asked me to write you this letter to assure you that your friend Buddy is very happy and safe here in our little cottage in the Grimms' Forest. We are calling him Budistiltskin, and he seems to like that. Last week he caught a lovely trout with his new dad, and we had it for dinner. Budistiltskin was so proud!

We do not know if a fully human child can learn magic, but when he is older, Rumpelstiltskin intends to train him in the family business if it is possible. Budistiltskin is so bright and willing to please that he may just surprise us all and become a full-fledged magic worker one day! No mother could ask for a better son, and Rumpelstiltskin hasn't stopped smiling for weeks.

Maybe in time you will wish to visit your friend in his new home. As happy as he is, I'm sure Budistiltskin misses you and other old friends.

I hope you are as happy as we all are; if not, ask the nice people who care for you children to send you here and we will adopt you too. As for me, I will accept as many as will come. Always remember.

Take care, and eat your vegetables.
Kindly,

Sarahstiltskin